It Continued with the Cowries

Jane Ross Potter

Goose River Press
Waldoboro, Maine

Library of Congress Card Number: 2023932523

ISBN: 978-1-59713-254-1

First Printing, 2023

Cover design by Brandi Doane McCann at ebook-coverdesigns.com

Author photograph by Melissa Davidson

Published by
Goose River Press
3400 Friendship Road
Waldoboro ME 04572
e-mail: gooseriverpress@gmail.com
www.gooseriverpress.com

Also by Jane Ross Potter

Fiction

Because It's There (2007 Indie Excellence Finalist)
Margaret's Mentor (Book One of the Birsay Trilogy)
Symbol Stones (Book Two of the Birsay Trilogy)
The Secret of Finlay Village (Book Three of the Birsay Trilogy)
Sharkbait
Seeking the Medicine Buddha
It Began with the Marbles
Frances vs. the Ice (short story)
A Year of Moments (short story)

Prologue

From the website of the *Kilvellie-by-the-Sea Weekly News*:

Kilvellie-by-the-Sea, Scotland. Kilvellie police are investigating yesterday's death of an elderly local man. He fell from the clifftop near the popular Beachside Cafe and was pronounced dead on the beach below at two o'clock in the afternoon. Although the police do not suspect foul play at this stage, they have issued an appeal to the public for any photographs or video footage taken near there in the hour before the man was found. Something in the background of a picture or video may provide an explanation for the fall. Absent other evidence, the police speculate that the man stumbled while getting up or walking away from his usual bench near the cliff edge.

This tragedy will no doubt lead to a renewed public demand for guardrails or fencing along the cliff, especially in busy areas such as the parking lot. That parking area serves both cafe customers and beachcombers, who access the beach by the wooden stairway located near where the man is presumed to have fallen. Visitors walking the coastal path also park in that area.

More details about the man and his sudden passing will be published in the next print and digital edition of this newspaper. Meanwhile, the public is urged to help the Kilvellie police by providing any video or photographs taken in the area of the parking lot, the clifftop coastal path, or the beach, yesterday between one and two o'clock in the afternoon.

Chapter 1

A full week had passed since Alistair Wright's last visit to Kilvellie, a seaside town north of Dundee, Scotland. He had planned for it to be, literally, his last visit, and was relieved to be back in his temporary Scottish home, a cottage on the coast of Fife. The cottage was owned by his American fiancée Margaret Milford, and they were living there together while making decisions about their future.

Much was up for discussion: should they return to their real homes in Portland, Maine, and start planning a Portland wedding? Margaret's parents, and most of her friends, were in the Boston area, so that made logistic sense. However, they had become engaged in Scotland, and he knew that the residents of the nearby village, Finlay, were hoping to attend the wedding. Alistair thought back to several weeks earlier, when he imagined marrying Margaret in the little picturesque church in Finlay, the ceremony conducted by the local minister who had become a good friend and confidant to both Alistair and Margaret.

In addition to deciding where to marry, they had to choose where to live. Between them, they had the resources to spend a couple of years at the cottage in Finlay, but that meant loosening their professional ties in Portland: Alistair's private investigation business which he'd built up over the years, and Margaret's career as a young attorney at a law firm in Portland.

Margaret's supervisor Hamish, and the firm's partner-

Jane Ross Potter

ship, had been understanding when Margaret's uncle died the previous spring and left her a cottage. Their understanding had continued when Margaret, working remotely, had still managed to orchestrate a major, and lucrative, win in a lawsuit that Hamish was handling. But that understanding couldn't last much longer.

Alistair looked out through the beach-facing picture window, absently taking in the waves of the Firth of Forth, the wet sand glistening in the morning August sun, and the calling gulls. It was an idyllic existence, in terms of location. The cottage was two miles from Finlay Village, with access by either walking along the beach at low tide, or driving the recently-cleared disused railway track route. A fifteen minute drive north brought him to St. Andrews, the vibrant university town he never got tired of exploring, and Edinburgh was to the south, close enough for day trips.

Why would he ever need to leave, he wondered, not for the first time. But the visit to Scotland had only ever been that, a visit. He hadn't chosen to settle in Scotland, but his stay kept being prolonged by various projects and events that he and Margaret, together or separately, couldn't resist. He knew this limbo situation couldn't go on indefinitely, with both of them avoiding a firm decision to stay or go.

He heard the shower running in the bathroom off the adjoining bedroom, indicating that Margaret would soon join him at the table for breakfast. She hadn't initiated a discussion about moving back to Maine, so he decided it was up to him.

In fact, Margaret hadn't talked about anything serious since her return from Orkney, the group of islands north of the mainland Scottish coast. Her visit had coincided with his time in Kilvellie, but other than telling him she was in Orkney to provide background for a magazine article, she hadn't offered much.

Margaret's ties with Orkney were complex. Alistair knew she loved visiting the islands, with their wealth of Neolithic

2

stones and tombs, their natural beauty and opportunities for hiking, and, more recently, their important role during both World Wars. However, earlier that summer, she'd fallen into a dungeon below a crumbling palace ruin, then risked her life to crawl through a long, dark tunnel, only to emerge to daylight and a young man threatening her with a knife.

All had ended well, but Margaret's claim to fame for not only helping to discover a lost architectural feature, but also a hidden cache of stolen gold coins from the first millennium, meant that she had become an authoritative source for any reporter or writer investigating the stories. Alistair knew she was tolerating the attention, if only because she was a stickler for getting facts reported correctly.

He also knew that every hour she spent with a reporter, or demonstrating where she fell into the dungeon and where the tunnel emerged at the shore, meant another hour she could have been billing to a client for her law firm. In his career and hers, there was no escape from the hard truth: time was money, but time was limited.

The hairdryer began droning, and Alistair poured himself another cup of tea. He fumbled with his cell phone. There was a piece of unfinished business from his visits to Kilvellie, an awkward call he simply had to make to the police. And the longer he put it off, the more awkward it became. But now he had a short reprieve as Margaret emerged from the bedroom, ready for the day. He slipped his phone into his pocket.

Chapter 2

Margaret's curly red hair was glowing in the morning sun, and she'd tied it back in a ponytail. She wore jeans and a cream linen tunic, with indoor felt clogs on her feet. Alistair smiled at her as she sat down, touched the teapot to make sure it was hot, and poured herself the first welcome cup of tea of the day.

"Do you need to make a call?" she asked. "You had your phone out before I sat down." She was surprised that he was still in his bathrobe, a warm navy blue terry robe from a shop in St. Andrews. He must have been up early, she thought, and hadn't wanted to wake her by rummaging for clothes in the bedroom.

He hesitated before replying. So far, he hadn't told her about his unfinished business, about the burden he carried, and decided now was the time. It would help to ease them into a discussion about their immediate future.

"Actually, I do, but it's not something I've told you about yet. Do you want to hear it now, or do you need to work first?"

Alistair thought he knew the answer: with Margaret's boss and colleagues in Maine, five hours behind, she usually had her mornings free before she had to check for anything urgent.

"I don't need to work this morning, not law work anyway. If it's a long story, should I make us a new pot of tea? You must have been up for a while."

Alistair poured the dregs, strong from steeping, into his

cup and handed the empty pot to her. "Thanks. And I'm sorry the kitchen counter isn't fixed yet. I had planned to work on it while you were in Orkney, but I'll get right back to it, I promise!"

Margaret laughed. "No hurry, I won't disturb whatever you're doing."

He just nodded his head. He actually hadn't started on the kitchen at all, part of his avoidance of anything new that could extend their time and prevent a realistic decision about returning to Portland. And his recent days of sleuthing in Kilvellie, being reminded of the kind of work he enjoyed back home, reinforced his reluctance to start any cottage remodeling.

When Margaret returned with the fresh pot of tea, Alistair began the story he'd kept from her until now. She listened with increasing interest, so engaged that she took few sips from her cooling tea.

"You know I told you that the town, Kilvellie, used to be famous for its glass factory, and now it's famous for the sea glass, the beach glass that people come from all over to collect?"

"Yes, and I want to go there and look for glass!"

Alistair glanced at the shelving against the nearby wall: on it were numerous jars of multicolored sea glass collected by Margaret's late uncle, on the nearby beach. He felt like saying that she'd inherited plenty of glass, but resisted the temptation.

"Margaret, you may not want to collect glass there when I'm done with the story. The glass factory was productive from the early nineteen twenties until the nineteen nineties. Their best work was done in the twenties and thirties, when they turned out vases using skills and techniques that someone brought from Venice, from Murano specifically. I've seen the vases. Some in *millefiori* design, just gorgeous. And valuable now. Anyway, after several decades, the cliff edge erosion was making the location unsafe. It was far too expensive to move or rebuild the factory, so it closed down and was demolished." He stopped and took a long drink of tea. "But that's not what I need to tell you. During the Second World War, there were a series of attacks on the factory. A few young men, too young to go to war, went on rampages through the factory and they tossed all the glass they could get their hands on over the cliff..."

Margaret interrupted. "So *that's* why the sea glass there is unique? Because it began as beautiful glassware?"

"Yes, that's part of the story. People who don't know the background only see the positive side to the colored glass pebbles and shards they collect. And sell, and use to make jewelry. The negative side is that the sea glass is evidence of criminal activity that went on for most of the war."

"But how could it?" Margaret cried. "Why did the local police and the townspeople let the factory be trashed like that?"

Alistair shook his head. "It baffles me too. One explanation is that the factory was built by a former German soldier, who'd fought against the British in the First World War. He was injured badly at the front and ended up in a British ward. While he was recovering he met a Scottish nurse, and after the war he moved to Scotland where they married and had a family. Maybe the townspeople saw the factory as a legitimate target when Britain went to war against Germany again. But another explanation is that there were no able-bodied men left in the town to protect the factory..."

Margaret let out a groan. "Well, there would have been able-bodied *women* I would think. If the factory provided jobs for their sons and husbands who were off fighting, they'd have had a strong motive to keep the factory secure until the war ended."

"Good point, of course, but for whatever reason, protecting the factory was left in the hands of one young man, who they called the factory guard. His bad eyesight kept him out of the military, but he was deemed capable of guarding a building."

"But it didn't work, did it, if the place was still looted?"

Alistair paused to drink more tea and consider how much to tell her.

"Here's where the stories diverge. Some people think the guard may have colluded with the vandals, or that he was forced to let them in under threats to his family. Whatever the explanation, he emerged from the war with a stash of valuable glass vases and other glass items. When he was moving into a care home a few years ago, his granddaughter sold the glass for him and he's living in luxury accommodations. An old manor house in the town."

Margaret took a sip of tea and shook her head. "It sounds to me like he was unjustly enriched by his work during the war years. Sorry, I'm speaking legalese. He basically had his granddaughter sell stolen goods. Does she know where the glass came from, or maybe you don't know the answer to that. Maybe she's innocent in it all?"

"I spoke to her just once, and that conversation is what's giving me so much anxiety about the phone call I have to make."

Margaret touched his forearm for a moment. "I know you've been a bit quiet since we both got back last week, but I figured you have a lot on your mind, with the cottage renovations and thinking about our wedding. I had no idea you're feeling stressed. You should be sharing these things with me!"

He smiled. "I know, but there's one piece I can't share yet until I make a call to a police officer I know in Kilvellie. When all this is over, I want to invite her here. You'll get along well. It's her last job before she plans to retire, but policing the town is more challenging than she expected. It's not all beachcombing, ice cream, and fish and chips." He stopped and sighed. "And now I'm going to give her some news she will *hate*."

Chapter 3

Margaret went to the kitchen to prepare breakfast, leaving Alistair to make his phone call. She hoped it wouldn't take him long, because she had something to discuss with him, something that had a bearing on whether they would stay in Scotland for longer, or return to Maine. As she waited for the toast to pop up from the toaster, she thought back to her recent visit to Orkney. It felt like the islands were weaving a web around her, preventing her from thinking about anything else. And now she had a request that she was having a hard time turning down.

Although raised in America, Margaret had been born in Scotland to Scottish parents. With Margaret on her own now and working in Portland, her parents spent more and more time in Britain, and her father assisted the royal family now and again, diplomatic issues as far as Margaret knew, as her father didn't reveal much. One of the princes, in his late twenties, was soon to marry a young woman who lived in Orkney, and on Margaret's most recent trip to Orkney, the prince had been there also.

During a casual dinner, he'd told Margaret about his latest project. He was already taking a leadership role in helping the British regain their sense of civility and civic pride, and the village of Finlay was the recipient of an award for civility. As an avid beachcomber, the prince had turned his attention to Scotland's coasts. Increased tourism in remote areas was causing formerly pristine beaches to become dumping grounds for waste, including the ubiquitous plastic

8

bottles and other plastic items that could prove fatal to marine life.

Margaret knew that beach clean-up projects were popular, but the prince had something else in mind, in which the collection of trash would be incidental to the real incentive: a competition to find natural treasure on Scottish beaches. After hearing the prince's idea, Margaret was eager to get involved. But, realistically, could she put her career on hold for another couple of months to collect *cowrie shells*?

When she returned to the dining table, carrying a tray of toast, jam, marmalade, and butter, Alistair was sitting immobile, staring at the phone in his hands.

"Was that enough time to make your call?" Margaret asked. She thought he looked shaken.

"Yes, but the person I need to talk to isn't available. There was an accident yesterday that resulted in a death, so she and her sergeant are both out looking for witnesses. They have an officer from another station handling the office calls."

"A car accident?" Margaret waited for his reply while she arranged the food and dishes on the table, then refilled their teacups.

"No, it sounds like someone may have fallen over the cliff. I hate to say it, but I'm not surprised. There's nothing to prevent people from getting too close to the edge, and it's eroding away, so..."

"Was it an elderly man?"

"I don't know. Did you see something in the news?"

She opened her laptop. "Possibly. I was reading about access to some of the Scottish coastline last night. There's an online petition to install guardrails along the more dangerous cliff edges." She stopped while she found the information, then summarized it for Alistair.

"It's the same town, Kilvellie. An elderly man was sitting on a bench near the edge of a cliff one minute, and then he was gone. His body was found lying on the beach below. No one claims to have been near enough to see it happen, but so far it's not being treated as a suspicious death."

She looked up. "Poor old guy. He probably lost his balance. Horrible way to go."

"Does the report give a name?" Alistair asked, his voice far away, as if he was dreading the answer.

"No, only that he's local, not a tourist."

Alistair turned his phone over and over in his hands, and finally he looked through his contact list and pressed the number for his private investigator friend Adam. They had worked together on a recent case in Kilvellie, involving a missing teenage girl. But beyond that, Alistair had a specific reason to call Adam: Adam's mother was the senior officer in the Kilvellie police station.

Alistair listened: Adam had seen who was calling, and knew why.

"Hi Alistair, I assume you're calling about the news from Kilvellie. The identity of the man hasn't been released to the public yet, but it's Ronald Wilson."

"Was... was..." Alistair hesitated. He and Adam knew something of the man's involvement as the glass factory guard during the Second World War, but Alistair had another layer of information, the secret he had yet to share with Adam's mother. "Was it really an accident?"

Adam's voice was reassuring. When Alistair had first met Adam in the spring, Adam's strong Scottish accent and word choices had taken some getting used to, but now Alistair was able to tune in quickly and follow the conversation without interrupting for explanations. "As far as we know, aye. I've spoken to Mum a couple of times. No one has come forward saying they actually saw him fall. As you know, the bench he always sat on is at the far side of the parking lot, and people around the cafe would have had to be looking toward the cliff at that precise second."

"So," Alistair mused, "no real-time witness..."

"Nae so far, but Mum's appealing to anyone who was in

the vicinity to check their photos and videos, in case there's something in the background. It's a long shot, but someone might have inadvertently captured the fall while they were filming their wee bairns nearby, or scenery."

Alistair sighed. "I agree, it is a long shot. We'll probably never know. Poor old guy."

"Aye, although maybe better a sudden death than lingering for months or years with a terminal illness. But I agree, a sudden death will be difficult for his family to adjust to."

They ended the call with the usual promises to get together soon, although that might be a while, given Adam's busy work schedule in Inverness, a long day trip from Finlay.

"That sounded intense," Margaret commented, looking at Alistair's face as he stared out at the beach, his eyes half-closed and his forehead wrinkled in confusion.

He turned to her and his face softened. "It's tragic for the man and the family, but it actually renders my dreaded phone call moot. That's the right legal term, for a situation changing so that a course of action is no longer relevant?"

"Close enough," Margaret agreed. "And if the point of your *dreaded* call is now moot, can you tell me what it was about?"

"Yes, and I know I don't need to say this, but please keep it to yourself."

Margaret smiled. "If you know nothing else about me, Alistair, you know I can keep a secret."

Chapter 4

Alistair and Margaret cleared away the breakfast dishes, and Alistair decided he needed coffee to stimulate his mind while he told Margaret about the last hours of his second, and he'd hoped final, visit to Kilvellie. During those hours, he'd felt his mind pushed to the limit to try and make sense of conflicting facts, if they were facts at all.

While the coffee was brewing, he went to the bedroom and threw on jeans and his favorite gray St. Andrews University hoodie. He'd never wear it to go out, for fear of looking like a tourist—he was too old to pass for a student—but wearing it at home gave him a cozy sense of belonging.

With coffee in hand, he returned to the dining table. He realized it would help to have a map of Kilvellie handy, so he printed one from his laptop. Margaret sat next to him at the table and he placed the map in front of them.

"I've already told you about the glass factory and the young men, six of them we think, who repeatedly pillaged it and threw glass over the cliff. Well, everything pointed to them being young men from Kilvellie, or nearby, who resented the idea of a German, who'd fought the British in the First World War, having a successful business in their town. If they'd been old enough to enlist, presumably they would have done so, but maybe they had older brothers or fathers fighting over in France or Italy, or Africa, and they had to let off steam somehow."

He stopped to drink some coffee and re-orient himself with the map. Using his pen as a pointer, he continued.

"The locations matter for what I'm going to tell you. The town itself is here, the beach is at the east side of the town, and the Beachside Cafe is to the north, about halfway along the cliff."

"How do you get onto the beach?" Margaret asked.

"The land slopes downwards, going south to the town, so you can access it from a ramp in the town. There's also a long set of wooden steps from the beach up to this parking lot. It's where the glass factory used to be."

He stopped and thought. "Oh, and there's another set of steps up the cliff at the far north end of the beach. It was mainly put there as an escape route for people who risked getting caught on the beach during high tide."

"I'll keep that in mind!" Margaret interjected.

Alistair pointed again to the parking area on the map. "The man who fell, he used to sit on a bench here. His granddaughter would drive him to the cafe, then he'd hobble over to sit on the bench for a while, with his memories I was told, while his granddaughter and her young child would have a half hour or so at the cafe."

Margaret looked up at him. "How do you know all this?"

"It's part of a very long story of what I was doing in Kilvellie. I promise I will bore you with it all soon. But to get back to the old man, he was the grandfather of the sergeant in the police station there. And the woman who brought the old man to sit by the cliff is the sergeant's sister. I got bits of the story from both of them, but they have different versions. The grandson, his name's Desmond, he said he grew up disliking the grandfather, Ronald. Ronald had moved in with Desmond, his sister Emily, and their parents. According to both grandchildren, Ronald's mind had been damaged during the war. Not like on the battlefield, but his unsuccessful efforts to protect the factory from the vandals had left him mentally stuck in those years, still battling."

"It sounds like he was a very unhappy man. It must have been difficult having him in the family home."

13

"Yes," Alistair confirmed, nodding his head. "It got so bad that as soon as Emily and Desmond took off for university, their parents moved and the grandfather stayed on alone in the house. That is, until he couldn't look after himself and he went into a care home."

Margaret thought for a moment. It seemed a bit extreme, in her experience, for a married couple to have to move out of their home, simply to accommodate one aging parent.

"Why didn't they get home help for him in his own house? That's one of the benefits of aging in Scotland, getting help to enable people to stay at home."

"Good point, but according to Desmond's father, Ronald could be mean and rude, and that made it uncomfortable for people to come in and help. So Ronald moved himself into a fancy care home."

Alistair pulled up the website for the Seaview Manor Home on his laptop. "It's located a few blocks inland from the coast, but it still has a view of the water, and it was convenient for Emily to visit and take him out."

"Wow!" Margaret exclaimed as she looked at the pictures of magnificent gardens, elegant rooms, and the descriptions of the food available to the residents. "Ronald, the grandfather, must have had a good income to afford this place."

"He didn't, that's the point. This is the man I mentioned earlier who accumulated a lot of valuable glass during the war, and his granddaughter Emily sold it for him in the past few years and he used that money to pay for this place."

"Oh, sorry, I didn't put two and two together. So *Ronald* was the glass factory guard?"

"Exactly," Alistair confirmed. "But here's how I got involved last week. Ronald's grandson Desmond, the police sergeant, was staying at Emily's for a couple of nights while he was moving to a different apartment, and he noticed boxes with recent auction records, including the vintage glass Emily had been selling. Adam went through one of Ronald's other boxes and found that he'd kept diaries during the war, with records of the days the factory was vandalized, and lists of glass that apparently he was given or he took. Way back then, the pieces were each unique, so Adam and I managed to match them up with the ones Emily sold to fund his comfortable life in the care home."

Margaret drank some tea and stared at the care home website.

"So," she ventured after a few moments, "this is what you alluded to earlier. Ronald lived in comfort thanks to the sale of stolen property? Wartime theft?"

"It looks like it. We don't know for sure that he didn't receive it legitimately, for example maybe the factory management paid him in glass, but there's no record of that, at least that I've heard. He also wrote the names of six men in his diaries, on the dates of the vandalism."

"Good, so with the diaries, could the police still go after the men, if any are alive?"

"We talked to the police officer who heads the Kilvellie station, Helen Griffen, and she decided that it would rake up too many bad memories. There could be people living in the town whose parents or grandparents knew the young men, or other people who had colluded and also got some of the stolen glass."

Alistair stopped and sighed. "Have you seen the television show Foyle's War?" he asked.

"Yes, my parents watched it. In your situation, do you think Foyle would still expose the vandals' identity, all these decades later?"

"That's the question. But we decided not to. Well, I mean, Helen decided not to, after she and Adam and I went through the pros and cons. I made the point that with no evidence of loss of life, it was all property damage, and maybe too much time has passed to hold young men, teenagers at the time, accountable. Or even to make their names known."

Margaret looked up and smiled. "With just that set of facts, I think I agree with you. It's one thing to still go after wartime criminals in their eighties and nineties who were responsible for killing, but somehow, tossing glass over a cliff doesn't rise to the same level, that's what I think."

"Good, I'm glad you would have concurred, with your legal background." Alistair stood up. "I need more coffee before we continue."

Margaret was ready to finish her tea and make a start on the day. "Isn't that the end of the story? With the old man, the factory guard, now dead, it sounds like he was the only witness, so even if the vandals were found, you only have his diary evidence of their involvement, right?"

"I wish that were so. But there's another part of it, and only I know. I should have told the police right away, but I was having arguments with my inner Foyle!"

Chapter 5

Alistair returned to the dining table. Margaret had also gone to the kitchen for a fresh mug of tea. She brought back a dish of shortbread.

"Brain food," she explained. "This story is getting too convoluted for me to follow."

After a long drink of coffee and a satisfied, "Ah, that's better," Alistair resumed the story by pointing again at the map.

"The last day in Kilvellie, my mind was at rest about the old man and the factory attacks, but I was still feeling unsettled. I missed having you to talk to, so I was wavering between driving south to Finlay and waiting for you to get back from Orkney, or driving up to catch a ferry and meet you. I thought maybe I could help with whatever you were doing. So I drove north through Kilvellie, and made a split second decision to stop at the cafe I mentioned before." He stopped and looked at Margaret, a questioning look on his face.

"Does that happen to you?" he asked. "That sense of not being able to make a decision, and your body kind of makes it for you?"

"Sure it does. Like when I crawled through that tunnel from the palace in Orkney. My brain said I should wait and keep yelling for help, but all the while, I was on hands and knees and crawling toward what might have been a very nasty end, stuck in a tunnel."

"So you understand when I tell you that the car just about pulled into the parking lot of its own volition. I got

17

some coffee and a box of pastries, then it was so nice out, I sat outside the cafe while I tried to decide what to do next. I could see the old man on his bench by the cliff, but I had no reason to walk over and talk to him. Then suddenly, I felt someone sit on the bench next to me. I recognized her from Desmond's photos—it was his sister Emily."

"Did you tell her who you were, and what you'd learned about her grandfather?"

Alistair smiled. "Margaret, I'm sure you know the answer, I didn't. I just told her my name. But she seemed to be in a mood to chat, so I listened. I won't repeat all the details, but she told me that her grandfather had confided something to her, and only to her. He thought she would understand because her husband is in the military. The story she told is that the six young men who vandalized the factory were Germans. They supposedly told her grandfather, the guard, that the factory founder had stolen equipment and supplies from their own family glass factories in Germany, right after World War One. Then the founder somehow shipped all that stuff to Scotland and built his successful factory in Kilvellie. In their eyes, they were simply getting revenge on him."

"What?" Margaret shook her head. "I thought everyone knew that the vandals were local boys, but they weren't caught or prosecuted because people in the town might have been quietly benefiting, or at least looking the other way since the factory was built by a German man, an ex-soldier?"

"Yes, that seems to have been the party line, if you can call it that. The factory owner came back from being interned as an enemy alien, and then after years of closure, he managed to get the factory up and running again in the nineteen fifties."

"So did *he* at least try to get justice, some kind of compensation for the damage?"

"No," Alistair said. "According to everyone I spoke to, the owner just wanted to get back to business and not live in the past. Unlike the factory guard, who seems to have let those years define, poison even, the whole rest of his own life."

"And did those six young men, the vandals, just slip away? Go back to Germany, if that story was true, or get absorbed back into their families if they were local, and keep quiet?"

Alistair sighed deeply, then took Margaret's hand. "This is what's been keeping me up at night, agonizing over whether to talk to the police officer, Helen. Emily finished her story by telling me that one night, during one of the glass rampages, her grandfather snapped. I still find this horrible to believe, but she claims that he told her he pushed all six of the vandals over the cliff, when they were lying at the cliff edge, relaxed and laughing, tossing glass into the waves below."

"Oh, my God. Could that be true? No wonder the old man couldn't adjust after the war. Did any of the six men survive?"

"Not from Emily's telling. At high tide, the water covers the beach and the waves smash against the cliff face. Any of the young men who didn't drown right away would likely have been knocked unconscious or killed outright by the force of the water against the cliff. And before you ask if their bodies were found, even if they were, there was so much loss of life at sea in those war years, no one could have suspected they'd been shoved off a cliff. With the old man as the only witness, he obviously kept quiet for decades."

"Poor you." Alistair released Margaret's hand so they could each have a comforting sip of tea and coffee. "That's a huge burden. You were all ready to tell Helen, the police officer, about your conversation with Emily, and now the man has died before you had a chance?"

Alistair sighed again and shook his head. "It's not right to say I didn't have a chance. I've just been torn about it. Part of me feels like it's not my place, as an outsider, and all my information is hearsay. But if there *are* six young men dead, at the hands of a man who was still walking free and living in comfort in the care home, don't they deserve justice even after all this time? There must have been parents grieving when their sons didn't return home that night, or the next weeks or months."

"Maybe," Margaret agreed, "but young men lied about their age to enlist. Whether German or Scottish, if anyone did wonder what had happened to a son, a brother, whoever, it would be reasonable to think they were killed in battle and buried as unknowns." She looked at the map again, then up at Alistair. She could see that he was feeling strained from relating the tragic story.

"Alistair, it sounds like Emily is the only remaining source for this idea that her late grandfather killed six men. If you don't say anything to the police in Kilvellie, and if Emily keeps it to herself, then this could be the end of it, right? I mean, with the old's man's death, as tragic as it was?"

"Not quite." Alistair pointed to the map again. "After Emily left with her grandfather, I realized I really wanted to be with you as soon as possible, so I continued driving north. I noticed a small chapel beyond the cafe and I stopped to think for a moment. There were memorial plaques on the walls inside, and a man who works as a guide there translated one for me. It was in German. It listed the same six names from the grandfather's diary, I mean, Ronald the factory guard, and it said the men were dedicated to the deep in the North Sea in nineteen forty-four. The plaque also said it was witnessed, but the name of the witness has been scratched out."

Alistair showed Margaret a photograph of the plaque he'd taken with his phone, but with the glare from the windows on the shiny brass surface, the names weren't clear, and the texture of the scratched area was lost.

"And before you ask," he continued, "the guide has no idea when the plaque was installed, who installed it, and who crossed out the witness's name. I tried searching online for the names, but nothing came up specific enough to the town, or the era."

Margaret was silent for a moment, then spoke in a soft voice. "That's written documentation of the deaths, so a whole different scenario than Emily's hearsay story. Wow. You really have a dilemma."

"Yes, but with the factory guard dead, murderer or not, do I have an obligation to say anything to the police about what Emily told me? I need your legal take on this. The names are on public view, so a visitor to the chapel could look into it if they chose. Although, there may be nothing helpful online. But that's kept the balance tipped in favor of not saying anything to Helen. The names are written on a plaque in *her* town, and I'm just someone who passed through. It's not my place to call attention to the plaque, is it?"

Margaret sipped her tea while she thought for a moment.

"Well, you know the back story to why the names are there, if Emily is telling the truth. What if there *are* six families in Germany, or here in Scotland, whose descendants still wonder what happened to an uncle, or a brother, during the war? And any of those boys could have a younger brother or sister still living and wondering about their missing brother."

Alistair smiled. He knew she'd reach that conclusion, but it had helped to talk it through. "You're right, Margaret. So maybe, with the old man dead, this would be the time to make a public appeal for relatives of those boys? They wouldn't have to be told the boys might have been murdered, just that they died in Kilvellie in a fall from the cliff. That's perfectly believable, considering it's what just happened to the old man."

"What *probably* happened," Margaret corrected. "Now that I know more about the man's past, if Emily was telling the truth, then maybe a relative of one of those boys tracked Ronald down and decided to kill him."

Alistair stood up. "I need a mental break. But even if a family member traced the boys' presence to Kilvellie in the nineteen forties, how could they possibly know what happened that night, if Emily is correct about him shoving the boys off the cliff, in the dark?"

He slumped back into his chair. "Oh no, what if there *was* a witness like the chapel plaque says, and that information was passed down and someone traced Ronald and was able to identify him as the guard? I had been thinking the witness was really Ronald, and he'd had the plaque installed out of remorse, but then scratched his own name off to protect his family. Maybe there was a *separate* witness on the clifftop that night?"

"Alistair, listen." Margaret's voice took on a serious tone. "Speaking as a lawyer, you have *got* to go to the Kilvellie police and tell them all this in person. They may want to interview you on the record. If there's *any* chance that the old man was pushed off the cliff, no matter what he did in the war, that itself is still murder. And other than Emily, you seem to be the only one who could come forward to identify a motive."

After considering Margaret's rational advice, Alistair said he would, but that he'd want her to go with him for support. She was right, this was too important for just a phone call.

"First thing tomorrow morning," he declared, "we'll drive up there. I mean, I hope you'll come along to encourage and support me. I doubt Helen will be around today, based on what the officer at the station said. It's less than an hour away, and even after all I've told you, maybe you can have a look for sea glass on the beach."

Margaret smiled to herself. She still hadn't told Alistair about the project that she was considering, but this would be a chance to check Kilvellie as a beach for targeted shell collecting. Now that Alistair was getting involved in Kilvellie again, albeit perhaps just for a day or two, she'd reveal her news on the drive there in the morning.

Chapter 6

The next morning promised a sunny day, perfect, Margaret thought, for visiting a new beach. She had to remind herself to control her enthusiasm: the only reason for the trip was to give Alistair a chance to tell the Kilvellie police something he really should have told them a week before.

As befitted his somber task for the day, Alistair wore a blue shirt, a navy tie, and a lightweight tweed blazer, although he tempered the business casual look by wearing his usual black jeans. He wore black loafers, but brought running shoes to change into in case he accompanied Margaret to the beach. His black hair was neatly styled; Margaret appreciated that he always took time to look his best, whatever they were doing. She wore a long white cotton sweater over a denim skirt, and brought jeans and water-proof sandals for her beach visit.

The previous evening, Alistair had explained what he'd learned about beachcombing at Kilvellie: the odds of finding a prize piece of glass before someone else did meant searching at the water's edge as the tide receded. Margaret had done her diligence online and printed a copy of the day's tide chart. Being optimistic, she brought along several sealable plastic sandwich bags for her finds.

Parked outside the cottage was their third in a series of vehicles. On arrival in Scotland months earlier, Alistair had rented a standard sedan, then switched to a longer term lease when he realized he'd be staying on. Soon after that, the village had given Margaret permission to clear the overgrowth from the two-mile stretch of former rail tracks, enabling vehicle access from the village to her cottage. Alistair exchanged his sedan for a well-used Land Rover that could handle the rough path.

The Land Rover wasn't comfortable for long trips, so with no date set to go back to Maine, he and Margaret had bought a used Saab convertible, metallic gray with a navy roof. The weather was rarely conducive to driving with the top down, but when it was, the investment was worth it. Today was one of those days.

As soon as they'd reached the main road leading north from Finlay, Margaret broached the subject of her recent Orkney trip.

"I haven't committed to anything," she assured him, "but if it fits with your plans, I'd like to help the prince."

"Actually, I'm glad you mentioned plans," Alistair responded, glancing at her. "I don't know if you're waiting for me to take the lead on discussing what we're going to do in the next several months, or if you have some ideas. I just don't want us to each wait for the other person to initiate a discussion."

"I feel the same!" Margaret said, relieved. "I don't want to rock the boat of our comfortable routine in Finlay, but I know we have decisions to make soon. I'll explain what the prince needs, or wants me to do, and then we can discuss whether I should agree or not, and if I do agree, how much time to devote, and maybe you'd want to get involved too."

Alistair laughed. "I'm not saying another word until I know what the project is!"

"To put it simply, the prince has two goals. One is to inspire people to take better care of Scotland's beaches. Not just a yearly or twice-yearly beach clean-up, but make it a daily habit. Like if you're walking the beach, pick up any trash you see when you see it. Not leave it for someone else. And the second goal, which is really the carrot, is a competition to find groatie buckies. People will pay to participate and that money goes to charity."

Alistair tapped the steering wheel a couple of times. "Where have I heard that term? Wait, didn't it have to do with the prince getting stuck near a tidal island, and Hamish rescued him?"

"Exactly. They're small cowrie shells and in Scotland they're called groatie buckies. People get fanatical about collecting them, but serious collectors are reluctant to disclose their good collecting spots. That's my task for the prince. He's going to lead one of the collecting teams, and he thinks I can help by doing research online and identifying where the best groatie buckie areas are. It would involve studying photographs, learning about groatie buckie ecology, where they live, that kind of thing."

"And for this you went to college and law school," Alistair said. "Nice work if you can get it!"

Margaret nudged his elbow. "It's for charity, don't knock it."

"And in addition to your research, would you also help collect the groatie buckies?"

"I'd like to of course, but from the little I've learned so far, it could mean traveling to remote islands."

She waited, expecting Alistair to raise an objection. She knew that he worried about her when she was away, although he was trying to temper his PI-trained urge to check on her. This time it seemed he had no serious concerns with her plans.

"I can help," he said. "I'm worried that when we eventually go back to Maine, Scotland will fade away in my mind, like Brigadoon, and I want to experience as much of it as I can first."

"So," Margaret ventured, "you don't mind staying on a little longer? Aren't you missing your investigative work back in Maine?"

"I am, a bit," he agreed. "But another month or two won't matter..." He paused for effect. "Not if it's for charity!"

25

A sign for Kilvellie-by-the-Sea soon came into view. Approaching from the south, the brick police station was one of the first buildings that Alistair saw, and he pointed it out to Margaret.

"I'll park near the station, then we can walk to the bakery and get some tea or coffee to bring with us. Does that sound good?"

"Sure. The police won't mind you just stopping in?"

He reassured her as he pulled into a parking spot on the main road, just beyond the police station. "No, they run quite a casual unit. Professional, but casual. In fact, the right-hand side of the building is a residence. Helen was living there when I left last week, but she was thinking of moving to somewhere more private."

"Sounds like Hamish Macbeth," Margaret muttered to herself as she unbuckled her seat belt and opened the door.

"Och aye, it is a wee bit," Alistair said, to her surprise, in a mock Scottish accent. He'd never been keen to watch British comedies, especially ones from so many years back, but maybe he was learning to adapt.

A few minutes later, with paper cups of tea in hand, they stood at the front door to the police station. Alistair rang the buzzer and then tried the door, which opened easily, so he was glad that someone would be there to speak to him.

Inside, he introduced himself to a female police officer who was occupying Helen's desk, and she stood up to greet him, remembering him from his call the previous day.

"I was hoping to find Helen, I mean, Officer Griffen," Alistair explained.

"She's mentioned you. I expect her back shortly, so you're welcome to wait in the conference room."

"You mean, the interview room?" Alistair asked. That's what it had been called during his recent visits, anyway.

"Probably the same thing," the officer said as she opened the door to a room off the main office. Alistair and Margaret took seats at the round table.

"From what Helen's told me, I'm guessing you're here about the death?" the officer asked.

Alistair hesitated. "I, um, I've some information about Ronald that I just learned recently and I hadn't had a chance to share it with Helen. I'm hoping she won't be too upset at the delay."

While Alistair was speaking, Margaret slipped the tide table from her backpack and was trying to discreetly look at it. The young officer glanced down and saw what Margaret was doing. With a grin, she said, "Next low tide is in three hours, so if you wait an hour, then head to the beach, you'll have your pick of the glass that's just been uncovered by the waves. Sorry! I shouldn't presume, but most outsiders are here for the glass."

Margaret laughed. "I'm sorry too. I know Alistair is here on serious business, and there's been a death, but I want to take advantage of being this close to the beach and the glass. It's my first visit to the town."

"I'd better get back to my desk," the officer said. "If it's all right with you, I'll leave this door open. The room can get a little claustrophobic otherwise."

Alistair told Margaret more about the town while they drank their tea and waited for Helen to return. Through the conference room doorway, Margaret glanced around the station; the main office held Helen's large desk facing the front door, and a smaller desk by the far wall faced into the office. Behind that desk was the door into Helen's adjoining residence. There was a kitchen area just visible at the back of the station. The station walls were mainly bare, apart from what looked like regulation police information posters and signs. An institutional gray metal cabinet stood against the wall next to the second desk.

The conference room itself was less standard-issue than the office area. The table accommodated four chairs and not much more, and there was a desk with information leaflets about the town, and photocopies of a local map. The walls were decorated with vintage-looking posters of the beach, the cliffs, and an old steam engine train. Margaret imagined it was designed to be a pleasant room for interviewing witnesses, although the strong bars on the window sent a clear message to anyone secured in the room.

A few minutes later they heard the front door open, and Alistair recognized Helen's voice. He stood up and went into the office to greet her. Margaret knew that Helen was Adam's mother, and she searched for a family resemblance. While Adam was tall, lanky, and sported bright red hair, his mother was shorter, stouter, and gray-haired. She wore her uniform, but Margaret imagined that, in street clothes, she'd blend in well with the cafe owners and other devoted businesswomen who kept small towns going in good times or bad, always a cheery word for friends, and a welcome for tourists. Margaret liked Helen immediately.

After introductions, Helen made herself a mug of tea and joined Alistair and Margaret in the conference room. She hesitated at the door, and Alistair silently indicated that she should close it. He assumed the visiting officer would be discreet, but he didn't know what direction their conversation might take.

To start on a casual note, Alistair commented that the interview room seemed more welcoming than when he'd visited previously. Helen glanced around. "Oh, aye, it was too institutional for my liking, so I did a wee bit of decorating. I may officially interview someone now and again, but anything that could get confrontational would take place at a bigger station, with better security. Anyway, I've started calling it my conference room."

Alistair was about to begin his explanation for visiting, when Helen said, "So you've heard about poor Ronald."

"Yes, just the brief report in the news. And I spoke to Adam yesterday."

Helen shook her head. "Of course you did. I knew the identity of the victim wouldn't stay confidential for long."

It Continued with the Cowries

Alistair raised his hands in protest. "I didn't tell anyone else, truly. And Margaret won't reveal anything we talk about, but if you'd prefer to just talk to me, that's fine."

Helen smiled at Margaret. "I have heard good things about you. But do you really want to be indoors on such a nice day, hearing about people you don't know? I'd suggest a walk on the beach, if Alistair doesn't mind you going alone."

Margaret wondered what could be dangerous about going to the beach alone, but put that thought aside. She was tempted to leave, then decided to stay and listen. After all, Alistair had asked her along for support.

"From the tide chart, I think it's too early to look for glass anyway," she said.

Helen glanced at the clock on the wall: eleven o'clock. "How about if we talk now, then we can grab some lunch, then the beach? Alistair can come back here with me if we need to continue our discussion. Frankly, I don't know yet what he wants to tell me."

Alistair began with profuse apologies to Helen, but she quickly cut him off.

"Alistair, unless *you* pushed Ronald off the cliff, you have nothing to apologize for, and I can't imagine anything you say will affect the conclusion about his death. As of now, no one has provided photographic or video evidence that anyone was near him just before he went over the cliff. It's being treated as a tragic accident, and not unexpected in an elderly man who was unsteady on his feet. Between us, I don't think the old guy should have been left alone so close to the cliff edge, but I understand that's what he wanted, and it was a long-term part of his routine, so there we have it. I suppose for his granddaughter, who took him there most days, she might not have noticed a slow deterioration in his balance."

Margaret was reminded of her own parents, and how she'd placed an unscheduled video call to them one evening and caught them behaving quite strangely. She thought that they were both suffering from dementia, which she hadn't noticed before, but there had been a simple explanation: marijuana-laced brownies that they'd eaten, unawares.

With that image in mind, she spoke up. "Helen, are you looking into his medications? I wonder if he could have taken too much of something and it made him shaky, or dizzy? I don't know if the coroner will do anything like a tox screen on him."

Helen raised her eyebrows. "That's something we didn't consider, I admit. The coroner said that with the severe injuries from the fall, it wasn't possible to determine if he'd been dead before he fell, like from a stroke or a heart attack. The family hasn't requested an autopsy, and so far I don't think the coroner is planning on one."

Alistair turned to Margaret. "Are you thinking he could have been given too much of a medication, maybe intentionally?"

"Goodness, no," she clarified, "I just meant, I obviously don't know what meds he takes, if any, but I have seen my parents affected by marijuana they accidentally ingested. They were both unsteady on their feet and my dad was staggering around the house. It was terrifying until I learned the cause."

Helen had a small notebook at hand and she jotted a reminder to look into the man's medications. She sighed. "Maybe you have a point, Margaret, to have his blood and tissues checked. It would have to be done soon, with the fast deterioration of most drugs. I'll think about it and decide after our meeting."

She sipped her tea, then addressed Margaret again. "I don't know if Alistair mentioned this, but the man who died, Ronald, is the grandfather of my sergeant, name's Desmond, and the father of my predecessor here, his name's Richard Wilson." She hesitated, then added in a low voice, almost sheepishly, "Richard and I are dating."

Alistair smiled. "I'm glad that's working out. I like Richard."

"You can see how awkward this is," Helen continued. "It's hardly an arms-length situation."

"But it's up to the coroner, isn't it, or the procurator fiscal?" Alistair asked. "I don't know exactly how this decision would be made. I mean, to determine how much post-death investigation to do, or to record it as an accidental death, no foul play?"

"Yes, that's not my decision to make," Helen confirmed, "but I have an obligation to pass on any information I get that could indicate that it wasn't an accident. Margaret's suggestion is only that, with no evidence, but something must have triggered her even raising the issue."

"It was just because of what I saw with my parents, when I had a video call with them," Margaret mumbled, now wishing she hadn't said a word. It was one thing to offer her opinion in a law firm setting, with senior associates and partners to serve as a buffer, a filter before anything she said was acted on, but here there was no filter. Now she worried that Helen was taking her comments too seriously, given her legal qualifications.

She tried to backpedal. "If my mother had been standing at a cliff edge, and not in her kitchen with soup boiling over on the stove, she could have easily slipped over the edge. That's how unsteady she was. But I'm *not* suggesting Ronald had been using drugs! Oh, darn it, I should have gone to the beach and not sat in on your discussion. I'm not really helping, I am?"

Helen stood up. "You are helping, both of you. When Alistair was here last week, it was this kind of conversation, with no holding back, that helped us make some difficult decisions. Believe me, I'm glad you're here, Margaret. Now, I need to refresh my tea. How about you two?"

Margaret felt a little better about speaking up. She watched Helen open the door to the conference room, and wondered why she didn't ask the police officer outside to fetch more tea. Margaret had certainly fetched plenty of coffee for people in her early days at the law firm, but perhaps this station was more egalitarian than that. In any event, when Helen stepped out of the conference room holding her mug, the officer leapt to her feet and offered to bring fresh tea and biscuits for the meeting. Thanking her, Helen handed over her mug and returned to the room.

She smiled at Margaret. "I wouldn't have asked for that, but when it's freely offered, I don't say no!"

They chatted about the beach and the town until the refreshments arrived, then closed the door and resumed the discussion.

Chapter 7

Helen steered the conversation to the reason for Alistair's visit; he took a long drink of tea, then sat back and began.

"I could set the scene and explain how the conversation came about, but you're so busy I'd better get to the point first. Ronald's granddaughter Emily told me that, according to Ronald, he killed all six of the factory vandals. In nineteen forty-four I think it would have happened. If it's even true..."

He stopped suddenly when he realized that Helen was almost choking on her tea, and she held a paper napkin against her mouth while she regained her composure.

"Good *heavens*, Alistair. Whatever I thought you might tell me, that was not on my list. How long have you known this?"

"As I said earlier, I feel terrible and I have to apologize for keeping it to myself. Emily told me a week ago. I happened to sit on a bench with her on my way out of town, near the Beachside Cafe. It was completely unsolicited. In fact, I really didn't want to hear more about Ronald and his war years, not after all we discovered."

Helen sipped her tea, more calm now, thinking and processing as Alistair spoke. Margaret stayed silent, listening; she'd heard the story the day before, but had no idea how Helen would react to it, or what she would do with the information.

"I've been agonizing over it, Helen," Alistair continued. "Remember our discussion, back when we read the diaries, and we figured that property damage was bad, but at least there were no *deaths* during the factory vandalism? Well, what if Emily's story is true? What if Ronald did kill the vandals? I've been feeling ill over what to do with the information."

Helen sighed. "And now he's dead."

Alistair nodded. "Now he's dead. Even if I'd told you a week ago, and you decided to investigate it formally, he died too quickly for you to bring him to justice."

"But it's not too late to get closure for the families of those six young men. If the story is correct, anyway. How can we possibly verify it? I guess I can start by asking Emily if he provided any more details, but anything she says will be second-hand at best..."

Alistair broke in. "Sorry, Helen, there is one more piece of information, possibly verification. Have you ever visited the little chapel just north of town? It's not far past the cafe, on the right." He took out his phone to show her the photograph of the brass plaque.

Helen was shaking her head. "No, but I've seen it from the road. How does it fit in?"

"There's a plaque, a memorial, on the wall. I took this picture of it, but the details aren't clear. It's in German, and a volunteer in the chapel translated it for me. It says that six men were committed to the deep in nineteen forty-four. The names match the six names in Ronald's war-era diaries. The plaque at one time had the name of a witness, but that name has been scratched out. The volunteer said he knows nothing about the history of the plaque."

Helen made some notes in her notebook, then looked up at Alistair again.

"This is very disturbing, Alistair. I don't blame you for keeping it to yourself while you struggled with telling me, so please don't keep blaming yourself. I'm actually glad to be hearing it after Ronald died. Otherwise, I would have been in a very difficult situation. As Adam said when we were discussing the diaries, the idea of questioning a seemingly harmless care home resident in his last months or years is pretty grim, let alone arresting him."

Margaret was following the discussion, but had not planned to contribute again after her earlier awkwardness. However, something was starting to take root in her brain and she decided to share it.

"I know I'm far removed from all this," she began, "and I've never met any of the people you're talking about, but if I was evaluating the information in a legal procedure, I would have one more question."

"Please share it, Margaret," Helen said. "Sometimes it helps to hear from someone who isn't close to the situation."

Margaret continued nervously, "You haven't said as much, but it seems you're considering it lucky, oh, that's the wrong word, maybe fortuitous, that Alistair kept this information from you until after Ronald died. Although, I think he was planning to tell you soon anyway. But what if you turn it around: could Ronald have died *because* of what he did during the war? Emily repeated his confession to Alistair, a complete stranger sitting on a bench. Who else has she told recently? If the young men were local and still have family around, could someone have sought vengeance and, I don't know, maybe poisoned Ronald that morning, before he fell down the cliff?"

Helen and Alistair both stared at Margaret for a moment, their faces stony, and again she felt like she should have stayed quiet.

"You're absolutely right, Margaret," Helen said at last. "The timing can't be ignored. I now have a list of urgent things to do and people to contact. I'll have to bow out of lunch after all. Alistair, I'm sorry to do this but I should arrange a formal interview and you can go over in detail what Emily told you, then your visit to the chapel and what you saw there."

"It's fine," Alistair assured her. "I'll help any way I can. The fate of those six men has been haunting me ever since I spoke to Emily. Is it all right if I do a bit of investigation on my own, or am I now considered a witness, or even a suspect?"

Helen laughed. "No, Alistair, I have not for once considered you a suspect, unless there's some deep family history you're not telling me. If you, or both of you, can see what you can dig up about that memorial plaque, when it was installed, who commissioned it, maybe even who removed the witness name, that could go a long way to explaining things."

Alistair agreed to help on that point. Margaret used the station restroom to change into her jeans and sandals. After saying goodbye to Helen and promising to keep in touch, she and Alistair left the station, emerging into the warm midday sunshine.

Chapter 8

"Do you still want to get some lunch and go to the beach?" Margaret asked Alistair. "Or are there people you need to speak to? I mean, about the plaque, and the chapel?"

"I need to clear my head first, so let's get sandwiches at the bakery and we can sit on the beach." He pointed across the main road. "That fence marks where a sloping path zig-zags down to the beach. We can access it there."

As they walked to the bakery, Margaret asked Alistair how well he knew the town; he seemed at home, to know his way around.

"It's so small," he said, "it didn't take me long. I was here twice while you were up in Orkney. You can see that this main road only continues for about three blocks, and as far as I know, there's not much on the side streets in terms of shops. The town caters to visitors, the shops I mean, and there are some good cafes. The main appeal is the beach, so some of the businesses focus on serving people here to col-lect glass, like the clifftop cafe further north. That's where the long stairway was built to access the beach, that I showed you on the map."

As they walked, Margaret began wishing she hadn't spo-ken up in the meeting with Helen. She felt as if she'd intro-duced suggestions that were not based on anything factual, more like a brain-storming exercise in law school. But now Helen was looking into questions that, apparently, she had not considered before she spoke to Margaret.

"Two years ago," she admitted to Alistair, "I wouldn't have

had the courage to make suggestions like I did with Helen. I've developed more confidence speaking up, but I'm wondering if I went too far today. I know none of the people involved, so I really should have kept quiet."

Alistair took her hand as they walked. "Don't belittle your contribution! Between us, I think Helen is too close to the dead man's family to make objective decisions. If the man who died was a visitor, a stranger in the town, Helen and her sergeant might have been quick to look into foul play, or ask if his meds could have contributed, things you suggested. So really, I'm glad your comments nudged her to think about alternatives to a simple but tragic fall."

He stopped as they reached the bakery. "No more about Ronald for now, okay? Let's enjoy the beach and you can tell me more about your project."

Soon, with sandwiches and drinks in hand, they walked back and forth down the zigzag cement ramp to the beach, and sat on a large boulder at the back of the beach, with the cliff towering above them. The beach was more expansive than the beach at Finlay, and Margaret thought of how much she enjoyed the view of that beach from her cottage. With this far more dramatic spectacle available to residents of Kilvellie, she wondered why Helen, the senior officer in the local police station, was living in the station residence. From Margaret's brief visit, she could tell the residence windows had no views to speak of, certainly not a beach view.

Well, she decided, maybe Helen was only there for a short time while looking for somewhere that did have a view. And since moving to the Finlay cottage and working from home there, Margaret had learned that there was something to be said for working and living in the same place. She'd only had a short walking commute from her apartment in Portland to her nearby law office, but five minutes in freezing temperatures and Arctic-like sleet could feel like an hour.

She noticed that Alistair kept glancing to the left along the beach, his face seeming to cloud when he turned back to

It Continued with the Cowries

Margaret.

"Are you thinking about the beach glass, and how it ties in with the factory attacks?" she asked him. "I don't need to beachcomb here if it has bad associations for you." Although, she said to herself, she would like to check enough of the beach to rule it in or out as a place to look for groatie buckies.

"Thanks, but it's not that. I'm remembering another thing that happened on this beach. When I was here before, I ended up helping to solve the mystery of how a teenage girl disappeared about seven years ago. Don't worry," he added quickly, "she's fine, and in fact she's dating Adam now. I'll tell you more about that."

"She disappeared on *this* beach?" Margaret looked around nervously. Maybe Helen had been right about not going to the beach alone: was there quicksand?

Alistair pointed to the cliff wall to their left. "She got caught in a recess, a shallow cave, just along there, when the tide came in. Her family thought she must have been swept away during a storm that night, but she'd found a way out to safety. A misunderstanding about her family kept her away for the next seven years or so, then she was reunited with them when I was here. But the lesson is, respect the tides, and don't get caught with the waves approaching the cliff. No beach glass is worth the risk."

They finished lunch in silence, enjoying the sound of the waves and the calling of gulls. The tide was right to start their search for glass, and Alistair suggested they walk along where the waves were receding. In her jeans and sandals, Margaret was ready to step into the shallow water if she spied any treasures there.

As they strolled at the water's edge, Margaret talked more about the prince's latest passion, the combination of beach clean-up and shell-collecting competition.

"And not just any shells," she reminded him. "We're only interested in groatie buckies, the little cowrie shells. But at the same time, the contestants must pick up and remove any trash they encounter while collecting. There will be teams of people, and a deadline for submitting each team's final groatie buckie count. Plus photographs documenting trash removal. I don't know yet what the prizes will be, but it should be something meaningful, for all the time and the expense of travel."

"It sounds like the contestants will get a lot of exercise," Alistair said, stopping to take a couple of breaths. Despite being fit, he was noticing the extra effort it was taking him to walk slowly along the rocky shoreline, dodging waves and leaning over or crouching repeatedly to investigate a piece of glass.

"Ironically, it may be the opposite." Margaret pointed toward the far end of the beach. "As far as I can tell, there's beach glass all along here, so walking is a good way to find it. But for the groatie buckies, in some places they're concentrated in a narrow section of rocky beach, and people basically sit for as long as they can tolerate and rummage through layers of pebbles and sand."

By the time they each had a small bagful of glass, the rustic wooden steps up the cliffside to the cafe and parking lot were in view. Alistair had only bad feelings about the area, but Margaret was seeing it with fresh eyes, so he put his reactions aside and asked if she felt up to climbing the long stairway and getting a drink at the cafe.

She hesitated, staring up at the cliff high above. "Is this, is this where, where the man fell?"

Chastising himself, Alistair nodded. "I'm being thoughtless. We should turn back along the beach. He would have landed near where we are now, but with the high tides since then, there would be no point marking the location down here."

Margaret turned to him. "No, let's go up. Maybe looking at the place where it happened will trigger some ideas. At least, if *you* want to?"

It Continued with the Cowries

What won in the end, for Alistair, was his thirst, so together they began the long climb, and after a few stops to admire the sweeping views north and south along the coastline, they arrived at the top. Alistair pointed to where police tape was strung from the stairway handrail and around several stakes in the grass, cordoning off the bench where the man would normally sit.

"It *looks* like a crime scene," Margaret commented.

Alistair tried to be reassuring. "They probably have it blocked off to keep someone else from falling. Perhaps the edge has become too unstable. And I doubt very much that they'd look for shoe prints or a sign of a struggle—lots of people will have passed by here walking to and from the stairway." But in reality, he was deeply saddened to think that he'd sat on that bench not two weeks earlier, chatting with the old man like they had all the time in the world.

Leaving thoughts of the tragedy behind them, they crossed the parking lot; as they walked, Alistair told Margaret about the new glass museum that was going to be built across the street. A brightly colored banner announcing its imminent construction flew proudly over a derelict former holiday home development.

"That's yet another story!" he said, holding the cafe door open for her. "I hope Greta is still baking for the cafe," he added as they approached the glass-fronted case that was normally full of baked goodies.

But from talking to a young woman at the counter, he was disappointed to learn that Greta, whose family had been just scraping by for years, had given up baking for local businesses recently. Alistair thought he knew the reason: Greta and her husband Malky had received a windfall of vintage glass hidden since the Second World War. As a descendant of the factory owner, Malky was the legal heir, and now the valuable glassware would form the backbone of the new museum.

Alistair was momentarily disappointed that he wouldn't

41

be sampling Greta's excellent cream cakes, treacle tarts, and other calorie-rich concoctions, but then the young woman explained that Greta was helping design the snack bar for the museum, which would be run as an extension of this cafe. When it opened, Greta would resume her baking.

"We're grateful to be hired to run the snack bar," the woman said. "Last thing we need is a competing cafe set up across the street."

After perusing the meager selections, Alistair and Margaret chose packages of shortbread and bottles of Highland sparkling water. They paid, then walked outside to sit in the sun. Alistair steered Margaret away from the closest bench, mindful of the conversation he'd had with Emily on that bench, and how awful he'd felt after hearing her tale of Granddad's murderous rampage during the war.

Instead, they found a bench closer to the cliff and sat down to enjoy the view.

"Okay," Alistair said, "let's get some plans in place. How about if we devote the next month to our own projects. You can go hunt for your grubby buckets or whatever they are, and I'll try to help Helen sort out what happened to Ronald, and to the young men who may or may not have died at his hand. Although I still find it very hard to believe. Does that work for you?"

She laughed. "It's *groatie buckies* and you'd better get used to pronouncing the name properly. With a whole lot of luck, you'll be surrounded by them a month from now!"

Alistair looked out at the North Sea, thinking that they had made a little progress in terms of their immediate future, but it brought them no closer to the big decision: stay in Scotland, or move back to Maine? Oh well, he decided, maybe the next month would help them decide.

Chapter 9

Back in downtown Kilvellie, Officer Helen Griffen finished her own lunch at her desk, then set off along the main street to visit the late Ronald Wilson's family solicitor. With Margaret's comments fresh in her mind, she decided to investigate Ronald's will, assuming he had made a will. Perhaps Margaret was right, and despite no forensic evidence pointing to foul play, maybe it shouldn't be ruled out at this early stage.

The solicitor, a Mr. McMahon, had offices on the second floor of a grand converted Victorian house on the east side of the main street, so she expected that it would have good views of the sea and coast. She opened the front door, original as far as she could tell, and well-maintained; green-carpeted stairs faced her beyond the lobby as she entered the building. She took a moment to look around: crown molding on the high ceilings, a chandelier still hanging over the entryway, looking out of place in the converted office building. More original-looking doors led to private offices on the main floor.

The house must have belonged to someone who had made their fortune in coal or shipping, she imagined, and the chandelier would have witnessed elegant social gatherings, its light illuminating the jewels of the guests. But behind all the glamour, she knew that in this town, the fortune of the long-ago owner was likely based on back-breaking work by hundreds of coal miners, or countless poorly paid sailors.

She walked up the stairs and found the door open to Mr.

McMahon's office. His desk sat in a large bookshelf-lined room, perhaps a former library, and he stood to greet her. After shaking hands, he barked to someone in the adjoining room to fetch tea and biscuits. Surrounded by thousands of books and old ledgers, some of which might date back a century or more, Helen felt herself grimace at the reminder of what life must have been like for servants in this great house, with the occupants yelling orders at young parlor maids and footmen. She was not impressed by McMahon's disregard of modern courtesies.

Her judgment had been misplaced. From next door emerged a woman in her sixties, Helen thought, wearing a tweed skirt suit. Her graying brown hair was shoulder-length and held back with a tortoise-shell headband. In a no-nonsense tone, she asked the older-looking Mr. McMahon, "Is that three teas, or two, your lordship? You didn't let me know if I'm joining your meeting." But the woman was smiling as she asked, so she was clearly not bothered by McMahon's apparent rudeness.

Mr. McMahon introduced her as Ms. Endicott, also a solicitor. She said to Helen, "Dinnae get the wrong impression. As often as not, I'm the one hollering at *him* to make the tea! And please, call me Elise. His lordship here is Claude."

With tea served and explanations of the office tea etiquette out of the way, Elise returned to her own office, ready to join them if the conversation warranted. Helen settled back in a comfortable wingback guest chair facing Claude. It was upholstered in a William Morris floral design, and Helen was already having thoughts of doing the same for her furniture once she was no longer living at the police station. She wondered if the chair was original to the house...

Claude interrupted her thoughts, pen and paper at the ready. "When you called, Helen, you said you wanted to discuss Ronald Wilson's will, and identify his heirs?"

"That's correct. With his death so sudden, I want to make sure I understand the family situation. As far as I know, he

leaves behind his son, Richard Wilson, and his two grand-
children, Desmond and Emily. As I'm sure you know,
Desmond is the sergeant working with me. He is single, and
Emily is married, with one son. Does that all sound correct?"

"Yes," Claude confirmed. "Ronald owned no real estate at
his death, and as far as I know he has nothing significant in
bank accounts. His will leaves almost everything equally to
his two grandchildren, with a donation to a local charity."

Helen thought for a moment. From what she knew, in
recent years Emily had done far more than Desmond to help
their grandfather, and perhaps was entitled to a larger share
of the estate. But if Emily had benefited financially from selling the now-vintage Regenbogen Factory glass that Ronald
had somehow acquired during the war years, maybe in
Ronald's mind that made up the difference.

"Seems odd," Helen ventured, "nothing to his son? He's
skipping a generation?"

"That's my understanding. Perhaps, since Richard had a
full career as a police officer and he owns the family house,
as well as property in Spain, Ronald felt that Richard was
well cared for, and that the younger generation could make
better use of his remaining assets."

"And what assets are there?" To Helen, it sounded like
there was nothing much to inherit that could have been a
motive to shove the poor old man off a cliff.

"Just his belongings at the care home. I believe he fur-
nished his room himself, and may have acquired some art-
work after he moved in." Claude stopped for a moment.
"When Ronald was signing his will, he muttered something
about boxes at his granddaughter Emily's house, but then he
told me it was just old papers and not worth mentioning in
the will."

"When did he sign his current will?"

"It was when he moved to the care home, four years back.
Although, I should mention that he came in a few days ago.
I hadn't seen him since he signed the will. I assumed he'd

become more infirm over the years, and when he called me, I offered to meet him at the home, or on the ground floor here, to save him the trip and walking up the stairs. But he was a feisty old chap, and insisted on climbing the stairs. He could grasp the handrail firmly. Emily helped him up."

With a lawyer's meeting so close to Ronald's death, Helen began taking notes of the timeframe. "Did Emily sit in on that meeting?" she asked.

"No, she went to do some shopping, and I called her when we were finished. He was here for an hour or more. Between us, I think he enjoyed being in town and talking to people he didn't see every day. We had two rounds of tea as I recall."

"And cake!" came a loud voice from next door; obviously Elise was attuned to their conversation.

"So," Helen said, leading the conversation back to the will, "did Ronald make a change to his will recently?"

"Nae, he didn't, but he brought in a sealed envelope that he wanted the recipient to open as soon as possible. The more interesting part of the visit, in my view, was that for part of the time, he was sitting in Elise's office. I had a brief interruption for an urgent matter, so Ronald went next door and chatted with Elise, for maybe ten minutes."

"More like fifteen!" came the voice again.

"Okay, fifteen minutes. But the point is, when he came out again, he told me he had remembered something and needed to write another letter, but it was to be secured with his will and only opened on his death."

"Has the letter been opened?"

"Not yet," Claude replied. "It concerns someone at the care home, another resident, at least, that's what Ronald told me at the time."

Now, instead of calling out from the other room, Elise appeared in the doorway and leaned against the frame, arms crossed over her chest.

"You're forgetting part of it, Claude. Ronald became agitated when he was sitting in my office. He didn't write the second letter at the time. He told you he had to visit Emily, then he came back here, and *that's* when he wrote the second letter, the one for the care home resident."

Helen was consulting the calendar on her phone, then looked up. "He came back here two or three days before he died?"

Claude and Elise glanced at each other, seeming to reach an agreement. "Yes, that would be correct," Claude acknowledged. "I hadn't written that second visit in our appointment book. I think maybe he just stopped by. Sorry, Helen, my memory is getting a bit rusty. I probably should think about retiring."

Elise laughed. "Och, Claude, away w'ya. Helen, he's been saying those very words since I started here ten years ago."

Helen felt like she'd learned all she could, at least until the two mystery letters were opened. Maybe they'd have some helpful information, although chances were, she wouldn't be told what was in them unless Ronald's death turned out not to be accidental.

The fact that Ronald wrote two confidential letters recently, including one shortly before his death, seemed suspicious. She hated to think it, but could he have been planning suicide? With Alistair's recent story about Ronald's possible role in six deaths during the war, she had to consider that Ronald might have found the memories too difficult to endure. Or, perhaps the old man simply wanted to die on his own terms, and not spend months or years bedridden and losing his independence. It was a lot to take in.

She thanked the two solicitors for their help, and was standing up to leave when Claude removed a small white envelope from Ronald's client folder.

"This has me puzzled," he said. "It's the letter that Ronald must have written at the care home, judging from the return address on the envelope. This is the one he said should be opened now, and not wait until after his death."

He handed it to Helen, and she was so surprised she fell

back into her chair. Instead of a proper address on the envelope, the shaky handwriting, presumably Ronald's, said, "For Alistair, the American who spoke to my granddaughter Emily on the bench by the clifftop cafe."

"I've no idea who that is," Claude continued, with Elise nodding her head in agreement. "Ronald was insistent that we didn't ask Emily about this mysterious American, so one of my tasks for today is to go to the cafe and ask if he's a regular customer. They might know how to get in touch, or even a last name would help."

Helen shook her head and smiled, handing the letter back. "No need for that. I'm sure the man you want is Alistair Wright, and he happens to be in town today. I know him, and if you want me to, I can call him and ask him to stop by. Although, I sure am curious about why Ronald would write to him."

Claude returned the envelope to the folder. "Bang goes my excuse to leave the office and go to the cafe on official business, but yes, please call him. And it's fine with me for you to be present when he opens the letter, as long as he agrees. Or he may take it away to read on his own."

While the two solicitors watched, with undisguised curiosity about the recipient of the letter, Helen called Alistair's cell phone number and waited for him to answer. To her disappointment, it went to voice mail; she left him an urgent message to call her.

With nothing else to do until Alistair called back, Helen thanked the solicitors and headed to her office, her mind occupied by the continuing twists in Ronald's recent history.

Chapter 10

While Helen was meeting with Claude, Alistair and Margaret had finished their snack at the cafe and walked back to town. They decided to return to the car and drive north, to visit the chapel. There, they could look more closely at the brass memorial plaque with the names of the six young men, fate unknown.

As he had a week before, Alistair parked the car in the small roadside parking area. He led Margaret along a grassy path to the chapel entrance. He was glad to find the door propped open, and he stopped for a moment to switch his phone to silent and avoid disturbing the peaceful atmosphere. Like before, soft voices of chanting monks could be heard from speakers located near the ceiling.

Margaret wandered around the interior, looking at memorial plaques and stones, and admiring the carved light-colored wood of the wainscoting. Alistair went straight to the brass plaque on the right-hand wall of the chapel. Sun shone through stained glass windows, so the engraved names were easy to make out. He again wondered about the plaque, with its secret history: was it random vandalism, or was there a deep meaning behind the angry scratched lines, the obliteration of the witness name?

He stepped away from the plaque and looked around for the volunteer guide he'd met on his previous visit. The guide had been unable to offer any information about the plaque, but Alistair hoped that, with additional questions, he might learn the name of someone who could provide the context.

Margaret finished looking around, and she joined Alistair where he was sitting in a chair near the plaque. He'd grabbed two blue canvas seat cushions from a shelf in the entryway.

"That's the one I'm interested in," he said, standing up and showing her. She lightly ran her fingertips over the scratched-out area, then they both sat down again and thought about the plaque.

"I wonder if it could be restored," Margaret suggested. "Could the engraving be visible from the back, maybe?"

"I hadn't thought of that. I was more concerned with finding someone who knew who'd commissioned and installed the plaque, and when. I imagined several scenarios. If Ronald did push six young men over the cliff during the war, as he told Emily, maybe he became remorseful over it and he had the plaque made and added his name as witness."

"And then someone in his family scratched it out?"

"Maybe, but then there's another possibility, that someone really did witness Ronald killing the men, and *that* witness put up the plaque, but Ronald scratched the witness's name off later?'

"And of course there's the question of why the plaque is in German," Margaret added. "It supports the idea that the men who died were from Germany. But maybe whoever commissioned the plaque was German?"

"It wouldn't be surprising in this town," Alistair agreed. "Many families trace back to the nineteen twenties and thirties, when the glass factory employed so many specialist glass makers. They liked it and stayed on and had families."

A crowd of chattering tourists in a group, judging from their name badges, began streaming into the chapel, accompanied by their guide. Alistair and Margaret stood up and replaced the seat cushions. Alistair recognized the guide from his first visit to the chapel, but with the group tour beginning, he couldn't quiz the guide about the memorial plaque.

As he and Margaret waited by the front door for a chance

to leave, Margaret could hear several of the tourists wondering if Mary Queen of Scots had worshiped in the chapel, and she smiled to herself. The guide had overheard as well, and he gathered the group together in the entryway and pointed out that as the chapel had been built in the late nineteenth century, the earliest queen who might have visited was Queen Victoria, a full three centuries after Mary Queen of Scots.

The group dispersed, slightly chastised. Under his breath the guide whispered, "And Rizzio was not murdered in the corner, folks."

Margaret laughed out loud, then quickly apologized to the guide. "I'm glad to see that *someone* is aware of Scottish history," he said to her with a grin and a wink, then walked further into the chapel to point out features to the group.

Outside, Alistair asked Margaret what she was laughing about. "It's a bit of history you'll learn when you visit Holyrood Palace in Edinburgh," she explained. "Mary Queen of Scots had an Italian secretary named David Rizzio, and he was murdered there. Legend has it that there's a bloodstain that cannot be washed away."

A bit like Kilvellie, Alistair thought to himself: the proverbial stain of misdeeds resonated here through the decades as well.

Before they walked to the car, he turned his phone back to ring, and saw that he had a message from Helen. He listened, called her, and arranged to meet her at a lawyer's office in Kilvellie. He didn't share his reaction with Margaret, but he had a bad feeling; if Ronald's solicitor needed to meet with Alistair and Helen right away, maybe foul play was gaining traction as the explanation for Ronald's clifftop fall.

As they drove south, past the cafe and the site of the future glass museum, Alistair thought back to suspicions from his previous visits to Kilvellie, that the abandoned holiday home site where the museum was being built might hide a body from the early nineteen forties. Or more than one body.

Alistair, Adam, and Helen had followed up on this suspicion and were relieved to find, instead, a load of valuable glassware hidden underground during the war. Luckily, no sign of a body on that visit. But once the bulldozers got to work, was a gruesome find in the near future?

That moment would be all too soon, he thought, as he drove along the main road of Kilvellie and found a parking spot near the building where the lawyer's office was located, where Helen would be waiting. Leaving Margaret to have a look around the shops, Alistair said he would call her when he was finished, and he entered the office building and climbed the well-trod carpeted stairs.

Chapter 11

Glad of a chance to explore the Kilvellie shops on her own, Margaret began on the west side of the main street, with a plan to walk the three blocks of shops on that side, then cross over and explore the shops on the North Sea-facing side. One, a new-looking building advertising open craft studios, she'd save for later, otherwise she might spend all her time in it.

Her northwards stroll didn't take long: most shops sold souvenirs or Scottish-theme items geared toward tourists. She spent a few minutes looking around a shop that sold handmade sweaters and vests. Seeing nothing designed by her cousin Jeannie, she took note of the shop owner's name; she'd let Jeannie know it could be another outlet for her popular knitted garments. From there, she crossed the main road, heading to the craft studios.

The building itself was only a few years old, and housed workshops and salesrooms of all varieties. On the ground floor, Margaret enjoyed peering in through the interior floor-to-ceiling windows and seeing printmakers at work, wool spinners surrounded by fresh fleeces and spools of colorful yarn, and a studio that specialized in handmade books. After finishing on that floor, she climbed the open central staircase to the second floor and discovered side-by-side glass studios: one had a sign for sea glass jewelry, and the other sold sea glass.

A young woman working at a bench in the jewelry studio glanced up, waving when she saw Margaret and standing up to welcome her in. Margaret hesitated; she didn't need any jewelry and she was content to look in the windows, but she didn't want to be rude. She approached the open door and said hello.

"I'm mainly window-shopping," she explained, hoping to avoid any awkwardness when she left without buying anything.

"That's fine," the woman said. She looked to be in her thirties, with straight blond hair tied back in a ponytail, a perfectly symmetrical face, and a pleasant local accent. She extended her hand. "I'm the jeweler, Christy. My brother William has the studio next door. He's the one to see if you need any loose sea glass. Or beach marbles, you know, weathered marbles."

"Really? I have jars of sea glass where I live, but I've never seen a beach glass marble."

"From your accent, I assume you mean, where you live in America?"

Margaret smiled. "Close, but right now I'm living down the coast, in Fife. Finlay Village, if you've heard of it. An uncle left me his cottage, and he obviously spent a lot of time collecting glass over the years, well, decades."

Christy's eyes took on a covetous look. "Why don't I take a break—we can go next door so you can see some marbles. In fact, if you have time for a quick cup of tea, I'd love to hear about your glass collection."

Margaret shook her head. "It's hardly a collection. Just jars and jars of the stuff. All colors. I thought about arranging it in patterns to photograph and sell online, but that's a low priority right now."

They reached the open door to William's studio; it was more spacious than Christy's, without all the jewelry-making equipment.

"Will?" Christy called out, and after a few moments, a young man in jeans and a well-tailored white shirt, a male version of Christy's blond good looks, emerged from an adjoining room. He held a teapot in one hand and two mugs in another.

"Oh!" he cried. "I thought it was just you, Christy. Would your customer like some tea as well? I can fetch another mug."

"I guess I've timed my visit well," Margaret said, introducing herself to William.

They all sat together at a wooden worktable, tea and biscuits at hand, and Christy explained to William that Margaret wanted to see some beach glass marbles. William reached along the table and pulled a shallow white pottery dish close so that Margaret could look. In it sat about twenty well-weathered glass marbles of all colors.

She couldn't help but ask if they were for sale; she'd never seen anything so exquisite.

"They are," William replied, "but they are a small investment because they're so rare. Do you want the whole spiel?"

"If you have time. I already told Christy I was just window-shopping, but now I'm rethinking that!"

William picked up a clear frosted marble that had strands of different colored glass swirling together inside. "This is a handmade marble, about a hundred years old. It was washed around in the North Sea for most of its life, and ended up on the beach here. I might as well tell you, I sell marbles like this for hundreds of dollars each."

Margaret was glad she didn't have a mouthful of tea, "I'm, I'm afraid that's a bit outside my budget. And seeing the whole group of them together, I don't think I could stop at buying just one."

"You don't have to *buy* them," Christy added helpfully. "They are down there on the beach for anyone to pick up. But it can take months to find a marble like this, in perfect condition and uniformly frosted. William and I live in town so we're out on the beach two or three times a week. It would be very fortuitous for a first-time beachcomber here to find a valuable marble."

"Still, it would be worthwhile looking carefully, now that I know what to look for," Margaret said. "I had a short walk on the beach this morning. I'd show you what I found, but I left it in the car."

William seemed very interested in hearing about her finds, and he spoke quickly. "Did you find any pieces with raised lettering? Most of the glass on the beach is from the old glass factory glassware, and we're always on the lookout for pieces that were once the base of a bowl or a vase, with the glass factory name. Regenbogen."

"German for rainbow," Christy explained.

Margaret sipped her tea and thought about the pieces she'd found. A few were multicolored glass pebbles, jewels to her, but none with lettering that she could remember. While she was thinking, Christy told William about the jars of beach glass that Margaret had inherited, some of it sitting in the cottage for decades.

"What are you planning to do with it?" William asked.

"I had thought about selling it on the internet, but, I don't know, would you like to take a look at it? I suppose there could be lettered pieces in it. My uncle mainly collected on the Fife coast, but who knows, maybe he came up to this beach now and again."

Christy and William looked at each other, nodding their heads, then William looked back at Margaret.

"That would be great," he said. "I sometimes buy glass in bulk, and Christy could look for pieces for her jewelry. A piece that could work well as a pendant, or matching pieces for earrings, could be worth more."

"Yes," Christy confirmed, "especially, bright colors likes reds and deeper blues, and dark turquoise."

"There's all colors in the jars, mixed up," Margaret told them. "A few weeks ago, a friend took hundreds of blue pieces out and photographed them for me in kind of a sunburst pattern. I never got around to listing it for sale."

"Hundreds of blue? Wow! *Where* is your cottage?" William

was getting more excited by the minute.

"It's in Finlay, about an hour south of here by car. You're welcome to visit anytime. I'm going to be traveling in the next few weeks, but if my fiancé is home, you could visit then."

After exchanging contact information, Margaret finished her tea so she could let the two glass experts get back to work. "Did you come here just to look for sea glass on the beach?" Christy asked as she gathered the mugs.

"No, in fact, sea glass wasn't even my goal. I'm looking for good groatie buckie beaches."

"You'll find one or two on this beach," said Christy, "but I don't collect them. I find it's difficult to look for different things at once. You have to compartmentalize, so your eyes adjust to searching for certain shapes and colors."

"Sounds like it's worth my time looking, but I mainly came along with my fiancé. He needed to talk to the police about something. It has to do with investigating that tragedy, the old man falling off the cliff."

Margaret sensed a sudden chill in the atmosphere; William's mouth fell open, and Christy stopped what she was doing.

"The *police*?" Christy whispered, looking alarmed. "We thought it was an accidental death. What more do the police have to do?"

"Oh, I don't know," Margaret murmured, realizing she shouldn't have mentioned it. For all she knew, they could be related to the man and she'd stuck her foot in it. "I'm sorry, was he family?"

"Nah," William replied, "but I suppose in a way we can thank him for our livelihood."

"*Blame* him more like," Christy blurted out. "He was supposed to guard the glass factory during World War Two, and he did such a lousy job that tons of glass products were thrown over the cliff by a bunch of hoodlums. That's why there's all this unique sea glass to collect. Our inheritance chucked over the cliff. And then we almost lost our sister too..."

She burst into tears, put the mugs back on the table, and ran next door to her studio. Margaret stood by in shock, then recovered enough to apologize to William.

"I'm so sorry. I really had no idea I was touching on such a sensitive subject."

William smiled sadly at her. "It's not your fault at all. Of *course* people who visit the town this week are going to mention the death of the old man. But Christy is basically right. The factory was repeatedly looted during the war years, and the man who just died, Ronald Wilson, had been hired to guard it. Some think he colluded in the thefts and kept glass for himself. But the truth is, if the factory had stayed intact and profitable during the war, it would have had several decades of success ahead of it, and our dad, who's the grandson of the founder, would have had a decent inheritance. Instead, our family grew up quite frugally, and from the time we could walk, me and my two sisters were out collecting glass for Dad to sell. My youngest sister almost died on the beach during a storm..."

He shook his head and let out a long sigh. "I don't know why I'm burdening you with this. It's a sunny day, you should be on the beach looking for marbles."

He lifted the dish of beach marbles. "Please, choose one. It sounds like we'll be able to do business with the sea glass at your cottage, so consider this part payment in advance."

After getting William's assurance that he really wanted her to take a marble, Margaret quickly selected one with swirling blue strands. She'd already decided on it, if she were to buy one. William placed it in a small felt pouch, then handed it to her.

"Enjoy. And since I mentioned our sister, I should tell you that it did have a happy ending. Eventually, anyway. She'd escaped from the storm and lived in St. Andrews for seven years. She never came home during that time because someone from the police had filled her mind with the idea that

Christy and I were a threat to her. All we did was run along the beach to get help before the waves reached the cliff, but it was too late. For seven years we thought she'd been washed out to sea, and blamed ourselves, so it will take a while to move beyond that. It was devastating for our parents to think she was dead."

He stopped and sighed again; Margaret didn't know what to say in response to the tragic story.

"But Christy's right," he concluded. "Everything that happened to our family can be laid at the feet of the glass factory guard. I suppose they gave him too much responsibility, guarding it alone, but why didn't he ask the management for help? Guess we'll never know, now that he's dead."

Margaret was anxious to get away. She quickly thanked William for the marble and hurried back to the street. She glanced into Christy's workshop on her way out, but there was no sign of her. All Margaret could think was, she'd just met two people with a strong motive to kill the old glass factory guard: revenge. But why now?

She had to tell Alistair, but he wasn't picking up his calls. She could see the building with the solicitor's office further along the street and headed straight for it, wishing she hadn't gone to the glass studios. Then she thought of her precious blue, handmade, vintage beach marble, and felt a little better.

Chapter 12

Margaret hesitated at the front door of the elegant Victorian mansion that housed the law office Alistair was visiting. She compared it to her own impersonal law office in Portland, and wondered what it would be like to report to work each day feeling like you were walking into the setting of a Victorian novel. It might be fun, but presumably, it would be difficult to accommodate modern technology and not run afoul of the delicate interior, not to mention historic preservation requirements.

She'd calmed down from her visit to the glass studios, and decided it wasn't urgent that she interrupt Alistair's discussion with the lawyer. Instead, she crossed the road to the bakery, purchased a cup of tea, then sat down on a wrought iron bench next to the law office building to wait for Alistair. As William had said a few minutes earlier, it was too nice a day to be indoors.

***

Upstairs, Helen and Alistair sat in guest chairs facing Claude's desk. Elise had brought in a chair from her adjoining office. The discussion was growing more serious by the minute. After learning that Ronald had left a letter for him, Alistair mentioned Margaret's almost throw-away comment about checking the medications in the late Ronald's system; perhaps the letter was a sign of erratic behavior. The suggestion was being taken seriously by the two solicitors: not as indicating murder at this point, but if there was evidence that Ronald had overdosed or taken the wrong medication, that could suggest wrongdoing or mismanagement at the care home. That, in turn, could have implications for other residents. The police really should look into it, the solicitors argued.

"To be clear, I know it's not your decision to make, but you both advise a tox screen be done on his body?" Helen asked again.

"If I had a relative living in that care home, the answer would be a resounding yes," Claude replied. "And we owe no less a duty to the other residents, relatives or not."

"It's not just a wild guess," Elise added. "We both saw Ronald in the days before he died. I thought he was spry for his age, very steady. His hands didn't shake when he handled papers. In fact, his hand strength was good, judging from how hard he pressed down with the pen. His posture was good for his age. Even at the top of our stairs, I didn't see any risk of him wobbling and falling down."

She stopped and thought for a moment.

"Yes, I'm finding it hard to picture him standing up from the bench he sat on by the cliff, and being unsteady enough to pitch over the edge. He also seemed very aware of his limitations, and he always had hold of something to steady himself, like a chair back or his cane. Or someone's arm. I'm sure that when he got up from a bench outdoors, he held on to it to find his balance. Well, used to anyway... I mean, he did make it into his nineties." Her voice drifted off and she dabbed her eyes with a tissue.

"I agree with my colleague," Claude said. "Helen, can you tell the coroner and recommend checking Ronald's tissues and blood for any unexpected drugs, or higher than normal levels of medications, especially anything that could make him dizzy, or sleepy?"

Helen agreed, but offered a counter argument. "What if he had a stroke as he got up from the bench and he was unsteady from that? Or a heart attack?"

Claude considered her question for a moment. "It's possible, I'm no medical expert. But I expect it would be difficult to determine if a stroke preceded or followed his fall. He was found immediately, isn't that correct? So it would be almost impossible to distinguish, as we know he didn't lie on the beach alive for any length of time."

"Probably lucky he didn't, with all the broken bones and pain," Helen muttered. She excused herself and went out to the landing outside the office door to call the coroner. That done, she'd have the difficult task of explaining it to Ronald's son, her predecessor at the police station, and to his grandson, her sergeant. If she couched it in terms of making sure a medication mix-up at the care home wasn't to blame, on the grounds of protecting the other residents from a similar mix-up, perhaps they would understand. She hoped it was unnecessary to even hint at foul play. Not yet, anyway.

Returning to Claude's office, Helen was glad to see that the tea mugs and biscuits had been replenished.

"Next item," Claude said, "is the envelope I have from Ronald, addressed rather cryptically to you, Alistair. It was fortuitous that I mentioned it to Helen here on a day that you happened to be in town."

Alistair took the sealed envelope and turned it over in his hands, looking at the front and back. The paper was creamy and textured, and the return address was engraved, indicating the name and address of the Seaview Manor Home, the care home where Ronald had lived for his last four years.

Claude handed Alistair a silver letter-opener. "You can take it into the other office to read, if you'd prefer privacy. Or just take the letter with you."

Alistair shook his head and respectfully slid the edge of the letter-opener along the top of the envelope. "I'll read it to myself, then I can show it to you, unless it's purely personal, which I doubt. I only spoke to him once, and that was to discuss the old coal chutes. As Helen will recall, that conversation triggered a search for the ground-level exit where Justine Green escaped, seven years ago now."

He pulled two small folded sheets of writing paper from the envelope, and opened them flat. The old man's forceful penmanship was easy to read, although Alistair had to stop now and again to interpret the phonetic or Scottish spelling of words:

Dear Alistair,

I apologize for not calling ye by your proper name, but me granddaughter Emily only remembered you as Alistair. I expect you will recall speaking to her on a bench outside the caff, the one up by the big parking lot. Emily told me later that she'd passed on to you a story I'd told her about the war years when I was a guard at the auld Regenbogen Glass Factory.

That story was never for anyone else's ears, so I was disturbed that she'd repeated it. I don't know ye at all, and I want to make sure you don't take the story as fact. If you are an honourable man, I hope that you wouldn't repeat it anyway, especially not the ramblings of a young innocent lass ye don't know at all.

Why did I tell her a falsehood? Here's why. Emily, poor lass, is married to a decent man who for years has served in the military all over, who knows where all he gets these days. He's been telling Emily that it's often impossible to distinguish friend from foe in other parts of the world. He sometimes comes home on leave tortured with guilt, that's the words he uses with Emily, at killing civilians who he thought were carrying bombs, that kind of thing.

I can't speak from personal battlefield experience, but I've tried to explain to Emily that in wartime, a soldier has to make snap judgements, life or death, and mistakes happen.

Jane Ross Potter

She still couldn't come to terms, I guess that's the phrase she used, with her husband and his guilt, so I concocted a story to help her visualize it in Kilvellie context. I don't need to repeat the details since she said she told ye, but Alistair, swearing on my late wife's mem'ry, there <u>were</u> young men who caused immense damage to the glass factory in those hellish war years, but <u>I did not kill any German boys</u>, as God is my witness.

Yours sincerely,

Ronald Wilson

With shaking hands, Alistair folded the letter in two again and handed it to Helen. It was shocking to read the poor man's desperate plea from the grave, made even worse since Ronald had not intended it to be read after his death. Alistair clearly remembered the old man's voice, and he could visualize Ronald speaking these same words, his voice raspy but sincere.

Ronald *can't* have committed suicide, Alistair realized: if he had intended to kill himself, he wouldn't have cared enough about his reputation, his legacy, to have written to Alistair and made a special trip to the solicitor's office, up all those stairs, to deliver it in person.

He looked at Claude and Elise, who were anxiously awaiting some indication about the contents. He knew that Helen had not mentioned his conversation with Emily to them, so the possibility that their long-term client Ronald was a killer had never been raised in the lawyers' office.

Helen read through it, her face non-expressive, and then replaced it in the original envelope and handed it back to Alistair. She smiled at the two solicitors.

"Alistair met Ronald in the context of Justine Green's disappearance, something about Ronald remembering the old coal chutes that led from the cliff down to the beach. In the

64

letter, Ronald simply wanted to clarify something personal told to Alistair about him later. Alistair had obviously made a good impression and Ronald didn't want him to get the wrong idea about him."

Alistair kept silent while Helen twisted herself in knots trying to explain why the letter was not going to be shown to the solicitors. What she was saying was factually true, if a bit misleading for his comfort. But it was her town, her possible murder victim, her possible multiple murderer for that matter, and he would let her make explanations that she could live with later.

In any event, the letter to Alistair seemed to shed no light on the old man's possible murder, unless Emily had told the same story to someone with ancestral connections to one of the young vandals, and after taking it as truth, they had decided to kill the old man in revenge, even decades later. But that was a long shot, and easy to investigate with a quick word to Emily, asking her if she'd repeated her granddad's "confession" to anyone else.

A glance at the wall clock, and Alistair realized they'd been meeting for almost two hours. Margaret would be wondering about him, so he excused himself and went outside the office to call her.

"Are you having fun?" he asked, when she answered right away.

"I'm having some tea. I'm actually outside the lawyer's building, so I don't miss you when you leave."

Alistair asked her to hold on a minute while he went back to the others and asked if they had much more to discuss, since he had plans to meet Margaret soon. Claude wanted to go over the details of Ronald's last visit to the office, in case something had happened that they'd missed, and he said that Margaret, being a lawyer as well, according to Helen, was welcome to join them.

Elise, Helen, and Claude all stood up for a break and Elise went off to make more tea. Feeling frustrated, but not wanting to abandon Helen, Alistair went back out to finish his call with Margaret.

"It will be a while, another round of tea, so you're welcome to come up and join us. You might be able to help with the rest of the meeting."

Margaret glanced at her watch. "It's almost five o'clock. Should we find a B&B here and make it a night away? I've noticed a couple of interesting places for dinner."

Alistair agreed, then he called and booked a suite at an elegant clifftop hotel on the north side of town. Adam had stayed there and raved about it, so Alistair would treat Margaret to a romantic seaside getaway. It was the least he could do after dragging her down into the morass that was Kilvellie-by-the-Sea.

He wondered about just leaving, since he had the letter now, but Helen seemed to appreciate his input as she talked things over with the lawyers. Her usual sidekick, her sergeant, was Ronald's grandson, so she was having to tackle things alone. Mentally steeling himself for another hour or two with lawyers and the police, he waited while Margaret climbed the staircase, and they entered the office together.

Chapter 13

Alistair, Margaret, Helen, and the two solicitors, Claude and Elise, were seated around a table in Claude's office. With introductions finished and the requisite tea and shortbread served, Alistair was more than ready to get on with the meeting.

Margaret sat quietly, wondering what exactly was going on. As far as she knew, this wasn't one of Alistair's client-driven work assignments. She wondered if he was charging Helen for any of his time, or had he just become caught up in the drama?

And was Margaret expected to give legal advice? She had no background in Scottish law. In the same setting in Portland—a meeting with two outside attorneys to discuss the recent passing of one of their clients—Margaret's time and effort would be billed by her law firm, at a rate of several hundred dollars an hour. It seemed that if these two solicitors wanted legal advice, they should hire someone, and not bring her in simply because she happened to be in town with Alistair. But, she reminded herself, she'd come along on the trip to support him, so she'd just see how things evolved.

Claude cleared his throat and Margaret focused again.

"Our final topic," he began, "is Ronald Wilson's letter to one of the care home residents. As I mentioned earlier, he wrote it here, in his own hand, and sealed the envelope. He left instructions that on his death, the letter was to be given to the named resident. Unopened, if course."

"We have no idea what it says," Elise confirmed.

"And for Margaret's benefit, remind us," Alistair asked, "I think you said he came in a few days ago to bring the letter addressed to me, then while he was here he became agitated, he went to his granddaughter's house, then came back and wrote this second letter?"

"That's exactly what happened," Claude confirmed.

"I know I'm new to all this," Margaret said, getting caught up despite her earlier misgivings, "but did he explain why he hadn't written that second letter, to the care home resident, beforehand? He had access to writing paper and envelopes at the care home, so why write it here?"

"It's a mystery," Claude agreed. "Believe me, I've gone over and over in my mind the conversation I had with him that day, when he delivered the letter for Alistair. I can't think of anything we talked about that would trigger the need for the second letter. And if he did need to write it, why didn't he go back to the care home, write it there, and have his granddaughter drop it off here the next time she visited him?"

"It seems he needed to have that letter in your hands right away," Alistair offered. "Almost like he had a premonition that he wouldn't have another chance?"

Helen shook her head. "That brings us back to wondering if he committed suicide by falling over the cliff. But there's no evidence for that, other than the fact of the fall."

"And *this* letter." Claude held it up and waved it for emphasis before replacing it on top of Ronald's client folder on the table.

His letter to me argues against a conclusion of suicide, Alistair thought to himself, but he couldn't reveal the contents to the solicitors, not yet anyway.

Margaret glanced around the room, taking a look at Claude's desk.

"I'm sure you're very careful with confidentiality here," she said to Claude, "but could Mr. Wilson have seen something, like a name on a file, or anything that would have triggered his need to write the second letter?"

"Not that I can imagine," Claude replied. "Since you're an attorney, Margaret, you will understand that Elise and I are very careful with our client information. As a rule, I only have files pertaining to one client at a time on my desk. And before you ask your next question, Ronald wasn't in my office alone at any time, so he couldn't have poked around in drawers or file cabinets."

Helen picked up on Margaret's question. "Maybe it wasn't a file or a name he saw. What else? Do you have anything new, something that wasn't here when Ronald visited before?"

Claude motioned around the room with his hand and chuckled.

"It's an astute question, but as you can see, Helen, redecorating isn't high on our list..."

Elise broke in. "Remember, Claude, Ronald offered to wait outside while you had a surprise visit from another client. I came out of my office and invited Ronald to wait with me. It wasn't going to be more than a few minutes."

"That's right!" Claude declared. "Another symptom of my fading memory. It was when he came back out of Elise's office that he asked for paper to write the second letter. No, wait, I've still got it wrong. Emily drove him to her house, *then* back here to write the second letter."

"But, but, we didn't talk about anything important while he was waiting," Elise said, her eyebrows raised in confusion. "Just the usual: how his great-grandson is doing, I mean, Emily's bairn, and that Ronald was looking forward to attending the wee boy's third birthday next week."

"He didn't see any files on your desk, any names?" Claude asked, mirroring Margaret's earlier question.

"No, and anyway, he sat in a guest chair at the far end of the room. I sat in the other guest chair next to him. Even with perfect eyesight, he wouldn't have been able to read anything on my desk. And he was never alone in my office."

"But, still," Helen said, "*something* in your office seemed to trigger his mind, or his memory. I know it's an imposition on your privacy, but may I take a quick look in your office?"

Elise stood up. "Of course, it's fine." She pushed her door fully wide open so that Helen could go in and take a look around. Margaret didn't get up, but from where she sat, she found herself facing, through the open door, a large framed photograph on the wall. The sepia-toned formal portrait showed a man and a woman standing, and in front of them, also standing, were two young children, a boy and a girl. The girl was shorter and looked younger. She was smiling, but the boy looked like he wished he was anywhere but in front of the camera. He glared at the lens.

Helen and Elise returned and sat down at the table again.

"Nothing jumps out at me," Helen muttered. "Maybe we'll never know."

The group focused on refreshing their tea as they let this disappointment sink in, then Margaret spoke up again.

"The photograph through there, is that your family, Elise?" Based on the era of the clothing, Margaret could tell that Elise was unlikely to be the young girl in the picture, but perhaps it was her mother or grandmother.

Elise leaned and looked into her office again. "The one on that wall? I forget it's even there! No, that's a family photo from my predecessor. She's the young girl in the picture, with her brother and parents. She worked here until she retired, about ten years ago."

"Aye," Claude confirmed. "On her last day, I asked if she wanted me to wrap up the photograph and have it sent to her home, as it's a bit heavy to carry. She said that would be nice, so I took it off the wall. But she and I started laughing, because it was only then that we noticed how much the wallpaper had faded. The colors under the picture are bright, so it was obvious that a picture had been removed. She said I should hang it back up again, as she had the same one at home. We left it that I would return it to her when I found something to hang in its place, or we redecorated, whichever came first, and as you can see..."

"I know the feeling," said Helen. "When I was busy working in Edinburgh, these kinds of projects tend to be put off day by day, until suddenly ten years have gone by."

"I wonder," Margaret ventured nervously, "is there a chance that Mr. Wilson saw someone in the photograph that drove him to write a second letter?"

"I suppose it's *possible*," Claude admitted. "When clients are visiting either of us, we usually keep the adjoining office door closed, so that the other person isn't distracted by the conversation. Especially if it's something the client is reluctant to discuss. So it's likely that although Ronald had visited *my* office before, he'd never seen the photograph next door. I can't imagine what else in Elise's office could have had an effect on him, or let loose a forgotten memory."

The group sat in silence again, just the sounds of teacups being lifted and replaced, and the soft crunching of biscuits. Margaret felt the gears turning in her mind. There seemed to be a cause and effect situation here: Ronald had spent time in Elise's office, then went to his granddaughter's house, returning here to write a letter that couldn't wait. She wondered now, who did he write to?

She glanced at the envelope sitting on top of the file. In his clear writing, it said,

Confidential, to be given to Mrs. F. Ramsay, Seaview Manor Home, Kilvellie.

"What do you know about the recipient of the letter?" Margaret asked Claude.

"Other than she's a care home resident, nothing but the name."

"Maybe I should find out more about her, before the letter's handed over," Helen offered. "Do you have time? I can step outside and call the care home. I've met the manager."

Minutes later Helen returned with an answer. "Your Mrs. F. Ramsay is a resident who met and married another care home resident, but he passed away. She still goes by his name and first initial, like women did decades ago. Her maiden name was Kathryn Spears. Her first husband was…"

Helen stopped speaking as the faces of both Claude and Elise took on shocked looks. Claude spoke first. "That's, that's Elise's predecessor! I had no idea she remarried at her…"

"Don't say 'her age' please," Helen cut in, and Alistair smiled to himself, aware that sixty-something Helen was dating sixty-something Richard Wilson.

Margaret tried to connect the dots. "Ronald Wilson saw a picture of Kathryn Spears as a child, now Mrs. Ramsay, and suddenly he had to write her a letter? But he must know her, since he lived in that home, and so does she. Why write to her when he could speak to her?"

"Good point," Claude said. "And what does he need to tell her that had to wait until he passed away?"

Helen asked, "Mind if I put the kettle on again?"

Elise stood and picked up the teapot. "Sorry, the tea must be getting cold by now."

"That's partly it." Helen stood also, then leaned over and lifted up the sealed letter addressed to the former Kathryn Spears. "But mainly I want to steam this thing open."

Before the three lawyers and the private investigator could jump in with objections, she explained. "We still haven't ruled out that Ronald committed suicide. I think it's in our interest to know ahead of time what he had to tell her just before his death. I alone will read it and reseal it, but I will take it as evidence if it serves as a suicide note, or anything that has a bearing on his death. Okay by all of you?"

The rest of the group sat still; no one leapt up to grab the envelope from her. As soon as she and Elise left the room, Claude hesitated, then snatched up the plate of biscuits and announced that he was also going to the kitchen to get more shortbread.

Margaret smothered a laugh and she turned to Alistair.

It Continued with the Cowries

"What is this, a *how many lawyers does it take to make tea* joke?"

Alistair laughed too, then said he was going off to find a restroom. Margaret leaned back in her chair and sighed. All this time indoors with lawyers, and worse, the time unbillable, when she could have been beachcombing, she thought with dismay.

She still didn't know if Kilvellie beach had enough groatie buckies to make a return visit worthwhile. Christy had said that she'd found one or two, but then she hadn't been searching for them. Anyway, most of the North Sea coastline was bound to have a groatie buckie here and there.

Chapter 14

Margaret was surprised when Alistair returned almost immediately and closed the office door behind him.

"Quick! I'll explain later. Look for a notepad, or a notebook with blank pages."

They both looked around at all the surfaces in Claude's office—desk, credenza, conference table, and shelves.

"Should I look next door too?" Margaret asked.

"Sure, just be careful. I'm hoping for a pad of paper that Ronald used or leaned on when he wrote his letter to Mrs. Ramsay."

Margaret slipped into Elise's office, taking a position facing the photograph in case the others returned, and from there glanced around; she soon spied a pad of lined paper sitting on a small table by the guest chairs. Moving quickly, she picked it up, saw what Alistair was probably searching for, and while the main office door was still closed, she hid it in her backpack.

"You *found* it?" Alistair whispered, just in time, as footsteps could be heard approaching the office door.

"I think so. We need an excuse to get out of here before they notice it's gone."

They both stood aside while Helen and the two solicitors returned, minus tea and biscuits. Margaret was alarmed to see a kitchen towel clumsily wrapped around Claude's right hand; he was holding the hand tight against his chest with his left hand, grimacing in pain. But before she could ask what had happened, Helen announced, "I have to get back to the station."

Alistair took that as their cue. "We should get going too. Margaret and I still have to drive back to Fife."

With goodbyes all around, frostier than the mood had been during their discussions, Helen, Alistair, and Margaret left the office and hovered at the top of the stairs.

"I'll meet you downstairs," Alistair said. "I never did get to the restroom."

Helen and Margaret walked down the stairs in silence and waited outside on the sidewalk.

"Was it me, or did things suddenly get weird in there?" Margaret asked.

"Downright weird," Helen agreed. "Listen, are you leaving now to drive back? I can cover a night at a B&B or something. I really want Alistair's opinion, and yours too, on what to do."

Margaret couldn't help but smile: a mysterious kitchen encounter over a dead man's letter possibly leading to a solicitor's injury? She was hooked. "We're planning to stay at a hotel somewhere near town. Alistair mentioned driving back to Fife so we could leave the office quickly."

"I was agreeing with Margaret that things got a bit weird in there," Helen said when Alistair exited the office building and joined them. "Can you come to the station for a chat? Or, no, Desmond might be back today. Where can we go... I know, how about the clifftop cafe? We can get something and sit outside."

Margaret and Alistair agreed to meet Helen there in a few minutes. In their car, heading the short distance north on the main road, Margaret asked Alistair if he was going to reveal to Helen that they may have found the notepad Ronald leaned on to write his letter to Claude's former colleague, Kathryn.

"We should see what she says first. I overheard a bit of it when I went out the first time to look for the restroom. That's why I came right back and asked you to help find the notepad." He glanced at her and then at the road. "Margaret," he said softly, "I think they were *threatening* Helen."

"Over that *letter*? Is that how Claude hurt his hand? Was someone holding a knife?"

"Or a letter opener! They sure weren't arguing about biscuits. Okay, we're here. Let's hope she has an explanation."

With the car parked near the cafe, they got out to wait for Helen. Alistair looked across the main road to check how progress was coming along with the new glass museum. He could see heavy earth-moving equipment, and workers were erecting a wooden fence around the site.

"That's where we found all the valuable vintage glass that's going into the museum," he said to Margaret, pointing across the road.

"You still haven't told me the whole story. How about tonight, over dinner?"

"I will tell you soon," he promised. "Bottom line, we were just relieved to find glass and not a body, or bodies."

Margaret shivered. "Enough for now. This must be Helen." They turned to watch as a Range Rover, marked "Police," pulled into the parking area, and soon Helen joined them.

"I need something stronger than tea, but I'm on duty for a while longer. Let's go in and order." She held the door of the cafe open.

Margaret and Alistair both ordered soft drinks; as often happened in Scotland, by late afternoon they'd had their fill of tea. Helen ordered a coffee, and when they had their drinks, they went back outside and chose a picnic table at the edge of the parking area, far from other people.

"Okay, you need an explanation for all this confusion," Helen began. "Alistair, I saw you walk by in the hallway outside the kitchen, so maybe you overheard part of it. I had just finished steaming the envelope open when Claude literally pulled it from my hand. His wrist got scalded by the steam coming from the kettle spout. But instead of getting something to soothe the pain, he and Elise stopped me from leaving the kitchen. He said the letter is covered by client confidentiality and I'll need a court order to read it. I've rarely seen people who seemed so cooperative, suddenly turn on me."

"That explains his injured hand," Margaret said. "I was worried he'd been stabbed!"

Helen laughed. "Believe me, I was tempted, it was so surreal."

"It is odd," Alistair agreed. "They've had the letter in their possession for, what, two or three days? They could have looked at it before."

"Maybe they already did, but if it's something they think shouldn't be revealed to anyone, why would they tell us about the letter? They could have kept it in the file and no one would have known."

"This is just a guess, Helen," Margaret said, "but it seems that things took a turn when you called the care home and found out that Mrs. Ramsay, who the letter's addressed to, is really their former colleague, or employee, Kathryn Spears."

During the conversation, Alistair had slipped his pocket notebook out and was leafing through the pages.

"What are you looking for?" Margaret asked.

"Just a wild hunch. I'll need to do some research online first." He closed the notebook and put it away with no further comment.

"How am I going to get my hands on that letter?" Helen wondered out loud. "What if Ronald and Kathryn were close, and he's written a suicide note explaining things to her? I guess I'll have to get a court order and force McMahon to turn it over. If he doesn't *shred* it first."

Alistair nudged Margaret's arm, and she carefully eased the notepad out of her backpack.

"I could say that I was running low on notepaper and I grabbed some from McMahon's office, but..."

Alistair gently took it from her and held it horizontally, trying to catch the sun on it just right.

"Bingo!" he cried. "Helen, we think this is the pad of paper Ronald used, and the pen marks have left indentations in the page underneath. What is it people do, shade over it with a pencil? But you should take it, maybe there's a more advanced way to see what's written and preserve it as evidence if needed."

Helen's face lit up. "Brilliant work, you two! I feel like I'm working with Tommy and Tuppence."

Alistair let out a groan. "No, Helen, not more British sleuths?"

"I know who you mean," Margaret declared. "Agatha Christie, right? And her married couple detectives."

"Aye, that's them." Helen glanced at her watch and quickly finished her coffee, then stood up. "Let me work on deciphering what this says. If it is personal, and not a suicide note, I may just keep it quiet, so don't feel offended if I don't tell you."

"No problem," Alistair said. "Happy that Tuppence and I can help."

Just as Margaret was thinking they were free for the evening and could focus on discussing their plans for the next few weeks, Helen sat down again.

"Margaret, since this is your first time in Kilvellie, can I invite you and Alistair to dinner? Richard and I already have plans to go to our favorite bistro, and I'd like it if you can both join us. I promise, no more work conversations."

Feeling like she had no option, Margaret looked to Alistair to answer for them. "Sure, thank you, Helen," he said. "Although, Margaret may try to enlist your help with her next project!"

After finalizing plans to meet at the bistro at seven o'clock that night, Helen left.

"I'm sorry," Alistair said as he and Margaret returned to their car. "She kind of ambushed us. I can call her back and say something's come up with your work if you'd rather not go."

"It's fine. Maybe she knows a good beach for groatie buckies."

"Okay, next stop, check in at our accommodations for the night. I'm glad we both have a habit of taking extra clothes and things just in case we get stuck overnight somewhere."

The hotel would remind him of his enjoyable afternoon teas there with the dancer SarahBeth: another story he hadn't yet shared with Margaret. He suddenly realized he might have made a mistake booking into the same hotel, but it was too late to change plans now.

Chapter 15

When Alistair and Margaret checked in at the front desk of the luxurious Kilvellie Cliffs Hotel a few minutes later, Alistair was relieved that the desk clerk was not someone he'd met before. Feeling like things were looking up, he took the keys and they climbed the staircase up one floor from the lobby. Margaret was admiring the seaside decor: the framed photographs of shells, the comfortable-looking blue and white chairs and sofas in the lobby, and now, as Alistair held open the door to their suite, also tastefully decorated with a beachy theme, she exclaimed in glee.

"This is fabulous, Alistair! How did you know about the hotel?"

"Oh," he answered vaguely, "Adam stayed here for a night or two when he and I overlapped in Kilvellie, when you were in Orkney. I stayed at a B&B in town. It didn't seem right to stay in such a romantic setting alone."

She walked to the far side of the room to open the windows and hear the sound of the North Sea waves crashing against the cliff.

"You were right about avoiding the beach during high tide." She turned back to face Alistair. "Okay, I have enough time to shower, do my hair, and iron something to look presentable tonight."

He laughed. "It's just a casual bistro dinner. No need to go to any bother."

"It may be a routine day for you, but a night out in a new town, for me, means treating it like a special occasion."

80

It Continued with the Cowries

Alistair made himself comfortable on the sofa while she disappeared into the bathroom. Another whoop of joy, and he smiled to himself, realizing that she'd seen the Jacuzzi tub that he knew was included in the suite he'd booked.

He was, in reality, glad to have some time on his own. He had to check something that had been nagging at his brain ever since visiting the McMahon law office. He took out his pocket notebook and opened it to the page where, a week earlier, he'd written down the names of the six "vandals" recorded in Ronald's wartime diaries, from his years of guarding the glass factory. The third name down, there it was: Speyer, first name Franz.

Speyer/Spears: was it *possible*? Could the boy in the picture in Elise's office be one of the young men who vandalized the factory, and if so, did Ronald recognize the face when he was in the office for that brief time? Did that cause him to write an urgent letter to the elderly Kathryn Spears, now Mrs. F. Ramsay?

Alistair needed more information, specifically, the first name of the boy in the photograph, and more importantly, the contents of the letter. He hoped that Helen would shed some light on that at dinner, although she and Alistair had promised not to talk about the case tonight, if there even was a case at this point. Anyway, Helen couldn't discuss it in the presence of Richard, or any other member of the late Ronald's family. For now, he'd keep his suspicions, tenuous as they were, to himself, and try to enjoy the evening.

If only he had some other investigative work, perhaps he wouldn't be so drawn to the glass factory mystery and the six young men. But that thought brought him back to the conversation he needed to have with Margaret: when were they going to reclaim their pre-Scotland lives in Portland? Ever? To distract himself, he flipped through channels on the television until he found an old British mystery to watch.

Half an hour later, Margaret emerged from the bedroom and announced that she was ready. She certainly looked refreshed, her red hair loose and held back by a gold tone headband, and she wore a colorful tunic over black pants, and espadrilles with a slight heel.

"You look lovely!" he exclaimed.

She pointedly looked him up and down, hands on hips. "Aren't you going to change?" she asked, and then they both burst out laughing: the question reminded them of a day not long ago, in Orkney, when Margaret's cousin Jeannie, and Alistair too, got dressed up to go to a folk concert at a pub in the town of Kirkwall. Margaret hadn't changed out of her dusty hiking clothes, and she could hear the echo of Jeannie's voice in her own words.

"It's okay," she said, "you always look good."

"Thank you, I think. I'm sorry not to treat this as a special occasion, but I'll make it up to you next time, okay?"

She smiled. "I'll hold you to it."

When they reached the bottom of the staircase to the lobby, Alistair realized he could hear the familiar voice of the front desk manager who he'd met when he was helping SarahBeth. Taking Margaret's elbow, he guided her around to the back door, avoiding the lobby. "It's nearer the car," he mumbled, although he couldn't remember how true that was.

"I hope we don't stay out too late," Margaret said as they walked to the car at the side of the hotel. "Since we have that Jacuzzi, I want to have a good soak tonight."

"Fine with me. Although, Helen and Richard have a tendency to get into long anecdotes, and they reminisce about old British television shows. They told me I have a lot of catching up to do. Seriously, give me a sign if you think we're staying too long."

She turned and winked at him. "Don't worry, I will!"

Chapter 16

Margaret and Alistair soon reached the bistro where they were meeting Helen and Richard. They were early and the table wasn't ready yet, so they sat together in the bar area near the entrance. The bistro was modeled on a French streetside cafe: the front glass doors could be opened so that the interior was contiguous with the sidewalk on the main shop-lined street of Kilvellie, providing seating with fresh air, perfect for people-watching.

They chose to hold off on drinks, in case Helen and Richard wanted to order a bottle of wine. Alistair decided to tell Margaret that he'd been at their hotel before, but only for afternoon tea. It had involved meeting a ballet dancer, and the hotel staff might remember him in that context. But before he had a chance, Helen and Richard came breezing in.

Alistair stood up to shake Richard's hand, then he introduced Margaret.

"Glad to finally meet ye, lass." As Richard spoke, Margaret was amused at the incongruity of his deep tan and sun-lightened hair, with his local accent and clothing: he wore jeans, a navy cotton turtleneck, and a tartan waistcoat.

A waiter called Helen's name, and they were shown to a table for four near the back of the bistro. The rear window was also open wide, allowing the smell of the salty air and the sound of the waves to drift in. But the aromas emanating from the nearby kitchen were more Mediterranean than coastal Scotland.

"I feel like I'm in France, or Italy," Margaret commented.

"Aye lass, that's why I started coming here," Richard said.

Helen added, "Richard has been retired in Spain, so I think this is a reminder of home for him. On days like this anyway. It will be quite different in winter."

Richard grinned. "Aye, but I plan to tempt this lovely lady to spend as much time as she can in Spain. Things are usually quiet here in town, so my son, the sergeant, can handle it."

"You're trying to make me redundant," Helen complained. "Let's order, then I want to hear all about you, Margaret, and something Alistair mentioned about a project you have? With the royal family? Sounds fascinating."

"Sorry," Alistair murmured, turning to Margaret. "I told Helen that you might be helping the prince with his charity work, that was all."

They sipped wine while waiting for the food. Margaret was happy to talk about her new project.

"As you probably know, the prince is committed to improving the coastal environment in Scotland. He's engaged to a young woman up in Orkney, it was all over the news so you can't have missed it. His incentive to get people out collecting trash on the beaches and shoreline is that he'll reward teams who find the most groatie buckies."

"They aren't trash, though, your grubby buckets?" Alistair was teasing her; he was dismissed with a withering look before she replied.

"Of course not, just the opposite. But some of the best places to collect them are on remote beaches that require long walks to get there, and participants will be expected to gather any trash they find along the way, or while they're actually collecting."

"You're going to be crouched down for hours on end, straining your eyes for tiny shells?" Helen shook her head. "Seems a funny thing for a lawyer to be doing."

Margaret laughed. "Believe it or not, my main role is

research. People post things online about their groatie buckie hauls, like ten or twenty at a time, but they rarely reveal the location. It's usually listed as their secret island, or secret beach."

Alistair joined in. "Margaret has excellent research skills in her legal work, so I expect that if she applies that to finding peoples' secret groatie buckie places, she'll make it a success."

"And are you going to share this information with all the contestants?" Richard asked.

"Are you kidding?" Margaret lowered her voice. "I'm on the prince's team. Me and two other people from Orkney, plus Alistair if he wants to join in. So any research I do, it's only for our team."

Discussion about seashells and beach research stopped while the dinner was served, and food became the topic of conversation.

"This is a nice change from Indian dishes," Margaret said. "Don't get me wrong, I love Indian food, but this onion soup and the fried zucchini flowers seem so exotic now."

"Do you cook the Indian food?" Helen asked. "I can't imagine you have much time to cook, with your work."

"I confess, I don't cook as much as I used to. In Finlay, where our cottage is, we have a wonderful Scottish chef who specializes in gourmet Indian street food, if that's not an oxymoron. He runs the restaurant at the hotel, and they recently remodeled and opened again as kind of a destination gourmet experience. It's on the Fife coast, easy to reach from Edinburgh, and they're doing well so far. Not sure once the cold weather starts."

Helen glanced at Richard. "We'll give it a try soon."

When the dishes were cleared and coffees and teas ordered, Richard returned the conversation to shell collecting.

"Margaret, I used to collect groatie buckies as a child and teenager. Haven't done it for decades, mind you, but unless

85

things have changed, I can let you in on my secret place."

"That would be great!" Margaret's eyes widened in excitement. "Is it here, I mean, Kilvellie?"

"Nae, there's hardly any on this beach. Here, it's all glass. Getting to my secret place depends on the weather. It's a tidal island off a small island in the Inner Hebrides. There's an airstrip on the main island, couldn't even call it an airport, and flights go from Oban, weather permitting as I said. There's also a daily ferry in summer, from Oban. Takes about four hours and it makes one or two stops each way."

"Are there good accommodations out there?" Alistair asked. "I've heard it can be hit or miss on some islands."

"Again, it's been years since I was there, but I'll call folks I'm still in touch with and see how feasible it would be. Back in the day, when my family used to go, we'd rent a campervan and take it over on the ferry, then park in the holiday campground. They had showers, basic but clean. We'd take bicycles and spend a good couple of hours looking for shells, depending on the tide of course, then the rest of the day swimming and exploring."

"Sounds perfect," Margaret said, "as long as I can find somewhere nice to stay, like a B&B. I'm not really a camping enthusiast. I like my creature comforts."

"She's thinking of the Jacuzzi tub in our hotel room," Alistair added.

"I can relate!" Helen said, and Richard gave a long explanation of Helen moving into the police station residence simply because it had a Jacuzzi tub. Which in turn was installed at the insistence of Richard's late wife, after they'd moved out of the family home and left Richard's father Ronald to have it to himself.

With this topic raised, everyone fell silent.

"God bless the old man, may he rest in peace," Richard said at last, raising his wine glass. "Still can't believe he's really gone. I guess I shouldn't be out here enjoying myself."

Helen held his hand for a moment. "I'm sure he'd want

you to be enjoying life no matter what. Let's get back to your groatie buckie beach, where he must have enjoyed taking you when you were little. Do you think lots of people will have discovered it by now?"

"Thanks, dear. You always know how to cheer me up. Yes, my groatie buckie beach has a trick for safe access. The old farmer whose field is adjacent to it keeps, or used to anyway, a few Heeland coos. Highland cows to you Americans. Big sharp horns on those shaggy beasties. They were really as tame as kittens, but you'd never know it to look at them. The wily old farmer, he used to offer to keep them behind a fence, away from the beach, but he would extract payment in the form of a bottle of single malt."

Helen laughed. "He reminds me of Hamish Macbeth's old seer, always demanding gifts before he'd cooperate."

Richard laughed too. "Who knows, them coos may be long gone. Like I said, Margaret, I'll make some wee inquiries and let you know in the next day or two."

"Did you keep the groatie buckies you found? My mother in Boston has a bottle of them, about twenty or so, and she's kept them since childhood."

"Och, aye, mine are rattling away in the house somewhere. Come to think of it, you might as well have them for yer competition, eh? It's for charity you said?"

"I'm sure she has to collect them personally, right, Margaret?" Helen asked.

Margaret thought for a moment, then grinned. "Oh, I don't think we have written rules about that. It's not like anyone's going to check if contestants include shells they've found in the past. What are we talking about, five or ten for the average beach visit?"

Richard almost choked on his wine. "Lass, I think you'll find that's a slight underestimate if you find a really good location. Like I say, I'll give you what I can find at the house. Tell you what, if you and Alistair don't need to make an early start tomorrow, why don't you come over and I'll give them to you then?"

"That's very generous. I don't know when we're leaving. It really depends on whether Alistair needs to talk to Helen more in the morning."

Richard wrinkled his forehead and looked at Helen. "What do you and Alistair need to discuss? I thought his work with finding the hidden glass, and finding where Justine escaped, was all done?"

Margaret felt her face redden in embarrassment. She'd become so wrapped up in the groatie buckie discussion, she'd forgotten that Helen and Alistair had been making discreet inquiries about the death of Richard's father; obviously, Helen had not shared that information with Richard. But Alistair saved the day.

"It's nothing about that," he assured Richard. "I'm just making preliminary inquiries about possibly working over here as a private investigator, if Margaret and I decide to stay on in Scotland. I'm not sure how to go about it and I'm hoping Helen can give me some leads, since that's what her son Adam does."

Wow, Margaret thought, what a good line. Although, she wondered if it was partly true: was he really thinking of staying on and working in Scotland?

With dinner over, Richard insisted on paying the bill, then they all met outside on the sidewalk. Margaret glanced at her watch: nine o'clock. Still early enough for the long soak in the Jacuzzi she was looking forward to.

While she spoke to Richard to finalize plans to visit his house in the morning and collect the groatie buckie donation, Alistair took Helen aside, out of their hearing.

"Have you deciphered that letter, on the notepad?" he whispered.

"Yes. It's a shocker. But good thing that Ronald had such a heavy hand when he was writing. Can we talk in the morning?"

"Of course. And I may be on a completely wrong tangent,

but I realized that Kathryn Spears' last name could be an English language equivalent of the German name Speyer, and one of the names listed in Ronald's war diaries is Speyer. It's also on the memorial plaque in the chapel up at the end of town. What if, and I know it's a very long shot, what if the boy in the photograph at the law office is one of the boys who helped vandalize the glass factory?"

"You may be on the right track," Helen replied quietly. "I'd like to see the plaque for myself and take some clearer photographs."

"We could go to the chapel in the morning."

Helen shook her head. "No, that won't work. I need to be at the station all day tomorrow and the next day. I gave Desmond the rest of the week off, to help his sister clear his grandfather's room at the care home, and I didn't think I'd need someone to replace him short-term. I doubt the chapel would be open before eight tomorrow morning, and anyway I'd want to speak to the volunteer, or the minister, whoever's on duty. I'll have to go another time. Will I be able to identify the plaque easily?"

"I can describe the location, I think." Alistair looked up, trying to visualize the chapel interior. "There were a few in German. Let's see, it was maybe the fifth or sixth on the, um, the south-facing wall, counting from the back. Sorry, that's not very clear."

Helen thought for a moment. "Does the chapel have windows low enough to look in?"

"Yes, some stained glass at the front, then clear glass on both sides."

"So it should be possible to see the plaque from the outside?"

"I guess."

"How about if you drop Margaret off at the hotel so she can enjoy the Jacuzzi, then meet me at the chapel. We can look in the windows, and you can show me which plaque. Then I'll know when I go back when it's open, shouldn't take us long."

Alistair wondered about the urgency, but Helen usually had a good reason for what she did, so he agreed. With their plan set, they rejoined Richard and Margaret, then set off to their respective vehicles.

Chapter 17

Alistair told Margaret he had to discuss something in person with Helen, so he dropped her off at the front door to the hotel and said he'd be back soon. "Enjoy your bath," he called out as she walked away, smiling.

Once she was inside, he drove to the road, then made a right turn and headed for the chapel. He parked at the side of the road and waited for Helen. There seemed to be nobody else around. Soon Helen arrived, driving her own car, a new blue Mini.

"No need to draw attention by parking the police cruiser here," she explained.

Together they walked across the grassy area, following the path to the chapel. Alistair could see that the main door was closed, which he'd expected, but they checked anyway and found it locked. He led Helen to the left side, then he peered in through the first window, nearest the back of the church and the entrance.

"They must leave emergency lights on. I can see the far wall clearly, but I think we'll have a better view from the next window along."

He moved to the next window and looked back and forth, turning his head side to side.

"This is odd," he muttered. "I'm going back for my binoculars. Hold on."

Helen cupped her hands at the window and tried to see what had caught Alistair's eye, with no luck. She could make out a row of memorial plaques along the far wall, some brass, others of stone. The interior of the chapel was well-maintained, she was glad to see, and she looked forward to visiting soon when it was open.

Alistair returned and, raising his binoculars to his eyes, renewed his search for the right plaque.

He finally lowered the binoculars. "It's gone! It was there earlier today, when I brought Margaret. There's a printed sign where it used to be, saying it's been taken down for restoration."

"I suppose that's reasonable," Helen said, "with the scratched-out name you mentioned. Maybe they're going to smooth that over so it's not so obviously defaced?"

Alistair reluctantly agreed. "I suppose. The timing seems odd, that's all. But maybe when I asked about it last week, it reminded the volunteer and they've arranged for the repairs. Sorry, Helen, you'll have to take my word about the names on it."

They turned to walk back to their cars.

"I don't doubt you, Alistair. I'm sure you saw what you say you did. I'll investigate who's in charge here. There's no sign outside with a minister's name, like most churches have, so maybe it's more of a tourist attraction now, not a functional church with a congregation. Shouldn't be hard to find out."

They said goodnight at their vehicles, with Alistair promising to stop by the police station in the morning to learn about the contents of Ronald's letter to Kathryn Spears. Contents that Ronald's attorney was doing his best to keep secret.

***

Back at the hotel room, Alistair entered to find the air filled with a steamy fragrance: Margaret must be enjoying her bath, he realized.

"It's just me," he called to her; the bathroom with the

Jacuzzi was off the separate bedroom area, and Alistair sat on the sofa in the main room and thought about what to do next.

He and Helen had learned nothing more about the names from visiting the chapel, but they'd have a chance for discussion at the police station in the morning, while Richard took Margaret to his former family home to retrieve whatever groatie buckies he could find. At this stage, Alistair had no idea whether he'd stay involved with the goings-on in Kilvellie, or whether he'd be free to accompany Margaret on her beach visits.

That reminded him of Richard describing the remote island off Scotland's west coast: a beach guarded by fierce-looking but actually docile Highland cattle, and a farmer who liked his whisky. The idea of Margaret being there alone was disturbing, and for the first time Alistair wondered who else was on Margaret's "team" other than the prince. If she'd have company on the far-flung islands and beaches, he'd feel better about not going along as well. He'd ask her when she finished her bath.

He watched television until she finally emerged, wrapped in a thick navy and white striped terrycloth bathrobe; she was drying her face with a hand towel, and as soon as she took it down, he could see that she'd been crying.

"Margaret, what happened? Did you get some bad news?"

She perched next to him on the edge of the sofa, her shoulders slumped. He realized he hadn't seen her like this since they had a misunderstanding many weeks earlier, when he'd stormed off, suitcase in hand, thinking she didn't want to marry him. They'd moved beyond that, and he thought they were now rock-solid with their relationship. Their engagement.

In a small voice, such a contrast to her self-assurance of earlier in the day, she asked, "Alistair, who's SarahBeth?"

"Oh, no," he groaned. "Whatever you've heard, you have absolutely nothing to be concerned about. I've wanted to tell you all along but didn't get around to it. SarahBeth is just a client. She's the reason I came to Kilvellie in the first place, and I only took the job because you were up in Orkney. Someone I know in America knows SarahBeth's mother, and asked me to basically be on hand to help her on her first visit here. She's a ballet..."

"Yes," Margaret broke in, "I looked her up. She's young and pretty and talented..."

Alistair took Margaret's hand. "She's all those things, Margaret, I won't deny it, but she's on the move, on her way to stardom. Even if I was attracted, which I'm *not*, I would only ever be her..." He stopped while he tried to recall the word. "Her *avuncular*. Like an uncle! Like Poirot!"

Alistair's desperate attempt to find common ground with Agatha Christie's fussy little Belgian detective made Margaret burst into laughter, and the tension was gone. Alistair got a small bottle of wine from the minibar; he opened it and divided it between two glasses.

"How did you hear about SarahBeth?" he asked when he was seated again. "To tell you the truth, I thought her name might come up while we were here."

Margaret took a long sip of wine, then turned sideways on the couch to face Alistair, snuggling the bathrobe around herself.

"When you dropped me off, the woman at the front desk said good evening to me, and I stopped and said good evening, then she asked if SarahBeth was back from her tour. I said I was sorry, I didn't know who she meant, and then she got a bit red-faced. She told me that with Alistair, you, back in town, she thought that SarahBeth and her ballet troupe must be finished their tour of Scotland, and that perhaps SarahBeth had come to say goodbye to her family and new friends, before flying back to America, where she lives. She said, 'I'm so sorry, dear, I hope I haven't put my foot in it.' I told her it was all fine, but when I got upstairs and looked SarahBeth up on the internet, well, I admit, I got jealous."

Alistair held her hand again. "Margaret, you have nothing to be jealous of. It was only a work assignment. It did get complicated though, because SarahBeth turned out to be the long-lost twin of a woman from this town, the one who disappeared for seven years." He stopped and gently tapped his forehead. "Of *course*, you've seen her! Not SarahBeth, but her twin. Remember the coffee shop we go to in St. Andrews, the barista with all the piercings and tattoos?"

"*She's* SarahBeth's twin? I never would have guessed."

"The tattoos and piercings are all cosmetic, I mean, they can be removed easily. Long story short, she was staying away from Kilvellie all those years because the current police sergeant, Desmond, convinced her that her older brother and sister had left her to die in a cave. He thought he was protecting her. A huge misunderstanding in the end."

Margaret turned to sit upright and drink some more wine, then made a connection.

"Wait, is the missing girl the sister of the two glass artisans in town? I talked to them earlier today. The man, William, is interested in seeing the glass in the jars at our cottage. In fact, he gave me something."

She hesitated, remembering Christy's outburst, her apparent antagonism toward the glass factory guard, Ronald. Hours earlier, Margaret had been impatient to convey the information to Alistair, but if she told him now, he'd want to pass it on to Helen right away. No, Margaret decided, the evening was for the two of them, and discussion of possible suspects could wait.

Instead, she got up and grabbed her pack, then retrieved the felt pouch. "Hold your hand out," she said, and Alistair complied. She tilted the pouch, and out rolled the blue beach marble William had given her.

"It's gorgeous. Did you buy it? I know these handmade ones are expensive, not that I'm complaining."

"No, he gave it to me as an advance on buying beach

glass from my uncle's collection." She put the marble away in the pouch.

"So we're okay?" Alistair asked.

"Of course. I need to remember that your work as a PI is sometimes going to involve beautiful mysterious women, and I have to learn not to be jealous."

Alistair took a few more sips of wine, feeling relaxed again. Now that Margaret's mind was at ease, he had to do the same for himself.

"About your groatie buckie collecting trips, the island and the beach that Richard talked about, it sounds very remote. If you go there, will you be on your own?"

"I shouldn't be. Jeremy from Orkney is on the team. You know he's trustworthy. But before *you* get jealous, his girl-friend will be there also. It will be perfectly safe."

"Okay," Alistair conceded. "I'll go as well if I can. It will probably depend on my meeting with Helen tomorrow. I didn't have a chance to tell you yet, but she managed to read the underlying page on the pad that Ronald used to write his letter to Kathryn Spears, or to Mrs. F. Ramsay, same person. With Richard at dinner, she couldn't tell me what it said, but the term she used was 'a shocker,' whatever that means. And on top of that, the plaque is missing from the chapel, so I need to..."

"No more investigating tonight! I had a scroll through the television offerings earlier. There's an Agatha Christie series on, featuring..."

She left the thought hanging while she went to the mini-bar and returned with a can of roasted nuts and a chocolate bar.

"Not Hercule Poirot?" Alistair asked.

"No, our new aliases, Tommy and Tuppence." She grabbed the remote, and they settled in to binge on murder and snacks.

Chapter 18

At nine o'clock the following morning, following an elegant breakfast in the sunny hotel restaurant adjacent to the lobby, Alistair and Margaret checked out at the front desk. After a short drive south and along the main street through Kilvellie, Alistair parked the car in a visitor spot at the police station, and they both went inside. Richard was already there, enjoying a cup of coffee and waiting to drive Margaret to his house to collect the groatie buckies, assuming he could find them.

"It's a bit of a mess over there," he apologized. "My daughter Emily has been in and out, keeping it from getting too dusty, but no one has lived in it since the old man moved into the care home four years back. Guess now I should get on with selling it. I need to check first if my son Desmond wants to live there, although I doubt it, not with his bad mem'ries growing up there. Sorry," he said, shaking his head. "No one needs to hear all this ancient history."

Promising to be back in an hour or two, Richard ushered Margaret out the front door of the station, leaving Helen and Alistair to talk.

"Tea?" Helen offered, holding up her own empty mug.

"Sure, then I'm eager to hear about the letter." Alistair took a seat in a guest chair facing Helen's desk. He glanced around, thinking it was odd to be there again. A week before, he'd mentally said goodbye to Kilvellie forever, thinking he would not be back. How wrong he'd been.

Desmond, the young sergeant, normally occupied the

desk on the north wall of the station, opposite the conference room, but he was out, helping to clear his grandfather's belongings from the care home, as Helen had explained. His desk was tidy except for a heap of clear plastic bags. From where Alistair sat, he thought he recognized the old man's outer coat in one of the bags, so he guessed that the clothing had been returned to Desmond as next of kin. Perhaps Ronald's son, Richard, was leaving the post-death logistics to the grandchildren.

Alistair looked up to see Helen emerge from the small kitchen in the back of the station, carrying a tray with a teapot, two mugs, and a plate of biscuits.

"Let's sit in there," she suggested, tilting her head toward the conference room, and Alistair got up to open the door.

"Is that Ronald's clothing on Desmond's desk?" he asked. "The wool coat looks familiar, from seeing Ronald at the cafe parking lot."

"Aye." Helen placed the tray on the conference room table and unloaded the mugs and plates. They both sat down and prepared their tea using milk and sugar from the tray.

"The coroner would have kept the clothing if they suspected foul play," she continued, "but even if he was pushed, God forbid, there would be little point in trying to get fingerprints or hairs or anything off his coat. He wore it everywhere, and countless people might have touched it recently, hanging it up on a hook in the solicitor's office, and holding his arm to help him up and down the stairs. Or when he was around the care home."

"So," Alistair said, only half-joking, "no sign of a button being torn off during a clifftop struggle."

"Oh, *heavens*." Helen looked over at the clothing, as if seeing it for the first time. "I doubt that anyone looked! A button could have come off when he tripped or landed on the beach, or when the first people on the scene checked for vital signs. So even if a button or two are missing, I can't see that it would be helpful information at this stage."

"I guess you're right." Alistair helped himself to a piece of shortbread. "I've been watching too many mysteries on television."

Helen opened a file folder that had been lying on the conference room table, and handed a piece of paper to Alistair. She explained that she'd keyed in and printed the text of Ronald's letter to the care home resident, as the impression on the original paper had taken her a while to decipher. He read it with a sense of dread of what he might learn.

My dear Kathryn,

I have been too embarrassed and ashamed to tell you this, but now that I am gone and my family won't be subject to the shame of my deeds, I am writing to explain what happened to your brother. I know you have wondered about him for many decades and for that I am more sorry than I can say.

In 1944, he was among a group of six lads who Henry Green, or Heinrich Gruener as he was known during his internment, employed to help clean up after the destruction of the World War One memorial window at Henry's old glass factory. Henry hoped to gather as many names of the dead as could be found and construct a new window, adding the names of Kilvellie's men and women lost during World War Two as well. I was there helping to supervise the work, and I took a break indoors. Henry was up in the office. It faced the road, and he told me later he didn't see anything.

When I came back out the boys were gone. At first I thought they'd run off, but I noticed that the cliff edge, near where they'd been working, looked rougher than it had earlier. I got down on hands and knees and crept closer to the edge. The tide was in, and all six boys were in the water. Kathryn, I'm sorry, but they drowned.

I've kept quiet all these decades. I learned later that

*the boys had been evacuated from Glasgow at the start
of the war, but no one ever came to Kilvellie to bring
them back home, even after Normandy, when the
chance of Scotland being bombed was less than in 1939
and 1940. The waves were pounding against the cliff
and Henry and I could see the lads were all dead, either
drowned right off, or smashed against the cliff.*

*Of course we reported it to the police and they called
to get a lifeboat dispatched, but the tide had started
going out by then and no trace of the boys was found.*

*I don't expect that God will let me into Heaven, not
with what I've seen and done, but if He is merciful, perhaps I will see you one day, when your time finally
comes. I pray for that.*

Please forgive me.

Your friend, Ron

Feeling a chill, Alistair handed the page back to Helen,
who placed it in the folder.

"I simply don't know what to think," she said. "Ronald
told his granddaughter Emily that he killed six German lads
who had threatened his family and destroyed factory property. He told her they went over the cliff. Then he wrote you a
letter and said he had not killed anyone and that he'd made
up the story to help Emily understand the moral dilemmas
her husband faced, in military zones. And now..." She shook
her head and sighed, holding her hot tea mug close with both
hands for comfort.

"Who else knows this story, or this version, anyway? If
the local police were notified and a lifeboat really was sent
out, presumably there will be a record?"

Helen shook her head. "This morning I searched for a
police report. There is absolutely nothing here from that
year. And there should be. I found ledgers from nineteen

forty-three and nineteen forty-five."

"So it's been hidden? Suppressed?"

"Destroyed more like. And it was well before Richard's time, so there's no point asking him."

"But this is a big lead, don't you think? There must be records somewhere of the six boys who were evacuated."

"Not necessarily," said Helen. "I've read a bit about the evacuation of children from the cities to the countryside as war was breaking out. Some of it was well-organized, but some of it, not so much. I mean, in those days, people used tags tied with string to identify children, and where they were being sent. Siblings would be separated, either intentionally or by accident. Some were taken in by farmers and home-owners who used them as unpaid help. Other families were much kinder. And some went to group homes. I expect that's what happened here. Although I don't know where the group home would have been. Could be a building that was torn down in the intervening years, taking any written records with it."

"Do you know if Kathryn Spears has been given the letter yet?"

Helen gave Alistair a hard stare. "Do you really think the lawyers will hand the letter over, after they read it? They represent Ronald, and his family I understand, so they won't want this information to be made public."

Alistair drank the rest of his tea, thinking while he poured refills for both of them from the teapot.

"Ronald was still alive for at least a day after he gave this letter to Claude, right?"

"Yes," Helen confirmed. "What are you getting at?"

"It sounds crazy, but could Claude, or Elise for that matter, have wanted him dead? I mean, to keep him from telling this story to anyone else? It's obviously been kept secret for decades, and the missing police ledger for that year hints at a cover-up. The more I think about it, how would it look if news got out that a town where children were sent to be safe

101

during the war, had instead allowed them to fall off a cliff and drown?"

"And at a German-owned factory for that matter," Helen added. "Oh goodness, what a mess."

They sat in silence for a few moments, drinking their tea while they each considered what Ronald's letter had revealed.

"Do you think someone should examine his clothes after all?" Alistair asked. "If no one saw Ronald fall from the cliff, that means no one would have seen if he was attacked moments before. A stab wound, among all the fall-related injuries, could have been missed when his body was examined, if he fell on sharp rocks. Especially if there was no reason to look for one."

Helen sighed deeply and forced herself up from her chair. "Yes, I think we have to. I'll get the clothes and some gloves. We treat everything we touch as exhibits from this point on."

"Wait, I'm not qualified to do a forensic examination!"

Helen waved his objection away with her hand, as if batting the words from the air. "Och, it will be fine. The clothes are in bags now just to keep them tidy, but as for exhibits, they really have little weight unless we find a recent clean cut that could have been done with a knife or something. As I said before, lots of people have handled them in the past few days."

Alistair gathered up the tea things and placed them on the nearby desk. Not that he wanted to find evidence of murder, but it would be far more satisfying to spend his time investigating in Kilvellie, than searching for trash and seashells under the watchful eyes of Highland cows and tipsy farmers. And, most likely, in the pouring rain.

He had a sudden thought and opened the file folder to re-read the letter to Mrs. Ramsay. When Helen returned and arranged the plastic bags of clothing on the table, Alistair showed the letter to her.

"Ronald writes that Henry was in his office at the time,

and that the office faced the road. The area where the boys were picking up glass was on the other side of the factory, away from Henry's sight. I hate to suggest this, but Helen, what if Ronald *did* push the boys over the cliff, and the edge didn't crumble like he claims?"

She sat down again at the table. "How can we ever know the truth from that day? He claimed in his letter to you, Alistair, that he did not kill them..."

"Hold on." Alistair removed his own letter from his pack and showed her. "He said that he did not kill six German boys, but that doesn't mean he didn't kill Scottish boys. The letter is either very craftily written, or, I don't know..."

Helen thought for several moments. "We have to get possession of that memorial plaque from the chapel and try to find out who the witness was. That may be the key to what happened to those poor boys." She picked up the top plastic bag of clothes, and with disposable gloves on, began to open it. "Get your gloves on, Alistair. Let's at least try to rule out that Ronald was stabbed or something. That would make things so much more complicated."

Alistair grabbed a pair of clean gloves from the box Helen had brought in with the clothing, then stopped. "Helen, you don't suspect that Ronald's *family* had anything to do with his death, do you? If you did, you wouldn't have agreed to Margaret going off alone with Richard, right?"

Helen looked at him in surprise. "Jeez, Alistair, no, it never crossed my mind! But I'll give you Richard's address if you'd feel more comfortable following them over there. I can't leave the station unattended, unless it's for an emergency."

Alistair thought for a moment. Margaret disliked her judgment being questioned, and on previous occasions when he'd been poised to go and check on her, she'd been fine and his fears had been unfounded. Would Kilvellie's ex-senior police officer have any reason to harm Margaret, under the guise of picking up a jar or two of groatie buckies? Surely not. He put it from his mind.

"Nah, let's get this done for now. If Margaret's not back in an hour, I'll call her and see how they're doing."

Chapter 19

Just west of the downtown area of Kilvellie, Richard pulled into the driveway of a two-story house that, at Margaret's first glance, had seen better days. Nearby homes of the residential neighborhood looked occupied and well-maintained, with flourishing front gardens. She imagined the neighbors must consider Richard's unoccupied house an eyesore.

The house appeared small from the front, but on approach she'd seen that it extended well into the back garden, possibly an addition. There was an attached garage to the right, secured with a large padlock, but probably accessible through the kitchen or a mudroom.

If the interior was anything like the exterior, she wouldn't want to stay long. She imagined the usual horrors: spiders, hanging cobwebs, rats. But since they had made the trip for her, she felt it was premature to object to going in. Before she could unlock her seatbelt, Richard was around to the passenger side, holding the door open for her.

"Here we are, lass. I know it's not much to look at, being empty for several years."

"How come you didn't sell it or rent it out?" Margaret immediately regretted asking. "I'm sorry, Richard, it's none of my business."

"It's fine," he assured her as they walked along a weed-filled cobbled path to the front door, dodging rolled plastic-wrapped free newspapers that had been tossed onto the unkempt lawn from cars and vans. "Guess Emily hasn't been by in a few days," he muttered.

"Anyway, Margaret, the reason I kept it vacant was my old man, Ronald. He can, or could, be quite cruel and prejudiced. I was expecting the care home to call me and tell me to get him immediately. No idea how he lasted four years there, the way I used to see him treating the home help here."

"I guess that's part of the job in a care home," Margaret offered. "I've heard that older people can be difficult to manage if they have dementia, or delusions, so I'd think the staff would be trained to overlook or excuse verbal mistreatment."

"Aye, lass, you have a point. But I kept the house anyway, in case I had to move him on short notice and get him set up here again."

They reached the front door; it had once been bright red, but between the peeling paint and some splintered areas, it seemed almost menacing. She was trying to think of an excuse to stay outside, but she'd wait until he opened the door; surely the place would smell of mold, and that could be her out: allergies.

However, she was surprised to smell not mold or neglect, but a pleasant lemon scent.

"Come in." Richard held the door open for her. "The outside looks terrible but Emily keeps the rooms clean. She spent time here, I should have said, going through the old man's boxes and finding things for him." He stopped and sighed. "Guess all this will have to go now."

Inside, they passed the entryway to a small but gleaming kitchen, like a film set for a nineteen fifties production. Someone would pay good money for this kind of vintage furniture and fixings, Margaret realized.

Richard was mumbling to himself. "Groatie buckies, groatie buckies... where would they be?"

She didn't think he actually wanted an answer, so she kept quiet, but looked around the kitchen, hoping to see a small jar or two of shells on the windowsill or shelving.

"I used to have them in glass jars," he said, as if reading

her mind, "but then I worried that the old man might break the jars by accident when he was living here alone. What did I do with them after that...?"

He stood in the hallway, running his hand through his hair. He glanced up the staircase, then shook his head. "Nae, they wouldn't be in a bedroom, and I know I wouldn't have put them in the cellar, hate going down there."

He walked into the room across from the kitchen, the family room, Margaret guessed. A wide shabby (not shabby-chic, she noted) floral sofa was strewn with fading pillows that were destined for the trash. The sofa and two equally worn easy chairs faced an old television set on a rolling cart. In keeping with the decor of decades earlier, there was no sign of even a DVD player or an audio system.

However, on the far wall, she saw a glass-fronted cabinet with an assortment of china ornaments, bowls, and other bric-a-brac.

"Could the groatie buckies be in any of those bowls?" She pointed at the cabinet.

"Nay, lass, them bowls are far too small."

Too small? Margaret asked herself. Each bowl could hold at least four scoops of ice cream. How could a bowl like that be too small for his collection of tiny shells? For a large hoard of groatie buckies, even she would confront an army of rats in the cellar. She was on the brink of offering when she thought of the garage, and she went back into the kitchen and approached what must be the door into the garage.

Richard's mood changed in a flash. "Not the garage!" he cried angrily, then immediately reverted to his jovial self, seeing Margaret's look of alarm. "Sorry lass, it's a jumble of tools and things. Don't want ye to get hurt!"

Feeling wary at the sudden changes in Richard's behavior, she stepped nervously away from the garage door and was heading for the hallway, to go outside and call Alistair, when Richard announced, "I remember!"

He flung open the kitchen cabinet doors and started

removing biscuit tins, placing them on the fading yellow
Formica kitchen table. Each tin was round, about nine inches in diameter and three inches high. Margaret recognized
some of the scenic Scottish designs from her Boston home,
tins her mother kept out of nostalgia for her own childhood
in Scotland.

Opening one, Richard sighed with satisfaction, and
Margaret looked in. She almost fell over in shock: she'd never
seen, or even imagined, so many groatie buckies in one
place.

"My goodness, it's full! That must have taken you years
to collect."

"Nae, lass, each tin is from a week's holiday. There's
many, many, thousands here."

He lifted the edges of the remaining lids and glanced into
each tin to make sure none contained stale biscuits or cake,
but no, one after another, to Margaret's continued surprise
and delight, contained groatie buckies.

"You can have them all if you want, lass."

"If you're *sure*. Or how about if I use them in the competition and then give them back?"

"Nae, they're yours. With the old man gone, I need to
clear the house completely. I'm not taking any of this stuff
back to my home in Spain. Emily's already sold most everything worth selling, and Desmond isn't interested in anything here."

"Well, *thank you*, is all I can say. Thank you, Richard!"

He handed one of the tins to her. "Here lass, you start
carrying the tins out to the car. I'm going to take a quick look
upstairs for something Emily mentioned, some old diaries of
Dad's that he was asking about recently. Don't much matter
now he's gone, but apparently he was quite agitated when he
couldn't find them in the boxes at her place."

Margaret paid little attention to what he was saying, she
was so overwhelmed with her windfall. Carrying each tin
carefully to avoid the lid popping off, she placed them flat in

the back seat and floor of Richard's rental car. With the last one, she counted: twelve all together. Alistair won't believe it, she thought to herself as she waited in the sunshine for Richard to return. And it more than compensated for her time helping the solicitors.

While Richard was still inside the house, Alistair called her cell phone.

"Not checking up on you," he explained, "just wondering when you're coming back to the station."

"We're about to leave," Margaret assured him. She'd hold off revealing the extent of the groatie buckie stash until she got back. "Richard's gone upstairs for something, what did he say? Oh, yes, Ronald was looking for diaries the other day, at his granddaughter's house. Must have been important to Ronald because he was upset when he couldn't find them. Wait, does this relate to what the lawyers said, about..."

Alistair interrupted, "Yes, it would be helpful to know *when* Ronald was looking for the diaries, but don't ask Richard. I don't want him to think there's something important in them."

Margaret agreed, then ended the call when she saw Richard emerging from the house, shrugging his shoulders, palms up in a "no luck" gesture. He locked the front door, and after praising Margaret's careful arrangement of the biscuit tins, they headed back to the police station.

Helen offered to make more tea before Alistair and Margaret left for the drive back to Finlay, but both declined, as they were ready to head home. Alistair and Helen had carefully examined Ronald's clothes, and short of a very thin skewer being used to stab him on the clifftop, or a hypodermic needle, they found no evidence of an attack being responsible for his fall, or death just before falling. Of course, they hadn't ruled out a simple shove in the right direction, although no one had come forward to say they'd witnessed any such thing.

Alistair and Richard went outside to tape the tins of

groatie buckies closed, then transfer them to Alistair's car, and Margaret stayed inside chatting to Helen.

"I hope you come to visit us soon," Margaret said. "With all the groatie buckies that Richard is parting with, I don't really feel like tromping around remote beaches to find a handful more. But I do need to go back to Orkney and check on some work I've ordered up there."

"What is it?" Helen asked.

"I'm getting two handmade walking sticks, and on the top of each I'm having them attach an old silver cone-shaped cover, with Pictish designs. I need to take those to Orkney personally. I don't want to trust them in the mail."

"Too bad poor Ronald's cane broke when he fell. It looks like a nice one." Helen indicated a plastic bag lying on Desmond's desk, next to the clothing which she'd replaced in their plastic bags.

"It must have broken when he landed on the beach," Margaret agreed. "I thought they were made of quite strong wood, usually. Can I look?"

"Sure, take it out of the bag if you want. It will probably just be tossed away."

Margaret lifted up the bag; it contained two halves of a well-worn handmade walking stick, almost identical in length. "Kind of a waste. I don't know what anyone could do with it."

As she replaced the bag on the desk, one of the halves shifted to give a different view of the ends. "That's weird..." she said to herself, picking up the bag again.

She looked at it more carefully, then turned to face Helen. "Has something been done to this since it was taken from where he fell?"

"Not that I know of. Why?"

Margaret switched on Desmond's desk lamp and moved the sticks through a range of angles under the bright light.

"Helen, I hope I'm imagining things, but this looks to me like it's partly sawn through. Recently. The wood inside looks freshly cut."

They hadn't noticed the front door open; seeing Richard enter, Helen grabbed the bag from Margaret and replaced it on the desk, turning off the desk lamp at the same time.

"All set?" she asked.

Alistair came in next and said goodbye to Helen. "Keep in touch, will you?"

"Of course," she replied, then looked at Richard. "Be a dear and put on the kettle, will you? I'm ready for a cuppa."

When Richard disappeared into the kitchen behind Helen's desk, Helen grabbed the cane again and handed it to Margaret.

"Keep this safe in the bag for now," she whispered. "I'll call you later. I can't risk anyone touching it until I think about what to do next."

Alistair looked like he was about to ask a question, but Helen hurried him and Margaret out of the front door.

"Go enjoy the rest of the day," she said. "See you soon!"

***

In the car and heading south toward Fife, Alistair asked Margaret why Helen had given her Ronald's broken cane. "It's not much use for anything except firewood, is it?"

Margaret sighed deeply. "Unfortunately, it looks like it's been partly sawed through the middle. Recent damage, I mean. He may have been murdered after all."

Alistair gasped, and turned to glance at the bag where it rested on the back seat. The day had become cloudy and he'd put the roof up when he was outside with Richard. "This is awful! Helen and I examined his clothes, but neither of us thought to inspect the cane. I must be losing my touch. And now, Helen doesn't want Richard or Desmond to find it, is that why she gave it to you?"

"Exactly. It was spur of the moment, but she had to think fast. I'm sure she'll be calling you later today."

Jane Ross Potter

"But Margaret," Alistair cried, bringing the car to a screeching halt on the shoulder, "chain of custody! We shouldn't have that evidence. What was Helen thinking?"

Margaret turned to him, eyes wide, horrified at the mistake. "I'm so sorry Alistair, I'm the lawyer here and I should have thought of that! Should we go right back?"

"No," he decided after a moment, pulling the car onto the road again. "With Richard hanging around, and maybe Desmond will be in and out, she must think it's best to have it out of the office and the residence. Look, don't berate yourself. You were acting under instructions from a police officer, an experienced one at that. If you were a criminal lawyer, you might have immediately thought of chain of custody, but that's not your area."

They were silent as they continued south, following the signs to Dundee, then across the Tay Bridge and on to Finlay. Any other day, Alistair would have suggested stopping near St. Andrews for lunch, but he wanted to get home and secure the cane. With possession of evidence that Ronald might have been murdered, it seemed that Kilvellie wasn't ready to let go of Alistair yet. And Margaret likely wanted to get started counting her unexpected bonus of groatie buckies.

112

Chapter 20

Alistair and Margaret arrived home at their cottage in Finlay at lunchtime. After a quick meal together at the dining table, they spent the afternoon catching up on emails and telephone messages. Margaret had several messages, all related to the upcoming groatie buckie competition. She decided to return them the next day, hoping to have made a decision about the twelve biscuit tins of groatie buckies that Richard had given her.

She snapped a couple of pictures of open tins with her phone and emailed them to her mother. She was sure her mother would be as incredulous as she was. As far as Margaret knew, her mother's finds had always been one or two per beach visit, not more.

Later in the afternoon, as she waited for Alistair to finish whatever he was doing upstairs on his laptop, she took a jar of her late uncle's sea glass from the shelf, placed a utility towel on the dining table, and poured the glass out to examine what she had, hoping it would be of interest to William and Christy.

She remembered William's comment about finding pieces with the old glass factory's name. She had a quick search, but saw nothing resembling the name or even part of it, REGENBOGEN. She wasn't surprised. Unless her uncle had collected glass at Kilvellie, he wouldn't have found anything like that: chances are, pieces of glass from Kilvellie wouldn't travel this far south and come to rest on a beach in Fife.

Hearing Alistair's footsteps on the stairs, she shoveled

the glass pieces back into the jar and returned it to the shelf. She was wondering how many sea glass marbles William would part with in exchange for the glass... or maybe an elegant sea glass pendant from Christy's stock. Wishful thinking at this point, she decided. She shouldn't have anything more to do with two people who had not yet been cleared of wrongdoing in Ronald's death.

"Are you ready to have dinner soon?" she asked Alistair.

"Sure. I was searching online for information about the chapel in Kilvellie, and maybe something about the memorial plaques, but nothing helpful turned up. Just a few photos of the outside."

"No website for the chapel?"

"Not that I can find. Strange, in this day and age. They have a donation box and information leaflets, so you'd think they would encourage visitors."

"Why don't you ask Calum? As the local minister, he should know about churches in the region, right?"

"Maybe, but the chapel doesn't seem to be an active church. Still, I'll give him a call."

"Invite him to dinner, if you want." Margaret held up her phone. "I'm about to call the hotel anyway and order Indian food. I know he enjoys that."

Calum arrived an hour later, needing no convincing to come over and eat with them. Born and raised in Finlay, he'd been a good friend to Margaret and Alistair for a few months now, with their initial friendship developing over Indian meals. Calum's father had been the village minister before Calum, and now Calum had occupied that position for over half his life.

He'd walked the two miles from town, waving to Alistair driving the other way to pick up the food. Calum and Margaret chatted while she set the dining table and opened a bottle of wine. She was distracted by a ringing phone, but when she checked, it wasn't hers.

"Oh, Alistair must have left his behind. I wonder if I

should..." She was looking at the phone sitting on a table by the couch, trying not to be nosy, but when she saw Helen's name come up on the caller ID, she answered.

"Hi Helen, it's Margaret answering Alistair's phone. He's just gone out for a few minutes and forgot it."

"I can talk to you, Margaret. You've realized, I'm sure, I shouldn't have given you Ronald's cane. All I could think about was Richard not seeing it, or Desmond, but since it may be important evidence, I need to consider chain of custody and all that. Can I pop over and pick it up?"

"We could bring it tomorrow," Margaret suggested, glad that it would be out of their hands soon.

"No need. I'm just down the street. I asked in the hotel where your cottage is and they told me. Don't worry, I identified myself as police. They're not giving your location out to just anyone."

Margaret wondered if having police from another town ask for directions to her house wasn't suspicious itself, but she didn't say anything.

"Sure, come on along. And you're welcome to stay for some Indian food, if you don't need to rush back."

"That would be super, Margaret. Just a quick bite and then I'll leave you to your privacy."

"Don't worry about that." Margaret glanced at Calum and winked. "You'll meet another dinner guest, who's already here. In fact, we invited him over to pick his brains about the chapel, so you can join in."

While Margaret set a fourth place at the table, she told Calum about Helen's visit, minus mention of the broken cane. "I just met her. She and Alistair are investigating a mysterious brass plaque in the chapel that he wants to ask you about. It purports to be a memorial to six men lost in the North Sea in nineteen forty-four, but there are two odd things about it. It's all written in German, including the names of the men, and there was once a witness name, but it's scratched out. When Alastair first saw it a week ago, he met a volunteer guide in the chapel who claimed to know nothing of the plaque's history. And now, maybe even more oddly, the plaque itself was removed sometime yesterday afternoon or early evening."

"All very mysterious," Calum agreed. "In any event, I look forward to meeting your guest."

The kitchen door opened and Alistair walked in carrying a cardboard box, in which Margaret could see the usual array of containers. The spicy smell preceded Alistair and quickly filled the kitchen, a welcome distraction from discussions about Kilvellie. Margaret saw Helen's blue Mini through the open kitchen door. After quickly explaining Helen's presence to Alistair, she went outside.

"Just park anywhere!" she called out, pointing. Although the former train track route had been cleared of overgrowth from the cottage to the village, nothing had been cleared beyond the cottage, so it was as far as a car could be driven. Helen soon emerged from her small car, wearing jeans, running shoes, and a blue fleece vest over a white cotton turtleneck. She carried a folded plastic tote bag, presumably for collecting the broken cane.

***

Once introductions were taken care of, the four sat around the dining room table enjoying Chef Dougie's specialties.

"This is an unexpected pleasure," Helen commented as she finished cleaning her plate using a last piece of naan. "Yesterday when I said I'd try the food sometime, I didn't mean so soon. I'm glad it worked out."

"Do you have to get back, or do you want to stay while we talk to Calum about the chapel in Kilvellie?" Alistair asked.

"I don't want to barge into your evening more than I'm welcome, but I would certainly enjoy it, yes."

Calum helped Margaret clear the dishes from the table,

while Alistair rearranged chairs to make a seating area around the coffee table. "It's nice to be near the sea," Helen said to him, standing at the open front window that faced onto the beach. "I had a view of the North Sea when I first moved to Kilvellie, and now I admit I miss it, after moving into the police residence."

"Why did you move? If it's not impertinent to ask, I mean."

She laughed. "Adam blames it on the Jacuzzi, and the fact that my flat only had a shower. But I first thought about it one evening when I was walking home from a meeting in town. I picked up some fish and chips, and I realized that if I was still working in Edinburgh, I could have walked to my office and put in another hour or two while I was eating. But with Desmond living at the station, it felt intrusive to go back there and work in the evening. So I really moved so I could keep up my bad habit of eating supper at my desk, and the Jacuzzi was a bonus."

"But now you miss the view, and the sound of the waves?"

"Aye. I guess I can't have both."

"Is it a requirement for someone to be living at the station?" Alistair asked.

"Not nowadays, with mobile phones and texts and all that instant communication. Hmm, maybe that's a point. I could keep the residence vacant and use it now and again for guests and visiting officers, and I could live somewhere like the flat I had, with a view. I'd still have the option to work at the office in the evening. Thanks, Alistair, your sea view has helped me think this through."

"It's actually the Firth of Forth," he said, pointing out toward the water. "But at high tide the waves come quite close, like they do at the cliffs in Kilvellie. I hate to think what will happen to this cottage in the future, with the sea level predictions. So far the worst damage is to the steps up and over the sand dune, when there's a big storm."

Margaret and Calum returned bringing cups of chai and plates of the tiny spiced shortbread biscuits that Dougie had perfected to accompany his Indian meals.

Calum sat down on the couch, laughing. "I was about to reach for an old biscuit tin on the kitchen table, but Margaret warned me off. She opened it just enough to show me it was full of groatie buckies. Imagine the mess if I'd yanked the lid off and they went flying."

Margaret laughed. "I'll tell you what, instead of sitting here having chai, we'd all be on the floor in the kitchen to find every last shell!"

Turning serious, Calum asked Helen if she had a long drive home.

"No, less than an hour, but I don't like to be out too late. With my sergeant on compassionate leave, I need to be at my desk by eight tomorrow morning."

"You're in Kilvellie, is that right?"

"Aye, but I've been on the job just a few weeks. Kilvellie-by-the-Sea is the full name, which beats me because anyone can tell it's at the seaside."

"That's due to a grammatical misunderstanding. But if you want to talk about the chapel, I don't want to bore you with Pater's fascination with place names."

"Oh, please go ahead, Calum," Helen said. "I can always use anecdotes about the town that others might not have heard."

Knowing Calum's habit of stretching out his stories, Alistair and Margaret each took hold of their chai cups and sat back comfortably to listen.

Chapter 21

"It's not something I keep in my head," Calum began, "so when Alistair called and asked me about the chapel in Kilvellie, I got out Pater's old book of Scottish place name origins. It's out of print, and it was only ever a vanity press edition so I doubt you could buy a copy now. Anyway, there's been a town at the present Kilvellie site for centuries. In the eighteen hundreds, someone liked the area and they built a huge manor house about ten miles inland. They named it Kilvellie Towers, a bit of hubris obviously, but the name stuck.

"As time went by and confusion developed with the two names, the town of Kilvellie decided to rename itself, or rebrand itself I suppose, as Kilvellie-by-the-Coalfields. It's a wee bit like a town near here called Coaltown of Wemyss. In both cases, the coal mines have been closed for decades, but the names live on. And as you probably know, Kilvellie's early prosperity depended on the nearby coalmines.

"I am getting to the point," he said as he stopped for a long sip of chai. "So at both ends of town, they erected signs with Kilvellie-by-the-Coalfields printed on them."

He showed the group an old black and white photograph from his book. Then, laughing to himself, he said, "One day, along comes a truck driven by a clumsy driver, and he left this in his wake."

Helen, Alistair, and Margaret looked at the picture of the damaged sign which now read "Kilvellie-by-the-C" and this caused Margaret to break into laughter as well. "Oh, my goodness, I can tell where this is going. The instructions to replace the sign got jumbled and it became 'Sea' instead of 'C,' is that it?"

"You're close, Margaret. It took several months to get a new sign made, and by then everyone was enjoying the joke so much, they decided to rename themselves Kilvellie-by-the-C. Someone vandalized the sign at the other end of town, so it was Kilvellie-by-the-C in both directions. However, the town government thought it was frivolous, as this was now into the nineteen fifties and holiday travel was starting up again, so they had the town name officially changed to Kilvellie-by-the-Sea. That's what it was being called by people anyway, verbally, I mean."

Calum sat back and sipped his chai for a few moments before concluding his story.

"The sad irony is that the Kilvellie Towers building was severely damaged by fire during the war, and the rest was demolished. So the town of Kilvellie has no reason to keep the 'by the sea' designation now. It's the only Kilvellie around."

"Was the family safe after the fire, I mean, the family in Kilvellie Towers?" Margaret asked.

"It stopped being a family residence early in the twentieth century. The building was requisitioned during the First World War as a place for soldiers to recuperate, and of course, it played a role in Operation Pied Piper in the Second World War."

Alistair looked at Calum in confusion. "What, you mean they put on plays there?"

"No, Alistair, sorry, I forgot you're new to oor wee country's history. Operation Pied Piper involved the evacuation of huge numbers of children from cities early in the war, and just before, when there were understandable fears about places like Glasgow being bombed. Many children went to farms and individual family homes, but others were housed in groups, like at Kilvellie Towers. By the time of the fire, some of the children had gradually returned home, or gone to live with relatives further north, but it's believed a few may have perished in the fire. As you can imagine, the records back then were nothing like today."

"That's awful!" Margaret cried. "So there could be children still unaccounted for, from that far back?"

"I'm sure there are," Calum said, shaking his head. "But with the growing interest in researching ancestry online, I hope that, one by one, the fates of missing children will be traced."

After sitting quietly for a few moments, Alistair asked, "Calum, do you think there's a list of children who were sent to Kilvellie Towers?"

"Och, I have no idea. It was so long ago now. I suppose there could be, somewhere, but I wouldn't know where to begin."

"Sorry to interrupt," Helen said, "but I should get going soon. Calum, can I call you and ask you about the chapel?"

"Of course!" He gave her a card from his wallet. "This has my office and mobile numbers. And email, but that's a story for another day. Listen, I apologize for getting off the subject with my musings."

"Really, it's fine." Helen stood up and stretched. "I've been spending too many hours sitting. I'm overdue for some long beach walks."

"Yesterday I'd have invited you to look for groatie buckies," said Margaret, "but now..."

"Now you have more than you could have dreamed of, thanks to Richard." Helen finished the thought for her. "And before I go, Alistair, I think there's something you were going to give me?" She turned her back to Calum and Margaret so that she could discreetly hand the plastic tote bag to Alistair.

"I'll bring it to your car," he said. "See you out there."

Margaret distracted Calum with questions about Kilvellie Towers while Alistair retrieved the broken cane in its plastic bag, placed it in Helen's bag, and took the bag out to her car.

Jane Ross Potter

The fewer people who knew about the apparently sabotaged walking stick that had belonged to Ronald Wilson up to the point of his fatal fall from a cliff, the better.

Chapter 22

"Can I have a peek at the groatie buckies?" Calum asked Margaret, while Alistair was outside with Helen.

Margaret grinned. "Sure!" They went to the kitchen; Margaret had placed the tins on the large country farm table. Motioning for Calum to sit down, she did also, and pulled one of the tins toward her. The lid had a bucolic rural Scottish scene, with a thatched roof cottage, birds, and a golden field, punctuated by bright red poppies, stretching to a blue sky behind the cottage.

"Not my cup of tea." Calum ran his hand over the lid to feel the raised design and the manufacturer's name.

"Me neither, but my mother would love this. Maybe I'll take the tins to her when I've emptied them of shells."

"Richard, was it, the name of the man who gave you all this?"

"Yes, he said he has no use for them in his current home in Spain, and his two children also have no interest. With his father gone now," Margaret rambled on, while carefully easing the tight lid off the tin, "he'll sell or rent out the house, so he needs to clear it out anyway."

"What happened to his father?"

Margaret stopped and looked at Calum. "Oh, I forgot you haven't heard any of this. Richard is Richard Wilson, and his father Ronald Wilson is the man who unfortunately died in Kilvellie recently, when he fell down the cliff onto the beach."

"How horrible! I hadn't heard that news. Is the death suspicious?"

Now Margaret realized she had to tread carefully. "The police, well, Helen, who you just met, is quietly looking into it."

"Why 'quietly'?" Calum made air quotes with his hands.

Margaret sighed. "Helen is dating Richard, and Richard's son Desmond, who is the grandson of the man who died, is the sergeant at Helen's police station. So it's a bit close to home."

"Did Helen know Richard before she moved to Kilvellie? I got the impression she just started that job a few weeks ago, and was in Edinburgh before that."

Margaret thought for a minute. "Not that I know. Richard was the senior police officer before her, and they met when he came back from Spain for a visit a couple of weeks ago. They were attracted to each other and now Richard hasn't gone back to Spain yet."

Calum wrinkled his brow, put his elbow on the table, and cupped his chin in his hand.

"You're right, it does all sound too close for comfort. Why doesn't she ask another police department to investigate the death?"

"As far as any public information is concerned, it was a tragic accident. The old man, he was in his nineties. He liked to sit on a bench near the cliff, and he probably stood up, stumbled, and went over. No one was near him at the time. His granddaughter was across the parking lot with her young child, chatting with friends."

"Could it have been suicide?"

"Honestly, I don't know, Calum." Margaret was afraid that she'd get caught up in the story and mention Ronald's possibly sabotaged cane. To distract Calum, she resumed her efforts to open the tin.

"Can you hold it steady while I work on the lid?" she asked.

Soon, with gentle lifts all around the edge, Margaret separated the lid from the tin, and she and Calum stared at the groatie buckies, the tiny shells almost overflowing at the edges of the tin.

Calum whistled. "Wow, I've only heard of people finding one or two at a time. This is amazing... must have taken *years* to collect."

"That's what I thought, but Richard told me he used to find hundreds in one afternoon. He has a secret location on a beach on one of the Hebridean Islands. He said he'll get some details of places to stay and get back to me. But now, I don't see any reason to go that far!"

"How many do you think are in there? I can't imagine anyone has done statistics on how many groatie buckies a biscuit tin can hold."

Margaret laughed. "That's my next task, to count these. Since Alistair's still with Helen, can you give me a hand?"

She took a sturdy brown paper grocery bag from their recycling supply, then opened it and placed it upright on the table. Calum got up from his chair, seeing what she had in mind.

"Do you want me to hold the bag open, or pour?" he asked.

"I can pour if you hold the bag, thanks."

Margaret carefully lifted the tin and tilted it gently over the opening of the bag. Groatie buckies rolled and tumbled into the bag, evoking the gentle sounds of a rain stick.

"My plan," she said to Calum as she poured slowly, "is to use a cup measure or something I can dip into the bag, and I'll count how many are in a cup. Then I can just count cupfuls and extrapolate, should be close enough..."

She stopped suddenly and held the tin level again, then she placed it on the table. With the top layer of groatie buckies gone, she and Calum could see a square brown box nestled tightly in the tin, surrounded by the remaining groatie buckies.

"That was a good idea," she said, lifting the box to free it from the tin. "He must have packed most of the shells in here, so they wouldn't all spill if the tin tipped over."

Working quickly, she peeled aging, brown adhesive tape from around the edges of the box and opened the lid, folding it back.

Calum stared into the box. "Hmm, not groatie buckies, then."

"No, it looks like a glass bowl." Margaret lifted the item out to look at it more carefully.

Just then Alistair returned and saw what she was doing.

"Margaret, don't tell me, you've found more glass? I thought we'd seen the end of glassware squirreled away. Where is this from?"

They all sat down at the table while Margaret examined the bowl, cupping it in her hands. It was colorless, with floral designs in gold, or gold foil, fused between two layers of clear glass. Hairline cracks near the edge showed evidence of damage and repair at some point.

"It doesn't look like any glass the Kilvellie factory made," Alistair commented. "I've seen their old catalogues, and the stash of glass we found in the coal chute. I still have to tell you that whole story, Margaret. Anyway, if I were to guess, I'd say this is a bit older than the twentieth century. What do you think, Calum?"

"This may give us an answer." Calum reached into the box to remove a fading cream label, with wording in precise calligraphy.

He read it to himself, then gasped. "Margaret, Margaret, put it down immediately! Careful, careful!"

Alarmed, she did as he requested, pulling her hands away quickly.

"What, is it radioactive?" she asked nervously, standing to rush off and scrub her hands.

"No. Look at this." Calum handed her the label, and she sat down again to read it along with Alistair, who moved his chair closer to see.

It Continued with the Cowries

Bowl, c. 300-200 B. C., 14 cm,
Made in Alexandria (?)
Property of the Edinburgh Museum of Antiquities
On long-term loan to the Regenbogen Glass Factory

"Holy mackerel!" Margaret cried. "Have I just been handling stolen property?"

"Don't jump to conclusions," Alistair said, patting her hand. "You weren't to know that it would be in a biscuit tin."

"A biscuit tin full of cowrie shells!" Calum added. "That makes me think, were the shells being used as packing material, to protect the box and the bowl?"

"Well, they did that, but they also concealed it." Margaret took her phone from her pocket. "I'd better call Richard and tell him what we found."

Alistair held up his hand to stop her. "Wait, Margaret, he can't have known about the bowl, or he wouldn't have just given you the tins, right? Which makes me think this could be connected to the old man, Richard's father. What if he acquired this during the war, when he had access to the factory and there was all the looting?"

"Alistair's right," Calum said. "I know nothing about this glass factory and looting, but finding a well-hidden antiquity, museum property at that, is something you need to report to the police."

"Yes, I'll call Helen instead..." Margaret began, then stopped. "This is a mess! She's dating Richard. What if he could be accused of hiding stolen museum property in his house? She'd be in a real bind."

"How about if we contact the Edinburgh museum tomorrow?" Alistair suggested. "Maybe it could be returned anonymously. People do that sometimes, to avoid prosecution."

"I suppose," Margaret said. "But won't they check it for

127

fingerprints? Mine are on it now. This is terrible!"

While Alistair and Margaret thought about what to do, Calum had been eyeing the remaining eleven tins.

"Could... could there be more?" he asked. "Not to get distracted by another of my stories, but when I was in London a few weeks ago, I learned that some of the crown jewels were hidden in biscuit tins during the Second World War. I'm sure they were all retrieved, but..."

"But we'd better check!" Margaret said. "If we decide to return the first bowl anonymously to the museum, we can't at the same time hand in eleven biscuit tins without checking to see what's inside. Anyway," she added, smiling, "I need the groatie buckies!"

Chapter 23

After a short break while Alistair heated up more chai on the stove, he, Margaret, and Calum sat at the kitchen table, enjoying the warm, spicy chai, and staring at the other biscuit tins.

"The rest of them could just contain shells," Alistair reminded them. "We may be getting worked up over nothing. And Calum, we're taking up your whole evening. You'd said you were just popping over to join us for dinner."

"I can't even remember what my plans were for later tonight. Probably writing my next sermon, but this is far more interesting. So, you two, what's your strategy?"

"It's Margaret's groatie buckie windfall," Alistair said, "but one priority is to preserve it as possible evidence, although evidence of what, I don't know at this point. I'd like to put clean gloves on, open the remaining tins, see if any contain a box, and then open it carefully. We would only handle the glass with gloves on, if there even is any more."

"Makes sense to me." Margaret finished her tea, eager to get started.

Half an hour later, the three sat back in their kitchen chairs, all feeling a bit stunned. The clear bowl with the gold design had been joined by eleven other pieces of glass of various shapes and sizes, including more bowls, a couple of small pitchers, and what might be a drinking cup that was similar in design to the first bowl they found.

Each box contained an identification label, and the age of the pieces ranged from twelve hundred B.C. to the nineteenth century. Margaret's favorite piece was about two thousand years old and Italian: a bowl made from the kind of glass rods used in *millefiori*, but for the bowl, the rods had been kept intact and arranged in parallel undulating, multi-colored designs. She was having a difficult time resisting touching it.

"What now?" Calum's question echoed everyone's thoughts.

"I'm tempted to secure them in bubble wrap," Margaret said, "but I expect that could damage fingerprints, if that's even possible after all this time. I'm assuming these have been stored like this for decades, judging from the condition of the tape holding the boxes closed."

"Let's go back to the living room. I have a story that might help," Alistair said, picking up three whisky glasses on his way. Margaret and Calum joined him and soon they were all seated around the coffee table, small glasses of single cask malt whisky in their hands. They spent a few moments admiring the sun setting over the water, and the evening calls of the gulls as they settled for the night, then Alistair began his story.

"I mentioned that Helen and Adam and I found a stash of vintage Regenbogen glass hidden in a tunnel in Kilvellie, during the Second World War. We realized that it would have been part of the glass factory's inventory, if it hadn't been hidden from the vandals in the nineteen forties and then forgotten about. We also discussed who it really belonged to, and Helen came to the conclusion that it should go to Malky Green, who inherited what remained of the glass factory equipment and stock after the factory closed over twenty years ago. He's the grandson of the factory's founder."

"Do you think that analysis applies to the glass we just found?" Calum asked.

"Maybe. The man who recently died, Ronald, was a guard at the factory in the war years. Not an effective guard, unfortunately, and there were suggestions of collusion with the vandals. But if we give the old fellow the benefit of the doubt, could he have taken these museum pieces and secured them at home, to prevent the vandals getting them?"

"I guess that's a possibility," Margaret agreed. "But if that's the case, why didn't he return them to the factory after the war ended, explain what he'd done and why he did it?"

Alistair sighed. "Who knows? From all I've heard, his mind was never the same after the war. He'd witnessed so much hatred from those six vandals, whether they were Scottish or German, maybe we'll never know, since it does seem they died back then."

Calum put a hand up. "Hold on there, what's this about six people dying at the factory, am I hearing you correctly?"

"Alistair," Margaret said softly, "don't get carried away. You're getting into some confidential information now."

Alistair turned to her. "Yes and no. It's public that six men died in the North Sea near Kilvellie in nineteen forty-four. From the plaque, I mean. It's not public, not yet anyway, that they could be the glass factory vandals, but all the information is pointing in that direction."

He turned to look at Calum. "It comes full circle to why we wanted to talk to you tonight. The little chapel on the north end of Kilvellie has, or had, a brass memorial plaque to six men lost at sea that year. There was a witness name engraved on it, but that name has been defaced. It's unreadable now. Oh, and the writing is in German, and as of yesterday evening, the plaque was removed for restoration. The same day I went back to see it a second time."

"Calum, that's the plaque I mentioned earlier," Margaret said. "Do you know anything about the chapel? Is there a minister we could ask about the plaque?"

"I will look into it and get back to you both. But first, I want to raise an issue that's been bugging me. Alistair, Margaret tells me you like to play devil's advocate, and I'm surprised you haven't brought this up."

Looking flustered, Alistair asked Calum to explain.

"You've mentioned a small group of people in the context of the factory guard, the elderly man who just died. The main person investigating is Officer Helen Griffen. She's having to tread on eggshells because she's romantically involved with the old man's son, and the old man's grandson works in the police station, if I have all that correct?"

Alistair nodded his head. "So far, exactly right."

"Okay, Helen is in a sticky ethical situation. I'm frankly amazed she has anything to do with investigating the death, but I'm just a village cleric. What do I know?" He took a sip of whisky, then put the glass down and leaned forward, elbows on his knees. "Have you considered that Richard, the dead man's son, might have involved himself with Helen for this very reason, to make her less likely to suspect Richard and his children of having anything to do with the death?"

"So, Calum, you're saying this could all be premeditated, I mean, his friendship with Helen, is that it?" Margaret asked, a surprised look on her face.

"Exactly, Margaret." Calum leaned back in his chair and focused on his whisky.

"What a mess!" Margaret said, remembering Richard's reaction when she tried to access the garage at his house. She decided to keep that quiet, not paint Richard in even worse light, not yet anyway.

"You've got that right, Tuppence," Alistair agreed. Hearing the name, Calum looked up sharply.

"What did you just call Margaret?"

"Tuppence. And I'm Tommy. Helen told us we were acting like Agatha Christie's fictional detective married couple, so we're just playing along."

Calum finished his whisky, slapped his hands on his knees, and stood up. "Good luck with your detecting! I'll keep all this to myself, but I will see what I can ferret out about the chapel in Kilvellie. Expect a call if I learn anything useful."

Alistair and Margaret watched from the kitchen door as

It Continued with the Cowries

Calum, after declining a ride, headed back to town along the cleared old railway path, his flashlight beam sending ripples of light from one side of cutaway shrubbery to the other. Margaret felt a twinge of nostalgia, remembering that when she first moved to the cottage, the only access was by walking along the beach, or arriving from the nearby village by boat. She'd grown used to the loud putt-putting of Calum's outboard motor, so it was strange to see him return to town at a walking pace, and so quietly. *At least he's getting some exercise*, she thought to herself.

In the kitchen, Margaret and Alistair donned gloves again and replaced the glass pieces in their original boxes, then laid the boxes in a row on the table, far from the edge. An hour later Alistair was asleep, but Margaret's mind was in turmoil: she'd trusted Richard, had spent time alone with him in his empty house. Could Calum be right, thinking that Richard was only dating Helen to keep her suspicions at bay?

As Margaret fell asleep, she was thinking about her short episode of suspecting that Alistair had proposed to her because he saw her as a source of financial support, and a Scottish beachfront roof over his head. She'd soon realized that she'd misjudged him, but it had felt like a real possibility, during those horrible long hours.

She hoped that Helen was being objective about Richard, and not being lulled by dreamy notions of spending her retirement with him at his home in sunny Spain. Richard's father Ronald was dead, and someone had sawed halfway through Ronald's walking stick. If the immediate family were not suspect, who did that leave, she wondered: Christy and William?

Chapter 24

After saying goodnight to Alistair and checking that the still-bagged broken cane was secure in the back of her car, Helen drove slowly along the uneven dirt road, the former railway track, until she reached the paved road of Finlay Village. She thought back to when she'd first met Alistair, was it just a couple of weeks earlier? She remembered that he'd described Margaret's cottage, with its beach access, and how he'd helped to get the railway right-of-way cleared for vehicle access to the cottage.

Helen was glad that had happened before her visit; she would not have enjoyed an urgent tromp along two miles of beach, only to get stranded at the cottage by the tide or by nightfall. The road through Finlay was narrow, and Helen glanced back and forth at the shops on either side. Some looked new, with "Opening Soon" signs in the windows. On her right, the white paint of a floodlit church gleamed: Calum's church, she figured.

At the end of the row of shops she came to the hotel where she'd stopped briefly for directions to Margaret's cottage: "Grand Reopening!" was blazoned on a banner hung above the entrance to the parking lot. Beyond the ten or so cars, Helen could see people sitting at picnic tables under umbrellas, and a sign for the restaurant. Must be the source of the Indian food she'd enjoyed at the cottage, she realized, and definitely a place to bring Richard.

She continued on until she saw a sign for the road heading north, and once she was zooming along the wider road, she relaxed and thought about the evening. As it turned out, she hadn't learned anything about the Kilvellie chapel from Calum after all, but his description of the town's name origin had been fun to hear, and something for her to tuck away when she needed an anecdote for a visitor.

Now it was time to be serious. She'd let her guard down and violated her professional standards by sending Margaret and Alistair home with the single piece of evidence that Ronald's fall might not have been an accident. At the time, with the broken cane sitting on her sergeant's desk—worse, Richard's son's desk—her only thought was to make sure neither Richard nor his son saw it until she'd had a chance to study it. Chain of custody worries had arisen in her mind as soon as Alistair drove off, heading back to Finlay.

On Helen's drive south to retrieve the stick, she'd concocted an explanation of why the stick ever left police custody, if someone asked. It involved a slight lie, but only she would know; well, Alastair and Margaret would know also. It meant shifting the time of discovery back by a couple of hours. Helen rehearsed the story in her mind, and she would ask, or tell, Alistair and Margaret to join in the variation from the truth. She would have told them tonight, if Calum hadn't also been there.

Instead of Margaret noticing the sawed area on the cane at the police station, she would have noticed it when she took the cane home. Helen was sure she could come up with a reason for that: maybe Margaret was going to use the wood in a craft project. And with the old man's death believed to be accidental at that point, why would his broken cane be of interest to the police?

Glad that she could probably get away with that mistake, Helen turned to the reason for it in the first place: her professional life had collided with her private life. Maybe she should kick the evidence up the chain of command tonight and hand the nascent investigation and the broken cane over to someone else? But if she went along with her own story

135

about the cane, she only took re-possession of it that evening, so she could wait until tomorrow.

That settled, she let her mind drift to the broader question: who had a motive to speed up Ronald's demise? She could probably rule out inheritance. Richard was comfortably off, as he owned a home in Spain, at least, that's what he'd told her, she reminded herself. By all accounts he owned the former family home in Kilvellie, now unoccupied, as well as land where the glass museum and holiday cottages would be constructed. Helen couldn't envision a scenario in which Richard benefited financially from Ronald's recent death.

Richard's two children, Emily and Desmond, also seemed to be living comfortably. Emily was married and had a young child, and from what people had told Helen, Emily and her family lived in a large, newly decorated home, and Emily could afford to dress like she was working in a fancy office, even though she worked from home.

Desmond was the only one who could probably use a bit of money, but he had his police sergeant's salary, hope of advancement, and a free place to live for the next few months, thanks to Helen swapping places so that she could live in the police station residence. Desmond was now in Helen's former short-term apartment, and since she'd paid six months' rent in advance, she was letting Desmond stay rent-free.

No, the family looked clear in terms of motive, at least from a financial point of view. Not that the old man had much to leave behind, Helen remembered. His stay at the pricy care home had been financed with the money Emily raised selling vintage Regenbogen glassware that Ronald had somehow obtained during his guard years at the factory. This part was too murky as far as Helen was concerned: had he stolen the glassware and hidden it for decades? Had he been paid in glassware by the factory management, who would likely have been cash-poor during the war years?

It seemed that Emily hadn't asked her grandfather how

he got the glassware. She was happy enough to photograph it, list it on eBay, and funnel the money to him. Did she keep a portion of the money? There were conflicting stories about that. Anyway, if Emily was still selling the last of Ronald's glassware, and benefiting financially, surely that gave her less incentive to wish him harm. His death meant that his possessions would be catalogued and tallied up as part of the estate.

Helen remembered something else about Ronald's stay at the care home. When he first moved in, he'd paid for three years in advance. The care home management had been able to use that advance payment toward getting started early on a planned expansion. And in thanks for the up-front payment, they'd let Ronald stay on for a fourth year without paying the monthly fee.

She thought she might be on to something. Up until his fall, Ronald had been in good health for a man of his age. Was the care home management getting fed up with him living there for free? Presumably they could now rent his room out to a new resident, one who would pay. Could it be that simple, Helen wondered—a case of "follow the money?"

At least she had a tentative plan of attack for the following morning: visit the manager at the care home, express condolences, and perhaps chat to some residents. Emily and Desmond would likely be there clearing out Ronald's room, but Helen had every reason to visit, following up on his death.

The first sign for Kilvellie-by-the-Sea came into view, five miles south of the town. Helen chuckled, thinking she might restore the signs to their former version, Kilvellie-by-the-C. At least it could make for some light-hearted news about the town, following the recent story of a death on the beach, and the vehement but short-lived social media-fueled outrage about the lack of cliff-edge barriers. She shook her head: most of the people repeating and magnifying the outrage had probably never even been to Kilvellie.

Closer to Kilvellie, she called Richard. "Listen, I have a lot to do tonight, so I'll check in with you tomorrow, okay?"

To her relief, he said he was out with some old pals, reminiscing about his father, and he completely understood. "Enjoy the Jacuzzi, lass," were his parting words.

A day at a time, she decided, as she parked her car at the police station and took the broken cane in, to reunite it with the old man's bagged clothes. No need to risk damaging the relationship just yet.

Minutes later, with the station locked up, she was running the water to fill the Jacuzzi tub. But before she could fully relax from the day, she called the last person she could rely on who she hadn't yet caused to jeopardize a potential murder investigation.

"Adam," she said when her private investigator son in Inverness answered the phone. "I need your help... again!"

Chapter 25

Margaret and Alistair were finishing breakfast in their cottage in Finlay the next morning. They looked forward to getting back into their routine of housework, emails, and beach walks. But before they could discuss their plans for the day, Alistair's phone buzzed with a new text, from Adam. It was brief: "Pls call me ASAP, ta."

Alistair went to the kitchen, and while he waited for water to boil for his coffee, he called Adam back.

"What's up, Adam? Is your mom okay?"

"Yes, she is, but it sounds like she's in a real bind with the aftermath of Ronald's death. I'm going down to Kilvellie to help her out. She also wants me to explain something to you, on her behalf. Any chance you could drive up and meet me there? I know you just got back yesterday."

Alistair felt deflated. Why wouldn't that town let him go? But he couldn't let Adam down; over the past few months, they had developed a strong history of looking out for each other. "Of course," Alistair assured him, trying to keep the reluctance from his voice. "Where and when do you want to meet? It will take me about fifty minutes to get there, maybe more depending on traffic."

"How about the cafe across from where the glass museum is going in? It's easy to pull off the road and park there. I'll leave in about an hour, so let's aim for noon."

Hoping the answer would be "no," Alistair asked, "Should I plan on staying overnight in Kilvellie? Margaret and I stayed at your fancy hotel the night before last. I can see why you

139

like it so much."

Adam laughed. "I don't think you'll need to spend the night. I just want to talk some logistics face to face, and you can explain what's been happening so far. Mum's interested in the mystery of the memorial plaque disappearing from the chapel wall and she wants me to help with that. Seems like you and Margaret are the only people who've studied it up close. Recently anyway."

With plans set, they ended the call. Alistair fixed his mug of coffee and carried it back to the dining table, where Margaret was busy on her laptop.

"Work?" he asked. Although Margaret's work schedule was light following the major win for her law firm in Portland, she kept up to date with news from the firm and how her clients were getting on.

She looked up. "No, I'm checking on the museum that loaned the glass pieces to the Regenbogen Glass Factory. If it was no longer in existence, that would add to the dilemma, but it must be doing well enough that they've added a gift shop and a cafe."

"Good reasons to visit." Alistair stood and looked at the website with her, then sat down to drink his coffee.

"The website has the name and contact information for the director," Margaret said. "All seems to be up to date. What do you think? Should we drive over to Edinburgh and hand in the glass anonymously?"

"What, wear disguises and place a mysterious package on the information desk? They'd probably get the police to detonate it somewhere, in case it's a bomb. Think again, Tuppence!"

Margaret laughed and got into the spirit. "So my new approach to life is, what would Tuppence do? I guess it's a change from my old habit of wondering what Samuel Johnson would do."

She refilled her tea from the teapot and held the warm mug in both hands while she considered their latest challenge. "Do you think we need to involve Helen?" she asked.

"It's so messy, with her and Richard in a relationship, and he's the one who gave you the biscuit tins. But with a possible murder looming over everything, I think we have to tell her. I can't imagine that Ronald was killed over some old museum glass, but who knows at this point."

He stood up again. "Anyway, I can talk it over with Adam. That was him on the phone. I'm sorry to say, but he wants to meet me in Kilvellie at noon. Something we have to discuss in person."

"Should I come along?" Margaret asked. She realized she didn't really mind: it would be another chance to look for groatie buckies on Kilvellie beach, and maybe even find a sea glass marble.

"It's up to you, Margaret. I'd enjoy your company of course. I don't plan on staying overnight, but we should go prepared just in case."

Margaret closed her laptop and went to the bedroom to pack a new set of overnight clothes and supplies, including her beach sandals. She considered what to wear for the drive up, and decided on casual beachwear: jeans and a cotton sweater, with running shoes. If the visit involved any more meetings with solicitors or the police, they'd just have to deal with her seaside attire.

Alistair cleared up from breakfast, then got ready as well and packed his overnight bag. By ten thirty, they were in the car and heading north again.

"I've been imagining how Tuppence would approach your case," Margaret said as they drove through Fife, heading for the Tay Bridge.

Alistair glanced at her. "Remember, Tuppence didn't have the benefit of computers, Google searches, eBay sales records, and cell phones, so you need to imagine doing without all those resources."

She groaned. "Oh, if you insist. But one approach is the same. Who stands to gain financially by Ronald dying sooner rather than later? I'm phrasing it that way for a reason. If someone did damage Ronald's walking cane to speed up his demise, they must have been willing to wait until he had an accident. In fact, maybe he didn't even need to die. Maybe it was enough for their purposes if he broke his hip, or back, and was hospitalized."

"Yes, follow the money. All goods points, my dear. It's reminding me what Helen told me and Adam, about Ronald's stay at the care home. For the past year, he's been living there without paying any fees, because he paid upfront for three years when he moved in. But that was four years ago. If he doesn't have the money to pay for a fifth year there, maybe someone at the home decided to nudge his exit forward to free up the room?"

"That's horrible, Tommy, but it makes as much sense as anything. From what I've heard so far, I can't come up with any reason his immediate family would want him dead. His family basically gets on with their own lives, without expecting to inherit much, right? And from what you said, his granddaughter does a lot for him. Well, did a lot for him."

She hesitated, then decided to share what had happened at Richard's house. "Listen, Alistair, I know we're trying to rule out his immediate family, but something is making me wonder about Richard. When I went to his house to get the groatie buckies yesterday morning, he didn't want me looking in the garage. In fact, he was adamant about it. Practically blocked me from opening the door into the garage. It's accessed through the kitchen."

Alistair glanced over again and looked at Margaret. "On its own, I don't think that's suspicious. Goodness knows what all he's got in there, maybe even..." He stopped to let her complete the picture, from their experience at the Finlay cottage.

"Oh, no!" Margaret felt a chill as she pictured the dozens of boxes in a well-hidden cellar below her uncle's cottage. Alistair's suspicions had all been for naught, but he had taken on the task of checking the boxes for, as a young man in Finlay sheepishly called them, "girly magazines."

With that thought in mind, Margaret decided not to mention the garage to Helen; she'd leave that up to Alistair. Anyway, if an official investigation was launched, someone would find out soon enough what was behind the padlocked garage door. With daughter Emily a frequent visitor to the empty house, perhaps Richard had secured the garage to prevent her from going in.

They were quiet as they drove across the Tay Bridge. Margaret remembered crossing the bridge with her cousin Jeannie, months earlier, and learning about the Tay Bridge disaster in the nineteenth century. The rail bridge had collapsed with a train on it, full of passengers, and there were many deaths. Margaret was glad when whatever mode of transport she used, be it car or train, brought her safely to the other side of the water.

The road now headed northeast and they would soon reach Kilvellie. "Let's talk about the care home scenario a bit more," Alistair suggested. "Even if someone in management there decided to damage Ronald's cane enough that he would fall, and it would look like an accident, how could the police prove it? Presumably, if the culprit used a saw or some kind of serrated blade, they'd be astute enough to dispose of it, or at least take it from the premises."

"And anyone could bring a tool with them to work, so it probably wouldn't help to search for tools at the care home, looking to match a blade with the markings on the cane and do forensics on everything."

"Maybe we should go to the care home and see if we can chat with some of the residents. Who knows, someone may have seen something that they didn't think to question at the time. After all, we and Helen are the only ones who know about the cane."

"And the person who sawed it," Margaret noted.

"Right. So, imagine, what if a resident happened to notice

a nurse, or one of the managers, carrying Ronald's cane in the days leading up to his death. It normally wouldn't seem suspicious, but it could be, given the timing of his death. Even better, carrying a cane to or from Ronald's room. That would be a start."

Margaret thought for a few moments. "Maybe Adam will have some instructions from Helen. Do you want me to be there for your meeting with him?"

"You can say hello, then stay if that's his preference. At this point, I don't know why he couldn't tell me over the phone."

Soon the signs for Kilvellie came into view, and after driving straight through the town, Alistair made a right into the parking area where Adam had suggested they meet. A tall, skinny red-haired man in a black fleece jacket and jeans rose from a nearby bench and strode across the gravel to where Alistair had stopped the car. Margaret hadn't seen Adam since they returned together from Orkney a few weeks earlier, and she was looking forward to catching up.

After greeting Adam, Margaret offered to get drinks for her and Alistair, giving Adam a chance to explain to Alistair why he'd been summoned back to Kilvellie. While she walked toward the cafe entrance, Adam and Alistair sat on the bench.

"Before Margaret gets back," Alistair said quickly, "do you need to talk to me alone, or can she stay? Either way is fine with her. She's just as happy to go beachcombing and shopping."

"I'd like her to stay for a few minutes at least. Mum asked me to convey a message to both of you. After that, it's up to you and her. I mainly want to brainstorm and help Mum out of this mess, and Margaret will probably have ideas from the legal side. But she may not want to get embroiled in it."

Alistair sighed. "I'm afraid she's in it up to her neck. I'll wait until she gets back so we can explain. But bottom line, she's been in a house that really should have been sealed off for searching and maybe fingerprints, and she's in possession of something from the house that could connect back to the war and Ronald's guard work at the glass factory."

Adam exhaled and shook his head. He took a long drink from his coffee flask. "Does Mum know all this?"

"She knows that Margaret was going to the house. It's got to do with collecting groatie buckies."

"Wait, wait," Adam cried, laughing. "Time out. How do cowrie shells relate to Ronald's death?"

"Margaret can explain better. Here she comes."

Adam shook his head again. "I can already predict Mum's reaction to what you just told me." He began to speak and Alistair joined in: "What fresh hell is this?"

Chapter 26

Margaret was laughing too as she handed Alistair a large take-out cup; she sat next to him on the bench and took a sip from her cup. "What are you two doing, channeling Dorothy Parker? I'm still getting used to being Tuppence."

"Wait, you don't mean Tommy and Tuppence, do you? I feel like I'm trapped in some complex BBC production here," Adam complained. "What's with the groatie buckies? And who's Dorothy Parker?"

Alistair explained that Helen had dubbed Margaret "Tuppence" after the fictional wife/detective dreamed up by Agatha Christie. Then he told Margaret that the "fresh hell" line had been uttered by Helen recently, when she, Adam, and Alistair went off at midnight in search of a possible body buried at the abandoned holiday home site across the road from where they were now sitting.

Margaret took over when Alistair finished speaking. "I need groatie buckies for a shell-collecting competition. It has to do with the prince and his fiancée in Orkney, but I can tell you later. Dorothy Parker was a writer in New York City, and that 'fresh hell' quote is attributed to her."

"Okay," Adam said, "now that we've got all that sorted out, let's start by discussing the broken walking stick, or cane, that was bagged up along with Ronald's clothing after he died. Mum, needless to say, feels, well, she *knows* she made a mistake asking you two to take the stick with you yesterday. I can understand her wanting to keep Ronald's son Richard, and the sergeant, Desmond, from looking at it and noticing it was partly cut through, I mean, before she had a chance to consider the implications. But she could have locked it in her residence or something. All his clothes and the stick should have been secured from the start."

"I know, Adam," Alistair agreed. "Lots would have been done differently, and much as I admire your mother, I do think her friendship, or her relationship, with Richard has, I don't know, it's..."

Adam broke in, raising his voice. "Let's be honest here. It's screwed up a murder investigation! I know she's my mum, but she hasn't been thinking straight. Ronald's death should have been treated as suspicious from the start, then work backwards and conclude it was an accident. Instead, Mum and the coroner have treated it as an accident, based on his age and being unsteady on his feet and all, but now they've lost a few days of investigation time. And the prime piece of evidence, the partly-sawed cane, is suspect because chain of custody is messed up."

"I feel terrible about that," Margaret mumbled, and Alistair said he did too.

"Mum wanted to call you last night and say she's got, and forgive me, her words, a 'cunning plan,' thank you Blackadder. Then she realized something: if another station takes over from her and investigates the death from the start, they may learn that you two had the broken walking stick even just for a few hours. If that's bookended by multiple calls between your phones and Mum's, it looks even worse for her."

"But we can't undo what we did," Alistair argued. "Our fingerprints will be on the bag, at a minimum."

"Wait, I haven't told you her cunning plan. If things go south and other officers ask about chain of custody of the cane, the plan is that you and Mum delay the discovery of the damage by a few hours. Under that scenario, Margaret still sees the broken stick in the police station, and because at that point the death is deemed an accident, Helen gives

Margaret the stick, oh, I don't know, maybe to use in a craft project. But when you get home to Finlay, you look at it more carefully, see that it's been sawed, and Helen comes to pick it up. That would correlate in time with her call to you last night. Am I right in thinking you never took the cane out of the bag?"

"Yes," Margaret replied, "so any fingerprints on it should be intact."

"I guess I can live with that explanation," Alistair conceded. "It will be consistent with the cane's actual movements, and I think Tuppence here can be convincing about wanting the broken stick for the wood. You should see some of the stuff she brings home from beachcombing."

"Tommy!" Margaret hit Alistair's arm playfully. "I've told you before, I pick up trash when I'm out on the beach. I'm not *collecting* it."

With the main reason for Adam's conversation with Alistair and Margaret out of the way, they sat quietly for a few moments and looked out toward the cliff.

Alistair broke the silence with a long sigh. "I can't believe it was just a couple of weeks ago when I sat out there and chatted to Ronald." He pointed to the stretch of police tape that still cordoned off the cliffside benches and surrounding grassy area. "Poor old guy. I can only hope he had a stroke or a heart attack and wasn't aware of going over the cliff."

"Sadly, I think we'll never know," said Adam. "At the time, there was no evident reason to do an autopsy, and now it probably would be too late to distinguish, physiologically anyway, a stroke that occurred on the clifftop, and damage to his brain and arteries that happened when he landed on the beach."

Margaret shivered. "If you guys are going to talk about this kind of detail, I'd rather not be here. It's too depressing."

"Sorry, Margaret. Just picking up on what Alistair was saying. Please stay, and let's go over what we know so far."

Adam took a pad of paper from his backpack to take

notes, and Alistair took out his pocket notebook.

Adam began, "Mum can't think of any motive the immediate family has for Ronald's death. I know she's too close to some of the family to be making that kind of judgment, but I agree with her. Even after reading Ronald's war diaries from his time as a factory guard, that didn't really impact his own family, right? I mean, apart from the poor guy being mentally trapped in the war years, not engaging with his own grandchildren when they were young."

Alistair nodded his head. "I agree, and even if his son Richard and his two grandchildren resented how he impacted their family life, that was long ago. Why would they take revenge, if that's what this is, when the old guy probably just had a few years, or maybe months, left?"

Adam jotted some notes. "Okay, for now, we'll put the immediate family aside. Next, we have Malky's family to consider."

"Remind me, who's Malky?" Margaret asked. She was tempted to tell Adam about Richard's locked garage, but since Alistair hadn't mentioned it, she would follow his lead.

"I'll explain the family history later," Alistair assured her, "but briefly, he's the grandson of the factory founder, Henry. Malky's potential inheritance was diminished by the loss of stock during the war years, and the years the factory was closed to repair all the damage. I expect he has a simmering resentment of how it affected his own family, but again, they've had the windfall of all the valuable glass that was hidden from the vandals and only found, by us I might add, last week."

"Wait," Margaret said, "I met his children a couple of days ago. The glass artists, William and Christy, I think?"

"That's them," Adam confirmed. "But they seem to be successful businesspeople at this stage. Why would resentment of the old man suddenly manifest itself now?"

"Has anyone talked to William and Christy yet? I mean, in the context of investigating Ronald's death?" Margaret leaned forward and looked back and forth at Alistair and Adam.

"Mum hasn't mentioned them as possible suspects." Adam wrote their names on the pad of paper. "I guess they can't be ruled out."

"Someone should talk to them," Margaret continued, leaning back on the bench. "Christy seems to have a lot of anger just under the surface. She got very upset when I was talking to her and William. I mean, upset to the point of raging about their childhood in poverty, and their sister going missing. It sounds like she's barely keeping it together. At one point she starting crying and ran next door to her own studio. I didn't see her after that."

"When was this?" Alistair asked. "You didn't mention it to me before."

"It was the day we first arrived in Kilvellie, and William gave me the blue marble. Remember, you were meeting with Helen at the solicitor's office and I was looking around the town. I didn't set out to talk to them about anything sensitive, but they invited me to have tea and show me some sea glass, then I guess the conversation naturally went to how there's so much unique sea glass here, and the wartime damage to the factory. Christy seems to blame it on Ronald. But that's old history, right? Why would she, or they, want to hurt him now?"

"This is something to be explored." Adam tapped his pen on the pad. "I'm wondering if we should meet with Mum and continue the conversation in her presence."

"Hold on," Alistair said. "I can think of one thing that could explain the timing. Justine's reappearance."

"You mean, Christy and William's missing sister?" Margaret asked.

"Yes. Her disappearance involved both Richard and Desmond. Richard was tied up in it because he was the senior officer at the time, seven or so years ago. We're back to a conflict for Adam's mother. My suggestion is, let's keep hashing this out ourselves and try to identify some leads, then go to her. At that point, I think she'll have no choice but to step aside and have a new team come in for a thorough investigation."

"I agree," Adam said. "But first, I need some food. Shall we get something from the cafe here and move to a picnic table and just keep going?"

With agreement from Alistair and Margaret, the threesome picked up their belongings and headed to the cafe. Margaret felt a little ill at ease having lunch so close to the scene of poor Ronald's fall, but perhaps, for Alistair and Adam, it was a way to keep focused on learning and exposing the truth behind his death.

Chapter 27

Alistair, Margaret, and Adam chose a picnic table halfway between the clifftop cafe and the cliff edge, on the outskirts of Kilvellie-by-the-Sea. As a break from talking about the old man, Ronald Wilson, who'd fallen to his death from the cliff just days before, Margaret was telling Adam about her plans to visit remote Scottish beaches and collect groatie buckies. Their conversation was interrupted by a woman's voice: "Adam! I *thought* that was your car!"

Helen came marching up to the table. "I was heading to the chapel and saw your car in the parking lot. Mind if I get a sandwich and join you? And hello, Tommy and Tuppence. Glad to see you're on the job."

Without waiting for an answer, she headed to the cafe.

"She's not in her uniform," Alistair commented, as he watched Helen's retreating back: she wore black trousers, with a deep purple tunic and a matching purple scarf that fluttered behind her in the breeze.

"She's in *tourist* mode," Adam explained, shaking his head. "Makes sense if she's going to poke around the chapel. Wouldn't want to make it look official."

"I thought she was trying to put some distance between her role in investigating Ronald's death, and contact with me and Margaret?"

"Just phone records, texts, that kind of thing. No one will notice her sitting here having lunch, not out of uniform anyway. She'll just blend in."

"I know what you mean," Margaret said. "I guess it can

152

have its advantages in a murder inquiry."

Helen soon returned, carrying a tray with a cheese and tomato panini, a large cup of tea, and small bags of assorted potato chips which she put in the middle of the table. "Brain food. Help yourselves, so I won't feel guilty eating a bag myself."

Before starting, she quietly asked Adam, "Did you deliver my message about the cane?"

"Aye," Adam confirmed. "Message received by Tommy and Tuppence."

They all laughed, then Helen lifted her sandwich. "While we eat, Margaret, I'd love to hear more about your groatie buckie quest. Have you started counting the ones in Richard's biscuit tins? I'm curious about how many a tin will hold."

Margaret looked to Alistair for a cue; he raised his eyebrows and shrugged his shoulders.

"We have to tell her, Margaret. Now's as good a time as any."

Helen stopped mid-bite. "Tell me what? The tins had something awful in them, is that it? Moldy cake?"

"No, Helen," Margaret said, "just the opposite. We don't know what to do about it. Each tin held a surprise. There were groatie buckies, but there were also boxes with glassware. And not glassware made by Regenbogen. Much older pieces, on loan from the Museum of Antiquities in Edinburgh, to the Regenbogen Glass Factory. I have a feeling the boxes have been in storage for a long time, judging from the old and flaking tape keeping them shut."

"Not glass again," Helen moaned. "How do you know all this about them?"

"Each box has what looks like a display label identifying the piece, with geographic origin and the age. Some are over two thousand years old. Well, according to the labels."

"Do you think they could be fakes?" Adam asked.

"I've no reason to suspect it," said Margaret. "What, do

you think the glass factory people faked a display of museum pieces to impress customers? Seems to me that the glass they made was impressive enough on its own."

The group ate in silence for a few minutes; Margaret could tell that Helen was thinking through the implications of her discovery. And how Richard might be involved. It was all Margaret could do to keep from mentioning the garage, but Alistair continued to stay quiet about it.

"Margaret, does Richard know about the glass?" Helen asked. "I mean, did you and he open any tins at his house yesterday morning?"

"Just to check for groatie buckies. At home, I opened one completely to show Calum, and he was helping me transfer the shells into a bag when the box was revealed."

Helen stopped eating again. She was making little progress with her lunch at this rate.

"*Calum* knows about the glass too?"

"Sorry, yes, he does. I'd assumed the box in the first tin would just have more groatie buckies. But once we found that piece of glass, I was curious to see if any other tins had glass. They did, twelve pieces in total. We handled the boxes with gloves after the first one."

"And all from that museum in Edinburgh?"

"According to the labels, yes. We checked the museum website. It looks like it's still open, so, I don't know, do you think we should return the pieces? Maybe anonymously?"

Helen shook her head and replaced her half-eaten panini on the paper plate. "I'm losing my appetite. Too many questions. How did the glass end up in Richard's possession? Was it stolen from the factory during the war? In fact, I remember in all my conversations with the Greens, I mean Malky and his two older children, none of them mentioned items on loan from a museum. Malky's daughter Christy seems to be the glass factory historian, so if there's any written record, she should have come across it by now."

Helen thought for a moment. "I had a few dealings with

the museum when I worked in Edinburgh. All very pleasant, discussions of security measures, that kind of thing. How about if I call and verify that they did loan pieces of glass to the factory here, probably decades ago? And maybe there's more of it at Richard's house. I'll ask my contact if he knows the full extent of the loan. At least then we'll know if the pieces should go back to the museum. I won't reveal that we have the pieces, or that they might get caught up in a murder investigation."

"How could they?" Adam asked. "It sounds like Richard didn't know they were there, or he wouldn't have given Margaret the biscuit tins, would he? And as far as I've heard from Desmond, his sister Emily has been all through the old family house, looking in every room and every box for glass to sell on eBay, for her grandfather."

Helen laughed. "I guess she didn't think to look in the biscuits tins. Something to note for the future!"

"Well," Margaret said, "in her defense, if you can call it that, if she'd lifted up any of the biscuit tin lids, she would have seen that the tins were packed to the rim with groatie buckies. You'd have to be either very determined or very imaginative to suspect the groatie buckies themselves were hiding something."

Alistair held Margaret's hand for a minute. "That's my Tuppence! It's her determination that led her to find the Pictish silver in her kitchen, and the gold coins buried under a shop way up in Orkney."

"And now possibly stolen glass," Helen added. "It complicates the investigation, Margaret, and I'm realizing, your fingerprints will be in the house where Ronald lived before he went to the care home, so I truly hope it doesn't get included as a potential crime scene."

Adam looked at Helen with an expression of relief. "Mum, are you ready to turn the investigation over to another station?"

"Oh, Adam, I know I should, but I hate to see Richard, his

son and daughter, maybe his daughter's husband, who has a prominent position in the military, coming under suspicion of killing the old man. An outside team will cause so much disruption to the peaceful life of the town."

"And," Margaret ventured, "they'd have to question William and Christy Green, right? Now that I've told Adam how Christy reacted when we spoke at the glass studio, and the resentment she has against Ronald, you have to share that with a new team, I would think. Sorry, I don't have experience in criminal law, but I did study evidence in law school."

Adam crossed his arms on the table and leaned forward to try and persuade Helen.

"Mum, Margaret's right. And she's a lawyer! The longer you wait to get a proper team in, the longer people have to come up with alibis and make sure their stories match up. If more than one person was involved, that is."

Helen finished her tea, then addressed the group. "Yes, son, I hear you loud and clear. Problem is, I truly don't think Ronald's family is involved, and I'm not saying that because I'm seeing Richard socially. I also can't imagine Christy, the sea glass jeweler, sawing through Ronald's cane. She has so much to lose if she's arrested. And when and how would she get access? The old man used to go back and forth between the care home and the cliffside bench, with just the short visits to his solicitor's office. How on earth could Christy or William get hold of the cane long enough damage it?"

Everyone sat in silence, then Adam spoke up again. "What do *you* think happened, Mum?"

Helen looked pleased that her son was encouraging her input, instead of questioning her judgment.

"I think we need to look closer to home, and by that I mean closer to the *care* home. Remember, Ronald's been living there for a year, maybe more, without paying any fees. What if the management decided he'd overstayed? They couldn't exactly tell him to move out, not in a town where his son is an ex-senior police officer, and his daughter works and cares for a young child, with a husband in the military. It would not look good if the home expects to get future residents from this town."

"So they used a short-cut to ease him out?" Margaret suggested. "I guess if he fell and was badly injured, they could shuttle him off to hospital, get the NHS to pay for his care, and free up his room that way."

"That's where my suspicions are," Helen confirmed. "They had access and opportunity, to sabotage his cane I mean, and they have financial motive." She glanced at her watch. "Och, I really need to go. I closed the office for a lunch break so I could visit the chapel, but I can't leave it closed any longer. You three, put your heads together and come up with a plan to investigate my suspicions about the care home..."

Adam interrupted. "But *Mum*! You can't put it off any longer, getting a proper investigation started! You know that the first few days after a death are crucial. I can't believe you're having to hear this from me."

Helen stood and looked down at Adam. "I know, son. Give me one more day. If we haven't solved this by nine o'clock tomorrow morning, I promise, I will step aside and turn everything over to fresh eyes. And on my list for today, I'll call that museum in Edinburgh and ask if they loaned glassware to the factory. Easy yes or no question, I would think, then we can take it from there."

After Helen left, Alistair could tell that Adam was irate over her obstinacy.

"Listen, Adam," he said, "your mother may have some confidential information that she isn't sharing with us, not yet anyway. Can't you trust her for one more day, to do the right thing? I, and I'm sure Margaret as well, will help all we can, even if it means suffering one more night in the darned fancy hotel."

That got Adam laughing, and he pointed to the cafe.

"Okay, the next round of tea and coffee is on me, and when I get back, you two, Tommy and Tuppence, had better have a game plan in place for today."

"Bring back some treats!" Alistair called to Adam's back; Adam didn't turn, but raised his hand with a thumbs up gesture.

Chapter 28

Leaving Adam with his pals Margaret and Alistair, Helen returned to her car in a determined mood. She had forgotten to bring the rest of her panini with her and was still hungry, so she looked forward to getting back to the station, changing into her uniform again, and rummaging in the kitchen for some biscuits. On the plus side, she now had a deadline to work toward: nine o'clock the following morning.

After learning about Margaret's discovery of museum property among the groatie buckies, she knew she had to distance herself from Richard, for the moment anyway. His late father, the glass factory guard, was at the top of her list for having hidden the museum glass pieces. If Richard had known, surely he wouldn't have handed the biscuit tins to Margaret. But nothing was clear at this point.

The museum glassware was distracting her from other lines of investigation she had to follow, and perhaps she could deal with it with a phone call or two. She checked the Antiquities Museum website to get the telephone number. Judging from the images, the building had changed a lot since her last visit, several years back. She pictured the enjoyable meetings with the then-director, as they sat at a table in the apothecary garden courtyard around which the museum was built.

She could still smell the sun-warmed herbs: the rosemary, mint, thyme, and oregano, and the lovely teas that the museum created from antiquarian book recipes. And she remembered the medieval-style espalier fruit trees trained for countless decades to grow along the walls in the garden. But when she returned her attention to the website, she was horrified to see that the entire garden was gone, replaced by a concrete expanse on which a tacky outdoor cafe now stood. The website gave no sign that the historic garden had been recreated elsewhere. The museum boasted a large gift shop, replacing the former desk which had sold postcards and booklets, but no toys, umbrellas, and other products making it look like any other store.

More disappointment from her call to the museum: none of the staff she remembered were there, nor did anyone have information about lending glass items to a company in Kilvellie, a town that none of them had heard of anyway. The conversation had even ended in an admonishment.

With the young curator's words echoing in her ears, "We expect return of any museum property promptly, or we will take legal action," Helen took out her old address and phone book from her Edinburgh working days, glad that she'd hung on to it. She found the home telephone number for the former director she knew from the museum, and hoped he hadn't moved. She had no cell phone number for him.

"Marcus?" she asked when a man answered the phone.

"Aye, that's never you, Helen, is it? Been years! Are you retired?"

Helen was thrilled to reach him, and they fell into their familiar pattern of conversation.

"Some days I wish I was! I left Edinburgh and took a new position in Kilvellie, on the coast north of Dundee. Just been here a few weeks but it's already driving me demented."

"How can I help? Sounds like this isn't a social call."

"No, but we can catch up another time. Maybe meet for tea in Edinburgh someday, like we used to. I was sorry to see on the museum website that the herbal garden is gone, replaced with a caff?"

"Oh, dinnae get me started," Marcus grouched. "The museum was acquired by a large company. They started out running the gift shops and restaurants in smaller museums, and before you knew it, the gift shops and cafes got bigger and the actual exhibit space got smaller. Tail wagging the dog it is, these days!" He laughed, but Helen could tell there was no humor behind it.

"I'm so sorry, Marcus. But I'm calling to challenge your memory. It was before your time, but do you have any knowledge of the museum loaning some old, very old, glass pieces to a business here in Kilvellie? There used to be a famous glass factory, Regenbogen. Or Rainbow Glass it became known as, after the war."

"Aye, it does ring a bell all right," Marcus replied right away, and Helen whispered a silent *thank you* as she leaned back in her desk chair and listened.

"As you say, it was before my time. I only started working there in the nineteen seventies, but I remember, we used to rotate the exhibits, keep some things in storage and change them out every few months so local folks would have a reason to visit more than once. There was a shelf in the most secure part of the storage room, with a sign on it saying that the pieces normally there had been loaned indefinitely to the Regen—whatever it was—glass factory. Don't know the name for sure, but what you said sounds right."

"Can you remember when the loan would have taken place?"

"Aye, lass, before the war. I mean, probably in the nineteen thirties, earlyish that decade. The reason I remember is, we eventually took that sign away and started using the shelf for other things. One of the staff members contacted the factory, maybe in the eighties, to see about tracking down the pieces. Not that we especially needed them back, if they were being put to good use, but just to keep track. We were told that no one at the factory knew where the pieces could be. The founder, forgot his name, he was gone, dead, I mean, and apparently the factory had been looted and attacked during the war. Was it bombed? I never knew the details. So

161

Jane Ross Potter

in the end, we assumed the pieces were stolen, or more likely
damaged and tossed out. So much happened in the war..."
His voice drifted off.

"This is very helpful, Marcus. It sounds like there is no
one left, I mean, from your museum, who could identify the
pieces. Do you think any photographs were taken before the
glass was loaned out?"

"Och lass, I dinnae ken that. I will tell you though, when
the new company took over the museum, they did a grand
clear-out of the paper archives. Everything's digital these
days, they said. I was hoping they'd get the old records
scanned, but they didn't want to spend the money. They had
the former management, people like me, look through papers
for anything really important, mainly to support provenance
of the more valuable pieces in the collection, but everything
else was tossed out. Shredded, what have you."

Helen stayed quiet while she debated with herself
whether to tell Marcus that the loaned pieces had survived
the war, intact as far as she knew. Then she imagined Adam,
already suspicious of Richard, listening in on the conversation, and decided not to disclose that information yet.

"Marcus, can you keep this call confidential for now?"

"Och aye, lass, ye know ye can trust me, from our old
days of working together. And who would I tell? I'm not lifting
a finger to help that lot of money managers over at the museum now, not even if they paid me."

"Okay, I'll make a trip to Edinburgh soon to see you.
Might bring a colleague with me. Will you be in town during
the next week or two?"

"Aye lass, it would be good to meet you again. Did you
keep your flat, in the New Town I think it was?"

"Yes. I'm not sure if I'll sell it or rent it out. Although, with
the mess I'm creating here, I might be out of a job and back
there before you know it!"

Marcus laughed. "I can't imagine it's that bad. You
always were a good copper."

Helen laughed too. She enjoyed reconnecting with a kindly contact from the old days.

"Well, in a nutshell, an elderly man died here a few days ago. It looks like an accident, but I just found evidence that he might have been, shall we say, eased on his way. I'm dating his son, and the old man's grandson is my sergeant. Can you top that?"

"Nae lass, you're in it thick! I can't wait to see ya. And regards to your boy, Adam, I think his name was?"

"Aye, your memory's as sharp as ever. He's in town helping me, and he'll be happy to hear we've spoken."

Helen ended the call feeling like she'd finally accomplished something, and a narrative with a positive spin was forming in her mind. She had earned another cup of tea and some chocolate biscuits, and retreated to the office kitchen to consider her next move.

Chapter 29

While Helen was at her office investigating the museum glass, Adam, Margaret, and Alistair formulated a plan to visit the care home and see what they could learn about the late Ronald Wilson. And, although it was a long shot, find some evidence that his cane had been borrowed, misplaced, or seen in the possession of someone with no reason to have it. Adam called the manager, Carolyn Wortham, and introduced himself as a friend of Ronald's family, and said that he and other friends would appreciate the chance to chat with residents who'd known Ronald, mainly to gather material for his funeral service.

The manager, who knew Adam's mother Helen, had no objection at all, in fact welcomed the visit. They left Adam's car in the parking lot and drove in Alistair's car to the care home, located a few blocks west of the main part of Kilvellie. Adam remembered his mother's description of it, from her visit with Richard. At that time, Ronald was still alive, and Helen and Richard had been investigating how Ronald could afford such luxury in his old age.

Inside the elegant two-story foyer of the Seaview Manor Home, Margaret and Alistair stared in awe at the huge chandelier, the wide red carpeted stairs that divided at the top and led right and left around a balcony, and the marble floor with its carefully but casually distributed Turkish carpets. "Doesn't look like any care home I've ever seen," Margaret whispered to Alistair, while Adam went to the reception desk to gain entry to the resident area.

With name tags for each, they were directed through a door marked "Staff Only," where they briefly met with Carolyn Wortham.

"We're all devastated that poor Mr. Wilson is gone, and so suddenly," she said. "Most of the residents will be in the sun lounge waiting for their afternoon tea. I know it's a bit early, but we do the lunches at eleven-thirty and by now they're ready for a spot of tea."

Alistair kept his thoughts to himself, but he was quickly realizing something: suspicions of the care home were probably misplaced. Otherwise, the manager would be unlikely to allow them free access to the other residents. He was anxious to speak to Kathryn Spears, but felt it was premature to single her out. Anyway, he couldn't reveal his reasons, that Ronald had written to her urgently just prior to his death.

Carolyn stood up and escorted her three visitors back to the lobby, then across and into a large south-facing circular room with views out to the landscaped grounds. Residents were dotted around the comfortable-looking chairs and sofas, in twos and threes, chatting quietly. Margaret could see few walkers, wheelchairs, and other accoutrements of old age, but perhaps the home catered to people who were still reasonably mobile.

Guiding the visitors to a group of three elderly women, Carolyn introduced them, then left them to chat.

Alistair and Adam pulled up three additional chairs and they all joined the group. Alistair and Margaret had decided in advance to keep quiet; if they were supposed to be friends of Ronald's grandchildren, the American accents might confuse the residents.

"I hope you dinnae mind the wee intrusion," Adam began in a soft voice. "We're hoping to learn a bit about Ronald's time here. He didn't say much to his son or grandson, and he was here for, what, four years?"

"Aye," one of the women said. "But we cannae tell ye much either, sonny. Ron kept himself to himself. He rarely joined us here after lunch. Preferred his own company. And most days, his wee granddaughter, Emily, would pick him up and take him out for an hour or two in the afternoon."

"So none of you knew him well, it sounds like," Adam said. He glanced at Margaret and Alistair, hoping for ideas.

"Hang on laddie!" Another of the women joined the conversation. Adam leaned in to hear her quiet voice. "He was good pals with one resident. Ye should talk tae her."

Adam looked around the room. "Can you point her out to me?"

"Nae, she's not down here today. Stayed in her room, she's that upset."

Adam hesitated; he wanted to ask the woman's name, but if she really was upset, he didn't want to intrude on her privacy.

The woman who'd spoken up was on her feet, slowly straightening her back and finding her balance. "Be good for her tae have some company. Come on, I'll take ye to her. And yer pals. Quiet folks, aren't they!"

Just outside the door to the lounge room was an elevator, the door disguised as a regular room door. The woman pressed the up button, and the door slid aside to reveal an elevator barely big enough for two people. "You come with me, laddie, and your friends can get it when it comes back doon."

"Can they get to where we're going by the stairs?" Adam asked.

"Aye, should have realized they'd be fit enough for that." She pointed to the staircase at the back of the lobby. "Just back there, up the stairs, then follow the balcony around. We'll see who gets there first."

Alistair and Margaret waited until the elevator door slid closed, then they made their way across the lobby and up the stairs. "I feel like I should be wearing a ball gown," Margaret commented as she stopped halfway up to look across at the chandelier. Alistair smiled and took her hand for a moment.

166

"Or a wedding gown," he whispered, and she squeezed his hand tightly in reply.

The wide white-railed balcony followed the contour of the circular lobby, and Margaret and Alistair turned to their right at the top of the stairs, meeting Adam and the woman, who they learned was named Angela, outside the elevator.

"Follow me, you spry young people," she said, and led the way down a well-lit corridor to the residents' personal rooms. The door to one stood wide open, and Alistair could hear voices inside: Ronald's grandchildren Desmond and Emily, he realized. He wasn't sure how he'd explain his presence to them, but luckily they didn't see him, so he continued on.

At the next door, Angela knocked lightly, then opened it. "Kathryn? It's me, Angie. I brought you three visitors to talk about Ron. I hope you don't mind."

Margaret hesitated, thinking it would seem like an invasion if they all went in, but a clear voice rang out from inside. "Aye, please come in. I'd like to meet all of you." Angela held the door open wide, and Margaret followed Alistair and Adam in.

"I'll leave you to it," Angela said. "Please say goodbye when you go. I'll be in the sunroom."

Margaret and Alistair shared a grin: according to the nameplate on the door, they were about to meet the resident they'd wondered about at the solicitors' office, the intended recipient of Ronald's mystery letter.

Chapter 30

A diminutive woman sat by the room's south-facing picture window; she seemed comfortably ensconced in a large wingback chair, with a knitted patchwork shawl around her shoulders. Her face was wrinkled and pale, and her eyes were red-rimmed, from tears Margaret expected. So this was the care home resident Ronald had written the letter to. She and Alistair couldn't let on that they knew about it, but it was fortuitous to have a chance to meet her.

"Sorry I cannae stand up tae greet you," Kathryn said in a surprisingly strong voice. "Please, move chairs around and sit where I can see you."

Margaret took surreptitious glances around while Alistair and Adam moved chairs and arranged them in a semi-circle to face Kathryn.

"Tea or coffee?" Kathryn asked next.

"Only if it's not a bother," Margaret replied for the group. She looked around for a kitchen area or a tea tray. "Can I make it for everyone?"

Kathryn laughed gently. "Nae lassie, I just press this wee button and it appears."

Sure enough, when Kathryn pressed a button on the windowsill next to her chair, a male voice spoke up over an intercom system. "Yes, Kathryn, good afternoon. What can we do for you?"

"Hello Josh. I've got three visitors, can you believe it? And one's from America, a lass. Can we have tea and some cake?"

"Happy to help. I'll be there in about ten minutes."

Kathryn smiled broadly. "Like magic it is, eh?"

She leaned back and closed her eyes briefly, then opened them again. "Sure is quiet here without Ron. Who could have imagined it? Goes out one afternoon with his wee grand-daughter, just like most days, but this time he doesn't come back. They say he went peacefully, a heart attack while he was looking out at the sea."

Margaret felt an involuntary gasp: so Kathryn didn't know that Ron had fallen to the beach below. Just as well, she thought. Why should that image be the last that Kathryn would have of him? Much better to picture him drifting off, at peace, sitting on his familiar bench in the sun, facing the sea.

Alistair seemed agitated, Margaret thought, aware that he was fidgeting and couldn't settle. She decided to include him in the conversation.

"Let me introduce my fiancé Alistair," she said to Kathryn. "I know we both sound American. He's from America, but I was born in Fife. I've grown up in America, though."

Kathryn seemed happy to be distracted by asking about various locations in America, and reminiscing about members of her family who'd visited there in years past. Margaret realized that this conversation was not really helping achieve their mission, which was to investigate Ronald's death. As far as Kathryn seemed to know, he simply died suddenly and was gone, nothing at all suspicious about it. And no mention, from either Kathryn or Angela, of other recent deaths among the residents. She hoped it meant that their earlier suspicion about medication was probably on the wrong track.

There was a tap on the door, and a young man in a crisp uniform of aqua tunic and pants came in, pushing a tea trolley loaded with goodies. Absent the cakes, Margaret thought the man would look more at home working in a spa.

"Here we are, Kathryn. Would you like me to serve everyone?" He stopped the tray within reach of where the group was sitting.

Kathryn shook her head. "Nae, Josh, we can manage. I'll ring when we're finished."

With a slight bow, Josh told everyone that he hoped they'd enjoy the tea, then left and pulled the door partly closed behind him.

"Please help yerselves." Kathryn gestured at the tray, then grinned, a twinkle in her eyes. "I shouldnae be telling ye this, but I want to explain. The monthly fee here covers our room, three meals a day, laundry, minor medical care, all the essentials. But if we order things like tea in our rooms, it's a wee bit extra. I had a look at the bill one day, and I discovered they have a separate charge if a staff member serves the food. So from then on, I poured me own tea!"

Alistair, in his American accent, offered to be Mother, which amused Kathryn greatly, and soon they each had a cup of tea and a plate piled high with cake slices and biscuits. Feeling less awkward than when they'd arrived, Alistair casually nodded his head toward a large framed photograph that was sitting on the floor, leaning against a bookcase.

"Kathryn, do you need someone to hang up that photograph?" he asked. "After what you said about serving the tea, I'm guessing that the management charges extra for tasks like that."

"Och, that's kind of ye, laddie, but don't get the idea it's been sitting there for weeks waiting to be hung up. Nae, it's just been there a day or two. I used to work at an office in town, and they let me hang that family photo on the wall. When I retired, oh goodness, ten years ago now, old Claude took it off the wall, but the wallpaper had faded around it. I said he could keep it up until he redecorated. Well, all these years later, here it is! Took him long enough. I had a similar one at home, but of course most of my things are stored downstairs, since I have less space here. Och, listen to me going on."

It Continued with the Cowries

"We're happy to listen," Margaret said. She had also recognized the photograph from the solicitors' office. "If it's not too personal, may I ask who the people are in the photo?"

Kathryn sighed deeply and looked out of the window for a moment; Margaret felt bad that she'd struck a nerve. However, Kathryn turned back with a smile, sipped some tea, and said, "I can talk about it now. Been decades after all. That young girl, that's me, age nine. My parents are in back. And the boy... the boy was my brother. I adored him. He was a bit older, thirteen in the picture. This was afore the war..."

She stopped and took a handkerchief from her pocket to dry her eyes.

"Did, did he fight in the war?" Margaret asked gently.

"He was too young to enlist when war broke out, but he might have run off from the home..."

The *home* Margaret wondered to herself: had Kathryn and her brother both been sent away at the start of the war?

Kathryn picked up the story again. "You youngsters may not know this, but at the outbreak of war, the British government encouraged city families to send their bairns into the countryside, to be away from the expected German bombing. My mum thought I was too young to leave my parents, but my father insisted on sending me off to Canada to live with a relative. My brother by then had a group of pals. This was in Glasgow, did I say? Anyway, he wasn't having anything to do with being shipped off to Canada, no way. But he and his pals agreed to leave the city and go to a group home as long as they could stay together. That's what happened, and it was the last time anyone heard from him. Or from his pals."

She stopped and looked out of the window again. "Ironically, I could have died on the way to Canada, what with all the U-boats out there sinking ships. My parents, God bless them, they were now freed up to help the war effort and they went to London, got bombed and died there. I stayed in Canada until I was old enough to work, but I missed Scotland and I eventually came back."

171

Jane Ross Potter

She exhaled a deep breath and looked at the photograph. "Still miss him I do, miss all of them."

Chapter 31

Margaret, Alistair, and Adam worked their way through their afternoon tea treats and placed their empty plates on the trolley. All this time, Kathryn had been sitting quietly, murmuring now and again, seemingly in her own world.

"*We should go*," Margaret whispered to Alistair, who in turn nodded his head toward the door, indicating the same to Adam.

Adam leaned forward toward Kathryn and said gently, "It's been lovely having tea with you, but we don't want to tire you. Would you like me to call and have the trolley removed?"

Kathryn suddenly remembered she had company and perked up. "You young folks must have better things to do than listen to me rambling on about the past. But it sure was nice to talk. That's what I'll miss most. I've lost two husbands, and now Ron's gone. He didn't talk much about the war. I think he had a bad time of it. But we talked about lots of other things. Funny, now I think of it, we talked about my brother the last time I saw him. Ron sat in that very chair where you're sitting, lassie. I'd told him before about my brother going off to the countryside, but Ron asked me, for the first time I reckon, where exactly my brother and his pals had gone."

"And did you know?" Alistair asked, feeling a surge of adrenalin: finally, they might get some information.

"Aye laddie, I'm getting to that. The place burned down in the war, and I thought my brother might have died in the fire. Anyway, it wasn't far from here, Kilvellie Manor, or

Towers or something it was called. Same name as this town."

She leaned forward and pointed to the trolley. "Any more tea in the pot?" she asked Alistair, and waited while he poured her a refill, which she drank eagerly.

"That's how I landed up in Kilvellie, did I not say? When I came back from Canada after the war, I was twenty-one then, I tried to find some written record of my brother, but I was told all the records for Kilvellie Towers went up in the fire. It was the solicitor Claude McMahon's father I spoke to, he was very kind and said he unfortunately couldn't provide any useful information. I explained that I was going back to Glasgow to look for a job, but that I really had no ties there by then. By chance, the solicitor's office needed a secretary, so I just stayed on here and got married. Eventually qualified as a solicitor as well. And now, here I am still, two husbands later."

Kathryn finished the rest of her tea, then pressed the button to summon the staff to collect the tray. "Just give me fifteen minutes and I'll be up," came a cheery reply.

Alistair, Margaret, and Adam took that as their cue to stand up and start the farewells. They replaced the chairs in their proper places around the room, and Alistair casually picked up the framed photograph, turning it to the back, then making a point of feeling the weight. He replaced it in its position.

"Kathryn," he said, "I meant it when I offered to hang up the picture. Now I know about how heavy it is, I can get the right picture hook." He took a business card from his wallet, wrote his UK mobile number on it and handed it to her, then the three departed, leaving Kathryn with her memories.

Back in the lobby, they stopped to say goodbye to Angela, then made their way out into the sunshine of the late afternoon.

As Alistair pulled his car keys from his pocket, Adam asked, "What was all that DIY business, about hanging up the photograph? Surely the home has a maintenance crew on hand."

Inside the car, Alistair quickly started up the engine and glanced at Adam, who was sitting in the back seat. "We need to meet your mother, as soon as possible. Can you get hold of her?"

"What's going on, Alistair? We didn't learn a *thing* from that long visit."

"We did, Adam, believe me. All will be revealed soon."

Chapter 32

Minutes after leaving the care home, Alistair found a parking spot near the Kilvellie police station, then he, Margaret, and Adam went inside to meet with Adam's mother. When Adam had called her, she assured him that she was free to meet, and that the station was quiet.

Inside, Adam said, "I don't know what's up with Alistair. I thought we spent a long two hours drinking tea and eating cream cakes and keeping an elderly woman company. Alistair here seems to think he's made a breakthrough."

"Sounds like you don't need tea first," Helen said, sitting down behind her desk. "Pull chairs over and tell me all about it."

"Okay," Alistair began when he, Adam and Margaret were seated and facing Helen. "But please stop me if you think I'm way off base. Helen, do you remember when we visited the McMahon law office the other day, and the photo of Kathryn Spears' family was on the wall?"

"Aye," Helen confirmed. "Looked like it would be there for another few years, the rate they're redecorating. *Not* redecorating is more like it."

"And do you remember, they said that Ronald would have seen the photograph, maybe for the first time, when he went in to deliver the letter for me, and that after he saw the picture, he hurriedly wrote a letter to Kathryn, well, addressed to her married name, Mrs. Ramsay?"

"Yes to all of it. Where is this going, or are you testing my memory?"

Alistair laughed. "Sorry, it's not funny. Not for Ronald or for Kathryn." He took out his pocket notebook. "One of the young men whose name Ronald recorded in his wartime diaries is Franz Speyer. We're operating on the belief that Franz was one of the six factory vandals."

"Who Ronald may or may not have shoved over the cliff," Helen added. "Sorry, it's been a long day."

"It's fine," Alistair assured her. "Well, when we were at the care home this afternoon we talked at length to Mrs. Ramsay, alias Kathryn Spears. Claude McMahon had delivered the picture to her, the one that hung in her office for decades. The boy in the photograph is her older brother, Frank Spears. According to Kathryn, Frank must have been part of that Pied Piper project, sending children off to the countryside before World War Two. Frank apparently left Glasgow, along with some pals, headed for Kilvellie Towers."

Alistair stopped and turned to Margaret. "Remember, Calum told us that Kilvellie Towers functioned as a group home for the boys, before the fire?" Margaret nodded.

"Okay," Alistair continued, "again, I may be completely off base, but Kathryn spent the war years with family in Canada, and must not have come back to Scotland until the nineteen fifties. Her parents died in London in the bombing. She got a job as a secretary with the McMahon firm, working for the current McMahon's father, or maybe grandfather. She said she'd gone to the firm to ask for help finding paper records from the Kilvellie Towers group home, but they claimed there was nothing, all lost in the fire. Instead, they offered her a job, and since she had no family left in Glasgow, she settled here and married."

Alistair paused to retrieve a bottle of water from his pack and took a long swig.

"Now, if you'll accept my premise that Frank Spears was one of the six vandals who kept going back to the glass factory over a span of years, and that Ronald the guard had supposedly seen the boys around town, where were they living, when Kilvellie Towers was already burnt down? And even if they had been living there, how would they get back and forth to this Kilvellie, the town of Kilvellie?"

He stopped and took a deep breath. "I know it's a stretch, but what if those six boys from Glasgow never did go to Kilvellie Towers? What if they were sent here, to the town of *Kilvellie,* by mistake? And then stayed on, after learning that the Towers building burned down?"

The others sat in silence, and then Helen said, "You may be onto something, Alistair. I've been doing some digging myself today. Although I hate to think that anyone employed at the care home would have harmed Ronald, I did some research on the place. Turns out it's not locally owned. It was acquired last year by a bigger group who are buying up care homes and trying to run them more efficiently."

Adam nodded his head. "That would explain something that Kathryn told us. Apparently, the staff will deliver food, or afternoon tea, to residents' rooms, but they'll charge extra to stay a few more minutes and serve the food. Seems really petty to me."

"I agree, son. Anyway, I found information online that the care home building began as a fancy manor house, then in the Second World War, well, both wars, it served as a convalescent home for soldiers. But what ties in with Alistair's idea is this: it also served as a temporary home for evacuee children, kind of a staging point before they went off to live on farms or with local townspeople."

"So," Margaret said, "if Frank Spears and his friends were sent to Kilvellie by mistake, or maybe as a staging point, instead of Kilvellie Towers, they wouldn't have seemed out of place?"

"It all starts to add up," Helen agreed. "And from what I've been reading about the Pied Piper aftermath, some children went back home soon after the war broke out, but others stayed for the full five years. And since poor Frank's parents seem to have died in the war, and Kathryn says she had no family left back in Glasgow, there really was no one to trace Frank."

"Helen," Alistair asked, "can I see that transcript of the letter again, the one Ronald wrote to Kathryn right before he died?"

Helen took a file folder from a desk drawer, opened it, and handed the letter over. Alistair skimmed through it.

"I agree, it all seems to add up." He handed it back to Helen. "This letter is a bit of a coverup, for Kathryn's sake I think. Ronald doesn't mention that the brother helped vandalize the factory, and he puts a positive spin on what Frank was doing the day he died. I mean, that he was helping clear up the broken glass when he fell from the cliff."

"If that's what really happened," Helen said. "I can't find any record here in the station of police involvement. Remember, the ledger for nineteen forty-four, the year they supposedly died, is missing."

"Would the lifeboat people have records that far back?" Margaret asked. "It's such a big part of life on the coast in Scotland. Seems that a major incident of six young men falling over the cliff here would have been investigated and recorded."

Helen sighed. "I'd like to think so, Margaret, but if the police record is nowhere to be found in this office, then I don't have high hopes of a corresponding record existing among the lifeboat ledgers, or whatever they kept back then."

"So we keep coming back to Ronald's account of what happened to the six boys, or teenagers," Adam concluded. "Just going around in circles."

Helen glanced up at the office clock. "Five o'clock on the dot. I am officially off duty. Tommy and Tuppence, are you driving back to Finlay tonight?"

Margaret looked at Alistair, then back to Helen. "We haven't discussed it. I'll leave it up to him. He'd have to twist my arm to stay in that fancy hotel another night, though!"

Helen smiled. "Good. I'm calling them to book you a room

for tonight, and one for Adam, then we're going to dinner so I can tell you my news from this afternoon."

Chapter 33

Helen said she needed a few minutes to gather up her things in the residence next door and secure the office. Alistair, Margaret, and Adam sat and waited, chatting about the afternoon. The front door to the station opened, and in walked Emily and Desmond.

"Oh, hi Adam," Desmond said, not looking as surprised as Adam would have expected him to. "Is your mum here?"

"Yes, she's just getting something from next door." Adam stood, as did Margaret and Alistair. "I'm so sorry about your grandfather," Adam said, before making introductions. Margaret hadn't met Richard's children before, but Alistair and Adam knew Desmond.

Alistair remembered Emily from chatting with her on the cafe bench over a week earlier. He felt awkward now, especially after receiving the letter from Emily's grandfather, retracting the story he'd told Emily: his confession, really, about killing the glass factory vandals. He hoped Emily wouldn't remember him, but she clearly did, so he offered her his condolences.

Desmond hesitated, once the introductions were finished. "This is a bit strange. Em and I came here to ask Helen a question, but we might as well ask you all instead. What were you doing at Granddad's care home this afternoon? We heard your voices in the hall, then we saw you from the window when you went back to your car."

Margaret decided to take the lead, and the others could add more if they wanted.

Jane Ross Potter

"That was for me," she said. "My parents in Boston are thinking of retiring back here. They're both Scottish. I figured, since I was in town, I'd take a look at that facility. I was going to go in alone, but one of the residents, Angela was her name, said that Mrs. Ramsay could use some company and took us all up."

Desmond seemed to relax. "Oh, that makes sense. Yeah, poor Kathryn, I mean Mrs. Ramsay. She and Granddad were close, according to Em here. Em visited him more often than I did, I'm ashamed to say."

"Do you think it would be a nice place for your parents?" Emily asked Margaret, who was momentarily taken aback, then remembered it was their excuse for being there. She thought Desmond was surprisingly gullible, for a police officer anyway. After all, why would Adam be involved in checking a care home for Margaret's parents?

"Oh, um, yes, it seemed nice, the areas we saw. We ended up talking to Mrs. Ramsay for a long time, and she insisted on ordering a tea trolley. I didn't get to see much of the facility other than Mrs. Ramsay's room and the sunroom. And of course the lobby is lovely and elegant."

"Granddad was happy there." Emily took out a tissue and dabbed her eyes. "I sure will miss visiting him. I wish he'd had a chance to watch my bairn grow a bit older."

The group all turned when Helen emerged from the residence side.

"Goodness! I had no idea we had more visitors. Desmond, you aren't due back for a few days. And Emily, I'm so sorry. I hope you're managing well enough."

"Yes, thank you, Officer Griffen. Desmond and I stopped by to ask a question, but these people have answered it for us, so we can take off."

"Are you finished clearing out your grandfather's room at the home? It must be difficult, all his memories."

"It's taking longer than we expected," Emily replied. "In the days before he died, he got really worked up about something. He insisted that I take him to my house a couple of times, which he rarely visited, because he wanted to look through his boxes that I moved there from the family house. I didn't know if Dad would sell the house right away, and Granddad didn't want anything to be discarded yet. Anyway, the other day I brought all the boxes I have of his to the family room so he could look through them."

"Do you know what he was looking for?" Helen asked, as she knew that Adam and Alistair would want to know as well.

"Not specifically. There are just a few file boxes left now. I offered to help go through them, but he wanted to look himself. He kept muttering about diaries and something about old glass from a museum. I've been looking in his care home room for those things. Although, now he's gone, it probably doesn't matter."

Margaret felt her eyes widen, but she kept quiet, listening carefully to see where the conversation led.

"He was probably confused from seeing the banner for the new glass museum out on the road, don't you think, Em?" Desmond suggested. To Desmond's gullibility, Margaret now added a lack of curiosity. Or, she realized, maybe she was just used to Alistair's need to question everything, to turn it over and examine it from another angle.

"Oh, I suppose," Emily conceded. "Whatever it was, he got so agitated, he suddenly asked me to drive him back to the care home. We got all the way there and realized he'd left his walking cane behind at my house. I offered to go home and bring it for him that night, but he said he'd get it from me in the next day or two. He has a walker at the care home. Well, had a walker. He really only used the walking stick outside. The walker would have been useless on the gravel and grass up by the cafe…"

Seeing that Emily was close to tears, Helen broke in and asked if she and Desmond would like to stay for a cup of tea, since they'd been working all day. "Only if you have time, ma'am," Desmond said. "Do you all have dinner plans or something?"

"Nothing specific. Go and make yourselves comfortable in the wee conference room. Margaret, I'm sure, will help with the tea, right, dear?"

Margaret felt like she was taking part in a play in which she hadn't been told her role or her lines. She followed Helen into the kitchen behind the main office.

"I should invite people into the residence sitting room, it's more comfy," Helen said, half to herself, "but this is still a quasi-police matter so I want to keep it a bit formal." She lowered her voice. "Listen, Margaret, I have some information about the museum glassware you found, that I was going to tell you and the others tonight. But Desmond and Emily showing up is fortuitous. Will you please just follow my lead when we go back?"

"Yes," Margaret agreed, then quickly explained to Helen the excuse she'd given Desmond for being at the care home: she was investigating it as a possible home for her parents. She fell silent when they heard Desmond approaching.

"Can I help? Em's showing the guys her latest pictures of the bairn and all he gets up to. I've seen it in person so I left them to it."

"Good timing." Helen handed Desmond a tray to carry, with six assorted mugs, the creamer, and a bowl of sugar cubes. She dashed next door to her residence for a fresh packet of digestive biscuits which she asked Margaret to open and put on a plate, while she attended to the whistling kettle and pouring water into the teapot.

"Ready?" she asked Margaret, when the tea had steeped for a couple of minutes.

"Yes." But ready for what, Margaret wondered.

The conference room felt crowded, with the small table covered in tea things and biscuits, and six people around a table that seated four, trying to find space to put their tea mugs between sips. Helen decided to get right to the point and not prolong the gathering.

It Continued with the Cowries

"I had a chat today with an old friend in Edinburgh. You may not know, Emily, but I worked in Edinburgh for many years before I moved here a few weeks ago. This friend used to be a director at a small museum in Queen Street, in the New Town. It specializes in antiquities, and it's not as well-known as the big museums and galleries. Anyway, when I told him I'd moved to Kilvellie, he said the name jogged his memory from when he was still at the museum."

She stopped to sip her tea, carefully watching Emily's face for any sign that Emily knew what was coming next, but Emily seemed as attentive as the rest of the group.

"He said that the museum may have loaned some old glass pieces to the Regenbogen Glass Factory, probably before World War Two. Apparently, the pieces were never returned, but the museum didn't push the matter, after learning about the damage to the factory during the war, and then being closed for years after for repairs."

Still no word from Emily or Desmond, and Helen was relieved that Margaret and Alistair had the presence of mind to keep silent.

Helen sighed, as if it was no big deal. "Ah, well, never mind. I hoped maybe your granddad might have mentioned it. As far as I know, he was the only person still alive who knew the factory during those difficult war years."

Alistair was on alert, wondering if Emily would repeat the story she'd told him, about Ronald claiming to have killed the six vandals. But she kept quiet, seemingly lost in thought.

Helen finished her tea. "I hope I haven't upset you both with this talk. I'm sure it's painful being reminded of those times for your grandfather. Emily, you should get home to your wee bairn."

Emily had been staring into her tea mug, and now she looked up at Helen. "A lot of Granddad's memories were jumbled up, but he recently mentioned removing something valuable from the factory for safekeeping during the war. I assumed he was referring to the glass vases, the ones you

185

found in the coal chute, that Malky has now. But what if your museum friend is right, and Granddad *did* take something to protect it? I have no idea where it could be. I've been through every box in our old family home, and the ones at my house. Not the ones with papers of course, those were Granddad's private files, but I'm sure I would have come across anything of value, especially if it was glass."

Helen suddenly had a vision of Vera, the fictional Northumberland detective, saying, "Ah, pet, but you didn't think to look in the *biscuit tins*, did you?"

She was tempted, but that news could wait. Things were already falling into place without disclosing more than needed to Emily and Desmond, not yet anyway. Signaling the end of the impromptu gathering, she stood up, and the others followed suit. After repeats of the sympathy sentiments from earlier, Adam walked Emily and Desmond to the front door while Margaret and Alistair helped Helen to clear up.

Chapter 34

With the office finally secured for the evening, and Helen back in civilian clothes, she, Margaret, Alistair, and Adam walked along the main street in Kilvellie, ready for dinner. Alistair and Margaret had requested a return to the bistro where they'd eaten before, and Helen and Adam were happy to oblige.

Alistair was wondering where Richard was all this time; he'd been a constant presence at Helen's side, but perhaps Helen had asked him to keep a distance while she was occupied with the formalities after Richard's father's death. The museum glass and broken cane complicated matters.

The late afternoon was still warm, so they chose a table just inside the restaurant, next to the wide open glass doors. After studying the menus and placing orders, Alistair asked Helen how Richard was doing.

"I haven't talked to him since last night. I thought he might have been staying at Emily's and looking after her young son while she's clearing out Ronald's room at the care home, but her husband is home now on leave. Richard's probably over at their old family home, getting it cleared to sell or rent."

"It needs some work," Margaret commented. "I thought it looked quite run down. If no one has lived in it for four years, I suppose that's to be expected."

Adam steered the conversation to the task at hand: solving the mystery of the broken walking cane, and whether Ronald could have been murdered.

"During our visit to the care home today," Alistair offered, "I didn't get the sense that anyone was suspicious about Ronald's sudden death."

"Well, the residents aren't being told the truth," Adam added. "At least, not Kathryn, who we spoke to the most. She thinks Ronald died of a heart attack while sitting on the bench. She doesn't know he was found on the beach below the cliff."

Helen shook her head. "With news and social media, the residents are bound to find out soon. But back to the cane, I keep thinking about what Emily just told us, that Ronald left it at her house overnight, or maybe a couple of nights. That screams opportunity, to me anyway. Thoughts?"

"Opportunity, yes," said Adam, "but what's the motive, Mum? We've already been through this for Ronald's immediate family."

Helen nodded her agreement. "Maybe Emily's husband resented her spending so much time with Ronald. If her husband's only home on leave for short visits, I don't know, perhaps he'd have preferred it if Ronald wasn't so much a focus for her. Between listing and selling the old man's glassware, taking him to the cliffside most days, and visiting him at the care home? I don't know... I've never met her husband, and I hate to think he would be so cruel as that."

"Or maybe her husband didn't intend Ronald to die, just become injured enough that he couldn't go out any more," Adam suggested. "A broken hip would be the likely outcome from a fall, in a man of his age."

Helen looked over to see a waiter approaching with their meals. "Let's talk about this after we eat. I'd still prefer to rule out Richard's family's involvement before I bring in an outside team."

As they ate, Margaret asked Helen what she planned to do next about the museum glass in the biscuit tins.

"I'd like to get a couple of pieces from you, Margaret, and take them to show the former museum director in

Edinburgh. He can judge if the labels look authentic, and if the pieces could have been in the museum's collection, before they were loaned to the glass factory here."

"What other explanation could there be?" Adam asked.

"It's stretching things, I know, but maybe Henry and the glassmakers created replicas and displayed them, with fake museum signs. I don't know why he'd do that, maybe to add some evidence that the factory had connections with a reputable Scottish museum. Remember, when Henry first built and opened the factory, World War One was fresh in peoples' memories. Henry probably did all he could to show his alignment with Scotland, and distance himself from his previous life as a German soldier."

"It's an idea, Helen," Margaret said, "although I agree, it does seem like stretching things. I think the pieces are real, and your conversation with the former director supports that."

"But how did they end up in biscuits tins, at Richard's house?" Helen asked. "I wish I knew. If another team takes over, Richard's in for some difficult questions. And I didn't tell any of you yet, but the current museum management already threatened me with lawyers if the pieces still exist and aren't returned."

"Yikes!" Margaret whispered. "I don't want them in the cottage if you bring in outside police help!"

"Me neither," Alistair said, looking alarmed. "I feel like driving home tonight and bringing them to the police station immediately."

"No need for that," Helen assured him. "Margaret came by the pieces innocently, so neither of you would be in trouble. Just don't break any in the meantime..." She stopped when she saw a text message come in on her phone, which she had next to her on the table.

"It's Desmond. I'd better go outside and call him."

Helen returned moments later. "Desmond and Emily have a suggestion about the museum glass, following up on our conversation at the police station. If anyone knows about the factory borrowing glass decades ago, it would be Malky and his two older kids, especially Christy. She's studied the written records of the factory, and there might be photographs. A collection of museum glass could have been on display in the factory. At least, that's what Desmond and Emily suggest."

"That's a great idea," Margaret said. "But what about Malky's older kids as suspects? I mean, hurting or killing Ronald in revenge for his part in the wartime factory vandalism? Christy was very emotional about all that."

Helen turned to look out of the window, then back to Margaret. "Can't we treat these as separate issues? All we want to do right now is look at old photographs of the factory, see if we spy the museum glass. In fact, unless there's a written record of the loan among the documents Christy has, she and her family may not even know about it."

Adam had his phone out. "It's not too late to call them. Shall I get in touch?"

"Wait, son, I need to think of a reason for asking."

"You have one," Adam pointed out. "Your conversation with the director, that you told Emily and Desmond about this afternoon."

Helen smiled and shook her head. "That's not quite how things went. I called him in Edinburgh to say I knew about the glass, and could he confirm that it was borrowed from his former museum. *He* didn't bring up the subject."

"Doesn't matter, Mum." Adam enumerated points by counting off on his hand. "You had a conversation with the retired museum director, a question arose about glass loaned to the Regenbogen factory before World War Two, and has Christy seen any evidence for it in the pictures and records she's looked at. That's all true, right?"

"I guess," Helen agreed. "You three, order coffee and tea, whatever you want, and a cappuccino for me. I'll go and call Christy."

With Helen outside again on her phone, Adam looked like he was about to explode. "I'm going along with Mum for now, but I *really* don't like this, and now she's involving more possible suspects, getting all chummy with them over the loan of the museum glass!" He groaned. "I *wish* I'd given her an earlier deadline to turn over the investigation."

"I think it will be fine," Alistair assured him. "She's just asking about glass from decades ago. Chances are Christy will know nothing about it. And I truly don't see how the glass in the biscuit tins could tie in with Ronald's death."

"That's not it!" Adam persisted, his agitation growing, but he kept his voice low. "The house where the tins were located is Ronald's son Richard's, and Ronald lived there until four years ago. Ronald's grandchildren Desmond and Emily, who you must admit are suspects even though Mum doesn't seem concerned, had free access to the house all this time. Any decent detective would require the house to be sealed for investigation the minute Ronald's *unexplained* death was discovered. By having possession of items removed from the house soon after the death, you and Margaret are now within the sphere of being questioned. Even more for Margaret, since she was in the house, so they'll have to get her fingerprints to rule her out."

"You're right, of course," Alistair mumbled, ashamed of not coming to the same conclusions himself. He was about to go outside and ask Helen not to call Christy yet, when Helen returned, looking triumphant.

"Christy's still down the street at her studio, so she'll lock up and meet us. Everyone, scoot your chairs along to make room for another one."

Adam reluctantly shifted his chair closer to the other end of the table, while Helen asked a waiter to bring an extra chair and place setting. If anything, Adam looked even more furious, but he kept quiet. Helen was oblivious to the tension, and instead seemed pleased at the progress she was making.

The group was silent as the coffee and teas were served; minutes later, Christy arrived, noticed Helen right away, and approached the table.

"Oh! I didn't realize you had so many people with you." Christy recognized Margaret from her visit to the glass studios, and as she sat in the chair that Helen held out, she apologized for her emotional outburst during the visit. "I hope it didn't upset you too much," she added.

"It's fine," Margaret said. "William probably told you, he gave me a marble as down payment toward the glass that I said he can have from my cottage. Anyway, no bad feelings at all."

"Good." Christy pushed her bangs back from her forehead, and Margaret noticed her eyes looked clear, with no sign of prolonged crying. "Sorry I'm such a mess. I was working on jewelry all day and haven't had a chance to tidy up."

Margaret couldn't help but smile, looking at Christy's flawless face, her recently trimmed blond hair, and her silky pink blouse, which had elbow-length sleeves and a V-neckline that draped softly to frame her face. Like a walking advertisement for her jewelry, she wore a matching sea glass pendant: a teardrop-shaped piece of pink frosted glass expertly encased in a rose gold border, and hanging from a rose gold chain. Margaret couldn't see what needed to be "tidied up," and now she couldn't imagine the elegant and artistic young woman being capable of anything so untidy as a plot to injure or kill Ronald.

Her thoughts were interrupted when the waiter who'd brought the chair returned, asking Christy what she'd like to drink. After glancing around at what the rest of the group had, she ordered a cup of herbal tea.

Chapter 35

Christy's tea arrived, and she took time to drizzle and stir honey into it. She took a few sips, looking like she was finally relaxing after a long day. "Now," she said, "Helen, you wanted to ask about museum glass?"

"Aye, just something that's come up. I can't say how yet, but there are hints that your great-grandfather's factory, if I have the generations right, may have borrowed some glass from a museum of antiquities in Edinburgh. It would have been before nineteen forty, I believe. The Edinburgh people assume the glass was lost or damaged during the war. Does any of that ring a bell, from your familiarity with the old factory records?"

The herbal aroma from Christy's tea reminded Helen of the teas she used to enjoy with the former Edinburgh museum director, at the now non-existent apothecary garden. She imagined replicating the garden, if she bought a house of her own... or maybe at Richard's property in Spain, where the growing conditions for herbs would be better...

She snapped back to attention when Adam tapped her arm. "*Mum*, did you hear what Christy's saying?"

"Sorry, dear," Helen said. "I have so much on my mind. What was it?"

"It's fine." Christy repeated her comments. "I was just saying that I do remember reading in an old record book, that some glass on loan from a museum was removed from the factory for safe-keeping early in the war. I can look for the record book, although it may take me a while. It was likely nineteen forty-one. Or maybe forty-two."

Helen glanced over to see that Alistair and Margaret were trying to suppress smiles. But without disclosing the existence of what was probably the same glass, Helen asked Christy if she remembered anything else, and what she'd thought when she first read about the borrowed glass.

"Honestly? I didn't think much about it. I mean, by the time I was reading the records, probably about five or ten years ago, the factory was long gone." She stopped suddenly. "Wait, did it show up in the glassware you found in the old coal chute recently? That would make sense!"

Helen hmm'd and haw'd as she tried to formulate a reply. That vintage glassware had been turned over to Malky, for his own museum, and as far as she, Adam, and Alistair had seen during the recovery efforts, all that glass was made by Regenbogen. Anyway, if there had only been one museum loan, some or all of those pieces were now at Margaret's house.

"Not as far as I know, Christy. But I suppose it's possible. If Malky finds anything not made by Regenbogen while he's cataloging it, I hope he'd let me know."

"I'm sure he would," Christy confirmed. "If we know one thing about Malky, I mean, Dad, he wants to keep the factory record accurate, and tell the true history of it in the new museum. Finding glass from an Edinburgh museum would definitely be something he'd tell me and William about, since we're the most up to date on the old factory records."

Helen was sorely tempted to tell Christy that the loaned glass had probably been found, but first, Richard and his children Emily and Desmond had to be cleared of any wrong-doing in Ronald's death. Otherwise, the Wilson family home and the contents thereof, including the errant biscuit tins and all they contained, would become embroiled in the investigation.

With her mind set, Helen thanked Christy for coming to meet them, and talk turned to other topics. Christy asked

Margaret about her adopted village in Fife, Finlay, and said she hoped to visit soon with William, to look at the sea glass that Margaret's uncle had collected.

"I don't know if you're aware," Margaret said, "but Finlay won a Prince's Award for best small village earlier this summer. The village is using some of the prize money to establish new businesses in town, partly for employment opportunities, to keep people from moving away. There's interest in opening a sea glass shop, with jewelry made from Finlay sea glass. It seems that everyone in town has piles of it, passed down from parents and grandparents."

Christy's eyes lit up. "I'd love to speak to someone about that. Don't tell my family, but I'm getting bored with making the same jewelry year after year from the Kilvellie glass, well, the former Regenbogen glass. Fact is, there is a limited supply on the beach here, and it won't last forever." She was quiet for a moment. "And honestly, I am also tired of collecting glass on that same beach since I was little."

"I'm sure the village would be thrilled for someone of your experience to get involved," Margaret said. "Maybe you could help get a shop established?"

"I'll think about it." Christy sipped her tea and turned wistful. "For the past seven years, I never considered spending time away from home, let alone moving to Fife, or Edinburgh. When you visited us at the studio, Margaret, I mentioned about our missing sister. Well, now that she's back, and Mum and Dad are busy with planning the glass museum, I don't need to be around for support the way I used to. And with Adam dating my sister, Justine I mean, he's often here for support too."

Oh no, Alistair realized with a jolt. Margaret would put two and two together and figure out that with Adam dating SarahBeth's twin Justine, Alistair's story about being like an uncle to the young dancer SarahBeth was now suspect. Margaret was too smart to miss the connection.

Sure enough, Margaret spoke up right away. "Adam,

you're about the same age as Alistair, right?"

"Uh, sure," Adam replied, not knowing why Margaret was asking.

"And Justine is SarahBeth's twin, right?"

"Yes, um, that's correct also. But you haven't met either of them, have you?"

"I've seen Justine working in a coffee shop in St. Andrews." She grinned. "But so much for Alistair's claim that he's SarahBeth's *avuncular*!"

Now Adam realized what was going on: Margaret must have heard about Alistair spending time with the ballet dancer SarahBeth, and grown jealous. He had to help his pal out of this.

"Justine is mature for her age. Wouldn't you agree, Christy?"

"That's a good way to put it, Adam. Yes, she's still my younger sister, but after all she went through, she definitely has had more life experience than me."

Helen joined in. "And much as I love him, my son Adam is *young* for his age. So you see, Margaret, it's one thing for Justine and Adam to date, but Alistair and SarahBeth? He's called it correctly. An avuncular connection. *Definitely* avuncular."

Alistair put his hand to his forehead and exhaled a "*Whew*" before putting his arm around Margaret's shoulders.

"Anyway," he said, "if Adam and Justine are headed for marriage, I definitely couldn't date SarahBeth. Adam as a brother-in-law? No way!"

"Same back at you, Alistair!" Adam grinned and a round of laughter brought what began as a stressful gathering to a happy end.

Chapter 36

Outside the cafe, Christy said goodbye, promising to let Helen know if she came across references to glass loaned by an Edinburgh museum. With her departure, the group turned somber again.

Helen looked at her watch. "Just one night left," she muttered.

"Mum," Adam said, placing his hand on Helen's shoulder, "this is so stressful for you. Why don't you call another station now and get the officers who will take over up to speed? Then you can have a good night's sleep and focus on other work tomorrow."

She shook her head. "No, Adam, you granted me until tomorrow morning at nine o'clock, and I'm using every minute between now and then if I have to. Don't you understand, son, that my time in this town may be over after this?"

Adam took his arm down and faced his mother. "I can understand why you and Richard might not have a future together, but why would you leave the town?"

"I'll be accused of hiding evidence, of delaying an investigation into Ronald's death because of my personal ties to Richard. I would lose my professional credibility. Maybe I'd even be investigated!"

"Surely not," Alistair said. "Why on earth...?"

Helen turned to look directly at Alistair. "Because, Alistair, one could argue that it helps me to have Ronald out of the way. Now his son can sell the house and we can live off that money in luxury in Spain, or wherever. I have a motive, as does Richard."

"Mum, that's ridiculous," Adam cried. "You have your own house in Edinburgh to sell, and I'm sure it's worth much more than Richard's old family home here. No, Mum, *you* have no motive to kill Ronald."

Alistair spoke again when mother and son fell quiet. "Helen, if you had free rein to investigate *anything* between now and tomorrow morning, what would you do?"

Helen didn't have to think for long. "Ideally, I'd like to get into Emily's house and look in their tool box, or garage, wherever their tools are stored. The saw marks look fresh, so if I found a match, I mean, if that kind of comparison is even possible, we'd have our smoking gun, don't you think?"

"Maybe, but that doesn't identify who did it. Emily, her husband, or were they in it together? Or even Richard, much as I hate to suggest him."

"Mum," Adam broke in, "it's all conjecture. Without a search warrant, you can't just go in and demand to see their collection of tools."

"True," Helen agreed. "And I wouldn't want them to know we were suspicious, or it could be disposed of. If it hasn't been already."

"I have a crazy idea," Alistair said. "Do you want to hear it?"

Helen laughed. "I do, but I doubt Adam does."

"Try me," Adam countered.

"Okay. Remember when we were visiting Kathryn Spears at the care home and I offered to hang up the picture for her, the family photograph? Well, why don't I call Emily and say I'm staying in town tonight and plan to go back in the morning to do some minor work in Kathryn's room, and I would like to borrow some tools?"

"She might suggest you buy what you need," Adam argued.

"Not in the evening, nothing's open here. I'd say I need to get back to Finlay early tomorrow so I want to do the work first thing in the morning."

"I appreciate the offer, Alistair," Helen said, "but if you do find a saw that seems to match the marks on the broken cane, maybe looks recently used, then what? You couldn't bring it to me without destroying the chain of custody. I need to think about this more."

Alistair sighed. He was ready to solve the cane mystery and move on. "Well, call me if you decide you want me to try. I guess Tuppence and I will head to the hotel, but let us know if you have any ideas. I'm happy to help."

He felt uneasy about leaving Helen and Adam alone, as they so clearly didn't see eye to eye on Ronald's death, but he decided to take a break from thinking about the dilemma. It wasn't even an official case for him, he reminded himself, and he'd led Margaret into it also, causing her to spend several hours (non-billable, he was aware) using her legal expertise to help.

***

Half an hour later, Alistair and Margaret were settled into the same suite they'd had before. Margaret claimed the Jacuzzi tub; in the main room, Alistair opened a small bag of potato chips left over from lunch, poured himself a can of beer, and turned on the television. One station had a program on primate behavior: just what Alistair needed to take his mind off murder and lost museum glass.

He was half-watching while scrolling through emails, when suddenly an image on the screen caught his attention. He grabbed the remote, restarted the program, and fast-forwarded to the beginning of the scene, glad that the hotel had interactive TV service. Researchers had filmed an orangutan pick up a saw, and, for the first time as far as the researchers knew, figure out how to use it. Alistair could hardly believe his eyes, but there it was, an untrained orangutan sawing a thin tree branch.

Ridiculous to think an orangutan in Kilvellie could have sawn through Ronald's cane, but could a child have done it? More specifically, could Emily's child have done it? With time possibly running out on Helen's career and her relationship with Richard, Alistair put the program on pause and called her.

"Oh, Alistair," she said when she answered. "I'm sorry I didn't get back to you yet about visiting Emily and borrowing tools. I'm sitting here at my desk and I still haven't decided…"

Alistair broke in. "That's not why I'm calling. This will sound really odd, but I'm watching a nature show on TV, and they have video of an orangutan, untrained as far as I can tell, picking up a saw and sawing away at a tree branch. And using the saw properly, not banging it around."

"Okay, where are we going with this?" Helen asked cautiously.

"Assuming that Emily or her husband had the best opportunity to damage Ronald's cane, when it was there overnight not long before he died, why don't we consider whether their little boy could have done it? He's about three, right?"

"*What*? That's something I hadn't considered at all. In fact, I'd already been thinking I might just go over to their house tonight with the cane and ask them if maybe it got sawed by mistake, like when Emily's husband was in his workshop, if he has one. I mean, if I do nothing tonight, then tomorrow they are likely to be questioned by an officer or a detective who will not be as sympathetic as me. So if I go over there, I'm just giving them a warning of what's coming."

Alistair could tell he'd triggered Helen's interest. "On a more positive note," he suggested, "maybe you'll be able to head off any investigation from outside, if the little boy did play with the cane and somehow damaged it. Maybe he's got a toy tool set? I hate to think he had access to his father's tools."

"Good point. Let me call Emily now, and I'll be back in touch later. With any luck you won't end up doing a whole lot of DIY at the care home."

Helen was about to call Emily while she gathered her keys and jacket, but before making the call, she noticed a new text from Desmond, Emily's brother, so she called him first.

"What's up, Desmond?"

He launched into a torrent that she could hardly understand. "Please, can you come over to Emily's house? She's terribly upset and I can't calm her down. It's about Granddad."

"Of course! I'm literally walking to the car now. I'll be there as soon as I can."

She stopped short. She had no idea where Emily lived, so she called Desmond right back and got directions; the house was only ten minutes away by car, further south along the coast.

Chapter 37

As Helen pulled into Emily's driveway, she could see Desmond waiting for her on the front steps, waving madly. *Please don't let Emily be hurt*, Helen said to herself. She didn't think the young woman had been very distraught that afternoon, instead treating her grandfather's death as a sad loss, and she seemed capable of spending her days clearing the old man's care home room. She wondered what had upset Emily so much tonight.

She climbed the four wide steps to a large deck area, then in through the front door, taking in the opulence of the home. Inside, Desmond ushered her through an open door from the wide hallway, into an expansive open-plan family room, with a dining table at the far end. Beyond it was a glass patio door leading to the back garden, with swings and an assortment of toys on the well-maintained lawn. Closely-planted ornamental shrubs around the edges provided privacy, and presumably kept the young child from dashing off.

At the sound of whimpering, Helen turned to see Emily enter the room carrying her son, who was squirming and anxious to have his freedom. Emily's hair was disheveled, her blouse was half-untucked from her jeans, and she had obviously been crying. It was quite a contrast from her usual immaculate appearance.

Desmond invited Helen to sit in one of the comfortable-looking easy chairs arranged around a square wooden coffee table, the surface strewn with toys and children's books. Emily sat on the sofa, which backed onto a picture window facing the driveway where Helen had left her car. Desmond sat next to Emily and rested his hand on her forearm. The young boy escaped from Emily's arms and approached Helen, curious to meet the newcomer.

Helen acknowledged the boy, then he toddled off to find something to play with. Turning her attention back to Emily, Helen said, "I came as soon as Desmond called me. What can I do?"

"It's all my fault!" Emily cried out. "Granddad's dead because of *me!*"

She began sobbing uncontrollably; Desmond gathered her into a hug, shooting Helen a glance to indicate that this outburst was not a surprise to him.

Helen leaned forward in her chair. "Emily, dear, you were always so kind to him, taking him out, bringing things to the home. The manager told me you were very attentive to his needs. Why do you think you had anything to do with his death?"

Emily took a deep breath and calmed down enough for Desmond to release her. She realized that Helen was talking to her. "I'm sorry, Helen, I haven't offered you tea. Or wine? Never mind, you're driving. Oh, I'm so muddled!"

"Tea would be best. I'm going to the kitchen to make some for all of us, then we'll talk."

"Thank you," Desmond mouthed to Helen, and said, "down the hall on the right. Can't miss the kitchen. Everything for the tea is on the counter, milk in a small jug in the fridge."

While waiting for the fancy electric kettle to boil, Helen admired the modern kitchen, with a skylight, large windows over a gleaming stainless steel double sink, and something she guessed was what Americans called an appliance garage: a space on the counter for the blender, hand mixer, and toaster, with a roll-top cover to keep everything neat and out of sight.

The kitchen seemed to embody the organized, fulfilling

life that Emily was building for her family, and now Helen had no taste for asking about the cane, judging from the state the young woman was in. Once again, she realized her emotions were getting in the way, and she summoned her hardened Edinburgh persona for asking the difficult questions.

Soon the kettle indicator light flashed blue, and she poured water into three vintage floral Wedgwood mugs she found hanging from hooks under the wall cabinets. The teabags sitting in a bowl on the counter would have to do; she didn't feel like measuring loose tea into a teapot.

She retrieved the milk jug, matching Wedgwood, from the refrigerator, trying not to envy the abundance of fresh exotic fruits and vegetables behind the double doors. She'd never seen such thin asparagus, the bright green spears standing neatly at attention with their ends in a shallow dish of water.

She found a bowl of brown sugar near the kettle. Loading everything on a tray, she turned to the doorway, just as Emily and Desmond came in to the kitchen.

"Let's sit in here," Emily said, taking the tray from Helen. "Otherwise, Bobby will keep grabbing things off the coffee table."

It sounded sensible to Helen, so she followed the siblings' lead and sat quietly while they prepared their tea.

"Now," Helen said, "Emily dear, do you feel up to telling me what's upset you?"

"I should have realized it much sooner, Helen," Emily began. "I thought nothing of it the time. Granddad came over to go through some boxes, I've already said, and when I drove him back to the care home, he forgot his cane at my house, but he said he wouldn't need it that evening. So we left it that I would bring it when I picked him up in the next day or two, depending on the weather, to go and park near the cliff, like we usually do. I assumed the cane was leaning by the front door, that's where he leaves it, then he comes in and sits on the nearest chair."

Helen had a horrible sense of her suspicion being correct, but she kept quiet. She'd learn soon enough, then what to do with the information, that would be the question.

Emily sipped her tea, and with Desmond giving her support by draping his arm around the back of her chair, she continued.

"When I was putting Bobby to bed that night, I mean, the night Granddad left his cane, Bobby told me 'I saw Gramps' cane' or something like that. Bobby called him Gramps. I just thought he meant he *saw* the cane, Helen, like he had *seen* the cane, do you follow me?"

"Aye, Emily, keep going."

"Then the next day, or was it the day after, I really am muddled, when I was leaving to get Granddad at the care home, his cane was on the floor in the other room, lying half under the coffee table. I had most of my attention focused on Bobby, making sure he didn't run out the door, so I barely looked at the cane. I pulled it out from under the table, then I really don't think I looked at it again. I placed it in the car boot, I put Bobby in his seat, then we went and picked Granddad up."

"Humor me, dear," Helen said. "Can you explain exactly the sequence once you got to the care home?"

"That's what I'm going to tell you. Granddad was waiting at the front door of Seaview. Like he always does. He went out to the top of the steps with his walker, then I helped him down the steps and into the front seat and I put the walker in the foyer, so it would be there when we came back. Same as I usually do. Did..." She stopped and burst into tears again. "But he never went back! He died! Because of me!"

Helen now knew for sure what had happened. The little boy had sawn at the cane, left it lying damaged on the floor, and Emily had been too distracted to notice anything wrong with it. Instead, the damaged cane had been placed back in the trusting hands of her grandfather. But at what point? Helen needed to know.

Jane Ross Potter

"Have some more tea, dear, I'm in no hurry." *Actually, I only have one night left to solve this*, she said to herself, glancing at the kitchen clock.

When Emily couldn't stop crying, Desmond took over for her.

"I came over tonight to help Emily carry Granddad's clothes and things in from her car. We put Bobby in front of the television and I found a show about monkeys for him to watch. We knew it would distract him while we went back and forth to the car. Then at one point, Emily glanced into the living room where he was. There was some kind of monkey wielding a saw and trying to chop up a branch." Now Desmond's eyes teared up before he continued.

"Bobby was jumping up and down, pointing at the television, and saying 'I saw Gramps cane! I saw Gramps cane!' At first I thought the same as Emily, and I assumed he meant he had *seen* it, but then Bobby picked up his toy saw, which I've put in a plastic bag, by the way, and starting imitating the monkey."

"It was actually an orangutan," Helen added. "Believe it or not, I'm aware of that footage."

"That's why I think I've killed Granddad," Emily concluded, looking Helen straight in the eye. "We picked him up at the care home early that afternoon, like I told you, and drove to the cafe parking lot. Granddad said he was a bit tired and asked me to drive to the far side, near his usual bench. I helped him to the bench, him leaning on my arm, then I got his cane out of the car boot and didn't even look at it. I handed it to him and he laid it down within reach on the grass. Then he said I should park by the cafe and he'd walk back when he was ready. He always said the exercise did him good."

Helen asked gently, "So you think, the cane might have been, I don't know, partly damaged, if Bobby really did take his saw to it?"

"That's why I asked you over, Helen," Desmond

206

explained. "The day Granddad died, I remember the cane was broken in two next to his, his body on the beach, sorry Emily, and it never crossed my mind that it didn't just break *on the beach*. I don't know what happened to it after that."

"It's with his clothes in the evidence locker for you to collect when you come back to work."

"Evidence!" Emily looked up sharply. "*That's* what it is now. Evidence that I'm a bad granddaughter. Oh, why didn't I notice it was damaged?"

Helen cringed. She should have told Desmond and Emily that she didn't know where the cane was. She'd been so intent on retrieving it from Margaret's cottage, and now she'd missed an opportunity to give Emily some comfort. She had to try, at least.

"Listen, dear, you have nothing to feel sorry about. As far as we know, your Granddad was unsteady on his feet when he got up from the bench that day. In fact, didn't you just say that he asked to be driven right to the bench, that he felt tired? He probably had a stroke or heart attack out there and fell. I mean, without leaning on the cane at all. In fact, his friend Kathryn at the care home has been told he had a heart attack while he was sitting on the bench."

It didn't seem to help, and Emily kept imagining the worst. "But if the stick was sawed through, will I go to jail? What will happen to Bobby?"

Now Desmond spoke up. "Emily, you're not going to jail!" Then he remembered his boss was at the table. "Right, ma'am? Even if the stick broke when Granddad leaned on it, out by the cliff, no one intended him to fall, or get hurt, right?"

"I do need to think about this," Helen said, trying to reclaim her professionalism. "I can't ignore what Emily's just told me. But give me Bobby's toy saw, that you put in the bag, and I'll hold onto it for now."

She looked at the young woman, wishing she could relieve her distress. "I can promise you, dear, no one else is

207

showing up tonight in a police car to question you, so please don't be hard on yourself. Have a wee glass of wine, try to get a good night's sleep, okay?"

Emily mumbled her thanks, then went back to the family room to retrieve her son. Desmond silently handed the bagged toy to Helen, thanked her for coming over, and accompanied her out to her car.

Chapter 38

Half an hour later, Helen was sitting on the couch in her residence adjoining the police station. There was no fancy asparagus sitting in *her* fridge, in fact she was overdue a big grocery shopping trip, so she'd called ahead from outside Emily's house to order food to pick up from the Thai restaurant near the station. Now it was keeping warm in the oven while she reached a decision about the broken cane. Tried to reach a decision, anyway.

She had less than twelve hours until Adam's deadline. She wondered to herself why she placed so much stock in her son's sometimes rigid point of view when it came to ethical questions. He must have to make frequent calls of moral judgment, and ethical choices, in the course of his career as a private investigator. She was sure that, now and again, he'd learn something during a surveillance assignment that he chose to keep to himself, and perhaps not to reveal to the client who'd hired him.

With enough difficult cases in the coming years, maybe Adam would learn to be less decisive about what he perceived as right and wrong. He insisted that Helen had been wrong from the start, by not stepping away and asking another team to handle Ronald Wilson's death from the moment his body was found on the beach. By handling it herself, Helen had waded into increasingly murky territory, which was now difficult to back away from unscathed. Both personally and professionally.

She stared at the two plastic bags on the coffee table in

front of her. One, the bright yellow of the handle showing through, was little Bobby's toy saw. Helen hadn't examined it carefully yet, and didn't know if it could in fact saw through anything hard, let alone a sturdy walking cane.

The other bag held the two pieces of the broken cane, recovered from near Ronald's lifeless body on the beach; everyone who'd touched the cane that day must have assumed it broke in the fall. It had not been handled with gloves and placed in an evidence bag, but instead was lumped in with Ronald's clothes, which were presumably given a cursory glance at the morgue. With no evident knife tears or bullet holes, clothes and broken cane were together sent to Helen's office for Desmond to collect.

But thanks to Margaret's sharp eyes, Helen had learned that the cane did hold a secret: it most likely had not simply broken in two pieces when the old man fell. That discovery had been days after the death, too late to preserve the cane untouched as a possible cause of the man's fall. Fingerprints would likely be useless. Several people could have handled it over recent days, including staff at the care home, Emily and possibly her husband, her son, not to mention the various strangers and emergency medical personnel who rushed, too late of course, to the man's side on the beach.

An aroma of ginger and basil drifted over from the kitchen area, and Helen was tempted to put her decision on hold while she ate. *No*, she decided, she would enjoy her food more if she fulfilled her duty first. The problem was, she didn't know which way she wanted the evidence to fall. If Bobby's toy saw matched the serrations on the cane, it meant that Emily's story was likely true, as Helen suspected.

But if there was no match, then what? It meant that Emily shouldn't blame herself for not supervising her son, and not noticing the damaged cane. But it also meant that someone else had sawed partway through the cane, and she would be back to the beginning with identifying possible suspects. Adam would be right, an outside team should have been involved from the start.

Steeling herself, she put on disposable gloves and took each item from its plastic bag. Without laying either object on any surface, to avoid additional contamination, she aligned the serrated edge of the small saw blade and held it against first one broken edge of the cane, then the other. The cane had been sawed at an angle, not straight across.

A close enough match. And if her theory was correct, forensics would likely be able to detect microscopic pieces of yellow plastic in the wood of the cane, and tiny splinters of matching wood in the saw teeth. She carefully replaced the items in the bags, locked them in the evidence locker, then peeled off her gloves as she strode from the office to the kitchen, ready to seek comfort in the Thai food.

While she ate, she tried to quiet her mind with an old comedy show on television, but she couldn't shake the question: What to do next? Should she tell Emily that, yes, her little son had probably started the chain of events that may have killed his great-grandfather? Not decisively, but likely.

After all, the old man had occupied that same bench, several days a week, for four years, and managed to avoid stumbling over the edge. Statistically, what were the odds of him stumbling and falling on the one day that he used a partially broken cane? No, she concluded, there was a more likely than not cause and effect.

But what was the ultimate cause? A manufacturer who made a child's toy that could damage important grown-up possessions, such as a cane that kept an old man upright. Or the shops that sold these toys. Governments that approved them for children. Parents, or well-meaning friends and family members who purchased the toys. Parents or child minders who were distracted and didn't see the damage caused by the child. The next person to handle the damaged cane not noticing before it was too late.

The list seemed endless. Could anyone really be held responsible, under the law, for Ronald Wilson's tragic fall?

And if Emily was told that she was likely correct in her suspicion, it would haunt her the rest of her long life. Every time she looked at Bobby, she'd have the sickening reminder that he'd innocently hacked away at his great-grandfather's cane, thinking nothing of the damage he was doing. Would Emily tell her own husband? Would he blame Emily? Would their marriage fall apart?

And, less important but still a factor, would Richard, the old man's son, blame Helen for letting the heart-breaking explanation see the light of day? This, she knew, would doom the relationship.

The questions occupied her through the whole meal and lasted into a post-dinner cup of coffee. She was tempted to pour some whisky, but wanted to have a clear decision before she fell asleep. If only she could talk it over with someone, but with her sergeant in the center of his sister Emily's dilemma, he was out, as was Richard. She couldn't contact any former police colleagues without exposing herself to a possible charge of concealing evidence.

Adam was her usual go-to person for work dilemmas, but he was too close to this one as well. She felt that, whatever she decided, Adam would second-guess her, and their relationship would suffer. That darned orangutan, she thought. Yes, maybe blame him. Or her.

That's how all this started, she realized, with Alistair's call to tell her an orangutan could saw a branch, so why couldn't a small child? Well, he'd triggered this possible breakthrough, so he could be her sounding board. She knew he was discreet.

Then she remembered her worries about Margaret and Alistair taking the broken stick home, the museum glass in the biscuit tins from Richard's house, their removal to Margaret and Alistair's cottage, and whether multiple calls between Alistair and Helen could be misconstrued.

The heck with it, she only had one option, she decided. She hoped that they would still be awake, but just in case, she called the hotel and asked the receptionist to let Alistair know to expect a visitor.

After retrieving the two items from the evidence locker, Helen put on a black parka and baseball cap, and slipped out the back door. She took her own car, to minimize being noticed at the hotel. She worried that she might run into Adam there, but just in case, she mentally rehearsed a story about visiting Alastair and Margaret to discuss the glassware from the Edinburgh museum, which was now in Margaret's possession in Finlay.

Chapter 39

While Helen was on her way to visit Alistair at his hotel just north of Kilvellie, her son Adam was in the south end of town, enjoying a visit with his girlfriend Justine's parents Malky and Greta, and Justine's older siblings William and Christy. Justine was working in St. Andrews, but when he told her he'd be in Kilvellie, she insisted on letting her parents know, so he could spend a little time with them. An invitation to sample Greta's baked goods that evening was a welcome end to a stressful day.

Despite Margaret's concerns, he thought that William and Christy were unlikely suspects in Ronald's death, and he had no plans to mention the recent tragedy. William and Christy seemed devoted to their parents and to their younger twin sisters, and he couldn't imagine them crossing a line that would risk them being questioned by the police, let alone being arrested.

In fact, he was glad of the chance to take his mind off the fiasco his mother had created: her "quiet unofficial" investigation into Ronald Wilson's death. Nothing had been said about it at the Greens, so far, and Adam was relieved.

The Greens' family history was already entwined with the Wilsons'. However, Malky didn't seem to blame former police officer Richard Wilson, Ronald's son, for helping to cover up teenage Justine's disappearance during the storm seven years earlier. It was partly Malky's fault too, for insisting to Officer Wilson that Justine must have drowned and would have been swept out to sea, already dead. And Officer

Wilson's son Desmond, still a teenager himself, had discovered that Justine was found collapsed at the roadside early the following morning, soaking wet, bruised and bleeding, and muttering about William attacking her.

Fearful for Justine's safety, Desmond had taken her to sheltered housing in St. Andrews. Her injuries had left her feeling confused for weeks later, and she gradually succumbed to Desmond's protective care, deciding to stay on in St. Andrews after leaving the sheltered housing. She had recently made her way back north to Kilvellie and rejoined her overjoyed family, but she was settled at her job in St. Andrews and would continue that for now. During her re-entry into the life of Kilvellie, she'd met Adam, and despite his home and working life being based two hours further north, in Inverness, they were managing to maintain a good relationship.

Adam thought back to earlier that evening, and the image of Alistair dating Justine's twin sister SarahBeth. She had founded her own ballet company in America and was finishing a tour of Scotland, returning soon to New York. Adam simply couldn't visualize serious private investigator Alistair with the outgoing, flamboyant SarahBeth, whose clothing and posture suggested that she was about to leap onto the stage.

Margaret was more suited to Alistair: a bit shy, intellectual, and with a skill for analyzing unusual situations and coming to unexpected conclusions. A life of the mind, not a life of creativity and physical activity, like SarahBeth enjoyed. Anyway, Alistair was right: the idea of Adam and Alistair being romantically involved with siblings, let alone twins, would be far too much closeness. Better to stay as unrelated pals.

Taking another chocolate pinwheel biscuit from the plate that Greta was passing around the table, Adam focused again on the conversations around him. He could hear Christy, next to him, telling her father across the table about

215

the possible loan of glass from a museum in Edinburgh, to the old Regenbogen factory. Adam thought back to the dinnertime conversation between his mother Helen and Christy, and now he couldn't remember if Helen had asked Christy to keep the museum glass issue to herself for now. Well, whether she did or not, Malky knew, and Adam had quickly learned that once Malky got hold of an idea, he didn't let go until he had all the details.

The questions were coming fast, with Malky quizzing Christy.

"You're saying that Officer *Helen* was the one who first mentioned the museum loan? How could she know anything about it?" he asked, not for the first time.

"Yes, Dad," Christy replied patiently. "She said she'd been chatting with someone she knew in Edinburgh, might have been a retired museum director, I'm not sure. Anyway, she asked me if it sounded familiar. I told her I thought I'd seen something about it in the records from the nineteen forties, but I'd need to go back and check."

"We can do that now!" Malky cried, and, ignoring Greta's admonition that there was a guest present, he stood up.

"Greta dear, Adam's nae a guest, he's like family now! Anyroad, Christy, remember I borrowed some of the old factory records back from you, so I could find information to use in our glass museum? They're in my office. Let's go through them and look."

"I can help," Adam offered, "if it's not confidential, of course."

"Even if it were, laddie, that were so long ago, can't much matter now."

Malky left the dining room and was soon back, carrying two file boxes one on top of the other, and a shoebox overflowing with papers teetering on top.

"Make room!" he hollered, and everyone scrambled to move cups and plates out of the way before the boxes crashed down on the table.

216

"Malky! Do you need to do that in the dining room? And now?"

"Aye, dear." Malky stopped to kiss Greta on the cheek. "There's two more, but let's get through these first and maybe we'll find something."

Adam opened the file box nearest to him and peered in. "What should I look for?" he asked. He was reminded of looking through a box of factory papers that Desmond had found at Emily's house recently, and it held old Ronald Wilson's diaries from the war: diaries that documented the vandalism of the factory and the names of the six presumed perpetrators. He hoped there would be nothing sensitive like that in these boxes.

Malky noisily gulped some tea and sat down by the other file box, then he replied to Adam. "Couple of things. First, photographs of inside the factory in the late nineteen thirties, or very early in the war. The other would be anything with a label like 'Heinrich's correspondence from internment.' Could be an envelope, a folder, who knows. The guards had let Heinrich, I mean my grandfather Henry, write the occasional letter back to the factory with instructions for running it, maybe names of suppliers, that kind of thing. He'd been hustled away so fast, he had no time to go over everything with the staff left to run the place in his absence."

"*I* know what you mean," Christy said. "I've seen a few of those letters. I didn't read them carefully, they just seemed to relate to running the factory. And luckily they were all in English, even though he never learned to write it well."

"If he'd written letters in German from internment, that could have made things worse for him," Adam commented.

"Aye, laddie. Good point. But some of the factory workers back in those days prob'ly knew German better than English, them that had moved over during the nineteen twenties and thirties. Anyroad, at least we should be able to read any letters we find."

Malky pulled the lid off the box near him, dropped it on

the floor, and began rummaging around. Adam imagined a busy, determined squirrel in the same posture: eyes sharp, face pointed down, and front paws curled over to search through dried leaves for an acorn.

"Wait, dear." Greta put her hand on Malky's shoulder. "Let's do this systematically. I'll get a couple of empty boxes and you can move things over when you've looked. Don't just glance at papers and toss them back in the same box."

Soon the search was organized, thanks to Greta, and before an hour had passed, some useful items had been found. There was an envelope labeled as Malky had mentioned, and a stack of black and white photographs, their edges curling, that showed the interior of the factory, including office spaces and the main factory floor that had housed kilns, where all the glassmaking took place.

Adam sighed when he found a large photograph, also black and white, of the long-gone wall of windows that faced the North Sea. "I sure wish that had survived."

"I know," Malky said. "Just makes me ill that the vandals smashed it."

Christy put down the papers she was looking at and grimaced. "It's all the *guard's* fault. Why didn't he do a better job?"

"*Nein* Christy!" Greta's command made Adam jump. "We must not speak ill of the dead. You don't know what really happened at the factory. The old man had to live with it his whole adult life. He made life a misery for his family besides. So I don't want to hear anything bad about poor Ronald. You kids, you have *no idea* what people had to do to survive back then, in any of the countries, Britain, Germany..."

Her voice trailed off and, fighting back tears, she busied herself pouring another round of tea and refilling the biscuit plates.

"The war is never far from her mind, even now," Malky explained to Adam. "As you know, she was born in Germany. Years after the war ended, mind you, but she would have heard stories of survival that none of us can begin to fathom."

"Sorry Dad, sorry Mum," Christy murmured. "I know, with Mr. Wilson gone now, I need to let go of my resentment."

Adam had waited while the family worked through Christy's outburst, and now he said, "I may have found something." He handed a letter to Malky. "It's signed by Heinrich, and it's short, just one scribbled page, but I think he's talking about museum glass."

Malky took it and read aloud. "Angus," he began, then looked up and explained to Adam that Angus was Heinrich's oldest child, a teenager at the time of Heinrich's internment, and Malky's late father. He continued, "Don't forget to keep the burrowed glass safe. Get it away from the factory as soon as possible." Malky looked up again. "He wrote 'burrowed' but he meant 'borrowed,' don't you think?"

The others took turns looking at the letter.

"He couldn't have meant the glass that was hidden in the coal chute, that we found, could he?" Adam asked.

"Nae," Malky said. "Far as I know, that glass was only put there later, after it became clear that the vandalism was going to continue. The letter is dated in early nineteen forty-one. This is one of his first letters. So the glass must have been important."

Christy meanwhile had been looking through the stack of photographs.

"Dad," she asked, "can you get your magnifier?"

"Aye lass." Malky ran to his office and returned with a heavy magnifying glass which he handed to her.

She remained seated, examining a small black and white photograph in her hand, and the others stopped what they were doing and watched.

"I'll let you all look yourselves," she said, "but I've found some old photos of Heinrich's office. In one there's a wall cabinet, and there are some glass pieces that I'm sure weren't made by Regenbogen. There's a little label in front of each, and a couple of photos show the labels in close-up. Darn, I can't make it out, this magnification isn't good enough."

"Can I see?" Adam asked, and Christy handed the photos to him. He used the magnifier function on his phone to look at one of the labels. "It says that the piece is on loan from the Museum of Antiquities in Edinburgh. Let's see, there's a date, oh, that's not the date of the loan, it's..."

Excited, he looked up. "It says that piece is over two thousand years old!"

Everyone took turns looking through Adam's magnifier, and a ripple of gasps and astonishment filled the room.

"So what *happened* to the glass?" Malky asked, clearly frustrated at not solving the puzzle. "It wasn't hidden along with the vases in the coal chute, and it certainly wasn't among the remaining glassware from when the factory was dismantled."

"Margaret has it now," Adam blurted out, then he clamped both hands over his mouth for a moment. "Oh no, that's supposed to be confidential!"

Christy stared at him in confusion. "Do you mean the red-haired woman, Margaret, who's visiting from Finlay? She was at dinner earlier tonight, when I came to meet you, and she didn't mention it. Or do you mean a different Margaret?"

Adam jumped to his feet, his phone in his hand. "I need to call Mum. I'm *really* sorry, I should have said nothing."

While Adam called his mother, Malky, William, and Christy cleared the boxes from the table and returned them to Malky's office. Greta went to the kitchen to prepare a new pot of tea.

Adam returned to the dining room a few minutes later and slumped into his seat. "That's a relief. No harm done, and the good news is I can explain what I said."

"Wait for Greta!" Malky went to the kitchen to get a bottle of white wine and glasses, which he handed around the table. "Maybe I'm being premature, but I sense something to celebrate?"

"I hope so." Adam gratefully accepted the glass of wine from Malky while Greta took her seat again. He knew he had to drive later, but the alcohol would help alleviate the sense of panic from his indiscretion.

"It's one of these long stories," he began, "and Margaret can give you the background sometime. The relevant part is that she told Helen and Richard, Ronald's son, that she's participating in a competition to find groatie buckies on beaches in Scotland, and at the same time help clear trash and raise awareness for keeping the coastline clean. Since it's for charity, Richard offered her his collection of groatie buckies from his old family home. It's been unoccupied for four years, as you probably know. He and Margaret went to his house and he gave her several biscuit tins that he said were full of groatie buckies. She was thrilled, as you can imagine."

He stopped to take another drink of wine, and Malky asked, "How does this relate to the museum glass, son?"

"Dear, let him tell the story!" Greta admonished Malky, something she seemed to do often.

Adam continued. "Margaret and Alistair drove back to their cottage in Fife, in Finlay, and that night Margaret opened the tins to move the shells into bags, to count them I guess. Inside each tin was a sealed box, with very old tape around it, and when she opened the boxes, each one contained an old piece of glass, with the little labels that we just saw in the old factory photographs."

"She's nae keeping the glass, is she?" Malky cried.

"Of course not," Adam said quickly. "Margaret's a lawyer. She understands that she's not the owner." Now he improvised the explanation that Helen had hurriedly given him over the phone.

Taking a deep breath, he said, "You weren't told about the glass yet because it had been in Ronald Wilson's house, I mean Richard's house, but Ronald was the most recent occupant before he went to the care home. With Ronald's

221

death, Helen thought that his lawyers might have barred access to it while they took an inventory for his estate. Making the glass discovery by Margaret public, even to your family, could have been seen as removing assets from Mr. Wilson's house. Mum was just keeping this under wraps until the estate is settled. I hope that makes sense. I'm sure Mum can explain it better."

"So Ronald *didn't* steal it," Christy said, looking around the table. "Right? Based on the letter from Heinrich, asking Angus to safeguard the borrowed glass, maybe Angus gave it to Ronald, who was the official factory guard after all, and told him to safeguard it until Heinrich came back?"

"I wonder why they didn't just send it back to the museum in Edinburgh, where it came from?" Adam mused.

"Probably thought it would be safer up here in the north," Greta suggested. "After all, thousands of children were being sent into the countryside from the cities, expecting the cities to be bombed. A few boys from Glasgow, I think they were of German descent, ended up in town here by mistake, from what I've heard. Anyway, makes sense to me that they kept the glass in Kilvellie. And a biscuit tin is as good a hiding place as anywhere."

Feeling like a lot had been accomplished, Adam said he had to get going, as he had an early start in the morning. Soon he was in his car heading north to his hotel, the evening's discussions swirling in his mind.

Chapter 40

Comfortable in sweats, Margaret was hard at work on her laptop in the bedroom of their suite, while Alistair and Helen met behind the closed door that connected to the main room. Helen had arrived looking like she was on a clandestine mission, and after a few words of explanation from Alistair, Margaret was happy to leave them to their privacy and catch up on researching groatie buckie beaches.

Her excitement at having thousands of groatie buckies from the biscuit tins had soon been replaced with disappointment that the tins, the groatie buckies, and the museum glass might all be taken away as evidence for the investigation into Ronald Wilson's death. She couldn't think of another reason why Helen had to meet with Alistair so urgently.

On the other side of the door, Helen picked up the yellow child's saw and the broken cane, both still in their plastic bags. The items had spent an hour on the coffee table, while Alistair sat in a chair, with Helen on the sofa, discussing what the evidence implied. After a lot of back and forth, imagining different scenarios, Alistair had agreed with Helen: a child's damage to the walking cane was not concrete evidence of causation in Ronald's death, let alone intent to do harm. Helen had visibly relaxed at that point, and Alistair realized it meant that, after all, Helen wouldn't report the death as suspicious.

Alistair was getting up to let Margaret know the meeting was over when Helen's phone rang: Adam, sounding distraught, Alistair guessed, judging from Helen's attempt to calm her son.

"You said *what*," was her initial reaction, but she had come to an internal decision and eventually told Adam that he could go ahead. She ended the call, put the cane and the saw in her bag, then asked Alistair to invite Margaret in to sit with them.

With tea all around, plus a glass of wine for Margaret at her request, to dull the anticipated disappointment at losing the groatie buckies, Helen explained what had just happened at the Greens' house.

"Adam went there for a social visit tonight, and Christy started talking about our earlier discussion at dinner, when I asked her if she'd ever come across information about glass borrowed from a museum, you know, among the glass factory records. Of course, I should have realized she'd tell Malky, and knowing him, he couldn't rest until he'd dug through the paper files.

"They actually turned up lucky and found some photographs of a display cabinet, pre-war I believe, with the museum glass pieces and the same labels that you described, Margaret. And they also found a letter that Henry sent to the factory, early in his internment. He asked his son, who would have been Malky's father, to remove the museum glass for safekeeping. Adam sent me the pictures he took of the photos and letter."

She stopped to drink her tea while Alistair and Margaret took turns looking at the photos on her phone, then she relaxed back on the sofa.

"You can probably guess what happened. Adam got caught up in the excitement and said that you, Margaret, have the glass now. He immediately realized his mistake and called me. I figured, since there won't be an investigation into Ronald's death, not if I have anything to do with it, Richard's house won't be sealed off as a possible crime scene, and it's fine for Malky's family to know the glass has been found."

"But Helen," Alistair said, "how did Adam explain the delay in telling them about finding something important that had been in the factory? Margaret found the glass a couple of days ago."

"I told him to come up with something about the lawyers needing the house secured so they could check it for things to include in Ronald's estate, and removal of anything, even biscuit tins, could have seemed suspicious. I hope they'll have bought that idea."

"Oh, they will," Alistair assured her. "Malky's family has great respect for you and Adam, especially when you found all that vintage glass for them, and now they have things to put in their own museum."

Margaret was impatient to ask a question, and she broke in. "I missed the part about concluding that Ronald's death is not suspicious. What about the damaged cane?" She looked back and forth at Alistair and Helen.

Helen took a long time before she finally replied. "All you need to know, Margaret, is that no human sawed the cane with intent to do harm to Ronald. Is that satisfactory?"

"I guess," Margaret said, after thinking for a few moments, "although it sounds like a *very* fine line, legally speaking."

"Even if it is a very fine line, as you lawyers call it, I, as senior police officer for Kilvellie-by-the-Sea, where the death occurred, am comfortable on this side of it. We'll leave it at that."

Helen stood up. "I'll be in touch about the museum glass. I'll talk to my friend in Edinburgh, the former museum director there. But between us, if I have any say, I'm not giving it to the current museum managers. After what they did to the apothecary garden, they don't deserve it. Maybe it can be displayed in Malky's new museum instead. Anyway, hope to see you before long."

Alistair said goodbye to Helen and closed the door to the room while Margaret moved to the sofa, holding her glass of wine, brow wrinkled in confusion.

"I still don't understand about Ronald's walking cane, Alistair. It was deliberately cut halfway through! I saw it with my own eyes!"

Alistair casually walked over to the minibar and helped himself to a beer. He opened it and took a long swig, then sat down on the sofa, grabbed the remote, and switched on the television. He slowly turned his head to face Margaret, trying to look bored.

"What was that, Tuppence, something about a walking cane? Never heard of it." And with a sly grin he looked back at the television.

So that was it. Margaret would probably never learn who had sawed the cane, and why, and how on earth Helen had concluded there was nothing further to investigate. But she knew one thing: based on what Alistair had just said, that cane would, by morning, have ceased to exist. After all, why else was Helen dressed in black, if not for some clandestine nighttime evidence destruction?

Oh well, she decided, she'd get the story out of Alistair one of these days. She remembered her reaction at the McMahon solicitors' office, feeling annoyed at being asked for her legal input for free, and the demands Helen was making on Alistair's professional expertise, also unpaid as far as she knew. But now, after realizing that Helen had done something to, in effect, make the case go away, she was relieved that she was not being paid, and her name would appear nowhere in any records.

Chapter 41

Alistair and Margaret were up early the next morning. With their bags packed, they were finishing breakfast in the beach-theme restaurant beside the lobby. There was no sign of Adam in the restaurant, even though Alistair thought he'd stayed overnight in the hotel. Maybe he'd had too much wine at the Greens and bunked on their sofa, or in a spare bed. Alistair texted to say goodbye and that he hoped to see Adam soon.

As they lingered over their tea, Margaret decided to raise her concerns about Helen's sergeant, Desmond.

"It's none of my business at all, but Alistair, do you think that Desmond is a competent officer? It's just, I mean, I've noticed that he seems gullible, and doesn't really see beyond the surface. When he asked what we were all doing at the care home, and I said I was visiting as a possible place for my parents in future, he didn't question why Adam was there too. Then when Emily said her granddad mentioned looking for museum glass in his storage boxes, Desmond assumed the man was confused, after seeing the banner for the new glass museum."

"You're not wrong," Alistair said. "And you wouldn't know this, but Helen kind of inherited him. He was already working at the station when she took over, and she'd heard nothing negative to suggest that she should replace him. I think she saw his familiarity with the town and the locals as a plus, especially with her being new."

Margaret nodded. "That familiarity can work both ways,

though. I'm sure he's less inclined to suspect people he knows of any wrong-doing."

Alistair thought for a moment. "Actually, that helps put something in perspective for me. It relates to the Greens' daughter Justine. I think that Desmond's father Richard, the former senior officer, may also have a tendency to be gullible. Seven years ago, when Justine was left behind in that cliff recess on the beach, Malky thought she was dead, from what William and Christy told him. Justine had fallen and hit her head, and they claimed they found no signs of life. You've seen that beach, but not during a storm. The waves were almost at the cliff, so William and Christy had to leave Justine and run home along the very back of the beach. Anyway, the end result was that Malky, their father, assumed that Justine was dead and swept away in the storm. Richard, the police officer at the time, took Malky's story at face value, and there was no record made of the incident. Richard was trying to protect Malky's children from being suspected of causing Justine's death, especially if her body washed up with evidence that she'd been hit on the head before she died, which happened when she fell."

"According to William and Christy," Margaret corrected him.

"Yes, and that's why I say Richard was being gullible. He knew Malky's family well, and he apparently didn't entertain the idea that any of them could have deliberately hurt Justine, let alone killed her. But ironically, Desmond's gullibility then played into it but he took the opposite approach. Before Justine disappeared, he used to see her and William pushing and shoving each other on the beach, and he thought Justine was being bullied. Then, after she crawled to safety up through a coal chute during that storm, she collapsed unconscious at the side of the road. Desmond found her in the hospital and took over, convinced that William was responsible and that Justine would be safer somewhere else. That's how she ended up in St. Andrews."

"Making lattes for you."

"Silver lining, but no latte was worth what the poor woman went through. So, yes, I agree that Desmond is gullible, maybe a bit dense, and on top of that, a bit too sure of himself. It's as if he feels like he's an authority on the town, and doesn't need much training beyond that."

"I guess Helen has her hands full."

"She may flee back to Edinburgh soon. Policing here is not what she thought she'd signed up for!" He glanced at his watch. "Let's get out of town before she calls me about something else."

While Alistair carried the overnight bags to the car, Margaret went to the front desk to check out. She looked up to see Adam dashing down the stairs two at a time. He was wearing socks, his running shoes in one hand.

"Careful!" she called out. "Don't slip!" In a few steps he was standing next to her.

"What's the hurry?" she asked.

"I didn't realize you and Alistair were leaving so early," he said, catching his breath.

Margaret laughed. "It's not that early. We've already had breakfast. Alistair said he texted you."

"That's why I ran down to catch you. Can you stay long enough for a quick chat? I haven't eaten yet and I hope I can still get breakfast." The woman at the desk heard and smiled at him, nodding her head. "Of course, Adam," she said. "I remember, you're a friend of our dear SarahBeth!"

Margaret kept herself from saying anything, but she was getting a little tired of hearing how wonderful SarahBeth was. Alistair returned to the lobby. "Are you ready to go?" he asked Margaret.

"I was." She signed the receipt and picked up her credit card from the desk. "Adam needs to talk to us. Or to you, not sure. He's over there getting breakfast."

"I keep thinking I'm done with Kilvellie," Alistair muttered as he accompanied Margaret into the restaurant. "I promise to make it quick, whatever it is," he added in a whisper.

Adam was at a table set for four by the front window, and Alistair and Margaret sat down with him. "It won't take long," Adam assured them. "I heard something at Malky's house last night. It didn't register at first, but it's been keeping me awake. Then I did some research this morning."

He stopped to give his order to a young man who'd been hovering nearby. Alistair and Margaret each ordered a cup of tea to be companionable while Adam ate.

"I thought we'd solved that loose end," Alistair said. "You and I both talked to your mother last night. The existence of the museum glass pieces, which Margaret has at home, is out in the open. Well, not public, but the relevant people here in Kilvellie know now."

"Yes," Margaret agreed. "Your mum said she'd be in touch with me about the glass, after she speaks to someone she knows in Edinburgh."

Adam nodded, then took a long drink from the mug of coffee that had been placed in front of him.

"It's about the six vandals," he said, "the young men who seem to have died when Ronald was guarding the factory in the forties. Are you happy to walk away from that, Alistair? The other day, you told Mum your theory about the boys being evacuated from Glasgow and maybe brought here in error."

Alistair waved his hand in dismissal. "I was just rambling on. With the memorial plaque removed from the chapel wall, and with Ronald gone, is there any point in anyone, especially us, pursuing it as a missing persons case or something? I don't know where we'd start, with almost nothing to go on. Even Kathryn couldn't find out anything about her own brother."

Adam smiled. "I thought you hated loose ends, Alistair? Anyway, last night at Malky's house we were wondering why the glass on loan from the Edinburgh museum wasn't returned at the beginning of the war, instead of being hidden somewhere in Kilvellie. It was Greta who mentioned that lots of children were sent from the cities to the countryside, to escape from possible bombing of the cities, and that the glass would also have been safer in Kilvellie than in a building in Edinburgh, that might have received bomb damage."

"Makes sense to me," Margaret said. "And the glass did stay safe, whatever the motive."

"Then, Greta mentioned that some young men from Glasgow, of German family origin, had ended up evacuated to Kilvellie by mistake. Before you say anything, Alistair, it was literally one sentence in the midst of an emotional discussion about the museum glass, and thinking about poor Henry in internment. It really didn't click until I was back in my room last night. But it seems consistent with your theory, however wild you think it might be."

"So what are you suggesting?" From Alistair's tone, Margaret could tell he was reluctant to be drawn into another town mystery. Or shameful secret. "Have you told your mother?"

"No, she had some business that kept her out late. I haven't talked to her yet today. I was planning to go to the station after breakfast and tell her. Desmond's still on compassionate leave, until his grandfather's funeral is arranged, anyway."

Alistair sipped his tea and looked at Margaret with eyebrows raised in a question. She nodded her head. "If you both want to go and speak to Helen this morning, that's okay with me. It's a nice day and the tide's out. I can search for sea glass marbles on the beach. I agree, Greta's comment does seem like a promising lead, especially since the six names on the memorial plaque are German."

Adam quickly finished his breakfast, then headed out of the front door of the hotel with Alistair and Margaret. The plan was for Alistair to drop Margaret off across the road from the site of the new glass museum; she could access the beach by the wooden stairway, then walk south to the town.

Adam was driving to the police station in his own car.

After her beach walk, Margaret would meet Alistair at the police station, and if he was done earlier, he would walk north on the beach and they'd meet somewhere in the middle. After that, they would head back to Finlay. That was the plan, anyway, but as Alistair drove away from dropping Margaret off, he had a feeling that Kilvellie, and its secrets, wasn't finished with him yet.

Chapter 42

Alistair soon caught up with Adam outside the front door of the police station. "Once more into the breach," he mumbled as Adam held the door open for him. Alistair was dressed in jeans and a light blue shirt, and his running shoes; just days before, he'd thought carefully about what to wear for meeting with Helen, but with all that had transpired since then, clothes were the least of his concerns for this return visit to the station.

"It shouldn't take long. Anyway, Mum always has good coffee and biscuits."

Alistair shook his head. "You just had breakfast! I don't know how you stay so thin."

"I spend a lot of energy worrying about Mum. Especially this trip. Oh, don't get me started about Ronald. But her deadline's up, so she should have called in for help this morning."

Alistair realized, to his dismay, that Helen must not have shared her conclusion about the broken cane with Adam. But he wasn't surprised: Adam would surely question her decision to discreetly dispose of the evidence, such as it was.

Changing the subject, Alistair said, "Let's leave that for now and concentrate on those missing six young men from all those decades ago. I feel like each of us knows one piece of information, and if we gather it all together, maybe it will make sense."

As Adam expected, Helen had made fresh coffee for him and Alistair, and a pot of tea for herself. However, it wasn't the usual Earl Grey scent that Adam was used to.

"Is that herbal tea, Mum?" he asked as they took seats in the conference room.

"Aye, I've been remembering back in Edinburgh, when I used to meet the museum director I mentioned. That museum, the antiquities one, had a historic apothecary garden, I guess they called it their Physic Garden, with medicinal plants and herbs. It was in a square courtyard in the center of the museum building. There were a few wrought iron chairs and tables among the plantings, and the small cafe served tisanes and tinctures and herbal teas, all historically authentic. As far as I know anyway. So, I hadn't had herbal tea in a while and I got some at the tea shop up the street. Anyway, enough about tea for now. Let's get started so Alistair and Margaret can get home."

"Margaret's fine staying on today," Alistair said. "I dropped her off to take the long stairs down to the beach, then she'll walk along into town."

Helen looked at Alistair, over her steamy mug of tea. "Is that wise? I'd think she'd be upset visiting the area where Ronald died."

"She's tougher than she looks. Next time you visit us in Finlay, remind her to tell you about her narrow escape from a lost dungeon, and discovering gold coins in a cellar."

Helen laughed. "Okay, that's put my mind at rest." She picked up a pen and began a new page on a pad of paper. She looked back and forth at her two investigators. "Yes, I should be using my tablet for notes, but call me old-fashioned. Who wants to start? I need a detailed list of what we know and don't know about the lads who may have disappeared in the war, at the factory. We have so many open questions. We think one lad was Kathryn Spears' brother, to be confirmed of course, but who were the others? What were their real names and ages? Did they run away, did they fall over the cliff, or did Ronald and/or Henry push them off the cliff, much as I hate to think ill of those two men?"

It Continued with the Cowries

Adam began by describing what Greta had said the previous evening, and watched as his mother wrote, "Talk to
Greta" as the first item on the list. Alistair offered what information he knew: his discussion with Emily the previous
week, Ronald's letter to Alistair, "correcting the record" as it
were and denying that he had killed six German boys at the
glass factory in the nineteen forties. Helen produced her
transcription of Ronald's hastily-written letter to Mrs.
Ramsay, AKA Kathryn Spears, a letter that Ronald's solicitor
Claude clearly wanted kept from the police.

Alistair added that Kathryn Spears' brother, a young
teenager at the time, was lost during the war, according to
Kathryn. He'd been evacuated from Glasgow to Kilvellie
Towers, as far as Kathryn knew, an old manor home ten
miles from the town of Kilvellie, but that building had burned
early in the war, and all records were apparently lost.

Alistair also described the now-missing memorial plaque
that he'd seen, twice, in the seaside chapel north of Kilvellie.
The six names of boys, or men, engraved on the plaque,
matched the six names in Ronald's wartime diaries of the
looting in the glass factory, when he'd been a guard there.

Finally, Helen reminded them that those same six names
had been given to the care home, when the late Ronald
moved in four years earlier. He claimed the men were relatives who'd combined resources to pay for Ronald's stay in
the home, paying for three years up front, which itself was
unusual for someone of his advanced age. When Ronald's
son Richard had learned of the names recently, he denied
any knowledge of them, saying that if they were relatives,
they were very distant ones.

With her list complete, Helen placed the printed version
of Ronald's letter to Kathryn on the table so they could all
look at it. Alistair read the essential parts aloud:

"I have been too embarrassed and ashamed to tell you
this, but now that I am gone and my family won't be subject
to the shame of my deeds, I am writing to explain what hap-

pened to your brother. I know you have wondered about him for many decades and for that I am more sorry than I can say.

"In 1944, he was among a group of six lads who Henry Green, or Heinrich Gruener as he was known during his internment, had employed to help clean up after the destruction of the World War One memorial window at the old glass factory. Henry hoped to gather as many names of the dead as could be found, and construct a new window, adding the names of Kilvellie's men and women lost during World War Two as well. I was there helping to supervise the work, and I took a break indoors. Henry was up in the office. It faced the road, and he told me later he didn't see anything.

"When I came back out the boys were gone. At first I thought they'd run off, but I noticed that the cliff edge, near where they'd been working, looked rougher than it had earlier. I got down on hands and knees and crept closer to the edge. The tide was in, and all six boys were in the water. Kathryn, I'm sorry, but they all drowned.

"I learned later that the boys had been evacuated from Glasgow at the start of the war, but no one ever came to Kilvellie to bring them back home, even after the Allies landed in Normandy and it seemed the chance of Scotland being bombed was less than in 1939 and 1940. Henry and I agonized over what to do. The waves were pounding against the cliff and we could see the lads were all dead far below us, either drowned right off, or smashed against the cliff.

"Of course we called the police station and they managed to get a lifeboat dispatched, but the tide had started going out by then and they didn't find any trace of the boys."

Alistair sighed, shaking his head, and replaced the letter on the table. "Reading it again, after spending that afternoon with Kathryn, I feel so bad for her, never knowing what happened to her brother. But at the same time, I can't believe that this confession would give her any sense of peace."

"I agree," Helen said. "As I've thought about all this, it

occurs to me that someone must be working to keep this information from getting out. We had Claude grab the original of this letter from me after I steamed it open, and we have the fact of the nineteen forty-four ledger from this police station missing. And now, the memorial plaque in the chapel removed, supposedly for repair, but what if it's never returned to the wall? It's as if these boys, young men I mean, are being erased from the town's history."

"What about the lifeboat?" Adam asked. "Ronald's letter says they called out the lifeboat, but there was no trace of the boys."

"Maybe they survived after all?" Helen ventured.

"If Ronald's account is true, that they fell into the waves that were crashing against the cliffs, I don't see how," Alistair said. "Maybe today they'd have a chance, with that modern wooden stairway nearby, but back during the factory days, as far as I know, there was no escape route along the cliff. They would have had to swim a couple of miles to access the section of beach near the town, where the cliffs end."

Adam pointed out, "There was *one* escape route, the coal chute that Justine crawled up seven years ago, that opens onto the beach. But, now I think of it, it would have been virtually impossible to find the coal chute from underwater."

"And if the tide was receding," Helen continued, "they probably got swept out to sea quickly, even assuming any of them survived the fall into the water and could have been capable of finding that one route to safety. No, I think we should take it as fact that they died. Question was, where did they come from, how did they really die, and why does there seem to be a cover-up? At least, that's what it's beginning to look like."

"I can go back and talk to Kathryn again," Alistair suggested. "Remember, I offered to hang up a picture for her, that family photo, so I could stop in and see if she still needs it done."

"That's an idea," Helen agreed. "And I wonder if Claude

gave Ronald's letter to her. It seems he's obligated to, a request from a client to be carried out upon the client's death. How about if I talk to Claude, and Alistair, maybe you and Adam could visit Kathryn? Oh, I forgot, Margaret's on the beach and she'll be expecting to go back to Finlay soon."

"I'll call her and tell her to take her time on the beach," Alistair said. "I don't think she's in a big hurry to get home. In fact, with all those groatie buckies from Richard's house, maybe she won't need to go searching for them after all."

Chapter 43

Alistair and Adam headed off in Alistair's car for the short drive to the Seaview Manor Home. A call to the main desk had confirmed that Mrs. Ramsay would enjoy a repeat visit. Margaret had been understanding, and told Alistair she was happy to spend another hour or two on the beach, or looking at the shops. They'd find each other at lunchtime.

Helen did not have as much luck. After receiving no reply when she called Claude McMahon (or, she thought, maybe he saw who was calling and was avoiding her), she left the station and walked along the main street to the Victorian mansion that housed the McMahon law firm. A printed sign on the law office door, one flight up, indicated that the office was closed until the following Monday, and emergency calls would be taken by an answering service, with a local number provided.

"Darn it," she muttered, standing outside the building and wondering what to do instead. She was tempted to call the service and ask for Claude or Elise to return her call, but perhaps Adam and Alistair would learn from Kathryn if the letter had in fact been delivered. Or, Helen wondered, would Claude have substituted another letter, or not given Kathryn anything from Ronald? That led back to Helen's suspicion that something was being covered up.

She was about to return to the police station when she heard a woman calling her name, and she looked across the street to see Greta waving. She hadn't seen Greta for over a week, and noticed a change in her clothing. Until now, Helen assumed that Greta, thanks to her frugal lifestyle with Malky, had sewn her own clothes from Provençal-pattern tablecloths and other charity shop finds. Now she wore a stylish navy pantsuit with a matching blue and white scarf, and carried a designer-logo purse. Still possibly resale shop purchases, Helen thought, but less of a "make do and mend" wartime look.

After waiting for a couple of cars to go by, Helen crossed the street and joined her.

"What brings you into town?" Helen asked. "You and Malky must be so busy with planning the new glass museum. I heard that you're designing the cafe. I hope you'll be baking for it."

"*Ja.* Sorry, I mean, yes. I've just been speaking German for an hour with my German friends. It takes me a few minutes to switch back to English."

Helen hesitated; she really wanted to speak to the solicitors, but decided this was a chance to follow up from what Adam had told her. "Greta, do you have time for a quick chat?"

She watched Greta's face take on a worried expression.

"Nothing serious," Helen assured her. "I didn't mean at the station. Maybe the bakery, if that's convenient?"

The popular bakery and tea shop was nearby, and the two women entered and found a quiet table. Business had slowed between breakfast and lunch, and they were served quickly.

"What do you need to talk to me about?" Greta asked, looking nervous again.

Helen wanted to pat Greta's hand to assure her that there really was nothing serious, but didn't know her well enough. Instead, she explained that her son Adam had mentioned his visit to the Greens the night before, and that he'd repeated Greta's comment about some young men who were evacuated to the town of Kilvellie in the early years of the war.

"I think Adam said the boys, or teenagers perhaps, were from German families?"

"Oh," Greta asked cautiously, "are you wondering if they might have been enemy soldiers?"

"No, nothing like that. I only mentioned their background because it could be important for some research I'm doing. Have you ever visited the little chapel, it's near the cliff just north of town?"

"Yes, I have been there now and again for a wedding and a couple of funerals, but it was a long time ago. When Malky and I were first married, he still had some elderly family back then, but none left now."

"When you were in the chapel, did you ever look at the brass plaques on the walls, the memorial plaques, I mean?"

"*Nein*, no. It's a small chapel and always there were big crowds. I have never seen the plaques, you call them? Why is this important?"

"You know Alistair, I think, a friend of my son Adam?"

Greta thought for a moment. "Oh, yes, he's the man who helped SarahBeth, when she was hurt after the ballet. And wasn't he one of the men who helped identify her as Justine's twin? So yes, I know who you mean. Is he in town? I really should thank him properly. Invite him over for tea."

Helen decided not to confirm that Alistair was in fact in town, or the poor man would never get home. "Alistair visited the chapel recently. He showed me a picture he took of a memorial plaque with the names of six German men. The whole text was written in German, but a volunteer working in the chapel translated it for Alistair. I don't remember the exact wording, but in addition to the six names, it said that they had been dedicated to the deep, which I believe means they were lost at sea, in July of nineteen forty-four."

Greta had been listening carefully, and now she interrupted. "That would have been soon after your D-Day, is that correct? Maybe they drowned at Normandy? Oh, wait, you said the plaque is in German, with German names. Why is it

241

here in a Scottish church?"

Helen realized she was confusing Greta, and felt herself redden with embarrassment. What was she thinking, discussing events from the Second World War with this sweet German woman, whose parents and grandparents, God only knew, could have had roles battling the Allies? Or could themselves have fought at Normandy, on the other side.

"I'm *sorry* Greta, I'm being so insensitive. I need to finish telling you what the plaque said. If the six men did drown, and we have no proof of that, there was a witness who may have seen it, from the clifftop near here, in Kilvellie."

"Ah, now I see." Greta seemed to recover and took a long sip of tea. "And, who is this witness, may I ask?"

"That's part of the mystery. The witness's name has been scratched out. We don't know when the plaque was installed, nor do we know when it was defaced, to remove the name."

"Maybe we can go and look at it together? Since it's in German, perhaps I can read something in it that the volunteer didn't understand correctly."

Helen shook her head. "That's a kind offer, Greta, but the plaque has been removed for restoration. I haven't been able to reach anyone to ask about it. There seems to be no minister permanently attached to the chapel, and no website. I found a telephone number but it's answered by a message, at least the few times I've tried."

"I think I can help you at last," Greta said, smiling. "One of the women in my German group has lived here her whole life. It was her grandparents who came over, just after the Great War as you call it here. Probably to work in the glass factory, I've never asked her that. But her parents learned German, as well as English, and then she grew up speaking German fluently as a child. She joined our group to keep up her language. Most of us in the group were born in Germany, you see. We like it here, but we also enjoy speaking our childhood language."

"And do you think she knows something about the

chapel, your friend in the German group?"

"Oh, *ja*! That's why I mention her. She is, what you call it, the curator of the chapel. She must know the history you're interested in. I mean, the plaque."

"That's great. Do you think she would agree to speak with me?"

"I don't see why not. I know she's around, I just saw her at our meeting. Her name is Frau Endicott. Sorry, I only know her through the German group and that's how we address each other. Her first name is Elise. She works in the law office, in that old Victorian house."

It was too much to be a coincidence, Helen thought. She thanked Greta, not revealing that the law office was closed for a few days. She'd assumed that Elise was away, but perhaps not.

"You don't happen to have a home number, or address for her?" Helen asked. "I don't like to visit her at work when it's a personal matter, you know what I mean?"

"Of course!" Greta obligingly took out her phone and read the information to Helen. "I know I'm supposed to just press a button and send all the contact details to your phone, but I'm not very good with this new device," she explained.

As Helen sipped her tea, she pretended to be attentive while Greta described the progress with the new glass museum, but in her mind she was already planning a visit to Frau Endicott, and with any luck, some background on the memorial plaque. After the two women had finished their tea, they said a warm goodbye, with Greta reaching to shake Helen's hand.

"I have so enjoyed our chat, Helen. Please remember to tell Alistair to get in touch so he can come for cake."

Outside, they parted ways, with Greta heading across the street to visit her children Christy and William at their glass studios, and Helen to call Alistair and Adam to find out how they were getting along with Kathryn, Mrs. Ramsay.

Chapter 44

Helen's calls to Alistair and Adam both went to voice mail, so she left messages for one of them to call her when they had finished visiting Kathryn; presumably they'd both set their phones to silent. It was eleven thirty, so she decided she could legitimately close the police station office for the lunch hour. For her quick trip to the law office, which turned into tea with Greta, she'd left a sign on the door instructing any visitors to call her mobile phone if it was important, or to call 999 if it was an emergency. So far, it seemed she'd gotten away with leaving the station for longer than she meant to.

Inside, she tidied up her hair and replaced her hat, grabbed her satchel and a notebook, then locked the front door behind her, this time with the official "Closed for Lunch Noon to One" sign and the usual list of numbers to call for emergencies. She'd be glad when Desmond returned to work and the station would have someone on duty all day.

She'd recognized the street name when Greta gave her Elise's address, and felt confident that she could find it quickly by walking down a nearby street, past Malky's house, and then a right turn toward the harbor. She expected that the houses in Elise's part of town would have lovely views up and down the coast. Partway into her walk, Helen realized she should have told someone where she was going, and not rely solely on being reached on her mobile phone, but she wouldn't be gone long.

Thinking of her phone, she patted her jacket pocket, then

her shoulders slumped: she'd left it lying on her desk when she'd hurried into the station and back out again. Well, she was more than halfway to her destination now, so might as well keep going; maybe Elise wouldn't be home.

She turned along the street and looked at house numbers, admiring the well-kept gardens and neat facades of the single family homes. Not for the first time, she realized how lucky Kilvellie was to have avoided the derelict look of former coal-mining towns elsewhere in Scotland and in England.

She was nearing the correct house, based on the decreasing numbers, and she could see a woman crouching over and working in the front garden; she recognized Elise, although now in gardening clothing instead of the skirt suit she'd been wearing at the law office. In a denim shirt, baggy beige canvas trousers, and her brown hair swept up by a blue scarf, she looked at ease.

"Hello," Helen called out when she approached, and Elise stood up quickly. Her relaxed look of a moment before became guarded.

"Hello, Officer Griffen. Are you in the neighborhood on police business?"

"Perhaps," Helen replied, smiling. "May I speak to you for a minute?"

"Yes." Elise took off her gardening gloves and dropped them into a nearby wooden basket, then led Helen toward the open front door. On either side of the door, low bay windows faced the garden, and as Helen entered, she could see built-in seating areas in each; botanical-print pillows and upholstery served to extend the garden into the house.

Elise motioned toward a kitchen area further along the central hallway. "Can you have a seat in there? I'll have a quick wash and then I'll make some tea, only if you have time, that is."

Helen thanked her, but got the impression that the offer of tea was more for politeness, not because Elise wanted to sit down for a chat with the police. Perhaps the difficult inter-

245

action at the solicitors' office, over Ronald's letter to Mrs. Ramsay, had left a bad feeling. Helen hadn't missed that Elise referred to her as officer, not Helen, as she had done when they first met.

After what seemed a long time, ten minutes by Helen's watch, Elise returned. Helen was surprised that she had changed from her gardening clothes into jeans and a yellow cotton pullover, the kind Helen associated with cool weather beach wear. Her hair looked newly styled as well.

"You didn't need to go to any bother on my account," Helen said. She was sitting at the kitchen table, facing out at the back lawn, and beyond it, a view of the town harbor where fishing boats and pleasure craft bobbed in the gentle waves. Seeing the pier reminded Helen of the day when her sergeant Desmond had brought Malky Green and a teenage boy to the station after they had an altercation on that very pier. A dispute over a bucket of marbles. Was it only a couple of weeks ago? Helen felt like she'd been on the job far longer.

While Helen was admiring the view, lost in memories, Elise had prepared two cups of tea; milk and sugar were already on the table, along with a bamboo container of spoons and other silverware, and paper napkins in a green ceramic holder. As Helen poured milk into her tea, she thought she'd been right about the tea not being offered in friendship: other hosts would put a full pot on the table, a sign to linger and chat. The single cup, in contrast, served as an egg timer; finish the cup and then time's up.

Clearly, she had to get straight to the point. "Elise, I learned today that you work as a curator in the little chapel just north of town. A couple of tourists were there recently, and they expressed interest in a historic memorial plaque. I'm still new to the town, as you know, and I want to be in a better position to answer questions. Not in detail, mind you, I understand there is at least one volunteer there."

Elise listened with a growing look of confusion on her face. Helen wondered if she was talking to the wrong person—maybe Greta was mixed up?

But Elise finally responded. "As curator, I do have information about the chapel, yes. There's not much I can tell you beyond what's in the information pamphlets there. Perhaps your tourists didn't see them?"

"That may be the case, but anyway, when I went to look at that particular memorial plaque, it had been removed. For restoration, I believe?"

"Yes, possibly that was it. One plaque has been removed." Elise drank most of her tea in one go and put the near-empty cup on the saucer. "Sorry I can't be more help. I don't know how long the restoration will take, it's out of my hands. And if there's nothing else?" She edged her chair backwards as if to bolt.

"Um," Helen said, trying to prolong the conversation and move it toward their meeting at the solicitor's office, and the letter from Ronald to Mrs. Ramsay, but she realized she hadn't planned a believable transition. "Do you have any photographs of that plaque? Maybe in a pamphlet?"

"I'm afraid not," came the immediate answer. "Since that one is in need of repair, we didn't put a photograph of it in, and I don't have any here at the house. So if there is nothing...?" She shifted her chair back a few more inches and gulped down the rest of the tea, but was being just polite enough not to stand up while Helen was still drinking her tea. *Diplomacy by tea*, Helen thought to herself.

To delay her departure, she resorted to a time-worn excuse. "Mind if I use your toilet? I walked here from the station, and..."

"Of course," Elise said, a request that could hardly be refused no matter how much one wanted a visitor to leave. "I'll go out to the garden and gather my tools. I was just finishing up there. The loo is in the hall, under the stairs. But don't rush, finish your tea first."

With that, Elise stood up, took her own cup and saucer to the sink, and left to go back outside. *Strange*, Helen

247

thought, one minute she's hurrying the conversation along, and the next, she tells Helen to take her time. *And that's what I'll do*, Helen decided. In fact, she might as well take the long way around, by way of the living room that she could see through an opening in the wall of the kitchen. She was curious to examine the fabric of the window seat pillows: that would be her excuse, if Elise even noticed.

She finished her tea and placed the cup and saucer in the sink as her host had done, then picked up her belongings. In the adjoining living room, she glanced around at the decor; if Elise had been more welcoming, Helen would have asked for the source of her furniture and wallpaper, or perhaps a decorator had chosen everything. Helen had never been to Florida, but her immediate sense was that this was a Florida room, full of sun, with white wicker cushioned chairs, and decorated in shades of yellow and pink. Potted palms on stands softened the corners.

Her eyes were drawn to an untidy open cardboard box that sat on the floor next to the window seat. An item glimmered gold in the sun, and Helen wondered if it was a decorative mirror, something she'd been meaning to pick up for the station residence. Maybe the box was ready to take to a charity shop. She approached the box to have a look at the mirror, then realized she was looking down at a brass memorial plaque: in German. She pulled it out for a better look. Yes, there was the scratched-out name, the mysterious witness.

Glancing outside in case Elise was staring back in, Helen looked down at the box again, and this time she exclaimed aloud, seeing the missing police department ledger from nineteen forty-four. What on earth was it doing in Elise's house? She picked it up and headed toward the front door, preparing to confront Elise, but she turned at the sound of a man's voice. "Sorry, Officer Griffen, I can't let you take that."

Helen spun around, and now her confusion was complete: she was standing face to face with the other solicitor,

It Continued with the Cowries

Claude McMahon. It was little consolation that his scalded hand was done up like a mitten in a fresh white bandage. He was dressed casually, in jeans, a cream button-down shirt, and a quilted khaki vest that someone might wear for hunting in the country. As she heard Elise enter the house again and close the front door, Helen suddenly realized she *should* have told someone where she was going.

She didn't even have her phone with her to be located. And now a ghastly thought took hold: had the story about Bobby and the toy saw all been a distraction, and were the two people in the room with her the *real* culprits in Ronald's death?

Chapter 45

Adam and Alistair said a last farewell to Kathryn Spears, waving to her from the open door of her care home room. It had been a pleasant visit, but they'd learned nothing new. They hadn't overtly asked about receiving a letter from Ronald, but Kathryn was so chatty, she surely would have mentioned if Claude or Elise had delivered it.

Outside in the sun, they stood next to Alistair's car and checked their phones: each had a message from Helen, identical.

"Do you want to call or should I?" Alistair asked.

"I'll call her while you check in with Margaret. Looks like you and she can finally take off for Finlay."

But Adam only reached Helen's cell phone voice mail. A call to the police station main number also went to voice mail. He checked the time.

"It's almost one o'clock. She probably dashed out to get some food and can't answer while she's ordering, or talking to someone. Let's head to the station."

Neither of them needed any food; Kathryn had insisted that they have lunch served in her room, as her guests. The old dear was clearly missing her time with Ronald, so they felt it was the least they could do.

At the police station, the front door was locked. Alistair had reached Margaret, and she told him she was on the beach.

"Did you see Helen anywhere?" Alistair asked her.

"No, but I've been on the beach since I last saw you. Can't

you call her?"

"She's not answering her phone. Maybe she's in her residence. Her car and the police cruiser are both here." He tried the office number again while Adam tried her cell phone, and they looked at each other in confusion: they could hear both phones ringing inside the station.

"Something's not right," Adam said.

"Really?" Alistair asked. "She may be in the bathroom in the residence and isn't hearing the phone."

"No." Adam pounded his fist on the front door to the station. "The office phone also rings in the residence. She's had time to answer it by now."

Adam ran around to the back of the station and tried the separate door into the residence, but it was locked too. Returning to the front, he peered into the station through all the barred windows: the office and conference room were empty.

"What if she's had a heart attack in the residence side, or been taken ill?"

"Wait, Adam, if she's there, why is there a sign on the door saying she's at lunch? She would have taken it down when she got back, right?"

"Yes, but it's past her lunch hour. We have to check inside. Desmond must have a key to the station so I'll call him."

To Adam's relief, Desmond was on his way through town, heading to his sister Emily's to drop off more things from his grandfather's room at the care home. He said he'd be at the station shortly.

***

Minutes later, they stood inside the station, completely confused. There was no sign of Helen, no notes, no address where she might have had an emergency call. Desmond checked in with the local emergency dispatchers and with

251

the nearby police stations, and no one had any reports of emergencies that Helen might have been called to, or that involved Helen herself.

"I'll call Dad," Desmond said. "He's been clearing the old house to put on the market, so if he's there, he can get over here quickly. In fact, maybe they're together? I should have thought of that first."

Richard had not seen or heard from Helen, so he too drove to the police station while they brainstormed about what to do next. After discussing various options, they began calling around to people Helen knew. Emily hadn't heard from her today, nor had Christy, William, or Malky. However, Christy did volunteer that her mother, Greta, stopped by after having tea with Helen, but that had been a couple of hours earlier.

With Greta being the person who had seen Helen most recently, Alistair and Adam drove to Malky's house, hoping to catch Greta there, and even better, Helen.

***

Things were at an impasse in Elise's house. She and Claude had taken Helen back into the kitchen, and now Helen was sitting on the kitchen table banquette, her back to the window. Her two captors sat in chairs, glaring at her across the table. The police station ledger and the brass memorial plaque from the chapel sat on the table between them, after Claude had wrenched them from Helen's hands.

"This is outrageous!" Helen repeated, trying to keep her nerve. She'd faced down criminals in Edinburgh, but these two legal professionals scared her more, if only for the incongruity. "What is the *matter* with you two? What right do you have to keep me here?"

"What right do *we* have?" Claude demanded. "What right do *you* have, coming into someone's private home, looking around their private property and helping yourself?"

"I'm only interested in the police ledger," Helen insisted. "That's police property, and I've been looking for it. Why is it here?"

The two exchanged a glance before Claude spoke again. "Didn't Richard, I mean, former Officer Wilson, didn't he explain the situation to you?"

Helen looked at him blankly. "*What* situation?"

Claude shook his head in disgust. "You are in Kilvellie for all of five minutes, and already you've had Malky Green hauled into the police station, you've exposed young Desmond as a kidnapper, you've as good as accused Richard of covering up Justine's disappearance, and now you're poking around in Elise's house. Not to mention that on your watch, poor old Ronald Wilson went over a cliff and died. I hate to see what you'll do in your next two weeks on the job."

"That's right, Helen!" Elise took over, just as irate as Claude. "You came here from Edinburgh, with its fancy festivals, millions of tourists, museums, the lot. Kilvellie only ever had two things going for it. First, the coalmines kept lots of people employed. Then, the glass factory kept people employed after the mines closed down. Because of the glass factory, we were spared the fate of other towns that relied on the mines. Look around our town, you don't see shuttered businesses, graffiti, pawn shops, do you? No, we have a good thing going here and we intend to keep it that way."

"But, but..." Helen spluttered, "I want the same thing for the town! What is the problem?"

Claude shook his head. "The *problem*, Helen, is you. You're asking too many questions." He sighed and repeated, more emphatically, "What's the matter with Richard? He should have explained things when you took over."

The two captors fell silent. Helen sat and fumed, growing increasingly nervous. She was tempted to use the old cop show line that "back-up was on the way," but in Kilvellie, there was no back-up: there was her, now captive, and there was Desmond, on leave and clearing his grandfather's room, blissfully unaware that his boss might be in serious trouble.

And Adam and Alistair? They'd likely be wondering where she was, but would assume she was having a private lunch or meeting somewhere, with her phone turned off. She just had to wait it out, hoping her captors were not having murderous thoughts.

Chapter 46

A few blocks away, Adam and Alistair knocked sharply on Malky's front door.

"Oh, hello!" Malky cried when he opened the door. "Goodness, were we expecting you? Come on in, Greta's just taking a pie out of the oven." He stood aside, holding the door wide, but Adam said, "Sorry Malky, we're on a mission. Is Helen here by chance?"

"Nae, laddie. Like I said on the phone, I havnae seen her today."

"Can we speak to Greta?" Adam asked next, and Malky called to his wife. She joined Malky in the foyer, wiping her hands on a dishtowel.

She smiled expectantly. "Are you coming in for pie?"

"Nae, dear, they're looking for Helen."

"Oh, I haven't seen her for a couple of hours at least. We had tea in town."

"Did she say where she was going after?" Adam persisted. "The station is locked and she's left her mobile in there. We can't reach her."

"Let's see," Greta began, agonizingly slowly. "She wanted to get in touch with my friend Elise, Frau Endicott from my German group. We were talking about, oh yes, Elise's curator work at the chapel. Helen was interested..."

But Adam and Alistair were turning to dash away. "Thanks Greta!" Alistair yelled back over his shoulder. "We'll go to Elise's office."

"Wait!" Greta called out, but they were jumping into the

car and didn't hear her.

"What's going on?" Malky asked as he closed the door.

Greta sighed. "If they expect to find Helen at the McMahon office, they're out of luck. Elise took a few days off, she told me. She's probably at home working in the garden. I'll call and ask if Helen is there."

A call to Elise's home went to voice mail, but Greta didn't leave a message. "Let's drive over there and tell her Adam's looking for Helen. I need to return a baking dish anyway."

With a white porcelain pie dish in her hand, Greta accompanied Malky to their car and they drove the short distance to Elise's house, parked nearby, and approached along the sidewalk.

"Something's not right," Greta murmured to Malky, pointing to an upturned basket on the grass, with gardening gloves, seedlings, and newly picked carrots strewn about. "She never leaves her gardening things such a mess. I wonder if she's okay."

Closer to the house, they looked in the window and could see through the Florida room to the kitchen. They recognized Helen, in her uniform, sitting behind the kitchen table, almost as if she was trapped. She was facing Elise and Claude, who was on his feet with his fist raised and was yelling at Helen. His voice carried all the way to where Malky and Greta stood, shocked.

"This looks *bad*." Malky pulled Greta away and out of view from inside the house. "Wait here," he said, and he ran back to their car to fetch something, formulating a plan as he went; no point in calling the police, he realized.

***

Alistair and Adam stood on the steps leading up to the front door of the Victorian mansion that housed the McMahon solicitors' office, increasingly frustrated. With the upstairs office closed, where would Helen have gone next, they asked each other.

"I wonder if it was so urgent that she went to see Elise at home, wherever that is?" Adam asked.

"Let's call Greta back. If she's friends with Elise, she must know."

But calls to Greta and Malky's home number, and both their mobile phones, went to voice mail.

"I'm beginning to think the whole phone system has a glitch," Alistair mumbled. "Why is no one answering?" He looked up and saw Richard and Desmond, who were also searching the town, questioning shop assistants and cafe staff. Alistair waved for the father and son to come across the road.

"Anything?" Richard asked. "I'm getting so worried. It's not like her at all."

"And we keep calling the hospital," Desmond added, "in case she's been taken ill, but no luck there."

Adam explained about their conversation with Greta, but that the office door upstairs had a sign indicating that the office was closed until the next Monday.

Richard was visibly shaken. "I wonder if she's up there?" He peered up at the windows above the front door, as if to get a glimpse in.

"But the office is closed, Dad," Desmond said. "Why would they put the sign out if someone's up there?"

Richard put both hands on his son's shoulders. "There's things you don't know yet, son, that I will tell you eventually. But for now, we have to get in there and look for Helen. Son, run back to the station. We have keys for these old buildings in case they have an emergency. They've never been upgraded with sprinklers and such like most places in town. You know where the keys are, right?"

"Aye, Dad. I'll be back soon."

Desmond took off at a run; the police station was a few buildings away on the other side of the main street, and the three others watched Desmond clumsily dodge surprised tourists and shoppers. He was out of uniform, and Richard realized that bystanders might wonder if they should report him as a possible thief or shoplifter.

He took the initiative, walking up to some people who'd stopped to stare, cell phones poised in their hands. "Nothing's wrong, folks," he said loudly. "Just forgot my keys and he's gone to fetch them."

Fifteen minutes later, all four men were back on the street, having checked McMahon's office. Alistair called Margaret to give her an update, but the call went to voice-mail. He shook his head, frustrated at not reaching her. He assumed she'd wandered further north on the beach, away from the town, and perhaps the rising cliffs were interfering with cell reception.

He looked up when Richard spoke. "Helen's not in there, clearly, and neither are the solicitors. I suggest we start with Elise's house. It's just beyond where Malky and Greta live, so a quick drive."

They piled into two vehicles, Richard's and Alistair's, and Alistair and Adam followed Richard and Desmond along the main road, a left turn and past Malky's house, then a right. The road headed downhill toward the harbor, and Alistair slowed when Richard put his arm out of the window to point at a nearby open parking spot, which Alistair took. Richard parked a little further beyond, and they all regrouped.

"That's Elise's house two doors down," Richard pointed out. "It seems odd for the four of us to arrive at her front door, so how about if I take Alistair with me. I can't imagine there's anything wrong, but I don't want you panicking, Adam, since it's your mum we're looking for."

"And Alistair's stronger," Desmond commented. "I remember when they were pulling down the boulders on the beach..." But his comments went unnoticed as Alistair and Richard set off at a fast pace for the house.

258

Chapter 47

Unaware that help was on the way, Malky and Greta hovered in the side garden at Elise's, hidden from street view by a tall hedge that separated the front and back gardens. A narrow and well-trimmed archway through the hedge provided access back and forth.

"How about if I distract Elise, and if she moves away from the table, maybe Helen can get out?" Greta suggested.

"Aye, dear, I'm thinking the same. What do you usually do when you visit her? Do you knock on the front door?"

"No, her kitchen looks out to the back garden, so I go around the back and in the kitchen door. If I do that now, she'll see me through the window, since she's facing that way. If Claude goes to the door instead, I'll run back here and to the car."

"Good plan." Malky had a large paper shopping bag, the top rolled over, and something was shifting around inside. He was holding it closed with both hands. Greta decided not to ask what was in it: some fierce small mammal, a stoat or a weasel for all she knew. Malky must be improvising, one of his crazy schemes. She walked along the side of the house, and then, with a wave to Malky, she held the white pie dish up high to get Elise's attention.

Malky returned to the front of the house and silently tried the front door handle; he exhaled with relief, finding it unlocked, so he eased the door open until he could hear what was going on inside.

"Oh, no, it's Greta!" Elise cried to Claude. "And I left the back door unlocked, so she may try to come in. I'll get rid of her."

As soon as Elise was away from the table and opening the back door, Malky chose his moment. Opening the front door wide, he yelled as loud as he could, "Helen! This way! Now!"

He heard a shoving sound, and moments later Helen came running into the hallway, not looking back.

"Malky, thank God! I, I..."

"Not now, lass. Go to the garden, outta my way!"

With his first sight of Claude at the far end of the hallway, breaking into a run to catch Helen, Malky upended the bag over the hall floor. Hundreds of marbles of all colors ricocheted back and forth between baseboards, streaming like a rainbow of rapids toward where Claude had been joined by Elise.

Both screeched as the marbles rolled underfoot and sent the pair flying and landing in a disheveled mess on the floor. "Damn you, Green," Claude yelled as he struggled to untangle himself from Elise's flailing arms and get to his feet. But he needn't have bothered; Richard and Alistair arrived just in time to help the two former captors right themselves, then secured them on the kitchen banquette.

Malky stood by watching proudly while Helen returned, this time with Adam and Desmond, who she'd found waiting anxiously by the cars across the street. Helen crossed her arms and looked down on the two people who'd given her such grief during the past hour.

"Your choice," she said. "Either you tell me what you're up to, or I'm calling my superior officer to pick you up for formal questioning. My station is too small, so it's here or the city. *But,*" she added before either of the solicitors answered, "depending on what you say, I still reserve the right to have you taken away and charged with false imprisonment. And since I'm an officer, that is a serious charge."

Elise and Claude were sitting side by side, wedged in by the table, where Helen had been minutes before. Richard stood on one side of them, and Desmond on the other. Elise looked suitably chastised. Claude had regained his outrage, but waving the mittened hand about tempered the effect.

"What are you accusing us of? There was nae false imprisonment. We were just having a discussion. Maybe a wee bit heated, but just a discussion."

Malky interrupted. "That were no *discussion*, we heard the yelling from outside. Heck, other people prob'ly did too."

"If that's the case," Richard said, "someone may have called in an emergency. They were close to doing that in town when Desmond here went running to get the keys."

Helen pulled a chair away from the table and sat down, facing the two solicitors.

"Do you two want to clear this up quickly? Once reinforcements arrive, it will be out of my hands. You'll have to answer to the emergency services if they're on the way here, responding to a possible domestic dispute."

"Call and cancel it!" Claude demanded. "You know nothing's happened, no one's been attacked."

"Except by marbles, but who'd believe that?" Malky pointed out, clearly pleased with himself. Greta and Alistair were at that moment on hands and knees in the hallway, retrieving as many marbles as they could find and returning them to the bag.

"Okay!" Elise announced at last. "I'm ready to talk. I'm tired of all this secrecy. With Ronald Wilson gone, sorry Richard, sorry Desmond, no disrespect to your family, but his passing finally leaves an opportunity to right past wrongs."

Claude heaved a long sigh. "All right, let's talk. But just Helen and Richard can hear this, as the senior officers."

Adam stepped forward, crossing his arms over his chest. "I'm not leaving Mum here without support. I insist on being by her side, if her sergeant Desmond's not going to be nearby."

Elise turned sideways to whisper something to Claude,

and he gave in. "All right, you can all stay. Hell, might as well make it a party!" He shook his head in disgust.

"That's not a bad idea," Helen said. "Elise, can we at least make some tea or coffee for folks here? They must have been searching for me for ages."

She was tempted to suggest calling out for pizza, but kept her professional composure. So, with Elise's guidance as to where to find things in the kitchen, Helen and Adam soon had the kitchen table supplied with plenty of hot tea and plates of biscuits. "I'll reimburse you for the bickies," Helen said to Elise, who just grimaced.

Wicker chairs were brought in from the adjoining room, adding to the tea party atmosphere, and the group assembled to hear, at last, an explanation of the solicitors' bizarre behavior. Before sitting down, Desmond had stepped outside to call the emergency dispatcher for the area: in fact, no one had called in a suspected domestic disturbance at that address. He whispered the information to Helen, who just nodded. Their two culprits didn't need to know that yet.

Chapter 48

After taking several long gulps of the welcome tea, Helen pulled her chair closer to the table and opened her notebook to a fresh page. "If I had my phone I'd record this," she muttered to herself, "but with all this corroboration, I think we'll be fine. Anyway, I don't know what we're about to hear."

She jotted a few notes, then looked up.

"Okay, my first question for you two. What is it that Richard here, my predecessor, was supposed to tell me? Was it related to the police station, or something else?"

Claude took the lead. "It has to do with that." He waved his mitten at the nineteen forty-four ledger sitting at the edge of the table next to the brass memorial plaque.

"There were some crimes committed during the war, which the police investigated. My grandfather was a solicitor back then, representing the town, and let's just say, decisions were made to keep the details from getting out. We didn't want those people to live the rest of their lives with the shame hanging over them."

"What kind of crimes are we talking about?" Helen asked.

"Nothing really bad," Richard replied, joining the conversation. "I was told about it when I took over the station. Claude here keeps the ledger locked up in his office, the office that his grandfather occupied. It became a tradition that only the senior police officer and the town solicitor would know the truth of the wartime activities. A bit of smuggling, some illegal sale of meat from farms to get around the rationing. It was nothing serious like I say, but once the war ended and those same people returned to normal life, the town would have been in turmoil for years if those people had been arrested and jailed, their crimes publicly exposed."

"That's *it*?" Helen asked, looking back and forth at Claude and Elise, their expressions unreadable. "You terrified me to keep me from knowing that a police ledger from many decades ago has records of wartime sales of pork, and people cutting deals on the side? That went on everywhere! And why not just redact the names? You could maintain the record of wartime activities generally, but I agree, no one alive today needs to learn that their great-grandmother served black market sausages at teatime. I mean, it may be good television wartime drama, but that's all, right?"

There was no response, so Richard spoke up again.

"Now that Helen puts it that way, I don't really get it either. It was so long ago, and few if any of the perpetrators can still be around. So why do you keep up what you call the *tradition*? To be frank, I had forgotten all about it. That's why I didn't get Helen in on the secret of the missing police ledger when she started working here."

"I guess that clears things up," Helen said. "Now, I might as well take the ledger back to the station and store it with the others. Make the record complete."

Claude and Elise shared a long glance, and Elise murmured, "Richard, there's far more to it that you don't know. That's why we only want to disclose the background to you and Helen."

"Oh, let's just get it over with!" Claude declared. "I'm going to retire soon, everybody says I should, and that will be the end of it. If the town blows apart over what we tell you, so be it. Richard," he said, pointing at one of the kitchen cabinets, "get the whisky out. We'll need a wee dram for this. I will anyway."

Richard did as requested. Most of the group stuck with tea, and only Claude and Elise each took a glass. Helen knew she had to hold off until she got home, keeping a clear head.

It Continued with the Cowries

She was glad to see Richard, Adam, and Desmond follow her example. No need to add drinking on the job, with so many witnesses, to the mess that the day had become.

Alistair and Greta had been listening to the discussion from the hallway, and now they entered the kitchen. Alistair handed the brown bag to Malky. Adding some comic relief to the situation, Malky opened the bag and peered in. "Hope they're all in there! That's Henry's handmade ones, pre-war vintage. Each worth at least a fifty, maybe a hundred!"

Alistair felt his eyes widen and he was tempted to do a more thorough check of the floor, but instead, he fixed himself a cup of tea and one for Greta, and they sat down in wicker chairs near the back of the gathering.

Margaret still hadn't called or texted back, and Alistair was getting worried. He looked up the tide table for the afternoon. Seeing that high tide was not for a few hours, he forced himself to relax. The beach had plenty of sea glass collectors, so surely if something happened to Margaret, help would be at hand.

He focused again on the discussion. Everyone was listening, rapt, as the history unspooled in Claude's telling, back to the nineteen thirties.

"You probably all know that the glass factory had become famous, and many people in town worked there up until the war years. Few people in town minded that the founder Henry, Heinrich, had once been a German soldier. He'd proved himself a loyal Scot for almost twenty years, when war broke out again. Most of the men who worked in the factory went off to fight, but there were still people in town, woman and the older men, who trained up quickly and kept the factory going. All was fine until the authorities came for Henry and locked him up as a possible enemy alien. He was interned for most of the war."

Claude took a long swig of whisky and turned to face Richard.

"I don't know how much your father, may he rest in

peace, told you about his war years. He couldn't fight because of his eyesight, at least that's what I've always heard, but he was hired as the night guard at the factory. I don't know if he was hired before or after the first looting took place. He was the guard all through the war, but had been unable on his own to prevent the repeated looting and damage."

He stopped and thought for a moment before continuing, his voice softer. "It's honestly never been clear to me why more wasn't done to help the poor man, but I suppose, the lootings and damage happened randomly, once every several months, so it would have been difficult to justify posting enough men at the factory, night after night, in case the vandals appeared that night. And once they showed up, Ronald had no chance to raise an alarm and get help from the town, two miles away." He stopped again, then added, "I've always been suspicious that someone higher up in the town made the lads do it. That could explain why Ronald was never given any help."

Helen was tempted to move the story along, as Claude was mainly repeating the standard, publicly-known background, as far as she knew. But she didn't want to distract him by questions, so she sipped her tea and listened, taking notes now and again.

"You're probably all wondering," Claude continued, "why weren't the vandals rounded up and arrested? Well, one answer is that they disappeared again after each attack. Some folks said they just blended into the town. Others thought they might actually be Germans, and that could explain fear of confrontation. Or like I said, maybe someone in authority was protecting them. It wasn't until near the end of the war, when Henry was back in Kilvellie and was intent on knowing who'd done the damage, particularly to his beloved war memorial window, that there was a concerted effort to find the culprits. It turned out to be six lads from Glasgow..."

Malky interrupted with a loud, "It figures!"

"Malky," Helen admonished him. "That's not fair. Go on, Claude."

"Thank you Helen, sorry, Officer Griffen. I only mentioned they were from Glasgow for the context. They were wartime evacuees from Glasgow. They'd been among a larger group destined for a location ten miles from here."

"Kilvellie Towers?" Helen asked, remembering her recent discussion with Margaret, Alistair, and Calum at Margaret's cottage.

Claude looked at her in surprise. "Yes, although I don't know where you got that information. It's been kept hidden for so long. And if you know that, you probably also know that Kilvellie Towers burned down soon after the war started. The records were destroyed, so the documentation of which children had gone there, and which were missing and presumed dead, was a shambles. Disgraceful shambles. But luckily for six of the boys from Glasgow, and very unluckily for Kilvellie and the glass factory, these six boys had mistakenly been sent to the *town* of Kilvellie, not Kilvellie Towers."

He stopped for a moment, seeing Alistair and Helen share wide grins, then resumed.

"The mistake should have been discovered right away, since Kilvellie, this town, had no facility designated for housing evacuee children, but it did have a kind of staging area for them, Seaview Manor Home. Back then it was operating as a convalescent home for the military. The six boys somehow ended up living there, perhaps because they didn't realize they were in the wrong place, or maybe this seemed like a more pleasant opportunity than being in a towering old building, far from town, and a nicer place to pass their time in evacuation, however long it might be."

Now he stopped and gulped down the rest of his whisky. Helen was concerned that he'd keep drinking and turn belligerent again, but instead, he held up his mittened hand and asked if someone would make him a strong cup of coffee.

267

As Adam was nearest the kitchen, he volunteered. People took a break to check their phones, and to refresh their tea.

Chapter 49

The group reassembled on the chairs crowded around the kitchen table at Elise's house. Bolstered by frequent gulps of coffee, Claude resumed, and Helen hoped he would reach a conclusion soon. With no officer at the station for hours now, and her mobile phone left behind, she was concerned that important messages were piling up.

"As I was saying, after Henry was released from internment, he came back and was unbelievably forgiving of Scotland, of Britain, for locking him up, especially after all he'd done for this town. But he was absolutely livid that local lads, I mean, the young vandals, had almost destroyed his factory. He reserved his real fury for their desecration of the war memorial window. So he used all his contacts in town and asked around, and eventually found the six young men."

"Sorry to interrupt," Helen said, "but was the war over when Henry was released from internment? Wouldn't the six lads have gone home by then?"

"No, Henry was released in nineteen forty-four. He found the boys living in the convalescent home. Seems they'd ingratiated themselves there, helping with the meals and caring for the injured soldiers. He simply couldn't understand how these same boys would destroy a memorial to Scottish men and woman who'd fought and died on their behalf. He even wondered if they had been forced to, by someone in authority in town or at the convalescent home."

Claude seemed to be losing the thread of his story, and he looked around the room for a moment. "I guess I just said

Jane Ross Potter

that, did I, about suspecting someone had put the boys up to it? Oh well, it's impossible to know now. Anyway, I'd better get to the point." He pushed his now-empty coffee mug to the side and resumed talking after a sip from his whisky glass, which he'd refilled.

"Now, Richard and Desmond, here's where it gets uncomfortable. Ronald Wilson, the guard, was the only person who could positively identify those six young men as the vandals, and he reluctantly did so. He was afraid that they would enact vengeance on Ronald's family in town, but Henry persuaded him it was the right thing to do, then they'd be returned to their families in Glasgow at war's end, or before.

"Henry knew the boys couldn't reimburse him for all the damage, so instead, he brought them to the factory to work on getting it cleaned and restored, to eventually reopen. I think he hoped they'd reveal to him that they'd done the damage at someone else's urging. You're all familiar with the former location, right? Where the cafe parking lot is, by the cliff?"

People nodded their heads, so he continued.

"Picture the damaged factory still standing up by that cliff, the huge expanse of boarded-up windows facing the North Sea. There was an area of grass between that wall of the factory, and the cliff edge. It's where most of the glass from the windows had fallen and was still lying there. With Ronald standing guard, one day Henry told the six boys to search through the grass and find as many intact, or near-intact, names of the dead as they could. God only knows how they felt about it, whether they were terrified of this former German soldier and of Ronald, or whether they thought it was all a joke. Anyway, Henry leaves Ronald in charge and goes back to his office in the factory, facing out to the street. So he had no view of what the boys were doing. And before any of you ask, it was a Sunday, and no one else was believed to be in the factory that day."

He stopped and drank more whisky, and Helen could feel

270

the tension mount in the group. Some of them had heard a version of what came next, and here, finally, must be the authoritative version.

But no.

Claude shook his head sadly. "Who knows for sure what happened next? The story came out that Ronald took a quick rest break inside the factory, that was his explanation, and when he returned a few minutes later, he couldn't see the boys anywhere. He ran to get Henry, and they couldn't find any of the boys on the nearby streets. The lads hadn't gone into the factory, with only one door being used and it was kept locked, far as the police were told at the time. Finally, Henry and Ronald looked over the cliff edge, and they saw six bodies floating in the waves. It was a windy day, the waves were strong, and they could see that the boys were dead, probably all smashed against the side of the cliff. Of course, the two men tried to get help, but by the time a lifeboat could be called out and make its way across the waves, the tide was receding. No sign of the boys was ever found."

He stopped and glared at Helen. "That, officer, is the town's shameful wartime secret, not the sale of dodgy groceries."

***

The group sat in silence. Claude reached for the whisky bottle and poured himself another dram, topping up Elise's at the same time. She'd been nervously sipping from the glass, just listening along and expressing no surprise.

Helen finally asked, "It's been many decades since that event. Why are you so intent to keep me from knowing? Is it because poor Ronald has just passed away, are you concerned that he wrote it all down, and it will become public once his estate is settled? I just don't understand."

Elise spoke up, giving Claude a break. "Helen, think about it. The country was still fighting a horrific war with

Germany. To protect Britain's precious children, the country's future, from bombing in the cities, parents had sent them to the countryside. And here in this town, six of those evacuated boys were now dead from drowning, while cleaning up glass outside a factory owned by a German. At the time, the few people in town who knew about it decided to keep the whole thing quiet. Especially if there was suspicion, on Henry's part at least, that someone prominent had masterminded the vandalism."

"So," Richard ventured, "no effort was made to contact the poor lads' families back in Glasgow, at least tell them the lads were dead, not necessarily the circumstances? Just say they drowned in the sea, or something?"

"Ironically," Claude said, putting down his glass and joining the conversation again, "Henry *did* want their families traced. He hated what the lads had done to his factory and his livelihood, not to mention that of men coming back from the war, hoping to return to their pre-war jobs at the factory. It was closed for a long time before it was fully functional again. But Henry had more direct experience of war than some, having fought in the First World War, and he knew first-hand how agonizing it was for loved ones not to know the fate of their young men who'd gone away to fight."

"But he didn't do that?" Helen persisted, looking at Claude.

"As far as we know, the people in town, who knew about it, convinced him otherwise. Maybe they overdid the threats, if you can call it that, but perhaps he feared being sent back to Germany, leaving his Scottish wife and children behind. I mean, if word got out that the six lads died while working for Henry, after they'd trashed his factory repeatedly while he was interned, no one could prove he *didn't* have a hand in it, could they? I know all this because my grandfather was the town's attorney back then. It's come down through my father to me, the town's closely guarded secret."

"A *shameful* secret," Helen countered. "Not just the death

of the lads, that was bad enough, but even assuming they fell off the cliff by accident, it was shameful to keep that quiet all these decades, and not give their families a chance for closure. I won't even get into the question of whether someone had a hand in those deaths."

Richard looked at her warily. "You mean, my dad, Ronald, don't you?"

"I'm sorry Richard. I just as well mean Henry. He had motive, a need for revenge."

"But Helen, he wasn't that kind of man!" Claude exclaimed. "He had a huge capacity to forgive and look only to the future. And I really think he didn't blame the lads personally, if they were following orders from someone they feared."

"Aye," Malky chimed in, "that's all I've ever been told about Henry, my grandfather I mean. I'd be shocked if he had a hand in those lads' deaths."

Alistair cleared his throat, and everyone looked over to where he was sitting in a wicker chair, on the periphery of the group. He leaned forward.

"I know I'm just a visitor to your town, but I think this long guilty secret is unraveling now, isn't it Claude? When Ronald went to your office and saw Mrs. Ramsay's family picture on the wall, shortly before he died, he recognized the boy, didn't he? And he knew from talking to Mrs. Ramsay, Kathryn to him, at the care home, that she'd lost her brother in the war, when he'd been evacuated and she'd been sent to live in Canada. She thought he'd been evacuated to Kilvellie Towers, and when she came back from Canada as a young adult and discovered it had burned down years earlier, she must have assumed her brother had died in the fire, or been taken elsewhere and then his trail went cold when her parents died."

"You've been talking to Kathryn Spears, I take it?" Claude asked Alistair.

"Yes, but purely by chance, when Emily and Desmond

were clearing out Ronald's room next door." Alistair stopped, hoping Desmond wouldn't react to this slight diversion from the truth. However, he couldn't reveal, in front of Richard and Desmond, that when he visited Kathryn, he was also seeking clues about who might have wanted Ronald injured or dead.

Alistair continued, "I saw her family photograph there and she said you had brought it from the office, where it had hung for many years. I offered to hang it up for her, and when I was lifting it, I saw the brother's name on the back. It seemed similar to one of the names on the memorial plaque at the chapel, so I began wondering if it was the same person. You see, I'd also heard the story about Kilvellie Towers being confused with Kilvellie, the town, so a mix-up wasn't completely out of the question."

Helen leaned forward across the table to confront Claude. "So you knew *all along* that a woman you were working with, I mean, when Kathryn was working at your office, that she'd lost a brother and he was one of those six lads whose deaths were being covered up?"

"No!" Claude and Elise protested in unison. Claude explained, "It wasn't until you and Alistair visited the other day, and it reminded me that I really should take the photograph to Kathryn at the care home. Like Alistair, I turned it over and saw a name I recognized. I don't remember Kathryn ever mentioning his name."

Leaning back again and staring at the two solicitors in disgust, Helen continued, "Don't you think she deserves to know what happened to her brother? Maybe the families of the other five lads would be difficult to trace now, but you have one living family member, just a mile or two from here."

Elise nodded in agreement. "But what do we tell her, Helen? It's been going around and around in my mind. Do we tell her that people in Kilvellie knew, at the time, that her brother fell off a cliff in the nineteen forties, and during the decades that she held out hope that he hadn't died in the

Kilvellie Towers fire, we'd known all along he was dead from drowning?"

"Of *course*, not like that," Helen said, still fuming. She turned to face Richard. "I apologize for using your father's tragic death, but it seems he's taken that era with him. The war years of the glass factory. Maybe a case can be made that some new information has come to light following Ronald Wilson's death, with him being the last surviving factory worker from the war years, and somehow he knew about the deaths, and assumed the families had been informed? I know, I know, I'm fabricating things, but I'm trying to think of a gentle explanation for Kathryn, that is generally truthful."

"Wait a minute!" cried Desmond, at last putting the pieces together in his mind. "Did Granddad know all along that Kathryn's brother had died at the factory that day, when Granddad was there? He and Kathryn had rooms next to each other for *four years.*"

"I'm sure he didn't, sergeant," Claude replied kindly. "I can't reveal a client confidence, but your granddad only learned that just before his death. It was when he saw the photograph in Elise's office, the connection must have dawned on him."

"And that's when he wrote a hurried letter to Kathryn, to be delivered to her on his death," Helen added.

Now Claude leaned forward, looking directly at Helen. "Please, let Ronald keep that secret. Anyway, it's covered by client confidentiality. The contents of that letter I mean. It's not right to share it with all of you. Ronald wouldn't have wanted that. And," he mumbled, "I don't plan to give the letter to her. I agree with you, it's best that the information about her brother is delivered, ah, more gently."

Helen and Claude shared a look of understanding, as if he knew she'd found a way to learn what was in the letter, after he'd grabbed it from her when she'd steamed open the envelope at their office. The group fell silent again, with just

the sound of teacups on saucers, and the clink of the whisky
bottle as the two solicitors' glasses were refilled.

Chapter 50

Helen stood up, eager to bring an end to the tense gathering. "The families of those lads need closure. And this town has got to get beyond the secret that it's held onto for so long. Surely you can come up with a narrative that will reveal the names of six evacuees who died tragically during the war, and you'll, I don't know, offer to put up a memorial to them and honor their memory?"

"That's what Henry did, in the chapel," Elise pointed out. "He wanted to make the boys' real names known, but our predecessors reached a compromise, with the names and the memorial plaque in German."

"And the scratched-out witness name?" Alistair asked. "That's been bugging me since I first saw the plaque over a week ago."

Elise sighed deeply before answering. "Henry signed his name as witness, but as Heinrich Gruener. He didn't literally witness their deaths, but he saw their bodies in the waves below. I often think, if only that long wooden stairway had been in existence back then, you know, the one that goes from the car park down to the beach, maybe those boys would have survived. They could have grabbed the railings, the steps, I just don't know."

"And Henry and Ronald could have gone down the steps and tried to save them," Alistair added. "I've been there, and I know there's at least one life preserver hanging at the bottom of the steps."

"It is tragic," Helen agreed. "When were those steps installed? Was it recently?"

Elise shook her head. "No, Helen, it was that same week. Henry commissioned them, so in a way, the steps exist as a memorial to the lads. Well, they've been upgraded and replaced over the years, but the original steps? All thanks to Henry."

"Getting back to the memorial plaque," Alistair said, lifting it from the table to look more closely, "what is the story about Heinrich's name being scratched out?"

"The truth is," replied Elise, "no one knows. There's no record that I can find, as curator of the chapel, that makes a note of the damage occurring from one day to the next. Anyway, there's no security to speak of in the chapel even now, so someone could slip in when it was open and take a screwdriver to it, anything that would scratch brass."

Richard had been following the conversation and staring at the plaque in Alistair's hands.

"I never considered it before," he said, shaking his head sadly, "but it could have been my dad, Ronald. It was a long time ago now. In fact, I'd just received my driver's learning plate, and he was letting me practice around town. He asked me to drive him to the chapel and he said I could wait in the car, he'd just be a minute.

"He said something odd when he got back into the car: 'Thanks son, just had to protect his reputation.' I was much younger and thought nothing of it, except maybe Dad had some special request to ask God. But after hearing all this, I wonder if he did that to shield Henry, Heinrich, from connection with those six dead lads. But who knows what he was thinking, what triggered him to do it then, I mean, if it even was him?"

He let out a long sigh. "Aw heck, pass me a whisky glass. Let's have a toast to the old guy, long may *he* be remembered, even though he could be an ornery old so and so." He poured himself good shot, then lifted his glass. "To Dad, the

Regenbogen Glass Factory guard."

The room echoed in agreement: "To Ronald." And from Desmond, "To Granddad. Wish he'd opened up to us instead of keeping it bottled inside."

"Hear, hear," Helen said. "And with that, I think we've accomplished all we can for now. I'm mentally exhausted, and I expect that Elise would like to have her kitchen back."

"Are you going to charge us with anything, Officer Griffen?" Claude asked, standing and stepping out from behind the table, with Adam maintaining a distance between the man and Helen. The others were returning chairs to where they belonged, and carrying cups and plates to the kitchen counter.

"Nae, Claude. I had no idea of what's been simmering just under the surface for so long. You know, I had thought that Malky's family were the victims of the glass factory vandalism, because it set the company back by years, and in turn reduced profits and Malky's eventual inheritance. Malky's daughter Christy still resents old Ronald for being such an incompetent guard." She shook her head. "But now, I'm realizing that Ronald spent his whole post-war life keeping a dreadful secret, protecting Henry's reputation. The factory did eventually get back on its feet. If, instead, Ronald had made it widely known that six Scottish evacuees had fallen to their deaths while doing work for Henry, I don't know, maybe Henry would have been suspected of killing them and sent away for good, or just driven out of town with his reputation in tatters. That would have been the end of the factory, and the town might still be suffering economically to this day. Oh goodness, there's so much at play here. But no, sir, no charges. A misunderstanding is all."

Claude reached across the table with his good hand and picked up the nineteen forty-four police ledger. "What about this?" he asked Helen. "And before you say anything, I highly advise that you don't return it to the shelf in the station. There really are some wartime reports that, I suppose, could be embarrassing for the culprits' descendants, even now."

She thought for a moment. "You've looked after it well all these years. I know where to find it if for some reason the year is mentioned again, although I sure hope it isn't. Not on my watch, anyway." She glanced at the memorial plaque, still sitting on the table. "Keep that too, for now. We'll meet soon and talk about a fitting memorial for the six lads."

Leaving Claude and Elise to adjust to life post-secret, with a half-full whisky bottle for solace, Helen led the others out to the front garden.

Chapter 51

After goodbyes outside Elise's house, Richard and Desmond drove Helen back to the police station. Alistair stood by his car, unsure what to do next. If he drove back into town and started walking the beach, he had little hope of finding Margaret: she could be anywhere along the expanse, or in a cafe somewhere.

But wherever she was, it was getting late in the day, so he called the hotel and reserved their same suite from the previous night. He was trying not to think about the cost, but he decided that tonight really would be his last in Kilvellie: too many unpleasant associations for him. He ended the call and saw Adam, Malky, and Greta approach from Elise's front path, Malky grasping the precious bag of marbles with both hands.

"Malky and Greta have invited us over for a late lunch," Adam said. "Are you in, or do you need to drive back to Finlay now? I know we had lunch with Kathryn earlier, but all the drama has made me hungry again."

"I'd like to, but I still haven't heard from Margaret, and when I call I just get her voice mail. Maybe she doesn't have a signal on the beach, and..."

Malky heard the comment and interrupted. "Who's on the beach?" he asked Alistair.

"My fiancée, Margaret. She went to the beach hours ago. At one point she had cell phone service, but I haven't been able to reach her since we started looking for Helen. I assume

281

she's okay..."

"Was she looking for sea glass, or just out for a walk?" Malky asked next.

"She could be looking for groatie buckies. Is there a part of the beach where she might find them?"

Malky shook his head. "A few, maybe, but only at the very north end of the beach, where there's a section of rocky shore that extends into the sea. I suppose if she asked people on the beach, someone might have directed her there. But it's a long walk."

Alistair nodded. "That must be it. I guess there's nothing I can do except wait until she's back in cell service area. Maybe she'll call me to pick her up from that end of the beach."

"Nae, she cannae access the cliff there. She'd have to retrace her steps along the beach to the stairway up to the cafe," Malky said. "If she's gone to the far end of the beach, that would be at least two miles back."

Alistair's eyes widened. "Wait, I thought there was another stairway at the far end, for people who get caught by the tide?"

"Aye, sonny, but it's being repaired the noo. Some recent storm damage. Christy and William told me the other day."

"Is there a sign on the beach saying that the north stairway is closed?" Alistair felt a sickening dread creeping in.

"I doubt it. Few glass collectors gae that far north. They mainly stay between the town access and the stairway to the cafe, that's halfway along the beach."

Adam had been looking back and forth between the two men, listening with increasing concern.

"Alistair," he said, "we need to find her before the tide gets too far in. I have binoculars and I assume you have as well, so let's go to the cafe stairway and start looking from there. If we don't see her, we can drive north to the top of the closed stairway and look there too."

Malky offered to call Christy and William to help search

the beach, but Alistair thanked him and said to hold off. There was no reason to think that Margaret wouldn't be found quickly by a search with binoculars, then he could get on to the beach from one of the two access points, and bring her back to safety.

He remembered Justine's escape from a high tide by climbing up through a long-disused coal chute, but surely Margaret wouldn't be in danger of a similar fate. With promises to keep in touch, Adam and Alistair took off in Alistair's car, picking up Adam's binoculars from his car still parked in the beach cafe parking lot.

Soon they had run halfway down the beach access stairway and stopped on a wooden platform, which had benches for people to rest during the long climb up. Alistair scanned the beach to the north, and Adam took the south section; he had a more difficult task, as most of the beachgoers were concentrated on that stretch.

"We should switch places," Adam said. "You'll have a better chance of recognizing her amongst all those people."

Alistair did as requested, and checked from person to person. Before he'd finished, Adam cried, "I think that's her!"

Alistair turned again and faced north. Adam held his binoculars in one hand and pointed with the other.

"I can see someone sitting on the sand, facing the back of the beach and looking down. Is that Margaret?"

It only took Alistair a moment. "Yes, great work! I recognize her clothes from this morning."

Now having her in sight, he tried her cell phone number, but again it went to voice mail. Adam kept watch, and Margaret made no motion to answer the phone, so she clearly wasn't getting a signal. Alistair assured Adam that Margaret wouldn't have turned her phone off. "She's still officially working for the law firm," he said, "so she'll be getting work calls now and again."

She was too far away for their voices to carry. Alistair looked up the tide table on his phone again. The tide had turned an hour earlier, so although it wasn't exactly a race against time to get Margaret off the beach, that time would come if she didn't turn back and follow the handful of people walking southward at the water's edge on her section of the beach.

Alistair sensed other people running down the stairway and stopping, so he turned. Helen was accompanied by Malky and William.

"I feel responsible," William said. "She told me she wanted to look for groatie buckies. I didn't think she would go so far north on the beach. We've got to reach her within the next half hour, to get her back here safely."

Together, the group cupped their hands to their mouths and began yelling Margaret's name, but she was too far away. A couple of people near the base of the stairway looked up, but then continued on their way south to the town access.

"I'd better go down to the beach and start running toward her," Alistair suggested. "Maybe she'll turn back on her own."

"Oh no!" Malky cried. "Look, the lassie's up and she's still walking north! She didnae see us!"

"She must be relying on the other stairway for access. I wish I hadn't told her about it. I had no idea it would be closed."

"Alistair, I've an idea..." Helen walked back up the steps as quickly as she could, then returned with a bullhorn.

"Step aside, guys." She lifted the bullhorn to her mouth.

"Margaret!" she called, using the voice she would use to disperse a rowdy crowd in the Edinburgh streets at New Years. "Margaret! Turn around now!"

But this had no effect on Margaret, who kept walking.

"Does she have headphones on?" Helen asked Alistair.

"I doubt it. She enjoys the sound of the waves when she's on the beach. That's probably drowning out our voices."

"Let's try something else." Helen guided Alistair up the steps. The others waited to see if Margaret turned around, so they could wave and attract her attention.

In Helen's vehicle, Helen and Alistair drove north on the road, then across the grassy field near the chapel. Jumping out again, Helen stood as close as she dared to the cliff edge and bellowed down at Margaret through the bullhorn. Alistair watched through his binoculars, and was relieved to see that this, finally, had Margaret's attention. While they were driving north, she'd found another patch of sand that interested her and was sitting again, surrounded by her collecting gear.

"Turn back now!!" Helen yelled. "The emergency staircase is closed!"

Alistair motioned along with the words, frantically pointing south and waving the other arm to indicate that she should go back that way. He even motioned running, hoping she'd get the message.

Helen continued bellowing. "The tide's coming in! Go back to the cafe stairs! Now, Margaret! Go now!!"

Sighing a huge sigh of relief, Alistair watched Margaret's expression change. She smiled, gave a thumbs up gesture, and quickly gathered up her pack. They watched as she headed south at a brisk pace, then they returned to the car to rejoin the others at the cafe parking area.

Chapter 52

From the parking area at the top of the stairs, Helen, Malky, William, and Adam watched as Alistair raced down the stairs and ran along the beach to meet Margaret. Soon they were all gathered, with Margaret expressing her thanks to Helen for having such a commanding voice.

"You and your grubby buckets!" Alistair admonished her, but with a smile on his face. "You gave us all a terrible fright. I hope it was worth it!"

After profuse thanks to the group, Margaret took a paper coffee cup from her pack and snapped the lid off. "I found some, but a few were broken." She stared into the cup for a moment, then told everyone to hold out a hand.

"Keep your groatie buckies," Helen insisted, "you need them for your competition."

"I will," Margaret assured her. "I want to give you something else."

With her back to the group, she poured the contents of the coffee cup into her own hand, then turned and placed a frosted sea glass marble into each of the outstretched hands.

William was the first to react. "You found this *today*? It's a handmade one! This is as good as the best vintage ones I sell." He looked around at the other marbles, with his beach-combing instinct to compare finds.

"I got six," Margaret told him. "I remember you told me I'd be lucky to find one in such good condition."

"But Margaret," William protested, "you *really* want to

give away about a thousand dollars-worth of marbles?"

She nodded her head and turned serious. "I was down there with no care in the world, thinking I had enough time to cover the distance to the stairway at the north end. If Helen hadn't used the bullhorn to get my attention, I would have..."

She stopped and gasped. "William, I'm sorry, I wasn't thinking. That's what almost happened to your sister."

"It's fine, lass," Malky said. "You've got to be free to tell your own story without worrying it will bring back bad mem'ries for us."

He turned to Helen. "Better get some signs put up on the beach, warn folks that the third access route is not available. And that stairway needs to be fixed right away! We can't have other poor lasses like Margaret risk getting trapped."

"It's my fault," Margaret said. "I got so focused on digging through the piled-up shale. It's addictive. Once I found my first marble, I was hooked."

Malky invited everyone back to the house.

Alistair looked at Margaret, eyebrows raised in question. "I don't know about you, but I'm famished after all this worry."

Margaret laughed. "A likely excuse. I've been hearing about Greta's baking skills for days now, so I'm sure that's your real reason."

Malky and William left in their car, and Alistair and Margaret followed in theirs, with Adam in the back seat. Helen returned to the station to work on getting the beach access warning signs installed.

***

"I have soup ready," Greta said as she greeted the group at the door. "I'll heat up some focaccia bread I made this morning. Then fresh strawberry-rhubarb pie."

"Sounds great. Can I help you?" Margaret offered.

287

Greta, normally reticent to accept any help, acquiesced this time. Margaret took a few moments to look around as she entered the house. From the entryway, an open double doorway to the right led into a large dining room with an oval dark wood table of the kind Margaret had only seen in her grandparents' homes. Family photographs, some in frames decorated with sea glass, hung on the walls, and the room had windows that looked out to the street.

A hallway led straight back from the entryway, and Margaret could see several open doors. She assumed those were bedrooms, as the house was a bungalow, one level. She decided not to ask Greta for a tour later; she had a feeling that Greta and Malky lived modestly, and would not see a reason to give a near-stranger the run of their home.

While Margaret followed Greta through the dining room and into the kitchen, Malky took Adam and Alistair to his office in the back of the house, to show off his plans for the new glass museum. From the office, Alistair looked through the large south-facing window which overlooked the town harbor. "You have a great view from here," he said to Malky. "Margaret also has a cottage near the water, by a beach. I love having the fresh breezes come in, don't you?"

"Aye, and we're incorporating that effect in the new museum." Malky unrolled an architectural drawing, professionally done, of the proposed museum, and spent the next ten minutes explaining the features, and where various pieces of glass and vintage equipment would be displayed. There would also be a snack bar with an outdoor seating area, and a shop.

"My daughter Christy can sell her sea glass jewelry, and we'll invite other glass artisans to sell their work."

"Lunch is ready!" Greta called from the hallway, so Malky rolled up the drawing and ushered Adam and Alistair to the dining room in the front of the house, the table surface almost invisible under the platters of appetizers and breads that Greta had somehow conjured up in a short time.

"Sit down and eat while the soup is hot." No one needed to be asked twice.

While they ate, Alistair thought about Malky and his enthusiasm for the museum. Alistair didn't know Malky well, his information mainly coming from Helen's descriptions. After losing the glass factory to cliff erosion over twenty years earlier, Malky and his wife had lived frugally, choosing to stay in Kilvellie and maintain ties to their glass heritage, instead of moving away and starting anew.

Without regular work, they'd scraped by, with Malky selling off equipment and supplies from the dismantled glass factory, and Greta taking a variety of part-time jobs, plus her baking, which she sold to local restaurants. Their children had helped supplement the income from an early age, collecting the unique multicolored sea glass on the nearby beach for Malky to sell.

Yet, despite it all, Helen had said she found Malky to be consistently optimistic, seeing the good in people, and accepting small windfalls as if he'd won the lottery. And then he did, in effect, win the lottery. Alistair smiled at the memory of their recent discovery of dozens of vintage Regenbogen glass vases and handmade marbles, which had been secured underground during the war, safe from the factory vandals.

With the now-valuable glass deemed to be factory property, it was all given to Malky, and instead of selling some of it and going traveling with Greta, or moving to a bigger house, he planned to display it in his glass museum. Malky's goal in later life had been to have a museum to his ancestors, so that the story of Regenbogen glass, and its place in glass artistry of the twentieth century, would not be lost. Yet, just hours earlier, Malky had been willing to sacrifice a small fortune in vintage glass marbles to give Helen a chance to escape from Elise's house: the man certainly had his priorities straight.

Alistair also realized that Malky seemed to embody the spirit of his grandfather, Henry, and that returned his

289

thoughts to the strange events of the afternoon, when Helen finally got the story of the six factory vandals into the light of day. Someone had said, in passing, that the wooden cliffside stairway down to the beach was, in a way, a memorial to the six young men who had drowned there.

An idea came to him. If the town was ready to face its past, and publicly disclose the names of those six young men who had been evacuees in World War Two, maybe the stairway could be formally dedicated as their memorial? He'd suggest it to Helen. For now, though, he put memories of the difficult afternoon aside, and focused on the people around him and the next course that Greta was serving: pie and whipped cream.

Between courses, Alistair had helped carry empty dishes into the kitchen, and he noticed the wall clock that Adam had described from his own first visit. Instead of numerals 1 through 12, each hour had a piece of frosted beach glass of a different color. For a moment, Alistair thought of calling it to Margaret's attention, if she hadn't already seen and photographed it, then decided not to. He wouldn't want her to replicate it for their own kitchen back at the Finlay cottage. *I am done with sea glass forever*, he reminded himself, although not for the first time. But now he was even more sure, after the trauma of Margaret almost getting trapped by the high tide on the same beach that could have claimed Justine's life all those years ago.

Chapter 53

A week passed, and for Helen, life and police work in Kilvellie gradually returned to normal. Her sergeant Desmond was back at work after the funeral of his grandfather Ronald Wilson, the body having been released and no foul play suspected.

Helen had accompanied Ronald's son, retired police officer Richard, to the funeral. Richard was staying on instead of returning to Spain yet. In addition to helping supervise construction of the new glass museum on land he owned, he was clearing out his family home to sell.

Alistair and Margaret had returned to their cottage in Finlay, but not before Alistair offered a suggestion to Helen. He visualized signs to be installed at the top and bottom of the wooden cliffside stairway that led from the parking area down to the beach. After learning that the glass factory founder, Henry, had commissioned the stairway days after the six factory vandals had drowned at the base of that cliff, it seemed a fitting way to begin making the six boys' names and fates public.

Gradually, as the signs were photographed, shared on social media, and discussed out in the wider world, perhaps descendants of the families of those missing boys, evacuees during the Second World War, would find closure to the decades-old question of what happened to a long-lost uncle or cousin.

Or brother, in the case of Kathryn Spears at the care home, where old Ronald had spent his last four years. Helen had assured Alistair, with solicitor Claude's approval, that she would visit Kathryn and gently explain the recent discovery of Kathryn's brother's death by drowning in nineteen forty-four. Ronald's name would not be mentioned in the context, nor would Henry/Heinrich's.

And so, with Alistair busy on renovations at Margaret's cottage in Finlay, with Margaret off to the western isles of Scotland in search of even more groatie buckies, thanks to Richard's contacts on a remote Hebridean island, and with her son Adam back to Inverness and his work, Helen was looking forward to some time alone in her residence next to the station. She had to find somewhere else to live, somewhere more private, and that was high on her list of tasks.

At five o'clock, she closed her laptop and stood up. Desmond would work for another hour and secure the station for the evening. Then the front door opened, and Helen was momentarily annoyed that someone would arrive just as she was leaving. A man she recognized walked in, along with a younger man wearing a well-tailored gray business suit, and under it a white shirt with a perfectly knotted floral tie. Her eyes lingered on it: somehow, he'd managed to have only light blue show on the knot itself, with the floral pattern beneath it. A city look for sure, not the more casual attire of Kilvellie's professionals. He had wavy blond hair and an intelligent, wide-eyed look, and as Helen compared the two men, she saw a family resemblance.

The older man she knew: her captor of a week before, the solicitor Claude McMahon, still sporting a bandage on his scalded hand, but at least the comical mitten effect was gone. He apologized for arriving late in the day, and introduced his son, Giles.

"Please sit down." Helen indicated the guest chairs facing her desk, and she resumed her seat in her desk chair. "Would you like some tea or..."

Claude declined tea for himself and his son. "This should be a short visit..." Before he continued, he overtly glanced sideways at Desmond, who was following the conversation from his desk; Helen caught the implication, and asked if Claude would prefer to meet in private, in case a member of the public walked in.

"Thank you, Helen, that would be best."

Helen opened the conference room door and showed the two visitors in. She returned to Desmond's desk and said quietly, "I don't know what they want to talk about, but I'll tell you about it later if it's a police matter you should be aware of."

"Whatever," came the reply. Groaning inwardly, Helen reminded herself that she needed to help the young sergeant work on his communication skills.

She returned to the conference room and closed the door behind her. She was surprised to see the nineteen forty-four police station ledger on the table: the volume that Claude, as the town's solicitor, still kept it in his office, allegedly due to the sensitive nature of some wartime crime reports.

"I'm retiring soon," Claude explained, "and my son here, Giles, will be taking over. He's done his training and is ready to step in."

"I look forward to working with you," Helen said, as she knew that courtesy would be expected.

Claude patted the ledger. "Giles here wants to modernize my law practice, and since it will become his practice, it's fine with me. He suggested scanning our records, starting with the oldest ones. We'll be hiring a couple of law students to do the actual scanning, and the naming and organizing of the digital versions. But since this particular ledger isn't part of the law firm records, and it contains sensitive material, we want to ask you about it."

"Should I put it on the shelf here with the other ledgers? Is that why you brought it back?" Helen asked.

"No, we're here for two reasons. One is, while the students are scanning our records, we could have them scan your old ledgers. Consider it a public service."

"Desmond would like that," Helen said. "He complains that this office is too antiquated. I've thought about getting old records scanned, but without clerical help in the office, I didn't want to risk confidentiality by using an outside service."

"We will definitely maintain confidentiality in the law office. Now, to our second reason for meeting with you in private. I'm not going to comment, but I'd like you to read this entry." Claude opened the police ledger to a flagged page near the middle of the book, and Helen sneezed as the dust of decades was released.

"I see what you mean, Claude. Much better to have all this information digitized. Get rid of these moldy old tomes."

Claude turned the book so that she could read the page he'd indicated. It only took a couple of minutes for her to read the full entry, but it would take a long time for the information to sink in. She looked up at Claude.

"To be clear, *this* is the contemporary report of the six lads who went over the cliff by the factory? Not just bodies caught in the waves, were they? According to the report, blood was swirling in the waves around them, like they'd been beaten or stabbed. Or shot."

Claude sighed deeply. "Aye. The report documents Henry arriving at the police station that day with Ronald, in a panic. The officer on duty could hardly understand. Henry's spoken English was apparently good, but he reverted to German when he was stressed. As this report says, Henry and Ronald, the factory guard, saw the boys floating in the bloodied waves, and although it looked like the boys were not struggling or treading water, it might not be too late to save them. The officer called the lifeboat office, down at the harbor, and from what I've heard, the boat that could get out quickest was a fishing vessel that had just come in, and the captain volunteered to turn around and look for the boys."

"So," Helen asked, feeling renewed disgust at the whole episode, "does this mean there was *not* an actual lifeboat call-out, no official effort to find the boys, or the bodies at that point?"

"Remember, it was *wartime*, Helen. Maybe the local lifeboat was already deployed on a rescue, who knows. But there is no record in the lifeboat history for Kilvellie that they even knew about the call from the police."

"How do *you* know all this?" Helen demanded. "It's not written here in the ledger!"

Despite the rising tension, Claude maintained a reassuring tone, not the defiance he'd shown at Elise's.

"I know because Elise Endicott's grandfather was that fisherman. The fisherman reported afterwards that he got his boat along to the water below the factory cliff, although it must have been a struggle, cutting across the waves crashing against the cliff, and the tide receding. He said he saw nobody floating in the water, or trying to swim or holding onto a piece of driftwood or something. He brought his boat back and ran up to the police station, here, I mean, and said the rescue attempt had been unsuccessful and there was no sign of any bodies. He was told to keep the whole incident to himself. We only know because, much later in life, the fisherman told his daughter, who was Elise's mum. Elise knows because of the family connection, not because she works in my office. That's why Kathryn, Elise's predecessor, was never in on the secret, even though she worked in my office into her eighties. Amazing mind, that woman."

Helen sat back in her chair and crossed her arms. "So, between you being the grandson of the town solicitor who kept quiet about Henry's and Ronald's involvement, and Elise being the granddaughter of the fisherman who'd been told to keep quiet, the two of you became the latest guardians, if you can call it that, of this terrible secret about the town?"

"Aye, the secret that six lads, six evacuee youngsters from Glasgow, died here. Due to negligence, and maybe..."

"Maybe worse," Helen reminded him. "If some or all of

them landed in the water bleeding, maybe they *were* attacked on the cliff, then shoved over."

"Exactly, and that could implicate Henry or Ronald, or even both. Maybe they conspired. This is why I didn't want to share the story with the whole group, when we were sitting in Elise's kitchen. We've kept it from Henry's and Ronald's descendants."

"May I say something, Dad?" Giles asked politely.

"Of course, son, I want your agreement in whatever course we take with this ledger."

Giles began, sounding to Helen like he was making an opening argument in court in Edinburgh.

"When my father first told me about this ledger, yesterday, of course I was shocked. I had no idea that my home town, Kilvellie, could have played a role in covering up the deaths of evacuee children. If the boys did land in the water injured and bleeding, it sounds like the question is, did the guard Ronald attack the boys, or did the factory owner Henry attack them when Ronald went into the factory for his rest break, as he claimed he did?" He stopped while Helen and Giles both nodded their heads.

"I've been wondering, could there have been a third man? I mean, what if someone else attacked the boys and shoved them over the cliff edge when Ronald was inside the factory, and as far as the story goes, Henry was up in his office, facing the street, which meant he couldn't have seen it happen either."

Claude patted Giles' back. "My son's going to be a good lawyer, eh, Helen?"

"That he is," she agreed, although she couldn't tell if his "third man" comment was made in complete innocence, or if he was referencing the old Orson Wells wartime film for his own amusement. Either way, with his confident but calm tone, she imagined him very capable of knocking holes in the prosecution's case. Or defense, depending on who he was representing.

It Continued with the Cowries

"Giles reminds me of Alistair," she said to Claude, "the American private investigator. He sometimes takes what he calls the 'devil's advocate' approach to investigating. He raises uncomfortable questions and scenarios, but he's often correct."

Helen could tell that Claude was ready to move on to practicalities; he'd pulled the ledger toward him, still open at the date of the incident.

"My son makes a good point, but I don't see how the truth will ever come out now, not with the final witness we know of, and I mean Ronald, having passed away. So here's my suggestion, and Giles is in agreement. In your presence, we suggest removing the page with this report and shredding it here, in your office. Then we'll take the ledger and scan it with the others. If anyone ever wonders about a missing date for that year, my office can take the blame."

Helen stared at Claude in confusion. "But if you're prepared to do *that*, why wasn't that page with the entry removed decades ago?"

"I can explain," Giles said. "It's believable for your office, the police station, to say that a decades-old ledger is missing, or misfiled, or misplaced. But if one entry is torn or cut out, then the ledger put back on the shelf, that's evidence that the ledger was tampered with. No matter how carefully a page is removed, forensic analysis these days will detect a human hand at work."

"Plus, there'd be a date missing," Claude pointed out.

Helen asked for a few minutes on her own to consider the suggestion. She went into the office, and Desmond looked up.

She just shook her head. "No big deal, I'm just helping Claude's son Giles with some background. I'm sure you'll get to know Giles soon, with Claude planning to retire."

"Whatever." Desmond returned his attention to his tablet. It was all Helen could do to keep from shaking him into attention.

297

Chapter 54

In the small kitchen behind the office, Helen prepared a pot of tea and placed three mugs on a tray, then grabbed one more: she'd bring a mug to Desmond while she was at it. No matter how annoyed she was, office tea courtesy had to be followed. Outwardly, Desmond exhibited no curiosity or suspicion about her closed-door meeting with the town solicitor and his successor. In this situation it was to her advantage, but for police work, she wondered if she'd do better with a sergeant who had Alistair's innate urge to question everything, to be a devil's advocate for her.

But to the dilemma at hand: should she allow the erasure, forever, of a tragic event that happened decades earlier? She thought about the story Emily told Alistair, that her grandfather had "confessed" to her that he'd taken a hard object to the six vandals, stunning them and shoving them over the cliff. But in a heartfelt letter to Alistair, Ronald denied killing six German boys. Did that mean he'd killed six *Scottish* boys, or young men?

And now her mind moved on to Ronald's recent death, and his partly sawed-through walking cane that had led her on a wide-ranging speculation about who would benefit from his death, and who had motive. The evidence all pointed to Emily's young child Bobby who'd happily told Emily, "I saw Gramps' cane" – not "saw" as in sight, but "saw" as in cut through it. Later, Helen had compared Bobby's saw with the marks on the cane.

She was no forensic expert, but she was satisfied of a

match. So satisfied that she'd disposed of the broken cane, the only piece of physical evidence in a possible murder. Just days ago, she'd felt so secure in that decision, and now she cringed, faced with a similar scenario, but this related to possible murder of six men during the Second World War.

The comforting scent of her Afternoon Blend black tea blend wafted up from the teapot, bringing her back to the present. She was startled when Desmond was suddenly at her side.

"Sorry, ma'am, but Claude's wondering if you'll be back to the meeting soon."

"Aye," she said quickly, "tell him I decided to make some tea for everyone and I'll be there shortly."

"Can I carry the tray in?" Desmond offered, but Helen couldn't risk him seeing the page in the ledger that had his late grandfather's name, and asking about it. "No, thanks Desmond. In fact, you can get going if you want. I know you still have lots to do, helping get your dad's house ready to sell. I'll lock up here."

"Thank you, ma'am!" And without a moment's hesitation, without wondering why he wasn't to enter the conference room, even to carry in the *tea tray,* Desmond grabbed his tablet and phone from the desk and was out the front door without a backward glance. *Like a child released from school early,* Helen thought to herself.

His childlike behavior brought her full circle to Emily's child, whose actions might have caused Ronald's cane to break as he stood up from the bench. She pictured poor Ronald stumbling, maybe crying out in vain as he realized he was too close to the cliff edge. She forced the image of that terror from her mind, and now realized that if the tide had been in when he fell, he would have landed in water, and not on the hard, rocky beach.

Assuming no fatal stroke or heart attack before he fell into the water, perhaps he could have been saved. A life-preserver hung literally feet away, near the base of the cliffside stairway, above the high-water mark. Someone on the steps, maybe watching the surf and impatient to resume their beachcombing, would have seen or heard Ronald land in the water. If they'd acted fast, they could have tossed the preserver to him, while at the same time they or someone else could have called 999 on a mobile phone and summoned help.

And by the same reasoning, if the tide had been *out* when the six factory vandals fell, there would have been a dry scene with six bodies lying on the beach, and perhaps some of them, much younger and fitter than old Ronald, could have survived the fall. Or survived just long enough to tell what had happened. Had they been pushed? Had they been attacked while still on the clifftop?

Lifting the tea tray, she suddenly stopped: did it all come down to the tide? Was the truth about the six lads lost to history because the tide was in and they drowned, whereas Ronald's fall was well-documented, because the tide was out? And as an old man with weak bones, he died from the fall, whereas he might have lived if he'd fallen in water and help was near at hand, thanks to the steps and the life preservers, all installed by Henry.

Allowing those celestially-governed tides—events out of human control—to make the decision for her, she carried the tea tray to the conference room; the two McMahons had left the door open and were glancing out, probably wondering what was taking her so long.

She placed the tray in the middle of the table. "One of you be Mother, mine's milk and two sugars." She left the conference room again but soon returned, rolling a wheeled shredder in front of her, with a pair of scissors in her hand. She plugged in the shredder, then sat down and took courage from a few gulps of tea.

"I'm ready to shred that page," she announced. Then, glancing at the musty volume, added, "Heck, I'm ready to shred the whole ledger, but what looks like ancient history to

us, could be gold for a historian, so I know we have to preserve the other entries."

She took the scissors, opened the ledger to the flagged
page, and carefully snip-snipped along by the spine, the
blades noisily beginning the work. Then, with a final glance,
she fed the report of six bleeding men floating in the waters
of Kilvellie, beneath the towering clifftop glass factory, into
the unjudging, whirring teeth of the shredder as it completed
the work of the scissors.

"Wow!" Giles cried as he watched. "I have a horrible sense
of erasing history, but as Dad explained to me, sometimes it's
for the best."

"*Occasionally* for the best," Claude corrected. "Don't
make a habit of it, son. And if by chance someone recognizes
a name on the new sign to be installed at the stairway by the
cliff, and they come to your office, as town lawyer, after going
to the police station and learning that the digitized reports
from that year are incomplete, what will you tell them?
Remember, by then, the person might be quite irate. Or
heartbroken."

"Of course, I will be very sympathetic," Giles replied duti-
fully, "but I'll say it was all before my time, and although I
wish I could help, I understood that the old ledgers had been
destroyed once the pages were scanned in and organized."

"Good lad, but you forgot one thing, offer them tea first.
And you can always call me. Not that I'll be much help from
my beach home in Spain, but you can try!"

Helen smiled. "That's where Richard's retired to. Are you
moving there also?"

"Nae, I'll never leave Scotland, but I might move away
from here. Spend my retirement somewhere near a rocky
shore while my wife looks for groatie buckies."

"You're kidding!" Helen laughed. "At this moment,
Alistair's fiancée Margaret is out on an island in the
Hebrides. She got a tip about a good groatie buckie beach
there. Something about finding hundreds in an afternoon.

But she swore me to silence about the location."

Claude took out his wallet. "*Hundreds in an afternoon,* you say? What's your price?"

"Awe, Claude, put away your money. Silence has no price."

"Och well, worth a try."

"But you could ask Richard Wilson," Helen added. "That's who gave Margaret the tip. He might do the same for you after a couple of whiskies. But don't say I sent you."

Helen glanced over at Giles, who was busy on his phone. "Sorry Giles, I can get a bit carried away." She finished her tea and handed Claude the now-sanitized ledger. "You're sure that's the only entry that could implicate Ronald or Henry in the lads' deaths?"

"Aye, Giles and I, and Elise, have all looked through the other entries. I'm afraid to say, the rest is dull reading. It's the war context that makes them of historic interest. Just petty thefts, a few pub brawls, the usual policework in a quiet Scottish seaside town."

"That's why I came here." Helen sighed and shook her head. "I didn't bargain on what the past few weeks have brought, but I hope things will calm down."

Claude looked at Giles, who was still focused on his phone. Helen could already see that her future interactions with young Giles would be quite different from the chatty, casual approach of his father. The cups of tea. When he wasn't threatening her, that is.

"Son, be a good lad and take the ledger back to the office," Claude said. "I have some errands to do."

Chapter 55

When Giles had left the police station with the ledger, Claude stood with Helen at the front door. "I am eternally grateful to you for not pressing charges after Elise and I behaved the way we did at her house. It was completely out of character."

"It really is fine," Helen assured him. "The two of you inherited a terrible secret from your own parents and grand-parents. I can understand you resenting me coming in and demanding the ledger, asking difficult questions after only working here a short time. By the way, I never asked why the ledger was at Elise's in the first place. I thought you kept it at the office."

"Honestly? We were going to burn it, and get rid of the memorial plaque. Elise's son took it down for her. He's a vol-unteer guide at the chapel. But thanks to your intervention, we'll get the names of those six poor lads into the daylight. With old Ronald gone, there is no witness left to identify those boys as the vandals, and history can go forward with an abridged version." He fell silent.

"Which is...?" Helen prompted.

"They were six evacuee lads from Glasgow who had been sent to Kilvellie Towers, a place that burned down taking the records with it. The lads somehow made it to this town, helped out at the soldiers' convalescent home, and then trag-ically drowned. Perhaps they took a boat out, or perhaps they fell from the crumbling cliff when they were playing. Maybe they got caught on the beach when the tide came in. It will allow any surviving family to create their own narrative that the boys were happy up until just before they died, but at least that story will not implicate Henry or Ronald. Really, that's been our primary concern all along, I mean the bad publicity. Plus the tragedy of the deaths, don't get me wrong."

"I really do understand." Helen thought again about obliterating the evidence that three-year-old Bobby had damaged his great-grandfather's walking cane, maybe leading to the old man's death.

She placed a hand on Claude's arm. "I also feel strongly about not burdening subsequent generations, like Desmond's future children, and Malky's future grandchildren, with knowledge of ancient misdeeds at the factory. There has to be a line, don't you think?"

"Aye," Claude said, poised to leave. He patted Helen's hand and shook his head. "There has to be a line, Helen. I just hate to be the one *drawing* that line, but if not us, then who?"

And with that rhetorical question hanging in the air between them, he thanked her again and left, looking older and more burdened than when he'd arrived carrying the ledger and its now-shredded tell-tale entry.

She knew how he felt. She'd be haunted by the sawed-through walking stick for the rest of her days. Maybe she *should* tell her son Adam. After all, she didn't want to end up like poor Ronald, mentally burdened by a dangerous secret he'd kept for decades, and eventually becoming bitter and alienating his son and grandson.

From the open door, she looked out at the peaceful streets of Kilvellie, the visitors and townspeople alike enjoying the late afternoon sun, the gulls swooping and hoping to steal someone's fish supper, the salty air blowing in from the North Sea. The North Sea guarded so many secrets, and now she did too. She'd put off the decision whether to tell Adam. Instead, she went back inside and called Richard's mobile phone.

"Ready for supper?" she asked.

"Aye, lass. Meet you at our usual picnic bench?"

Smiling, she went into her residence to change out of her uniform.

***

She was locking the station front door, on her way out for the evening, when she heard her name; she turned, thinking it would be Richard, but it was Desmond, out of his uniform and wearing jeans and a rugby shirt.

"I'm just off to meet some mates at the pub." He stopped at the bottom of the steps up to the station entrance. "I went over to our old house, just to see how Dad's getting on clearing it. Boy, Granddad really was losing it before he went to the care home."

"What makes you say that?" Helen forced herself to ask, although she just wanted to meet Richard, who'd be waiting at the picnic table by now, and put thoughts of old Ronald from her mind. She walked down the steps and listened to the young sergeant.

"Strangest thing! Dad told me not to bother with the garage, he'd do that himself, but I figured I'd see what's stored in there. The kitchen door into the garage is locked and I couldn't find a key, so I got a bolt-cutter from the cellar to cut off the padlock on the front garage door. That key's probably been missing for years. Anyway, in the garage there were all these tree branches, like Granddad was making a nest or some such nonsense, and on the bench there was a toy saw, a bit like Emily's bairn's I guess! Granddad had been using it to cut the branches. Weird, huh?"

And with a wave, he was off again, not waiting for a response from his boss.

With shaking hands, Helen unlocked the station door again and flopped down in her desk chair. Her mind was reeling, her first thought being the now-destroyed walking

305

stick: *What have I done?*

And her second thought was, her sergeant did not have a suspicious bone in his body. If he was to be a successful officer, he'd need to be far less trusting. Surely any other copper would realize what the strange garage scene really meant: someone had planned it all in advance and practiced, and that someone had to be Richard, his daughter Emily, or her husband. Or even Desmond, but she was sure her sergeant was incapable of such skillful misdirection.

She thought quickly. If she cancelled dinner, Richard would likely go home and he'd have a chance to tidy up the garage as soon as he noticed that the padlock was gone. She had to keep the date. She'd say nothing to Richard of her suspicions, but she'd invite him back to her residence after dinner, then make a discreet call to her superior officer with an urgent request to send a team to Richard's house and secure the property, starting with the garage, as a prelude to opening a formal investigation of Ronald's death.

Then, tomorrow morning, she would tender her resignation. The disgrace would follow her forever: after a long successful career solving crime in Edinburgh, she'd managed to bungle a case of premeditated murder in a peaceful Scottish seaside town.

Chapter 56

As Helen walked from the police station to the picnic table near the fish and chip shop, she wondered how she would get through the next couple of hours, feigning ignorance of what Richard or his daughter or son-in-law had done. If it was Emily or her husband, perhaps Richard had no idea, in which case dinner should go smoothly.

But surely Richard knew something was suspicious about the garage, or he wouldn't have reacted the way Margaret said he did, when she suggested checking the garage for the groatie buckies. Helen just had to try and act normally.

Richard was waiting for her, a bottle of red wine and two glasses on the table. He seemed happy and relaxed, in a clean tartan shirt and jeans. No evidence that he'd made a start on clearing tree branches from his garage.

"We usually drink white, so I got this Spanish *Rioja* for a change. Hope you like it."

Helen sat down and smiled. She accepted a glass and sipped it, but she'd have to limit her intake for what she had to do later. Otherwise, after a couple of hours in Richard's company, she might lose her resolve, and not follow through with her decision about investigating Ronald's death.

She watched the waves and tried to relax while Richard went to the fish shop to pick up their suppers. She'd keep the conversation light, ask him back for coffee, and make the call while she was in the kitchen, out of his hearing. Then, she would keep him from going home for an hour or two, long enough for officers to secure his house.

She realized, she didn't know if he was sleeping at that house now, or still staying at a B&B in town, but she wouldn't ask. The less he knew about her role in what was to transpire that night, the better. Not that it would matter: she assumed this would be their last dinner together. Sad as it was, she had to follow the ethical standards she expected of everyone else. She had let her son down, but she'd worry about that later.

The fried haddock, as always, was excellent, and Helen indulged in plenty of salty chips to keep herself calm. If Richard noticed she was eating more than usual, he was polite enough not to comment.

When they'd finished eating, with the paper plates secure in the trash and out of reach of scavenging gulls, Helen was about to launch her plan and invite Richard back for coffee, but he poured refills of wine. He stared at the sea for a moment, before looking her in the eyes and saying he had something to tell her.

She had an involuntary moment of excitement, and then panic, that perhaps he was going to reveal his feelings for her, but to her relief, he didn't. Instead, he said he had a confession to make. Now her panic turned to horror: was he going to admit to damaging his *own father's* walking cane?

Finally he spoke. "Lass, let me tell the story my way, and no questions yet, okay?"

Helen nodded in agreement, although it might mean a long delay before she could put her plan in place.

"As you know," he began quietly, "I got to the beach that afternoon when Dad fell, just as the emergency crew arrived. You were walking around and taking statements from bystanders. You and Desmond, I mean. I was shocked, it was such a horrible end for the old guy. The medics said he would have died instantly, if he wasn't already almost dead from a heart attack or stroke up on the cliff. So that was some relief."

He stopped to drink his wine. Helen kept quiet. So far, none of this was news to her.

"When the medics were lifting him onto the stretcher, to carry him up the staircase to the ambulance, I noticed his walking stick lying in two pieces on the beach, and I just picked them up. I figured the stick had snapped, probably when he fell on it."

Helen forced her mind back to that terrible day on the beach. She remembered that the emergency services had been prepared to lift Ronald from the beach by helicopter, if they found any signs of life. But sadly, with no reason to rush him to the hospital, they had the time to carry his body up the staircase to an ambulance waiting on the clifftop. She tuned back to what Richard was saying.

"One of the other medics was gathering up equipment on the beach, and he offered to take the cane from me. As I handed it to him, I noticed the broken edges had some kind of regular pattern, so I asked him if someone on his crew had used a handsaw to, I don't know, maybe the stick had been pinning down a piece of clothing? I couldn't think what else.

"The medic glanced at it, then pointed down to the area around where Dad had landed. He said the marks could have come from scraping against a rough stone when the cane broke. Then he just stuffed the cane in a plastic bag to make it easier to carry, and he took off to catch up with the others. It sickens me now that I didn't even think to keep the broken cane, just out of nostalgia for the poor old guy."

Helen was fighting an urge to tell Richard what she knew, or what she thought she knew, but still kept quiet. Surely he wouldn't be telling her all this if he'd been the one who did the damage? But she asked him to wait while she tore a piece of paper from her pocket notebook. Without showing him, she wrote four words, then folded the paper and placed it on the table, under her phone.

"Just something I need to remind myself," she said. "Sorry, keep going."

After topping up both their wine glasses, Richard continued.

"I was at Emily's a few days ago. I kept away for so long, with her resenting how I'd treated my dad, and now she seems ready to try and restore our relationship. But Helen, how can I? I don't know how to tell you this, but I think someone in her home tampered with Dad's walking cane!"

He buried his face in his hands, and Helen reached over to grasp his arm for a moment.

"Tell me what you suspect, Richard," she said gently. "Or if you would prefer to stop there and speak to an officer from another station, I can call someone to meet you tonight." She indicated her phone, still sitting on the folded paper.

Near tears, he took his hands down. "Helen, if I tell another officer, you know what will happen. They'll take Em and her husband in for questioning, and where would the bairn go? Into temporary care? No, I want to tell *you,* and then if you decide to bring in outside officers, I will respect your decision. Truly. I had hoped our relationship would, well, become something lasting, but after tonight I don't see how it can."

"Richard," Helen pleaded, "don't get ahead of yourself. Calm down and tell me what you suspect."

He took a long swig of wine before continuing.

"I'd given the bairn a wee set of toy tools. Em had said he liked watching his father, the rare times he was home, doing repairs around the house, and I thought wee Bobby would enjoy having his own little plastic hammer, that sort of thing. They were bright yellow, I remember. I figured they would be easy for Em to find and put away after he'd played with them. So I guess, I'm making up for lost time by buying him toys, and I went back to the shop to get something else, maybe toy gardening tools. They were on display by the same tool set I'd already bought him, and I tell you Helen, my heart sank, because the teeth on that damned little saw reminded me of the strange edges on the broken ends of Dad's cane."

It Continued with the Cowries

"So, what do you make of this?" Helen forced herself to pretend this was all news to her.

"I couldn't believe it was possible for the toy saw to cut into wood, or I never would have bought Bobby that set of tools! I bought another of the same toy saws and I took it to my old house to try it out. I couldn't find any old walking sticks or canes in the house, so I dragged some tree branches into the garage and tried the saw on them." He sighed deeply. "God help us, but the cuts looked like I remembered on Dad's cane. Helen, that's why I think someone in my family, my *own family*, set out to hurt Dad. Maybe they didn't set out to kill him, just to hasten him on his way with a bad fall."

Richard's eyes were wide and he turned his head side to side as if he was trapped. Helen knew he was close to panicking.

She grasped his arm again to get him to focus. "Richard, listen to me! If we officially report this, they will want to know who had a motive to harm your father. Why on earth would Emily or her husband want to, as you call it, hasten his death? Or do you think someone visited the house and, I don't know, set them up?"

"I've been racking my brain, Helen, and I can't imagine any reason. I've come to the conclusion, and this makes me more sick than I can say, that my wee grandson, little Bobby, could have done it when no one was looking, when Dad was visiting Em recently. And I'm completely to blame! I bought him that damn tool set! So when the officers get here, tell them *I* did it, Helen! I'm begging you! Make up some story, like I was showing the bairn how to use the saw! Lie if you have to."

Helen sat still, her mind in turmoil. Richard had arrived at the same conclusion as her, based on the same facts. The cane had not just snapped when it landed on the beach; the teeth edges on the child's saw could cut through wood and were consistent with the broken ends of the cane; and the child had access to the cane. Oddly, she and Richard had

311

independently ruled out Emily and her husband, and focused on the child. That gave her some comfort that her decision was correct.

Richard was now fighting off tears, holding a handkerchief over his eyes. Helen gently took his hands away from his face and looked him in the eye. "Richard, I'm not going to call anyone. Read this." She handed him the slip of paper from under the phone.

At first he had a hard time focusing through his tears, so he read it again, aloud, then looked up at Helen. "You guessed it too? So you figured out that the cane was destroyed. But you couldn't have suspected *wee Bobby*, could you?"

"Listen, Richard," she said, taking the note back. "The cane is destroyed as in 'the evidence is destroyed.' With no cane, there's no case. It's *over*, Richard. The tragedy of it will always be with you, but I'd already investigated and reached the same conclusion. I was going to keep it to myself, to prevent you from knowing what your grandson probably did. But you solved it as well, and there's nothing I can say to undo what you know."

"How, how did you..." Richard spluttered. "Who else knows?"

Helen knew she had to explain how she found out; he might hear it from Emily or Desmond, then he'd wonder why she hadn't told him.

"Your Emily realized it after Bobby virtually admitted it. Desmond called me the other night and asked me to come to Emily's house as soon as possible. According to Emily, her son had told her a night or two *before* your father died, 'I saw Gramps' cane' and like anyone would, she took it to mean he had seen Gramps' cane. But then, and this will sound odd, Desmond and Emily were both at Emily's house when a television show about orangutan behavior came on. One orangutan had learned to use a saw to cut into a tree branch, and Bobby began imitating with his own yellow saw, calling out again and again, 'I saw Gramps' cane' which he'd said previously, so he wasn't just imitating what he was watching on the screen."

Richard shook his head in disbelief. "Oh, my poor girl, my poor Em! What did you say when she'd told you?"

"Like any sensible officer, I started by making tea. Sorry to be flippant, but Emily was beside herself with grief. She blames herself for handing the damaged cane to her grandfather, not realizing it was compromised. Maybe you didn't know, your dad had left his cane behind at Emily's one evening. A day or two before he died. So Bobby could have damaged it then."

"And Emily *didn't notice* when she put the cane in the car the next day?" Richard had an incredulous look on his face.

"Think, Richard! You've had children and you've been around Bobby. How carefully do parents look at things when they're packing up a car to go out with a child? Half of Emily's attention would have been on Bobby, making sure he didn't run into the street, and she probably gave the cane barely a glance when she grabbed it and put it in the car. She said she handed the cane to your father when she left him by the bench that afternoon. So the first time he could have used the cane, after the damage, was if he leaned on it to help himself up from his bench. And with the cliff edge so near, that may be how it happened. The saddest part of so many sad parts, is that he didn't first use the partly sawed cane when he was getting up from a chair indoors, when the resulting fall wouldn't have been fatal. Maybe some bruises, but nothing serious."

"And the cane's really gone? Permanently? What happened?"

"That's for me to take to the grave."

Richard's eyes widened. "You did that for my family? You *destroyed evidence*? Helen, this is your *career* you're playing with!"

Helen glanced around quickly in case someone had overheard. "Keep your voice down, Richard. I did it for Bobby. That child should never know that his great-grandfather's death was anything but a sad accident, at an age when the old man could have died at any moment anyway. And I can retire. It's not like I'm risking a long future career."

"But what about Emily?" Richard asked next, still not quite believing what Helen had done. "And Desmond? They told you they suspected that might be what happened."

"I haven't spoken to Emily since then," Helen admitted. "I'm hoping it will develop into one of those, I know, and you know, and I know you know, and so on, but we never actually acknowledge it. I hope she will be more careful about what Bobby plays with from now on, but what good would it do for this to be an open topic of discussion in their family? It's up to you, if you want to talk to her and explain what you suspect. I won't tell her you know, and I certainly won't tell Desmond. Oddly, he hasn't even mentioned it since he came back to work. Maybe he assumes that Emily was wrong in her suspicions, and has dismissed the whole idea."

She stopped and drank more wine before raising what, for Richard, would be another painful subject.

"This actually ties in with something about Desmond. I hate to be critical of your son, and I know he's still learning, but Richard, the young man seems to have no sense of suspicion, or curiosity. Do you know what he told me just before I met you for dinner tonight? He said he'd been over at your old house, and he'd found the branches and the toy saw in the garage."

"Oh, no!" Richard slapped his hand to his forehead. "He had no reason to go into the garage, not yet! Does he suspect that *I* damaged the cane? That's awful!"

"No, he didn't suspect you. Not only that, even after he'd been at Emily's when she realized that the cane might have been damaged in her house, most likely by her son, here's Desmond's explanation of what he found in the garage. He said his grandfather, your father I mean, must have dragged

314

the branches in *four years ago* when he still lived at the house, before moving to the care home." She shook her head. "How could that scene not have raised *any* questions in his mind?"

"Like..." Richard hesitated. "Like *I'd* been practicing with the toy saw, see if it would cut wood, before doing my own dad in?"

"Something like that. I'll need to find a training course to send him on."

Richard thought for a few moments before he spoke again. "Helen, I'm glad you raised the question of Desmond's competence, or lack thereof. I've also been hesitant to say anything, in case it came across as a comment on your training and supervision skills..."

She interrupted. "Richard, please speak freely if it would help Desmond's career development. I know it's awkward, being his father, but it can only benefit him. And the station."

"Thanks Helen. Here's what worried me recently. It was the day you visited Elise, and nobody could reach you by phone. You know that Adam contacted Desmond, who in turn contacted me. We all gathered outside the McMahon office building, and Adam and Alistair had gone upstairs and found the sign saying the office was closed for a few days. Normally I would take that at face value, but then I wondered if you were in there with one or both of them. Clearly, things were going to be different with Dad gone, the final witness to the factory vandalism. I don't know, maybe they hung up the out of office sign to prevent any persistent clients from banging on the door during a sensitive meeting."

"That makes sense, I guess. Go on."

"Anyway, when we were all outside the office wondering what to do, I remembered that the station has keys to that old building, for emergency access, so I asked Desmond to fetch them. He questioned that, and was ready to take the sign at face value. He had no suspicion at all that you might be in there."

315

"Or he had less motivation than you to find me." Helen smiled, then turned serious again. "I agree, it is another example of a lack of imagination, that things may not be as they seem at first glance."

Richard poured refills and they sipped their wine, both looking out to the sea for inspiration.

"Maybe he should spend more time with Alistair," Richard suggested, and Helen nodded. "But seriously, Helen," he continued, "I will not take it personally if you want to have Desmond reassigned and choose your own sergeant. Maybe it would be better anyway, if you and I..."

She smiled again. "Yes, if you and I continue to develop our friendship, it could look like a conflict to have your son working with me in that capacity. Well, we can think about that."

Richard pointed at Helen's phone. "Is this really over? No call to 999 to start an investigation into Dad's death? No repercussions for Emily or Bobby?"

"Not as far as I'm concerned. Poor Emily will have her suspicions the rest of her life. I tried to tell her that even if the cane had *broken* on the clifftop, her grandfather might have had a heart attack up there, and the fall could have been unrelated to the cane breaking. Maybe over time she'll start to think that way, and not blame herself."

"But it's really *my* fault, for buying him the toy tools."

"No, Richard. If you're going to shift blame up the ladder, then it's the toy manufacturers and sellers. It is not your fault that you relied on a product being sold as safe for children."

"I'll try to look at it that way." He sighed. "Well, Helen, this hasn't been the relaxed evening you were expecting, has it? What do we do now?"

"I really need to catch up on sleep, but if you're not disappearing to Spain tomorrow after what we've just discussed, how about same time same place tomorrow evening? Might as well eat outdoors while the weather lasts."

With the plans set, Helen walked back to the police station and let herself in through the residence door. Fighting tears of relief, she felt like she'd had a very narrow escape. And a new lease on life: she wouldn't resign tomorrow, and Richard was still a presence in her life after all.

Next stop, the Jacuzzi.

Chapter 57

The morning after Helen's emotionally wrought dinner with Richard, she began her day at the police station feeling confident, ready to tackle whatever came next. The remaining Kilvellie mystery, and she didn't want to belittle it, involved the six young men who had, according to the now-shredded police report and a memorial plaque, died in nineteen forty-four.

She hoped that, when the list of their names next to the officially dedicated beach stairway became more widely distributed, families would claim their missing young men, and have a chance for closure. If only there was more information available in the town, but the two solicitors, Claude and Elise, and their predecessors, had gone to great lengths to keep the facts hidden for decades.

Aside from that project, which might unfold over years, Helen had two immediate issues to deal with. First, her son Adam. She imagined him sitting in his home office up in Inverness, brooding over the fact that Helen still hadn't opened an official investigation into Ronald's death.

Maybe the solicitors were onto something, with their decision to entrust the town secret to one or two people in each subsequent generation. At least that way they had someone to discuss it with. Maybe Adam could be her confidant? No, she couldn't imagine him accepting, let alone approving of what she'd done, destroying evidence. Twice, she reminded herself: the broken cane, and the page from the old police ledger. Well, the second one was something he'd never need to know about.

Her other immediate problem was Desmond: how could she manage an efficient police station if her sergeant behaved like a kid who couldn't wait for the school bell to ring at the end of the day, and had zero capacity for critically judging a suspicious set of circumstances? Richard had been joking when he suggested that Desmond should spend time with Alistair, but the idea of having them work together on something police-related was not a bad one. She'd have to give it some thought.

The station office door opened, signaling the start of the day's minor complaints, questions from the public, and maybe an occasional social visit. She was surprised to see Claude McMahon again. They'd had a meeting recently, so she hoped nothing serious had occurred since then.

"I'm not stopping for long," he began. "My son Giles, at the office, suggested we start scanning your police ledgers. The law students are here, so we can get it done quickly. Maybe begin with the newest ones, since you'd be more likely to refer to them and it could help to have them digitized first?"

"Aye, that would be grand. Desmond's not in yet, otherwise I'd ask him to carry a batch over there."

"Nae problem, I'll take a few with me now, and I'll write down a list of which ones I take so you don't think they've gone missing too!"

Helen smiled, but she thought it was premature to make light of the recent events surrounding the missing nineteen forty-four ledger. At least Claude was trying to move beyond his embarrassing behavior. She took the five most recent volumes from a shelf and placed them on her desk.

"There's not much written in the past couple of years," she explained. "Desmond's been keeping his records on his laptop, so those ones shouldn't take long."

She watched while Claude wrote down the years of the ledgers on a sheet of paper, then signed and dated it. "Do you want me to sign it as well?" Helen asked.

"Och, might as well make it official."

He lifted the books up. "You wouldn't believe how much of this we have to get through, Helen. I didn't realize quite what Giles has taken on, scanning all the decades of our law firm cases. By the way, when I took the framed photo to Kathryn at the care home the other day, I stayed to chat. I thought she'd enjoy hearing about my reluctance to be dragged into the twenty-first century, with the scanning and the digitizing. She actually said it would be great if someone did that for the care home. For a moment I almost offered, but not without knowing in advance how much work it would be. Anyway, I'd need to coordinate with the manager, not a resident."

Helen looked at him in surprise. "A modern health care facility like that? Surely they do everything online these days."

"Oh, she didn't mean for the current facility. She said there's a storeroom in the cellar, according to one of the maintenance fellows who works there. Apparently they go back to when the place was a hotel, so there could be records of royalty and celebrities, all sorts. A bonanza for the historical society, I'd think. But as I said, I restrained myself from volunteering Giles and his team to scan all that old stuff."

Laughing, Helen walked Claude to the front door and promised to send Desmond over with another batch of ledgers soon.

Back at her desk, she looked up the care home website and clicked on the page that described the history of the building: from a private manor house in the nineteenth century, to a glamorous hotel between the World Wars, then serving as a convalescent home for soldiers in the nineteen forties. After that, the building had a good run as a hotel again, hosting celebrity events and the occasional royal visit. By the late twentieth century, those events had diminished in frequency, and with the growing number of well-heeled elderly, it had become a care home for those lucky enough to afford it.

Helen wondered about the records Claude had mentioned. It might be a long shot, but maybe there would be some information about the six evacuees among the convalescent home records, if such things still existed in the care home cellar. A project for Alistair and Desmond? Worth some thought, she decided.

Then she wondered, not for the first time, if Alistair was beginning to resent how much she relied on him. She'd given him a bit of money from her discretionary fund when he and Adam spent a few hours studying Ronald's wartime diaries, but she couldn't justify using police funds to look through the Seaview Manor Home's decades-old storage boxes. Not without opening an official missing persons case, anyway, and she doubted that her superior officers would divert resources to track down a handful of evacuees from decades earlier. It might eventually lead to closure and some public appreciation from families, but at the expense of investigating crimes affecting people today? Probably not.

On the other hand, Alistair did seem to be at loose ends: in the past three weeks, he had dropped everything to come to Kilvellie whenever asked. And, he hadn't been sure whether he'd accompany Margaret to remote beaches to collect cowries, so maybe he'd appreciate the offer of some challenging work while Margaret was away, even if he wouldn't be paid to do it.

Chapter 58

Alistair was eating dinner alone at home in Finlay, staring out at the beach and debating about whether to join Margaret on her groatie buckie quest. He just couldn't get up the enthusiasm for the long-promised work on her cottage, for some reason. Not enough of an intellectual challenge, perhaps. Collecting shells wasn't a challenge either, but at least he'd be outdoors and seeing some new parts of Scotland.

His cell phone rang: Helen. Why would she be calling in the evening? He thought they'd resolved all the strange twists and turns of Kilvellie's past, and that he and Helen wouldn't have much to discuss until Margaret was back, when Helen had promised to visit.

With trepidation, he answered the phone, then listened with increasing interest as Helen told him that the care home in Kilvellie had a storeroom with records of the building going back through its various iterations since it had ceased being a family home.

"I went over there today and the manager let me have a quick look in the boxes. I didn't say why, just routine police business, nothing to worry about."

"Since you're calling me, you must have found something of interest," Alistair said, then listened again while she explained that there were some file folders labeled "Evacuees," which gave her hope that they might hold information about the six boys, and possibly other children who were still unaccounted for since the war.

"What are you thinking, Helen? Can I help you look

through them or something?"

"You read my mind. You and Desmond, if you are comfortable working with him."

"I guess." He thought for a moment, his resolve to never go back to Kilvellie being challenged yet again. But at least it would be a form of investigative work.

"Yes, I'd like to help, and it's my own dime, as they say. Maybe I can drive up there tomorrow morning so we can discuss it together, with Desmond, as early as it works for both of you?"

"Perfect," Helen agreed. "Let's meet at the care home at ten o'clock. And lunch will be on me afterwards."

***

At five o'clock the following afternoon, Alistair was returning home to Finlay in a much better frame of mind than just twenty-four hours previously. He glanced in his rear view mirror at the file boxes on the back seat, and thought of the brand new scanner in the trunk, which he'd picked up in St. Andrews on his way home.

At the care home that morning, he and Helen had looked with increasing glee at the wealth of information hidden for decades in the file boxes. Most of it was unorganized, but there were World War Two-era photographs, including some that showed the same young man as in Kathryn's family portrait. A quick glance at the back of them revealed names and dates. There were several folders labeled "Kilvellie Towers," the place where those six boys should have been sent from Glasgow, and in a jumble of papers, there were lists of names, apparently of evacuees, and addresses in both Edinburgh and Glasgow.

Alistair had offered to not just go through the documents and photographs, but to scan and organize them at the same time. Once he'd done all that and had, he hoped, a timeline and a rough idea of who the other five boys were, besides

Kathryn's brother, and where they had lived pre-evacuation, the true investigation would start.

Desmond would help on that part; Alistair had quickly realized, at the care home, that the young sergeant just didn't have the curiosity and drive that had to be applied to the jumble of records. He'd had a quiet word with Helen, who'd agreed to let Alistair handle the organizing part.

He smiled, thinking there might even be a book in all this. Yet again, Kilvellie was not done with him.

***

Meanwhile, back at the police station in Kilvellie, Helen was tackling the final and most difficult task on her list: speaking to her son Adam. She reached him at home, glad that he wasn't out multitasking on a job, and could give her his full attention.

"What's happening with the investigation?" he asked right away. "You've had more than a week. Have you given Ronald's cane to an outside team and told them your thoughts about who could have damaged it?"

Helen felt a moment of irritation. So, no, *How are you after your ordeal at Elise's, Mum?*

"There won't be an investigation, son."

"But *Mum*," he whined, reminding her of his occasional childhood behavior when he didn't get his way. "Everyone who had access to the cane should be questioned. At their homes, if not in a formal interview situation."

"*Everyone?*" Helen repeated.

"Yes, Mum, everyone who had the opportunity to damage Ronald's cane, then investigate motives!"

Helen had been thinking about how to share enough information with Adam to get him to stop asking, and at the same time, minimize his knowledge.

"When you say *everyone*, Adam, would you include a three-year-old child in that group?"

It Continued with the Cowries

Now Adam was at a loss for words. Helen could imagine him sighing and thinking it through. He was well aware that Desmond's sister Emily had a three-year-old boy, and that the boy, and Emily, had often been together with Ronald, Emily's grandfather, including the days up to Ronald's death.

"You *don't* mean..."

"Just leave it, Adam, please, for the family's sake? I am confident that no one damaged Ronald's cane with the intent to do him harm, or kill him, do you understand? There is nothing further to investigate."

"I, I guess I understand now," Adam muttered. "I'm sorry I've been so hard on you."

"It's fine, son. You're still young now, but in a couple of decades, you'll probably have learned that there are lines you have to draw. They are uncomfortable, but it has to be done to keep families moving forward, and not get trapped by past deeds, like poor Ronald was. I promise that on my deathbed I'll give you the details."

"Mum! That's not funny. I won't second-guess you again. I've learned my lesson."

"Don't get me wrong, I'll always welcome your input, Adam, but this case is closed for any further discussion. Changing the subject, Alistair has a new investigation for me, did he tell you?"

"No, I'll call him now! I can't wait to hear about it."

Helen ended the call and breathed a long sigh of relief. Perhaps one day she'd tell Adam what she had discovered, leading to her conclusion about poor Ronald's death, but it would have to wait. For now, she had a romantic fish supper to prepare for.

Chapter 59

Despite enjoying a relaxed meal with Richard, and with all her self-appointed loose ends tied up, Helen couldn't sleep that night. So many tasks had weighed on her mind that she hadn't had a chance to mentally review passing comments people had made, and stray facts that had surfaced.

She finally got up and made a mug of cocoa, then sat on her sofa, feet up on the ottoman, and wrote things down as they surfaced in her wide-ranging memory. An hour later, finally feeling sleepy, she put away her notes, went back to bed, and slept soundly.

The next day was Saturday and she wasn't on duty, so she waited for a decent hour, nine o'clock she figured, and called Alistair.

"I hope you got the boxes home all right," she said.

"Yes, and I bought a snazzy scanner in St. Andrews en route. I've just started setting it up. Do you want to talk about the project now? I figure I'll organize all the paper files and photos, then scan them in a more systematic way. Should make it easier to set up digital files that anyone can search."

"Sounds great. I thought you were probably an early riser, but sorting out a scanner before breakfast is beyond my capability. Anyway, you're probably tired of me and Kilvellie melodrama, but I've only now had a chance to process some of the information that came to light in the past few days. Would you mind getting together so I can run some things by you?"

"Sure, how soon? I mean, I could drive up there today..."

She interrupted. "No Alistair, you've done plenty of driving for now. Can I visit you? Maybe get some of that good Indian food from the hotel to take back with me."

"How long do you think we need?" he asked.

"Sorry, do you have plans later? I shouldn't presume."

"No, just the opposite. Margaret's still away. We have plenty of room for guests, so if you, or you and Richard...?" He let the question hang in the air.

"I don't want to involve Richard in this right now. But if you can put up with me for a night, I'd happily take you up on the offer, and I'll even bring wine."

"Absolutely. Maybe we'll have a good sunset over the beach."

"Okay," she said, "how about if I come down there early afternoon. That way you can get back to your scanner, and we'll be able to talk into the evening."

"Anytime. If I don't answer the front door, check the beach. I often take my lunch or coffee out there."

Alistair spent part of the morning sorting out the guest room upstairs for Helen. He'd been using it as his office, but it didn't take long to move his belongings to his bedroom on the main floor, put fresh sheets on the bed, tidy up the bathroom, and wash and fold a clean set of towels. He knew it didn't come close to the luxury he and Margaret had recently enjoyed in Kilvellie, but with the beach view and sea breeze, it would be an improvement on sleeping in the police station. He wouldn't say that to Helen, though.

***

She arrived at two o'clock, looking comfortable in her jeans and a long-sleeved knit shirt, with a fleece vest. She was carrying an overnight bag and a canvas tote bag, which she placed on the kitchen counter. Once she'd unpacked two bottles of wine, her favorite snacks, and a few other goodies,

Alistair picked up the overnight bag and showed her to the upstairs suite.

"I like your staircase." She was holding onto the thick rope that served as a handrail. The stairs were fashioned of driftwood.

"I can't take any credit," Alistair said. "The cottage was exactly like this when Margaret moved in."

"I'm looking forward to hearing all about that."

He went back downstairs while Helen unpacked and familiarized herself with her home for the night. When she joined him a few minutes later, he'd brewed a pot of tea and placed it on the dining table, along with an assortment of biscuits.

"Do you want to talk about your ideas now, or relax first?" he asked, taking a seat at the table and pouring each of them a cup of tea.

"If you don't mind, I'd like to get my ideas out there for you to think about." She sat down across from him, then added milk and sugar to her tea and stirred it with a silver spoon. Alistair smiled, remembering Margaret's discovery of the Pictish silver in the same drawer that housed the silverware they used every day. He'd tell Helen the whole story later; so far, she'd only heard bits and pieces.

"The reason for the hurry," she continued, "is that it might help as you look through the materials from the care home, particularly the nineteen thirties and into the late forties."

Alistair grabbed a few sheets of blank paper from the supply near the printer and readied his pen. "Go ahead."

"There are two things that are bothering me about all we've heard."

Alistair was tempted to interrupt and ask, "Only *two*?" but he didn't want to break her train of thought.

"The biggest one is the destruction of the World War One memorial window. I don't know if you remember when you and Adam and I had dinner with Richard, and he worked himself into emotional meltdown describing how the vandals had smashed up that window?" She stopped, and Alistair realized she was waiting for his confirmation.

"Yes, I remember it very well. And especially, the image of townspeople the next day, crawling around on the grass below the broken window, looking for names of loved ones still intact."

"Aye, Richard really empathized with that scene. Now, I can imagine some bored youths who were moved far from home at the outbreak of the war. They're in unfamiliar sur-roundings, no idea how things will turn out for them. And who knows, maybe they were already trouble-makers back at home. Anyway, yes, I can see them succumbing to the temp-tation to smash up glass vases, and enjoy tossing things over the cliff. But deliberately breaking a memorial window to their own countrymen and women, people of their parents' generation who'd died just over twenty years earlier? It does-n't ring true, for me."

Alistair nodded his head. "I've had those same thoughts, Helen. I wonder if someone else broke that window and the young lads got blamed. It would have been natural to think they did all the damage."

"Exactly. That was *personal,* destroying Henry's pride and joy. I think the stories must be true, that he devoted himself to becoming a loyal Scot, putting his short history as an enemy soldier behind him. Creating and installing a memorial window to local people who'd died in the Great War, the one he fought in, was reparation in the best way he knew."

"Making glass."

She nodded her head. "Aye. For someone to break that window, they had to know it would also break Henry's heart, when he got back from internment at war's end. Or the year before, if we've got that correct."

Alistair took a few moments to sip his tea and stare out of the window before looking at Helen again.

"You may be onto something. The idea of his heart being broken. Remember the story that Emily told me, about her granddad claiming to have killed the six vandals..."

"Which he later retracted in a letter to you."

"Yes, which he later retracted. But in his letter to me, he didn't retract the bit he told Emily about the six vandals saying that Henry had looted their own family glass businesses back in Germany, just after the First World War. And didn't Greta tell you that the evacuees she had heard about, who went to Kilvellie, were from Glasgow but of German-origin families?"

"I remember you told me that. What are you thinking—if that part's true, maybe Henry broke someone's heart, not romantically I mean, but by destroying their glass business and benefiting himself, before he moved to Scotland and married Sheila?"

Alistair thought for a moment. "Maybe, but what if it *was* romantic? Did Henry abandon a fiancée back in Germany, and she or her family tracked him down to Kilvellie?"

"Or a wife," Helen ventured.

"What a mess! But I think we're onto something. Let's treat the destruction of the memorial window as a separate event from the other vandalism of the factory."

Helen glanced at the boxes from the care home, decades of records that Alistair had agreed to dig through, organize, and scan. "I really wonder if there's anything helpful in these after all."

"If there is, I will find it! Or more likely, Margaret, if she wants to help. So, first item, we have the memorial window mystery to solve. What else is on your mind?"

"You must remember since it was just a few days ago. Claude McMahon and I, I guess we're into the forgive and forget mode since then. Anyway, when we had that big reveal of the town's shameful secret at Elise's, he mentioned that he thought the lads, the vandals, were carrying out the destruction at someone's bidding. He thought it could be someone prominent in the town. Someone powerful enough to prevent or at least discourage investigation of the culprits."

"So," Alistair said, after thinking this through, "we need to imagine who would benefit from the repeated vandalism. From what I've heard, they did damage in the factory itself, not just to the glass products. If that's true, it could mean involving contractors and builders to repair the damage, right?"

"I assume. I doubt that the factory employed people for that kind of structural work, not once the factory was completed in the nineteen twenties."

"Right, so maybe, after the first phase of repairs, a local contractor realized they were onto a good thing, and *they* paid or forced the lads to repeat the damage months later?"

Helen smiled. "Once again, we need good old Foyle. But your idea has merit, for sure. I expect the local contractors and builders didn't have much work during wartime, I mean, few people would be building and renovating homes and businesses. But once they saw the potential for work restoring the damaged factory, they decided to cash in on wartime opportunities, like others were doing elsewhere?"

"That's a possibility," Alistair said. "Maybe we can look at Christy's stash of wartime records, see if we can identify repeat work by a local builder. Not that it would prove that they instigated the subsequent damage. How about another scenario: what if it was someone at the home where the young men were living, I mean, the care home now, but a military convalescent home at the time. Probably a long shot, but perhaps someone in charge there had fought in the First World War, and on arrival in Kilvellie, the first thing they see is a massive, and still flourishing, glass factory built by a former enemy, meaning Henry. Not to mention that Henry married a Scottish woman."

"That's a good hypothesis, Alistair. Someone in authority at the convalescent home would have been in a position to put the fear of God in six impressionable and vulnerable lads, from Glasgow or wherever they were from. And, this is just a guess, but if the six lads really were helping care for wounded soldiers and getting hands-on experience of what the fighting over in Europe was doing to men not much older than them, they could have been terrified that as soon as they were old enough, they'd be sent to the same fate, or worse. If the war went on much longer, I mean."

Alistair pointed to the boxes. "Maybe I'll find something to support your ideas in the records. I'm glad we're talking, because without these possible scenarios to keep in mind, a seemingly innocent letter or report could take on significance."

"Those were the main points I wanted to raise." Helen quickly finished her tea. "I'd love to walk on the beach while it's nice out. How about you?"

"Yes, that would be the routine if Margaret was here, so let's go!"

***

By the time they returned from the walk, Alistair was thinking about dinner, and whether they should eat at the hotel or order take-out for him to pick up. He asked Helen, and she suggested take-out, so they could both have wine.

"It's such a short distance from the hotel," he argued. "I could have a drink there and still drive back, or walk back."

Helen shook her head. "Nae Alistair, I'll be too tired to walk. I'm sorry, but when you go out to dinner with a police officer, you can't be getting behind the wheel after a couple of drinks. And I'm not foregoing my wine to be the designated driver!"

After perusing the menu with Helen, Alistair called in an order for pick-up in half an hour, and Helen said she would drive along and collect it. He was tempted to invite Calum so that he and Helen could continue the discussion about the Kilvellie chapel, but he decided not to, in case Helen wanted to talk more about going through the care home records. In just the past few hours, that project had already changed in focus, and he wondered what exactly he'd agreed to do. And how long it would take.

Maybe he'd made a mistake, especially if Margaret would be ready to get back to Maine when her groatie buckie trip was done. He hoped she wouldn't be dismayed to return to the cottage and find a massive project that he'd committed to. Oh well, he put it from his mind and decided to enjoy the evening with Helen. At least they had reached agreement about where the "investigation" was headed.

Chapter 60

Alistair was distracted by the front door opening and the aroma of Indian spices: Helen was back, and to his surprise, Calum was right behind her, helping to carry the food.

"Look who I found!" Helen announced. "I hope you don't mind, I invited him to dinner as well."

"Of course not." Alistair took bags of food from their burdened arms and arranged them on the counter. "And who else have you invited? This is far more food than we ordered."

"Och, I just suggested a few more things," Calum said. "Didn't want to arrive empty-handed. I also have some information about the chapel that you asked about."

"Oh, good. I've got a stack of boxes to go through, from the care home. They're records from before and during the war, so Helen and I are hoping there might be some clues about the six young men who drowned, like we were discussing the other night."

Over dinner at the dining table facing the beach, Calum explained what he'd learned about Kilvellie's chapel. It had been built in the eighteen hundreds as a church, but once places of worship of other denominations became established in Kilvellie and in nearby towns, the chapel itself lost members, and by the nineteen sixties, was no longer viable as a church. However, over the decades of its existence, it had become a place for memorializing those lost at sea, hence the brass plaques and stone memorials that Alistair had seen on his first visit.

The chapel became a charitable organization, with extra

support from its use for weddings and other events. Helen remembered Greta mentioning that she'd attended a couple of funerals and a wedding at the chapel, soon after she and Malky first married.

"I heard all this history from a minister Pater knew," Calum explained. "The man's retired now, but he steps in to cover when needed in several churches. By chance, he's helping with an event in Kilvellie tomorrow and he invited me to attend."

"At the chapel?" Helen asked. "I hadn't heard about anything scheduled there. Maybe I should have my sergeant Desmond on hand to oversee the parking."

"Nae, not at the chapel. It's an outdoor memorial service for the old factory guard, your Ronald Wilson. Just people who'd known him at the care home. It's to be held near the bench where he used to sit, overlooking the North Sea."

"Makes sense," Helen said. "The police tape was taken down recently, so now it looks back to normal."

Calum thought for a moment. "Say, Helen, would you like to go to the event with me? It's short notice, but I also just found out. And Alistair, you're welcome as well."

Alistair thanked Calum. "No, you two go. I have plenty to do here, and honestly, I'm not ready for that reminder. I sat on the bench with Ronald, and it's too soon to go back and focus on his death, in the same spot."

After dinner, Helen asked Alistair if she could stay overnight on Sunday night as well, so that she could ride to the event with Calum. With Desmond back on duty, she didn't need to be at the station early on Monday.

Plans set, Calum took his leave, and Alistair and Helen resumed their discussion about the boxes.

Chapter 61

The following morning, Sunday, Calum picked Helen up from Alistair's cottage at eleven-thirty. He had come straight from the morning service at his church, and wore a black suit and his white clerical collar.

"I can't go like this, in my jeans," Helen said. "We should have time to stop at my residence and I'll change quickly. It's in town so we'd drive by it anyway."

The clifftop service for Ronald was scheduled for one-thirty, and Calum agreed that they had time for the hour-long drive and a stop at her home. They passed the trip north pleasantly, sharing stories of their backgrounds, with Calum adding a couple of anecdotes about his friendship with Alistair and Margaret.

When they approached the main street of Kilvellie, Helen directed him to the parking area behind the police station.

"Won't be a minute," she said as she stepped out of the car and hurried to the back door into the residence. Normally, she would invite Calum in, but she'd left in a hurry the previous day and hadn't tidied up in case of a guest.

She emerged a few minutes later, wearing black pants, her deep purple tunic, and a matching scarf: she could use it as a shawl in case the afternoon turned cool. Calum returned to the main road and they continued north until the cafe and the parking area came into view. He found parking near the cafe.

"I see it's possible to park nearer the bench," he said to Helen, "but I'll leave space for the more elderly attendees to be driven right out there. I'm glad there are folding chairs set up."

After a stop in the cafe for a quick cup of tea, Helen and Calum walked across the parking area. They stood with other attendees behind the chairs. Helen nodded to a few people she knew, mainly local family members who had elderly relatives living in the care home where Ronald had lived. She also recognized the care home manager, Carolyn Wortham, and they exchanged warm smiles.

"That's the minister I know," Calum whispered. Helen looked beyond the seated guests, most gray-haired, some in hats from a different era, perhaps only taken from hat-boxes nowadays for funerals. She wondered what it must be like to attend funerals and memorial services for people of one's own age; well, she figured, she wasn't that much younger, so she'd find out soon enough.

Shaking away the morbid thoughts, she tuned in and listened to the minister. In somber clerical vestments, the man looked as old as some of the care home residents.

With his back to the cliff, he stood behind a lectern; Helen guessed it had been brought from the chapel. He must have gathered stories about Ronald from the residents, and judging from the occasional laughter, they seemed to appreciate the happy memories of Ronald.

Helen let her mind drift to other thoughts about this location, the former site of the glass factory. She realized that where the minister stood now was once a grassy area in front of the expansive glass factory windows. And the site of the tragic destruction of those windows, including the war memorial window, in the early nineteen forties.

Behind the minister was the cliff edge where six young men fell to their deaths. Decades later, poor Ronald met the same fate. She shivered, and Calum took her arm for a moment.

"It is a sad day, Helen," Calum whispered. "Always sad remembering the dear departed."

Helen turned to smile at him. "It's fine, thank you Calum." She was surprised at how comforting the touch of his hand felt. Was it because he was a minister? Or something else?

With a final hymn, the service ended and the attendees begin standing up, aided by younger friends and family members. Slowly, cars were started up and the attendees headed back to the care home where a tea was set up, according to the printed program of service.

As Helen and Calum approached the minister for introductions, they were distracted by a sudden movement to their left. The town had erected a temporary sign near the top of the stairway, announcing that the stairway would soon be dedicated to the memory of six wartime evacuees, teenage boys, who had drowned nearby.

A diminutive woman, her strength belying her appearance, was leaning forward in her wheelchair, waving her wooden stick back and forth in a wide arc, trying to topple the new sign. A younger woman, about Helen's age, was reaching out to intervene, but at the same time, avoid being struck by the stick.

Helen and Calum rushed to the scene.

"Dear, I'm the local police office, Helen Griffen," she said to the woman in the wheelchair. "Can you put the stick down for a wee minute and tell me what's upsetting you?"

The older woman ignored her, but was distracted just long enough for her companion to take the stick away, then introduce herself.

"I'm Pamela, and this is my aunt, Kathryn Ramsay. Officer, I have no idea why she's upset. She was fine during the service..."

"The sign!" Kathryn screamed. "Take it doon! Take it doon!" And she burst into tears.

"What's wrong with the sign, Auntie?" Pamela asked, kneeling by the wheelchair to listen.

"It will all come out now," Kathryn wailed. "All that secrecy, for nothing!" She struggled to get to her feet and reach for the sign again. Calum placed his hand on her shoulder to gently hold her in the wheelchair before she fell and injured herself in her distress.

"Take it doon, *please!*" she wailed again, looking up at Helen with pleading eyes.

"Of course, Mrs. Ramsay, we'll take it down for now since it's so upsetting to you."

Helen silently took Calum's elbow and guided him to the sign. He nodded, and together they rocked it back and forth until the wooden stake in the ground loosened. Helen laid it flat, face down. With that done, Kathryn told Pamela to take her back to the care home. "I need to tell ye somethin', dearie," Helen heard Kathryn say as the two women approached a nearby parked car, with Pamela pushing Kathryn's wheelchair.

"Do you have any idea what upset her?" Calum asked Helen, after Pamela had declined his offer to help get the wheelchair into the back.

"No," Helen said, "but I know who she is and a bit of the history. Let's put the sign in your car boot for now, until we find out why she objects to it so much. We can go to the care home and see if she'll speak to me. Or to us."

***

When Helen and Calum arrived at the care home, they parked the car in a visitor area and climbed the front steps into the elegant lobby.

"Have you been here before?" Helen asked. Calum stopped to stare at the towering marble-floored space, with the chandelier above, and the wide red-carpeted stairs at the back.

"Nae, but it looks quite fancy to be a care home. Must cost something to stay here."

"Aye," Helen said, nodding. "That it does."

Jane Ross Potter

A uniformed staff member directed them into the sun room, where the attendees were gathering for afternoon tea. They saw Kathryn in her wheelchair, near a window, and Pamela was at the buffet table. Helen approached Pamela and introduced herself properly.

"Do you think your aunt feels up to explaining why she reacted to the sign the way she did?"

"Yes, on our drive back here, she told me she needs you to know the truth. I don't know what's going on with her. I live in Canada, as you can probably tell from my accent. Kathryn had no children, and I'm her closest remaining family. My late father was Kathryn's brother."

Brother-in-law, Helen thought to herself, but she didn't say anything to Pamela. How could Pamela be the daughter of a man who, by all accounts, had died as a teenager in nineteen forty-four? Did he leave a child behind, born to a woman in Kilvellie who then emigrated to Canada?

Fortified by strong tea, Kathryn sat in the sun in her wheelchair and chatted to Helen and Calum, mainly stories she'd heard from Ronald, who she said she missed a great deal. Helen kept hoping Kathryn would mention the sign, but didn't want to raise the subject and upset her even more.

Kathryn fell silent, then motioned to Pamela so that she could say something private. Helen saw Pamela nod her head, then she turned to Helen.

"My aunt says it will be easier to talk upstairs in her room. She's having a difficult time with all the chatting around us."

Pamela pushed Kathryn's wheelchair toward the door. "I'll take her up in the elevator," she said to Helen and Calum. "It's tiny, so you can wait for it to come back down, or take the stairs at the back of the lobby. You'll see us emerge from the elevator. It's very slow."

340

Chapter 62

Following Pamela's directions, Calum and Helen left the sun room and crossed the lobby to the staircase. "I wonder if we should have brought our teacups," Calum said quietly. "I don't know about you but I have a feeling we'll need something for strength."

Helen smiled at him. "My son Adam has visited Kathryn twice now, in her room. If his experience is any guide, we'll be well cared for in the refreshment department."

"Really? And Adam didn't learn why that sign would have upset Kathryn so much?"

"Nae, Calum. You and I are in the same boat. We'll just have to listen."

As they reached the top of the stairs, they glanced along both sides of the open walkway that encircled the lobby below. To their right, they saw a door open, and Kathryn and Pamela emerged, Pamela first, walking backwards and pulling the wheelchair. Calum hurried along the walkway to offer his help.

Pamela accepted it gratefully. "These old elevators date from when the building was a hotel. They really need to be updated."

Calum crouched to ease the small front wheels of the wheelchair over the space between the elevator floor and the hallway. He thought for a moment of his trip to London, the "mind the gap" signs in the Underground, and wondered if something similar was needed here. "Is this the only elevator for the residents?" he asked Pamela.

341

Kathryn's hearing was sharp. "Nae, Reverend," she replied. "This is the wee elevator. There's a big one out of sight of the lobby, but this one is more convenient for the sun room. Sorry to be a bother, I should have suggested using the big one…"

Calum broke in, "It's fine, Mrs. Ramsay, and if I were you, I'd be using this nice one too. It's like being in a fancy hotel. And please, call me Calum."

Kathryn looked up at him. "Well then, you must call me Kathryn."

With the wheelchair now on the solid floor of the hallway, the group proceeded along a side corridor and stopped at the closed door of Kathryn's room. While Pamela was opening it wide to accommodate the wheelchair, Kathryn pointed to the adjacent door.

"That was old Ronald's room," she said, her eyes tearing up. "Sure do miss him. Room's still empty, but I hope my future neighbor is as friendly."

Calum held Kathryn's room door open, then he and Helen followed the aunt and niece in. Soon Kathryn was settled in her comfortable chair by the window, her knitted shawl over her shoulders.

"Would you like me to call down for tea?" Pamela asked her.

"Nae, lass, the staff are all busy with the guests. Can you make tea in my kitchen? There's the biscuits you brought me, too. And be a dear and take Helen with you while I have a wee word with the Reverend."

When Helen and Kathryn were in the small kitchen off the main bedroom/living room, Kathryn asked Calum to sit with her. He'd been glancing around, admiring the cozy environment Kathryn had created for herself. There was nothing institutional about her space; it reflected a long life of varied interests, judging from the bookshelves, the framed photographs, the paintings of local scenes, and the collection of small carved animals on a shelf.

Kathryn saw where he was looking. "Those are native carvings, from Canada. I used to live there, Calum, but I'll hold off on that, it's part of what I want to tell Helen. You can have a closer look at them later."

Calum sat in a chair facing Kathryn and waited for her to explain why she wanted to speak to him alone.

"With Ronald's sudden death," she began nervously, "I would like to ask for reassurance that something I've done isn't a sin..."

Calum lifted his hand to interrupt. "Mrs. Ramsay, Kathryn, do you not have a minister or a spiritual advisor who visits the home? I am happy to listen, but wouldn't you feel more comfortable with someone you know?"

She shook her head and smiled. "Nae, the reason I want to talk to you is that ye *dinnae* ken me, you aren't part of the toon." She stopped and looked upwards, pointing to the ceiling. "I won't hold you to it if I find my way into Heaven blocked, I'm just looking for some wee peace of mind the noo."

Calum smiled too. "I'm humbled that you are seeking my help. And of course I understand if it's something you don't want anyone local to hear about. You can rely on me."

Now Kathryn pointed to her family portrait hanging on the wall, in her direct line of sight; Calum turned to look also.

"That's me and my parents, and my brother Frank. Afore the war, of course. Last photograph of us all together." She stopped and dabbed her eyes with a handkerchief.

Calum turned back to face her, but held off asking any questions.

"I'll tell Helen and Pamela the whole story when they bring the tea. But Calum, Reverend, I want to know this. Some people in the toon here think that wee Frank died in the war. In World War Two, I mean. So many wars since then, we can't just say 'the war' now, can we..."

She shook her head and apologized for rambling. "Not that he died fighting, I mean. They think he died in nineteen

343

forty-four, near here. It's always been treated as a mystery. He was an evacuee from Glasgow, him and five of his pals. Some folks think they all died in the fire at a nearby evacuee home, and others think they fell over the cliff and drowned."

After a moment to compose herself, she looked directly into Calum's eyes. "They didn't die. They did some bad things during the war, but I don't know what they did. Just that it was bad enough for them to fake their deaths and have a chance to escape. To leave Britain and start anew. But the toon still thinks they died back then. Is it a sin that I've kept their secret all these decades?"

Calum struggled to process this new explanation, while offering comfort to her.

"No, Kathryn, their misdeeds, or their sins, if they did something sinful, are not yours. Did they... did they commit something unlawful? Did they... did they..."

"Did they commit murder?" she asked, finishing the thought for him. "Nae, I truly believe they did not. Fact is, Frank told me they had to leave before they were tempted to do something they would regret. All he told me, once he got to Canada, was that someone powerful forced them to commit vandalism. They were just lads, young teenagers, but they took the threats seriously, that they could be sent to the Front. They were living here, in this very building, when it was a military convalescent home. They saw the horrendous state of the lame and blinded men coming back from the fighting. Faced with nightmare images of their future, the lads fled and changed their names, partly to avoid being forced into the military before they were old enough, and also to avoid being prosecuted for the vandalism when the war ended."

Calum sighed deeply and looked out at the gardens beyond Kathryn's window. She clearly wanted some reassurance that her choice had been the right one, to protect her brother. During wartime, people had always been faced with difficult choices.

"Kathryn," he said gently, "it doesn't sound to me like the deception hurt anyone, did it? Obviously, it must have been very painful for your brother to walk away from the life he knew, but if he thought his life was in danger, he didn't have much choice. And if, by protecting his new identity, you also helped save his life, it sounds like you did the honorable thing."

He leaned forward and held his hands out, palms up. She placed her delicate, arthritic hands in his.

"From what you've told me, Kathryn, you haven't sinned. You were protecting family. A noble act, in my book."

She smiled, and he gently released her hands, then leaned back and closed his eyes for a moment before resuming the conversation.

"If you don't mind me asking, Kathryn, where were your parents during this time? Could they not help your brother?"

"Nae." She glanced again at the family picture. "Both died in the Blitz, in London. With Frank evacuated and me sent to Canada, they left Glasgow and moved to London to help the war effort. I never did learn what they did, but they were university professors, linguists, so perhaps they helped with translating. Didn't help for long, though, they died in the bombing."

Calum glanced up; behind Kathryn, he could see Helen leaning into the kitchen door opening, gesturing if they should return with the tea. He looked at Kathryn again.

"Kathryn, I'm happy to stay today and speak with you again, or I can come back another day. But we're probably both ready for our tea, you think?"

She smiled and nodded her head. "Thank you, I feel much, oh, lighter, perhaps."

Chapter 63

Seeing Calum nod his head, Helen retreated back into the kitchen. She and Pamela soon emerged with a tray, and once tea and biscuits had been served, they pulled up chairs and joined Calum and Kathryn.

Kathryn took a few sips of tea, then spoke to the group. "Reverend Calum here has given me great spiritual comfort. Pamela dear, I wanted you to hear this while we have these kind people here. I'm too nervous to tell you on my own."

"Tell me what, Aunt Kathryn? If it's something you'd rather not share with me, I understand. I don't want you to be upset, especially so soon after losing Ronald."

Kathryn shook her head. "Nae, it's *because* of Ronald's death, going so quick like he did, that I have to tell you while there's time."

She reached for a small pile of envelopes sitting on her window ledge. They were tied with blue ribbon. She handed them to Pamela.

"Before you read them, dear, I need to explain the background. You know your father, my brother, moved to Canada from Scotland, and settled there. You have always been told that he moved there as a bairn, well before the war, but that wasn't true."

She took a long sip of tea; now her hands were shaking slightly, and she carefully replaced the cup in the saucer.

"The name you knew him by, Gregory Scott, was not his real name. He was born Frank Spears, and I was Kathryn Spears, afore I was married of course."

It Continued with the Cowries

"Why did he..." Pamela began, staring at Kathryn in disbelief.

"I'm going to get to that, dear. At the start of the Second World War, children were evacuated from the cities to the countryside. For reasons only my parents really knew, I was sent to Canada. Your father, Frank, refused to go overseas. He was close with a group of boys in Glasgow. He agreed to leave Glasgow if he and his pals stayed together, so they were supposed to be evacuated to a place about ten miles from here. It's long gone, but due to a mix-up they were brought here, to this very building. Hard to imagine now, this fancy care home being a military convalescent hospital, but it was. So Frank and his pals, they didn't really mind where they were, as long as they were together, and they started helping out as best they could."

She stopped and took a long sip of tea, then pointed to the letters, still unopened in Pamela's hand, and continued.

"A senior officer at the care home turned out to have a real hatred for someone living in this town, in Kilvellie. He persuaded, well, forced Frank and his pals to go on nighttime raids against a nearby business."

She looked up at Helen. "The glass factory. But you must know this, since you'll have known about the sign being installed by the stairway."

"Yes," Helen confirmed, "I've heard bits and pieces, but I was told that the six poor lads drowned, that they fell over the cliff when they were picking up glass from the ground nearby."

Kathryn nodded her head. "Aye, the story held up all these decades. Frank wrote to me now and again during those war years. He didn't give me any details, probably afraid of censors reading his mail. Then not long before he and his pals disappeared, he wrote me a strange letter. It's in the batch that I just gave to Pamela. He said that he missed me desperately, and that he needed to find a way to join me in Canada. Remember, I was only in my teens myself, I had

347

no money, but the relatives I was living with, they were more than happy to help get Frank over to Canada, especially with our own parents dead by then. They arranged for his passage, but oddly, he'd insisted that they not use his real name. It wasn't until he arrived that he told me the truth, that he was fleeing for his safety, and needed to change his name so that, when the war ended, the police wouldn't go searching for him on account of the vandalism. He chose the surname Scott, to be a link with Scotland."

She fell silent, and Helen focused on refilling the teacups while she considered all this new information. Who had Frank been afraid of? Would Alistair find the answer in the boxes of old records?

"Frank was terrified when he arrived in Canada," Kathryn continued. "He was so terrified that when I was making the decision to move back to Scotland in the nineteen fifties, I told him I would help with the ruse, the cover-up I guess it was. I came to Kilvellie on the pretext of searching for what had happened to my missing brother. It was just chance that the McMahon solicitors' office needed help, and I settled in Kilvellie. As you can see, I never left. I assumed Frank and the other boys had passed completely from the town's awareness. No one alive to remember them, now that Ron's gone."

"But," Helen ventured, "with the sign at the cliff stairs today, you realized that their secret might not be secure?"

"Aye, and I'm sorry about bashing it with me cane! But it was such a shock. Names I hadn't read for decades, suddenly there on a sign for all to see. Helen, those six names, whether written in German or in English, those *names* did die in nineteen forty-four. The lads all went on to lead successful lives, far as I know. Pamela knows much more than I'll ever know about her own father, about the man that my brother became. He raised a wonderful daughter, I can attest to that!"

"The sign won't be installed after all, Kathryn," Helen assured her. "You're right, now that I know the real story from you, who learned it directly from one of those poor lads, it's time for that chapter of the town's history to come to a close."

Pamela was still sitting silently, fighting back tears and struggling to process this new information about her late father. She held up the letters. "Aunt Kathryn, thank you for sharing these with me. It will take me a while to adjust to what I thought I knew about Dad. I just wish he'd..."

"He *couldn't* share it with you, dear." Kathryn placed her hand on Pamela's arm for a moment. "He was deeply ashamed of what he'd done as a teenager, and sadly I think he never quite stopped looking over his shoulder, wondering if someone would connect him with the lads who supposedly died here during the war."

Calum smiled at Pamela. "I think many people wish they could replay their teenage years and undo things they said and did, at least, from what I've heard in confidence from my congregation members. I hope you won't think badly of your father for keeping his wartime-era experiences from you. Many, nae, probably most people of that era kept the truth from their descendants. They want to be remembered as the people they became later."

Kathryn had leaned back into her chair and her eyes were fluttering. Pamela stood up and gently tucked a blanket over her aunt, who mumbled her thanks.

"We should let the two of you spend time together," Helen said. "When do you go back to Canada?"

"Honestly, I think I'll stay and spend as much time as I can with my aunt. I'm a generation below her, but I've already lost a husband, and my children are off working far from home, so I can just as easily live here for a while."

"In that case, please do keep in touch. I live at the police station in town. I know it must sound odd, but it's temporary. The kettle's always on if you want to visit one day."

Pamela walked them to the door, and after expressing her thanks, she held up the letters. "I have a lot to catch up on and a lot to process."

Soon Helen and Calum were on the road south, heading back to Finlay, to relate the news to Alistair. Helen was very glad that she'd ridden with Calum, because she'd be unable to concentrate on driving. Everything she thought she knew about that terrible event outside the glass factory had to be reassessed. Yet again.

Chapter 64

As Helen and Calum drew closer to Finlay, Helen called ahead to Alistair to tell him they'd be back soon. He offered to heat up the left-over Indian food for an early meal, and she accepted gratefully.

After dinner at the dining table, with the sun still bright over the Firth of Forth, Helen told Alistair what they'd learned that afternoon. Alistair had poured each of them a dram of whisky.

"After the service, we met a woman, Pamela, Canadian accent. She was with an older woman in a wheelchair who turned out to be our Kathryn Ramsay. Kathryn was very upset at the new sign by the beach access stairs, with the names of the lads who drowned during the war. She insisted we take the sign down there and then. Pamela is Kathryn's niece..."

Alistair interrupted. "Must be a niece of her husband's, right, Helen? Or *one* of her husbands, since she was married twice..."

"Wait," Calum broke in, "we're getting to that. We all went back to the care home for afternoon tea. Then Kathryn invited us up to her room. I spoke to Kathryn alone for a few minutes while Helen and Pamela made tea."

He took a long sip of whisky, as did Helen, who then continued the story.

"Kathryn feels guilty about keeping a secret much longer and wanted to explain while she has a chance. It was brought on by that sign, about Kilvellie putting up a memorial listing the six young men who drowned..."

"Yes," Alistair said, "Calum, we'll tell you the long story, but we learned that Henry, the factory owner, had the stairway installed soon after the six factory vandals drowned, and it is being dedicated in their memory. Without identifying them as having anything to do with the factory damage, of course."

Calum held up both hands. "Please, let us finish. When the aunt, Kathryn, realized that the town is making the names public, by the stairway, she knew the time has come. So in answer to your question, Pamela is not a niece through marriage. She's Kathryn's niece through Kathryn's brother Frank..."

Alistair frowned and looked at Helen, then back to Calum. "*Really*? I thought he was a young teenager when he died..."

"*Wait*, Alistair," Helen interrupted. "Sorry, I didn't mean to raise my voice, but we're trying to tell you that Frank Spears, Kathryn's brother, did not drown in nineteen forty-four. According to Kathryn, *none* of those lads drowned. They had to escape from whoever had a hold over them at the place they were staying, so they faked their deaths. Pamela's only just learned this now, from her aunt. Frank, Pamela's father, moved to Canada and changed his name just as the war was ending, so his trail in Scotland ended after his faked death. He didn't want to be arrested and jailed for damaging the factory, but he didn't want to blame it on the person who made him and the others do it, or there would be possibly worse repercussions."

Alistair sat motionless, trying to comprehend, so Calum picked up the story. "We could tell that this news was a huge shock for Pamela, learning that her Scottish father who'd claimed to have emigrated to Canada as a child, was technically, I mean, decades earlier, a wanted man in Scotland. He'd told her nothing of this, and now he's gone so she can never ask him. I think the only reason Kathryn told her is because of the planned publicity surrounding the six sup-posedly drowned lads. Kathryn didn't want someone tracing the original name of Pamela's father, that is, Frank Spears, and connecting him with the man who he became in Canada."

"So," Alistair said, unsure what to think at this point, "does that mean the other five young men also changed their names and buried their Kilvellie past?"

"If Frank did that, obviously successfully, then I expect the other lads did as well," Helen said. "The point is, Kilvellie has to reconsider putting up a sign with the real names of those six lads. If they did all change their names, then went off and made something of their lives elsewhere and tried to put the war years behind them, why should that be revealed now? From talking to Pamela and hearing Kathryn's story, her lifelong secret, it's probably best not to publicize the names now and tempt people to start digging."

"But the names were already in public view at the chapel," Alistair pointed out.

"Yes," Calum agreed, "but you told me the sign was in German, and it was installed in an obscure chapel. Someone would have to know a bit of background to even notice the sign."

"Like Alistair did," Helen confirmed, "but only after he recognized those names from the old factory guard's diaries. May he rest in peace. And from talking to the town solicitor, Claude, that plaque will not be replaced on the chapel wall. Remember, it's been removed for restoration."

***

They all sat in silence, Helen and Alistair both shaking their heads as they processed the new version of Kilvellie's history.

"It will take a while for all this to sink in," Alistair said finally. "I used to think I was good at reading people, but

Kathryn had us completely misled. She was living in Canada in the nineteen forties and some of the nineteen fifties, so it makes sense that Frank fled to Canada in nineteen forty-four or soon after, then she helped with the new identity. And then, instead of going to Kilvellie to find records of him like she said, she really went there to bolster the fiction that he was dead. I mean, in case anyone was trying to find him and the other lads, bring them to justice back then."

"And by taking a job in the McMahon law office, she was in a good position to do that," Helen added. "What a tangled web."

Helen, Alistair, and Calum sat quietly again, gazing at the light of the setting sun over the water of the Firth of Forth.

"I guess you don't need to go through all those boxes, Alistair, now that we're not trying to trace six missing lads," Helen said. "I can take them back with me to the care home tomorrow. I wonder if Kathryn would be willing to talk to me again, and I can ask her what she knows about the other five lads, if anything."

"I can go with you," Calum offered. "Kathryn seemed comfortable talking with me, I mean, since I'm not from Kilvellie."

"I think it has to do with giving her spiritual reassurance, or absolution," Helen said, "but I'm not trying to pry."

Calum kept silent, but he nodded.

Alistair smiled. "Anyway, Helen, don't be in a rush to take the boxes back. Even if the six young men don't need to be traced after all, there's still the question of who had a hold over them, and was someone else responsible for breaking the memorial window. I could search for something about that."

Helen looked at Calum and grinned. "I think our young Alistair is in no hurry to get back to Maine, what do you think?"

Calum grinned too. "Aye, and maybe there will be a wedding in my church after all. Alistair, can I expect a call to set the date?"

"As long as Margaret will still have me when she gets back to all this, then yes!"

Calum topped up the whisky glasses.

"To Alistair and Margaret," he said, lifting his glass high, and Helen seconded it.

Chapter 65

Later that evening, with Calum safely home—he'd called to thank Alistair for another evening of Indian food and excellent whisky—Helen and Alistair made a start on what would be a long process of revising what they thought they knew about the glass factory during the war years. It would take a while, re-hashing the various versions, and trying to figure out who might have known all along that the six vandals had probably not, in fact, drowned. One of the six, at least, lived on to marry in Canada and have a daughter. They already suspected that the fisherman, who went right back out instead of a lifeboat, could have been in on it.

Alistair thought it made sense that Frank had gone to his sister in Canada after he'd faked his death, and that Kathryn's whole story about coming to Kilvellie in the nineteen fifties, supposedly to track down what happened to him, had been part of the plan.

With midnight approaching, Helen stood up and said she was ready to call it a night. She hesitated at the bottom of the staircase and turned to Alistair, who paused to listen as he gathered up the whisky glasses.

"I've realized something," she said, "maybe the saddest part of the whole sorry chain of events. Poor old Ronald went to his grave thinking he'd been responsible for those six lads drowning, by disclosing their identities to Henry. It haunted him his whole adult life. And when he saw the family photograph in Elise's office and realized that Kathryn's brother could have been one of those boys, he must have remembered his wartime diaries. He went to his daughter Emily's, maybe desperate to look at the names again. Then his cane was damaged by Bobby..."

She shook her head and sighed. "Poor old guy, in the end, maybe he met his death keeping Kilvellie's secret. And I suppose it means that Henry kept it too. He thought he'd seen six lads dead in the water, but unlike Ronald, who started his guard duties as an innocent young man himself, Henry had experienced the horrors of war, and he'd experienced internment. Coming to terms with six men drowning wouldn't have been so hard for him, after seeing so much death and cruelty. Plus, according to everyone we spoke to, Henry only looked forward, working toward better times. Poor Ronald let the past consume him."

"And now," Alistair continued the train of thought, "we've learned that the secret was probably a lie to begin with, allowing the six vandals to make a clean break from whoever had a hold over them. I just wish... I don't know, I wish Ronald had been told later that he hadn't seen six boys floating in the waves far below, but that he'd seen dummies, bags of clothes, whatever they used to get that effect."

"I agree, Alistair, but whoever helped them escape that day, maybe the fisherman, must have not trusted anyone else to keep the secret. They probably figured that Ronald had no motive to shield them, after witnessing what they'd done on his watch. For years."

"But Helen, if that *fisherman* was in on it, helping to fake the drownings, does that mean that his daughter, and then her daughter, our Elise, was in on the deception too?"

Helen just shook her head. "I wouldn't put anything past those two wily solicitors. Deception upon deception, it was. I don't think I told you yet, Claude McMahon and his son stopped by the station with the missing nineteen forty-four ledger. They showed me the page with the description of the six lads' bodies below the cliff. There's no harm in telling you now, but the report described the bodies as bleeding in the water, raising the issue that the lads might have been attacked on the cliff after all, not just fallen over accidentally."

"That would have been consistent with our suspicions, that perhaps Ronald, or even Henry, had in fact attacked the young men. Wow, no wonder the police ledger was hidden all these decades."

"Yes and no," Helen said. "It puzzled me, that if the police in the town back then really wanted to keep those deaths from being known, why didn't they just tear the page out? Claude's son Giles went on about how forensics could detect a page having been removed, and it was better for a whole ledger to go missing, blah blah, but you know what I think? After hearing the truth from Kathryn today, well, what I believe now is the truth, if those lads were so desperate to escape without ever being traced, so desperate that Frank's own sister Kathryn has kept up the pretense all these decades, well, maybe that page, with the report, was kept as evidence that the lads *were* dead, so that whoever had a hold over them wouldn't go looking. What do you think?"

Alistair just looked at her. "I'm beyond thinking, Helen. I need to start fresh in the morning and reconsider what I should look for in those boxes. Maybe tomorrow we'll decide we're both done with this whole multi-layered secret and return them."

"Maybe," Helen agreed.

Alistair hesitated, then added, "I realized something else. I'd suggested dedicating the beach stairway to the six drowned young men as a way to publicize their names, so that their deaths wouldn't be lost to history. So that the *truth* would come out. And do you know what, that is what's happening, but it's not the truth we'd envisioned at all. So maybe, Helen, we have helped, but instead of helping by *publicizing* their names, we're going to help by keeping the names hidden, so that the men those boys became, their new identities, will be protected."

"Good analysis, Alistair." She glanced up the staircase, then back at Alistair. "I look forward to waking up to the sound of the waves again. I wish the sea would just wash away all these terrible deeds and secrets. And now I have to make a very difficult decision. Do I tell Richard? Do I tell him that his father suffered mentally for decades, picturing those six drowning lads, when it was all a lie? That poor Ronald felt responsible for their deaths, but they didn't die after all?"

Alistair sighed deeply. "I just don't know, Helen. Nothing can change the past. Does Richard even have to be told?"

"Well, he'll notice that the memorial sign is not going up after all, so he's bound to start asking questions. Oh, I'll think about it overnight. Nothing to be done this late in the evening."

After sad goodnights, Helen slowly walked up the stairs to her bedroom. Alistair locked the cottage doors, then lay back on the bed in his room. He texted Margaret. *Come back soon and plan our wedding. Rev. Calum insists. And Helen.* He ended with a smiley face and a heart, not usually his style, but he knew she'd like that.

As he fell asleep, he felt an unexpected surge of relief that this cottage, this village, this country, could become his home, with no deadline looming to leave it and all its complicated history behind.

Epilogue

From the Obituary section of the *Kilvellie-by-the-Sea Weekly News*:

Kilvellie-by-the-Sea, Scotland. Local resident Ronald Wilson, 95, passed away following a tragic fall from the cliff near the beach access stairway at the parking lot just north of Kilvellie. A life-long resident of Kilvellie, for the past four years Ronald lived at Seaview Manor Home. He was well-liked by the staff and residents, and although he reportedly "kept himself to himself," his dear friend at the care home, Mrs. Kathryn Ramsay, has fond memories of their many conversations.

Although few people alive today would be aware, Ronald was once known in Kilvellie for his heroic efforts during World War Two. Unlike the many boys he had attended school with, who later fought valiantly in the war, Ronald's battles were closer to home. He would have proudly joined his friends on the Front, but his eyesight kept him out of the military.

He never publicly spoke of those years, but Henry Green, who founded the Regenbogen Glass Factory in 1921, praised Ronald for helping to protect the factory and the valuable glassware during Henry's internment during the early 1940's. Thanks to Ronald's efforts, Henry said upon his release, the factory had been able to keep in business through the war.

It Continued with the Cowries

As reported in this newspaper last week, a large stock of vintage glassware hidden secretly underground during Ronald's tenure at the factory has been discovered. It will go on public display in the Glass Museum now under construction, ironically, across the street from the former location of the factory. The museum fulfills a long-held dream of Henry's grandson Malky (Malcolm) Green.

After the war, Ronald went on to have a successful career as a security guard. His work included providing security at the many events held at Seaview Manor Hotel, prior to its conversion to a care home. Again, although Ronald never sought publicity, he would likely have met many stars of stage and screen, as well as royalty, as they graced the ballrooms of Seaview Manor in the post-war decades. As a final irony to Ronald's long life, he eventually enjoyed some of those same comforts, occupying a room at the care home that might once have housed royalty.

Ronald is survived by his son Richard, who many people know from his own years of service to Kilvellie as a senior police officer, now retired. He is also survived by two grandchildren, Desmond and Emily; Emily's husband; and a great-grandchild, Bobby. Desmond is following his father Richard's career path in the police force, marking three generations of Wilson men selflessly devoting their lives to the safety of our town.

Anyone wishing to make a donation in Ronald's memory is encouraged to support the work of the local lifeboat charity, as he requested in his will. Ronald's favorite bench by the cliff has been dedicated in his memory.

9 781597 132541